Unauthorized Confessions of a *Churchgirl*

by
Steven Darrell Bates

This is a work of fiction and does not in any way advocate irresponsible behavior. This book contains content that is not suitable for readers 17 and under.

Any resemblance to actual things, events, locales, or persons, living or dead, is entirely coincidental. Names, characters, places, brands, products, media, and incidents are either the product of the author's imagination or are used fictitiously. The author acknowledges the trademark status and ownership of any location names or products mentioned in this book. The author received no compensation for any mention of said trademark.

Edited by Pavita Singh, Effie R. Moran, & Kenny Crucial, KC Editorial

Cover image:
Images from Bigstockphoto.com
Cover Design by HWCC Author Services

I dedicate this book to my wife Tulane- it's a privilege to share my business, life, and love with you.

To my children Steven Jr. and Sarah – your growth provides a constant source of joy and pride.

To everyone who helped me achieve my dream. Thank you so much!!!

Steven Darrell Bates

Chapter 1

I could feel God's precious spirit slowly moving throughout the small overflow room. I could see people worshiping God around me, but it was like I was wrapped in a cocoon of warmth and happiness. My body was tingling from head to toe as an overwhelming presence of joy and peace flooded my senses. That's the way God's spirit made me feel. It felt like I was waking up on the first day of spring and in love. There was an uncontrollable feeling of elation that had my stomach doing back flips. I tried to remain still and enjoy the moment, but my body simply would not stay still. I swayed from side to side and praised the power of God silently. My feelings of pure ecstasy were suddenly interrupted by Craig as he approached me from behind. He placed his hands on my hips and slowly pulled my body towards his. His hard penis pressed against me and I felt God was trying to send up smoke signals and warn me about something. I quickly spun around and glared at him with disgust. This was not the time or place to be playing these types of games, and he knew this. I could not understand why Craig felt it was necessary to keep trying to seduce me this way. When I gave my life to Christ, I promised him that I would only serve him, and I meant every world of it. No matter how many obstacles Satan had thrown in my direction, I had always remained steadfast in my faith. It was just like Craig's ass to pull a stunt like this in church.

Craig tugged at my elbow and whispered in my ear, "Come with me! I have to tell you something."

I glanced around the overflow room embarrassed, hoping no one had seen us. Arriving late at a revival service was always so embarrassing because you were stuffed in the back where it was standing room only. This was one time that I was happy I was late, because no one noticed us leaving.

I held up one finger and followed Craig through the crowed room until I opened the door. The sounds of crickets and dense darkness filled my senses as the door slammed shut behind me. The muffled sounds of people still praising God could be heard as I quickly approached Craig. I wanted to let him know what type of scum he really was. It took a sick individual to interrupt God's spirit just to get his rocks off.

I placed my hands on my hips and prepared to tell him about how thoughtless he was, when he quickly moved closer to me and gently placed his hand on my stomach. "Now hold on Angela, I know that was stupid."

I hated when he flashed me that million dollar smile.

He placed his arms around my hips and pulled me closer and whispered, "I'm sorry, baby."

He kissed my cheek gently and whispered, "Come on, you know I was just playing. Don't be like this."

Every fiber in my body screamed for me to push him away. Seconds passed as I stood there and pretended to be angry. He continued to hold me and caress my body with his hands.

Craig continued to sooth me with his words. "Come on, Angie, stop acting like this. You know I was just joking with you. I was just trying to get a couple of laughs. I never meant to disrespect your faith, I was just having fun. If you think it's best to wait until we are married, then that's fine. If I've never told you, I think you're a strong woman for putting God first in your life. I apologize for doing and/or saying anything disrespectful about you or your faith. Now, I understand how much you are willing to sacrifice for God, and I will never act that way again. I want to love you unconditionally, without any strings attached."

Now I was confused! This was not the Craig I knew. The Craig I knew was the "give it to me baby" Craig. Now he was saying all the *things I had always wanted to hear from him. It was like I was in a theater watching a movie scene. I wanted to tell him I didn't care and I hate him, but my mouth would not open.*

Craig's warm embrace had my body pulsating with excitement as he continued to whisper to me. "Angela, you are the most important person in my life. I think about us getting married, having a family, and growing old together. I know you may not believe me, but I love you. I have always loved you and I will never hurt you again. Please give me a chance to prove it."

Now I knew I was in the middle of a dream! The words coming out of Craig's mouth were just too weird! I had known Craig since he was in the ninth grade, and the words love, marriage and family had never been part of his vocabulary. That was the reason why we had broken up—because his cheating ass couldn't understand the meanings of those words. I wanted to punch him for lying, but I couldn't. I just stood there glued to his every word like some lovesick, school girl in a fantasy.

Craig leaned forward and tried to kiss me, but I shook my head no.

I quickly glanced back toward the church and spoke frantically, "Are you crazy? Anybody could have seen us."

Craig smiled at me and led me toward the church garden behind the building.

The smell of sweet honeysuckles and jasmine crashed against my senses. Craig turned me around and continued to talk. "Is this far enough for you, or do we need to go further? I don't want anyone to hear you scream."

I playfully slapped his arm and pulled away from his embrace. I remembered how the hurt of losing Craig had made me withdraw from my friends and family and how easy Craig seemed to move on without even an afterthought. A part of me wanted him to say something terrible to wake me up from this lucid dream, but it never happened.

Craig held out his hand and slowly guided my lips toward his. I made one last attempt to pull away, but it was too late. Our lips touched and it was like every hurtful deed Craig had committed slowly dissolved. His tongue gently pulled at mine, causing my body to shiver with excitement. Craig slowly pulled away and stared deep into my eyes, causing me to blush and turn away quickly. Craig pulled me closer and began to gently sway my body from side to side as if we were dancing to an imaginary song.

Everything I was doing right now was wrong. There were certain rules that you followed in a Pentecostal church to avoid backsliding, and I had violated almost all of them. I was alone with a man and I had allowed him to isolate me from God's spirit. I felt silly for giving in after scolding him, but this time it felt different. For the first time, it didn't feel creepy. In fact, it felt really good, and I wanted more. Everything I had learned in Bible study about the Holy Spirit's protection disappeared. I slowly unbuttoned his shirt and he allowed me to touch his chiseled chest. I felt a sudden surge of energy rush through my body as he softly caressed me. The more Craig hugged and squeezed my body, the more excited I got. How did I get myself in this predicament?

I closed my eyes and quietly prayed to God. "Please Lord, hear my prayer and take this temptation away from me now in the name of Jesus."

I opened my eyes just as Craig tugged at the belt wrapped around my skirt. I felt helpless as my dress fell to the ground. I could hear muffled voices of praise coming from the church, but my mind was in full lust mode. Craig slowly guided my hand down his tight abdomen and rested it on his pants zipper. Craig leaned his head sideways and stared at me as if to say "Your move!"

In any other situation, I probably would have never thought about backsliding. But again, I had already dishonored every church rule to keep me from getting in this position. There was a small voice encouraging me to fight, but still, I unbuckled his pants and gave his

4

zipper a quick yank. Craig slowly pulled down his pants and underwear, revealing his erect penis.

I began to pray again for God to give me strength. "Anything but this, Lord. You said that if I asked in your name, it would be done. I need you to rescue me from this temptation. I can't hold on any longer."

Craig pulled me closer to his body and pulled my panties down. Everything felt so right, from his rippling muscles to his hard dick slowly sliding between my thighs but not yet inside. I grabbed Craig's arms tightly and closed my eyes as he pressed his body closer to mine. I shook my head no, but my body was swaying back and forth against him. With each thrust, my breath quickened as Craig studied my facial expressions and smiled.

The sound of the pastor's voice reverberated in the darkness, "Is there one who is willing to come and give their life to Christ?"

I could hear church members respond in concert, "Amen, Amen."

But Craig already had my body aching and begging to have more of him.

I continued to swivel my body on his erect penis until I whispered, "I want you inside me."

A devilish grin crept across Craig's face because he knew he was getting what he wanted. My faith in Christ had always given me the power to fight against any temptation, but tonight was different. All those times he had pressured me for sex, I had always resisted. Why, God, was I giving in tonight?

Embarrassed at what I had just said, I avoided eye contact with Craig by looking at the ground. Craig lifted me up into his arms and we both fell to the ground with our bodies entwined together. Craig quickly pulled his shirt off and unbuttoned my blouse. He nudged me backwards and my legs slowly parted as he positioned himself to enter me. Chills swept across my body as his mouth teased my nipples and he slowly pushed himself inside me.

I began to beg God for forgiveness and barter with God. "Please, God. I need your help. I will do anything if you take me out of this situation."

Begging to God only aroused Craig even more. It was like he was getting joy out of stealing me away from Christ. He repositioned my legs around his shoulders and methodically pressed deeper inside me. I clinched my arms around his neck and buried my contorted face in his chest. My body convulsed with every movement and I whimpered for mercy. My body had never experienced such intense pleasure. My muscles tightened as Craig glided swiftly in and out of me. My ears began to ring and my body stiffened just as I began to. . . .

"Excuse me, Miss, are you okay?"

The bright morning sun made it hard for me to see. I slowly focused on the voice of the stewardess tapping my shoulder. Awkwardly, I pulled my seat up out of recline mode and put on my glasses. There were two teenage girls sitting adjacent to me, staring at me and giggling.

Again, the stewardess asked, "Miss! Are you okay?"

I replied with my face flushed with embarrassment, "I'm fine, thank you."

The only thing on my mind was getting to the airplane's restroom before dying from humiliation.

Here I was again having devilish dreams instead of keeping my mind on God. But then again, that's how I had gotten into this situation in the first place. I quickly hurried to the tiny restroom and freshened up. I returned to my seat just as the pilot announced that we were on final approach.

I glanced over at Sha'qounda, who was sleeping peacefully, and I wondered how my life had become so complicated in such a short time. I had gone from innocent church girl to conspiring to bring down one of Atlanta's most famous churches. The funny thing about the whole situation is that I never really wanted to hurt anyone. All I had ever wanted from Bishop Tyler, Calvin, and Prophetess Stanford were love and respect. The only things that I received was tears and regret. They pushed me into a corner and had no other recourse but to fight.

I glanced out the small window as the plane touched down at Savannah/Hilton Head Airport. It was hard to believe, but this small area of Georgia had laid the foundation for who I had become. Baxley, Georgia was where my love of Christ first clashed with my curious thirst for all things worldly, especially bad boys. The irony of it all! Craig was the first stone that led me away from Christ, but here I was dreaming about him.

The first time I saw big-headed Craig, I thought he was so arrogant. He strolled into my tenth grade class and the girls started giggling like the latest teen idol had just walked in. He was tall with caramel skin and deep dimples that exploded off his cheeks. Craig wore the latest fashions, and when he walked past, I just wanted to brush against him. He was confident in himself, and it showed when he sat beside me and started up a conversation. I had to admit that he was the cutest boy I had ever seen, but I refused to acknowledge it. Craig asked if the seat next to me was taken. I wrinkled my face up and replied "yes" in a nasty tone. I wanted him to know for certain that I wanted no part of him.

I tried to ignore him as he walked to another seat, but he noticed me glancing and smiled at me. I frowned back at him as if he were disgusted by him looking at me. Craig turned away unfazed by my reaction and started talking to another girl who was mesmerized by his smile.

The rest of the morning was filled with glances from Craig and me trying my best to ignore him. It was almost as if he knew me, but was hesitate to approach. No matter how hard I tried to ignore Craig, I always found myself gazing at him. I wondered if he would ever approach me again, and that question was quickly answered. I was standing in line waiting for lunch when I saw Craig waving at me. He was walking in my direction and I nervously turned away. I tried to engage in small talk with my friends, but it was too late.

"Hi Angela! My name is Craig."

My friends looked at Craig and me in an awkward way and started giggling. My friends walked away making kissing noises, trying their best to embarrass me, and it was working.

Craig, unfazed by my friends' reaction, smiled at me, held out his hand, and introduced himself again, "My name is Craig."

Surprised that Craig knew my name, I nervously replied, "How do you know my name?"

Craig replied, "Carson Harden."

I remember Carson was best friends with my brother Steven during his freshman year at Clark Atlanta.

I responded by laughing and said, "Carson had a little snotty-nosed cousin who always cried when he didn't get his way. You wouldn't happen to be him, would you?"

Embarrassed by my question, Craig shook his head yes. We both laughed and I was able to relax a little because we had something in common.

I asked Craig, "How did you remember me from back then? We had to be in the third or fourth grade."

Craig's eyes brightened as he responded, "I never could forget you because you had those wired eyes like a cat."

I blushed at his comment and quickly glanced in the opposite direction. Family members had always made remarks about my eyes since I was a baby. My eyes were hazel brown, but sometimes they changed to a bright amber and gold when I was in the sun. As a child living in a small town, I just wanted normal eyes like everyone else. I hated trying to explain why my eyes were so different from everyone else's. As I got older, I learned to appreciate them because they complemented my looks. Craig told me that he had just moved from Atlanta with his mother. Atlanta gave Craig and me something else to talk about. I had always enjoyed going to Atlanta. Craig and I quizzed each other about Atlanta for what seemed like forever.

Craig would challenge me, "I bet you never rode Goliath at Six Flags."

I would respond, "Boy, please, I ride that old thing all the time. I bet you never rode the Batman."

He would respond with excitement in his eyes. "Batman! I've ridden Batman at least a hundred times."

Our conversation switched from Six Flags, to Stone Mountain, to all things fun in Atlanta. We never had an awkward break in our conversation. His cute looks and bright, intriguing smile had my stomach turning flips. Craig would lean in towards me when he laughed and I would nervously blush when he brushed against me.

Craig and I had a lot of fun together during that school year, but I guess he didn't see me as girlfriend material. I never pushed the issue, and during that summer, we just became good friends.

Craig's world was restricted like mine. Most of our friends took advantage of their summer vacation by spending endless hours at the outdoor pool at the recreation center. Our recreation center time was limited because most of the week was dedicated to vacation Bible school.

New Heaven Church of God became Craig's and my little discovery zone. Church became the link that would bond us together. New Heaven Church of God was a typical small-town church with about one hundred twenty members. My parents made sure I was at church for Sunday morning service. I had choir practice on Saturdays, and sometimes I would attend Friday night. Overall, I considered church fun. Craig, on the other hand was forced to endure the equivalent of church prison. His mother made him attend church Tuesday night, Wednesday night, Friday Night, and all day Sunday. Not only did I feel sorry for him, but even some grownups felt sorry for him. Craig's mother was an ordained evangelist and she was making sure that Craig was following in her footsteps.

At New Heaven, we were accustomed to the strict belief system. People in Baxley considered our small church to be harsh and overly rigorous. But that was nothing in comparison with Craig and his mother. The Hardens' literal interpretation of the Bible was alarming. His mother always wore a long white dress with a head veil, and Craig was not allowed to watch television or attend movie outings with other kids in the church. It was not unusual to see people at New Heaven shouting, praising God, and speaking in tongues. But you rarely saw a fifteen-year-old kid doing it.

We were used to hearing kids in the church testify about being saved and sanctified, but none of us ever spoke about speaking in tongues. That type of behavior was for older people in the church. Not only was he already speaking in other tongues, but he was also preaching. No one in the church actually believed Craig could really preach until we saw his first sermon.

Imagine sitting in church and all of a sudden a fifteen-year-old kid gets up and starts preaching like a grown man. When Craig spoke, it felt like God himself was speaking through him. He understood the word of God and he conveyed that message clearly to us.

Many people in church believed that God had a calling on Craig's life. Craig started out preaching once a month at our church, and those services attracted more members than any other service. Sometimes when he felt the spirit of God, he would fling his jacket off to the delight of the crowd. The church members and visitors would laugh and scream for more. At the end of the summer, I saw Craig preach at a revival service. At least one hundred sinners fell to their knees begging God for salvation because of the power of his sermon. That summer, Craig became a little superstar in Baxley. I was just happy to be his friend at the time. Little did I know that our destinies would lead us in separate directions, and that school year would be the catalyst.

I walked into eleventh grade homeroom and I could hear the adoring whispers from the boys. "Damn! Who is that? Ah man, that's

Angela. Angela? You mean skinny Angela from last year? Yep? Damn she fine! I bet I get her phone number this year."

Craig's eyes bounced happily up and down my body and I blushed from the attention. The summer between tenth and eleventh grade had been extremely good to my self-esteem. My lanky, bean-pole body had finally developed.

The hot Georgia summer had turned my normally light skin into an exotic copper shade. And my long, dark, wavy hair only added to my beauty. Over the summer, my father had also noticed the new crowd of boys hanging around vacation Bible school. The funny thing about fate is that it happens while you're busy making other plans. While my father was concentrating on keeping the boys away from me, he was pushing me closer to Craig.

Craig had always been a safe boy in my father's eyes. He was very respectful and almost spiritual to a fault. My father actually encouraged Craig and I to hang around each other. Everyone at New Heaven thought that it was so cute because we were connected spiritually. I was in the choir and he was the dynamic sixteen-year-old preacher. Our friendship was considered perfect in the church world. But with any situation, there is always the possibility of change, and by the fall of my eleventh-grade year, change had come.

I found myself more anxious and excited around Craig. Craig would pull people out of the audience to help prove a point during his sermon, and I would make every effort to volunteer. I just wanted to brush up against him. The Bible says, "If I could just touch the hem of his garment." Well, at the time, all I wanted to do was just be near Craig.

It was difficult being raised as a young Christian in a holiness church. We were taught to put Christ first and flee from the temptations of Satan. The problem was you never knew where the temptations would come from. The expectations of a saved, sanctified teenager were almost overwhelming. Everyone treated you like you had all the answers when you really didn't know anything. People just assumed you would make the right choice. Our parents built a bubble of faith around us and took for granted that nothing could tempt us. They believed that both of us being saved was enough to keep us focused, but it wasn't.

Our parents allowed us to go to the park after morning service, just to give us a break. If my parents had only known what was going on during those breaks. Both Craig and I were becoming more curious about our feelings. The problem is that we had no idea of what to do. Our kisses were awkward because we were trying to imitate what we had seen other people doing. Even though we didn't know what we were doing, it felt really good.

Most of the church members would be at the Music Pavilion listening to live jazz bands. The Music Pavilion was a covered stage and amphitheater located in a grassy bowl inside the park. It was a popular spot for concerts and events. Church members would bring blankets and picnic baskets and relax until the late service started. Craig and I would sneak off to our own secret spot. I loved being in that secret spot with him. The spot was a huge reservoir wall that overlooked the amphitheater. Most people hated the overlook because it was such long hike back to church. This was the place that Craig and I forgot about the church and explored each other. Craig and I would kiss and rub on each other until it was time for the long hike back to church.

I enjoyed those innocent moments with Craig. He would hold me tightly from behind and rub and softly squeeze my breast. I enjoyed letting him press against me until his penis was hard. I got into a habit of taking my pantyhose off before leaving for our rendezvous. The feeling of grinding against Crag was magical. Craig would nibble on my neck and message my body, causing me to shake with anticipation. Deep down in my heart, I knew what we were doing was wrong because of our Pentecostal upbringing. But I swear, those tender moments alone with Craig never felt like sin. We had convinced ourselves that as long as we never had sex, we were okay. All of that would change on Thanksgiving Day.

There was nothing like Thanksgiving Day in the small town of Baxley, Georgia. Pining your own Christmas tree from a nearby farm, greeting friends on Main Street as you dashed in and out of small shops looking for that rare gift, and watching the town Christmas tree light up for the first time were just some of the magical events that occurred in Baxley. On this day, my faith would be tested beyond anything that I had encountered in my short life.

To us, there was nothing odd about attending church on Thanksgiving Day. In fact, it was required. While our parents cooked and served meals to the homeless, I helped Craig conduct the young adult service. Young adult service encouraged us to worship Christ in a way that would attract younger people to the church. Craig's ability to galvanize young people was incredible. His knowledge of the Bible along with his ability to connect with the younger generation made him an ideal candidate for that year's event. Craig convinced local gospel hip hop artists to perform in the park. He gave an emotional message about being thankful and the crowd responded with a rousing applause. If you hadn't known, any better you would have thought that Craig was the headliner.

Craig introduced the master of ceremony for the musical event and exited the stage. He walked toward me and smiled as he approached. I was so proud of just being associated with Craig. People in the audience rushed in his direction, shaking his hand and patting him on his back. Craig just took it all in stride like it was nothing new to him.

When he finally reached me, he hugged me tightly and whispered, "Let's go for a walk."

Cheerfully, I agreed and he held my hand tightly as he escorted me through the crowd. I felt like the wife of a pop star. Eventually, Craig and I emerged from the crowd and their attention turned to the act on the stage. We soon found ourselves walking on the long path towards our secret spot. We exchanged glances back and forth and giggled because we knew what we were going to do.

When we arrived at the reservoir wall, we nervously looked around. Unlike on other days, the park was crawling with people that day, and anyone could walk up on us. I could still hear the music echoing in the background as Craig pinned me against the wall. I giggled as he tickled my neck with his soft kisses and his hands gently squeezed my butt. I could feel his hands slowly lifting my skirt and my breathing began to intensify. I was used to Craig feeling on me, but he had never tried to feel under my skirt. I quickly grabbed his wrist to stop him. Craig pulled me closer and continued to squeeze and massage my butt.

He whispered in my ear, "I just want to touch you in your panties."

I smiled at him and shyly shook my head no. He responded by gently peeling my fingers off his wrist and placing my hands around his neck. Craig than unbuckled his pants and pulled out his penis.

I pretended to be shocked and appalled by saying, "You are so nasty."

Craig, embarrassed, quickly placed it back in his underwear and smiled. I playfully punched Craig in the shoulder and he pulled my body closer until I could feel his erect penis nestled tightly against my vulva. Craig stepped back and I tried to pull him back toward me. He looked into my eyes and slowly unbuckled his pants while pulling out his penis. I pretended to be shocked and weakly fought against him, but in reality, I was curious too. Scared from all the tall tales that my parents had told me, I shyly peeked at my first dick.

Craig asked if I wanted to touch it and I timidly agreed. Craig slowly guided my hand down and placed it around his penis. He trembled with excitement and I flinched when it started to expand in my hand. I gently touched Craig's penis with my fingers, unsure if I was hurting him. I noticed that every time I touched the tip of his penis, he would wince and draw back. I also noticed that the more I played with it, the harder it got. Craig asked if he could rub it against me and I froze.

I was afraid to answer because of my faith and parents. I could hear my parents telling me that this was wrong, but Craig was already pulling me closer. His penis grazed my vulva as he positioned himself between my thighs.

The sexual energy rushed through my body as his dick rubbed against my panties. I could feel my legs trembling with anticipation of what was coming next.

I was confused and afraid and I felt guilty. I wished that I had never allowed him to touch me like this. It was my fault that Craig was out of control, and it was my fault that we were backsliding. Every thrust from Craig made me feel like a sinner. I could feel my panties moisten and my inner thighs tighten around his penis. The moisture from my panties made the thrust from Craig easier. Craig's eyes were closed tight and the frown on his face was intense. The more he pushed, the more I wanted to have sex with him.

After about three or four minutes of intense rubbing back and forth, I was on the brink of pulling my panties down when something strange happened. I felt the muscles in Craig's neck stiffing to a tight coil and his firm grip around my waist begin to tighten. His normal, deep, baritone voice gave way to soft moans. Craig's thrust intensified as he lost control of his body. He grunted one last time and released a steady stream of warm fluid between my legs. The extra dampness felt nasty between my thighs, but it turned me on. Craig's breathing became more erratic, and he staggered sideways as if losing his balance. I extended my arms to catch him and he awkwardly fell forward with his head coming to a rest on my shoulder. We held each other in an awkward silence. I wanted to ask Craig if we had just have sex, but I was afraid. We quietly straightened our clothes up as best we could and started the long walk back to the church. We held hands as we walked back to church, but it felt forced. Normally we felt comfortable with talking about anything, but that day was different.

We walked in silence trying to make sense of what had just happened. I stopped at a nearby restaurant and washed the smell of sex off as best I could. I threw my panties in the garbage and we proceeded to church.

By the time we arrived at evening service, it had already started. My father glared at us as we entered the church. I sat in the rear of the church and Craig slowly walked to the pulpit. I was so embarrassed that I was in church without panties on. I barely lifted my head to speak to anyone. I was always taught that a Christian should seek forgiveness, but I felt like there was no coming back from this transgression. I looked at Craig and his bright, normal smile had been replaced with a guilty gaze of regret.

My father asked Craig if he had a sermon for God's people, and for the first time ever, Craig said no. The guilty expression on Craig's face told all that he had backslid. My father looked at me, and it was like his eyes were burning a hole in my forehead. I think he knew Craig and I had done something wrong, but to what extent, he just did not know. During alter call, the entire church gathered around Craig while he prayed for forgiveness. I sat nervously in my seat wishing that Craig and I had never stumbled down that road. Later that night, my father asked me if I wanted to talk, and I shook my head no. There was no way I could let my father know that I had sinned.

The thing about being a teenage Christian is that you are taught to always look to Jesus or the Bible for answers. I searched for any scripture in the Bible that talked about the feelings I was having, but I couldn't find it anywhere. Craig and I saw each other the next Sunday and it felt awkward. The fun of seeing each other had turned into a daze of guilt. Craig and I finally had a conversation about what had happened. We both agreed that we could still go to the park, but nothing else.

That following Sunday, we both prayed for strength before going to the park, but still we ended up in the same predicament, I pinned against the wall while he soiled my panties with his sperm. Again and again, we asked God to forgive us of our sins, and we always ended up in our secret spot.

After a while, it got easy. I could praise God in church with a brown bag containing my wet panties and not hurt with guilt.

Craig became an even better con artist. One Sunday morning, my father asked Craig to preach in his spot during his absence. Craig preached one of the most passionate sermons about backsliding that I had ever heard. When we got to our secret spot, he came so hard between my legs that I thought he had a super soaker water gun for a penis. For a long time, I thought that it was something that I had done to make him cum so hard. I would later find out the truth.

At first it was just simple curiosity, and then overnight, Craig's attitude seemed to turn into the need to prove something. He started to pressure me more and more about having sex, and the things that he was asking of me were way passed our meager knowledge. One Sunday while pinned against the wall, I felt him pulling my panties down. At first it was playful, but then he became aggressive to the point of ripping my panties.

I was surprised because he never had been so demanding and aggressive. He wrestled me to the ground as if he were trying to force himself inside me. Craig only stopped after I screamed at him and slapped him in the face.

Craig laughed as he helped me off the ground and said, "I was just playing with you."

I laughed along with him, but in the back of my mind, I felt like things would never be the same.

I could tell something was bothering him, but he rarely talked about it. Then, Elder Early Madison began showing a lot of interest in Craig's mother. I wondered if that had anything to do with the change in his behavior. Elder Madison and my father were both ordained at the same time. In fact, sometimes it seemed as if my father and he were competing against each other.

My father would come home after church and complain about Elder Madison getting more shine than him. Sometimes my father would stay home almost as way of protesting. The Bishop would ask us about my father, and my mother would tell some lie to keep us in good standing with the church. I never really understood why my mother went out of her way to look good in front of a bunch of gossip hounds. It was almost like we had to be perfect because she didn't want our name in mud.

I always hated saying "yes ma'am" and "no ma'am" to bunch of cackling hens who thought they knew better. The same cackling hens were always trying to help Elder Madison find a good wife in the church. Elder Madison was young, attractive, and wealthy. Every single woman in the church wanted him. That's why everyone found it odd when he hooked up with Craig's mother. Not to say that she was ugly, but most people thought he could have done a lot better.

Craig's mother only dated Elder Madison for a short time, but I could tell that the relationship bothered Craig. He was especially bothered by the way his mother would force him to go with Elder Madison on trips. Elder Madison was more than generous with his money, especially to the young boys in the church. The girls in the church would get jealous about the gifts, but they were only offered to members of the youth ministers club. The youth ministers club consisted of boys ranging in age from six to twelve who were being raised in single-parent homes. Craig was older than most of the members in the young ministers club, but he was invited to chaperone because of Elder Madison's relationship with his mother.

Elder Madison would take the boys to Atlanta to see basketball games, take them on camping trips, and the most prized trip of all, Disney World. Craig was so excited to help chaperone during the first couple of trips. Then it was like he was uninterested in helping Elder Madison. In fact, he was so against going with Elder Madison that he would often be overheard cursing at his mother when she tried to force him to go. Craig eventually stopped preaching and sometimes would just skip Sunday service and meet me afterwards.

Then the rumors about Elder Madison began, but none of them were ever confirmed. Rumors or not, my father made it perfectly clear that my brother was to stay as far from him as possible.

My father would say, "Steven, don't ever get in that man's car. Something just isn't right about him."

I think everybody except my father was shocked when Elder Madison was arrested. My father just kept screaming, "I told you so," as Elder Madison's face flashed across the TV. The reporter said a nine-year-old boy had been molested by Elder Madison for years. I often wondered if Elder Madison had a part in Craig's sudden change of just being curious about sex to wanting to prove his manhood.

During the summer after my sophomore year at Appling County High School, my brother found me a summer job working as an intern at ESPN in Atlanta. The job was fast-paced and I met a lot of new people. Craig and I communicated over the phone and I felt like nothing had changed. He would tell me that he loved me and that one day he was going to buy me the biggest house in Baxley. During my first few weeks in Atlanta, unbeknownst to my father, I dreamed of having that same big house with Craig in Baxley. As the summer came to an end, I knew I could never spend the rest of my life in Baxley, Georgia. The bright lights and urban city feel of Atlanta had grown on me. I met different people with bigger dreams than just staying in a small town.

My junior year of high school came and went, and then Craig started making comments about us going to Georgia Southern University together. The university was only fifty miles from Baxley, and I wanted to go further away. I visited Georgia Southern with Craig to appease him, but I knew it was not for me. Then Craig found out that his careless attitude towards his grades was coming back to haunt him. His mother invested more in his athletics than in his education. I had to admit that Craig was a very good basketball player. Most

19

people in Baxley thought that he would be a huge basketball prospect. The reality was that he was a great basketball player in Baxley, but just average anywhere else.

On the other hand, my plans for college had already been in full swing since I was a sophomore. By the start of my senior year at Appling County, I had already received letters of acceptance from Virginia Tech, University of Tennessee, Baylor, and University of Cincinnati. The only reason that I was considering Cincinnati is that I had traveled there with my ninth grade debate team. I remember having such joy when I traveled to other places far from Baxley, Georgia. My dream was to attend Spelman College, and I would stop at nothing to achieve that dream.

Craig's dream of playing college basketball was dying quickly by the hour. His average basketball skills combined with his low grades equated to no scholarship offers. While my mother and father bragged at church about my college acceptance letters, Craig's mother seethed with jealousy. Whenever I went over to Craig's house, his mother would make sly comments about me not being better than anyone else in Baxley.

Ms. Harden's favorite line was, "Y'all can have a couple of babies, get jobs at the plant, and buy a nice used mobile home. Life don't get no better than that."

At first, Crag would stay out of the conversation, but then he started sounding like his mother. "Baby, we've been together for a long time. What's wrong with having kids now? I love you and plan on marrying you, so why wait?"

I was stunned because he sounded just like his mother. I continued to express my desire to leave Baxley. Eventually, Craig and I stopped going to movies between church services and he started talking to other girls at school. People in the church could see that Craig and I were having problems. What irked me the most was the way his mother would blame me. She would grab my hand and escort me to the altar as if I was doing something wrong.

As time went on, we began to argue more. I still remained true to Craig because I loved him. The straw that broke the camel's back occurred on prom night. For years, I had been so sure that when I lost my virginity it would be to Craig. We talked about having sex, but we had never gone all the way. At least one of us hadn't.

The protective father and preacher always made sure he talked to us about sex. My father would always stress to us that sex was a special commitment that should only be between married people.

But his street mentality usually made the conversation sound like, "If you touch my daughter, I'll kill you."

It began to seem like every sermon my father preached was directed at me. "Young people, I know prom is coming up. But always remember to put Jesus first."

And the church would respond with choruses of "Amen."

By the time prom night arrived, my mind was twisted in several directions. I wanted to respect my Christian upbringing, but I also wanted to make Craig happy. After days of going back and forth, I decided that I wanted Craig to be my first. I called him and told him that I had a special surprise for him after prom. That was the first time in a long time that I had heard excitement in Craig's voice.

Over the past couple of months, I had been the one initiating all the contact by phone. Most of the time he didn't answer or he would cut the conversation short. Those few months were very frustrating for a young girl in love. The sound of happiness in Craig's voice made me sure that this was the right thing to do.

Craig arrived at my house early and he appeared to be very excited.

Just as we were walking out the door, my mother spoke. "Craig, can you please wait in the car? I need to speak with Angela."

Craig walked out the door and my mother put her arm around me. I thought we were about to have one of those mushy moments when your mother tells you how much she loves you.

Instead, my mother smiled at me and then whispered, "Those new underwear are really cute, but still respect yourself."

I was so embarrassed! I had bought those sexy panties just for Craig. I thought I had hidden them pretty well. I should I have known I couldn't get anything past my mother.

My mother called my father and started walking toward us. I was mortified. Would my father kill me and Craig? Or would he just call off the whole night? I looked at my mother with panic in my eyes as my father arrived. Instead of telling him about my sexy panties, we joined hands and prayed.

After prayer, I walked out the house feeling free. I approached the car and smiled at Craig. I could feel his eyes on my body, so I poked my little butt out just a little further. I don't know if my mother told my father about my new panties, but I do remember my father bursting through the front door. He leaped off the porch just as Craig and I were pulling off. My father pounding on the truck, startling us, and Craig slammed on the brake.

I was so embarrassed when I heard my father yell. "My man, if my daughter's not home by 12:00, I'm coming to find you."

Craig's lips cracked into an awkward smile, but my father's expression was deadly serious.

Prom night started out uneventful, but that would not last. I was dancing and mingling with friends when I was approached by Stormy Underwood. Stormy and I were not friends; in fact, she ran in an entirely different circle. Her circle of friends were considered low grade. She lived in an area of Baxley known as "Black Town." It was your typical low-income part of any small country town. The four block area of town was packed with generations of low-income people who never made it out of Baxley. Steven and I were forbidden to go in that area. My father believed that side of town was like a black hole. Once you went in, you never came out. It was filled with crime and baby mammas. Stormy reminded me of a young Whoopi Goldberg with an attitude. She was a third-generation resident of Black Town with no plans to go anywhere. She hated me because she knew I was going places.

I was standing near the door with my friends when she came up to me. Stormy, accompanied by her group of Black Town inhabitants, looked at me with a smirk on her face. I turned away from them, but they continued to stare at me as if she knew something. The more I tried to ignore her, the more she whispered to her friends

After a few minutes, I finally asked sarcastically, "Do I have something in my nose or something?"

Stormy glared back at me with a smirk on her face and replied, "Naw, you okay, but I guess you haven't heard."

I turned toward Stormy and responded, "What are you talking about?"

Stormy glanced at me one last time with glee and walked away. I looked at my friends and just shook my head. As the night went on, I began to get more funny looks from other people in the crowd.

Concerned, I asked Craig, "Why are all these people looking at me all crazy?"

Craig responded by brushing it off and saying, "I don't know. I didn't see anybody looking at you."

My question seemed to make Craig nervous, because all of sudden he was ready to leave. Craig kissed me and whispered in my ear, "I love you. Come on, let's get out of here so I can get my surprise."

Craig's cute dimples looked like golf balls as he smiled at me and made his eyebrows dance up and down. I playfully punched his arm and blushed as I thought about giving away my precious virginity. I felt the bright light of the spotlight aimed at us as we continued to dance. Craig panicked and pulled my arm.

He was rushing me out the gym, but not before I heard cat calls of, "Da...ddy, Da...ddy."

I was so confused. I pulled away from Craig and stood in the middle of the crowd. Still dumfounded, I felt my best friend, Kennedy

Jones, pulling me in her direction. She grabbed me so fast that I nearly tripped over Craig's patent-leather-clad foot.

Kennedy rushed me out the gym door and pulled me close as she spoke. "Angela! I need to tell you something, and it's really going to hurt you."

Terrified, I responded, "What, Kennedy? What's going on?"

Kennedy took a deep breath and responded. "People are saying that Craig and Christy Mitchell slept together, and that she might be three months pregnant."

I can honestly say that hurt was one of the worse feelings I have ever experienced. It felt like somebody dropped a block of cement on my chest. I glanced back in the gym and saw Craig looking guilty as fuck. I loved Kennedy, but I had to hear it from Craig. Hurt and humiliated, I took the long walk back to Craig.

It felt like every eye in the building focused on me as I spoke. "So is it true? Did you get Christy pregnant?"

Craig looked at me as if he smelled rotten cheese and responded, "What are you talking about? You need to stop listening to rumors."

Not satisfied with his answer, I replied, "So did you fuck her?"

There was a long pause. The silence told it all.

Craig let out a long sigh and mumbled as he stared at the ground. "You got your life, and I got mine."

I wanted to slap the shit out of him. I assumed he was alluding to the fact that I was choosing to go away to college. Craig and his mother had made it perfectly clear that he would be laying his roots down in Baxley. Although they had made it clear, I was sure that I could convince him to leave. And even if he had decided to stay, I was willing to have a long-distance relationship.

Craig looked around the gym as if I didn't exist. I wanted him to say something, but I could tell he had moved on. I remember feeling so hurt and betrayed. It was like all my dreams were going down the drain and there was nothing I could do.

I felt my hand race forward and crash into his face as I spoke. "I hate you, motherfucker. You ain't shit."

I stormed out of my senior prom hoping I would never have to see my classmates again. If I could have left Baxley that night, I would have. Kennedy drove me home and offered to stay, but I declined. I was so hurt and humiliated that all wanted to do was hide.

I headed toward my door and my father greeted me. "What's wrong? What happened?"

I responded by shaking my head and saying, "Nothing, I'm just tired."

My father replied angrily, "Naw. Where that little motherfucker at? He did something, and I'm going to find out."

He opened the door and ran toward Kennedy's car. I was hoping he wouldn't snatch her out of the car thinking it was Craig. But at that point, I really wasn't thinking about that. I slowly climbed the stairs to my room and was met by my mother.

She approached me with concern and asked, "What's wrong baby?"

By that time, my eyes were filled with tears. I looked at her and then turned away, shaking my head. I was too upset to even talk. My mother started to follow me, but heard my father's voice getting louder outside. She ran down stairs and the door slammed shut.

I could hear Kennedy now explaining to my parents how that no-good Craig had broken their daughter's heart. I could hear them still mumbling as I dozed off to sleep. I was awakened from my sleep by my father's voice calling my name.

My mother interrupted him by saying, "Would you please leave that girl alone and get out of her room? We can talk about it tomorrow."

I could tell my father still wanted answers that night, but he reluctantly left the room. I pulled my covers over my head and tried to go back to sleep. The only thing on my mind was what Craig saw in Christy Bryant.

Chapter 2

Christy was two years behind Craig, and Craig's mother loved her. Craig's mother always thought that my family was snobs because we lived in a middle-class neighborhood. Christy lived near Craig in Black Town. Both Craig's and Christy's mothers had similar ambitions for their kids—move out of Black Town into a luxurious, double-wide mobile home. I tried to be strong when I saw Craig and Christy, but I often found myself in the bathroom crying. It felt like a cloud of doom was sitting over me. Craig's bright smile and tender kisses now belonged to Christy. All those happy days that we'd had together were gone. They had been taken by a loose project girl from Black Town. Whenever I saw Stormy and Christy, I just wanted to crawl under a rock and die.

Craig did his best not to flaunt Christy in front of me, but she made sure that I knew they were a couple. My father tried to comfort me by telling me that everything would be alright, but it fell on deaf ears. All I wanted to do was finish my last few weeks at Baxley and graduate. I wanted revenge, but I just didn't have the heart to do it. That would be the first time, but certainly not the last, that I found comfort in God.

My father had always placed Bible verses in my backpack since I was eight years old. I used to stuff them in a shoe box until I got older. When I got of age and received the Holy Ghost, I started putting them in a keepsake book. That book would be the lifeline that kept me strong. I would choose random passages every day to read and study. I became more active in the church and my faith grew stronger. By the time graduation came, Christ had made me stronger than ever. I was flush with self-esteem and it showed in everything I did.

I had a four-year academic scholarship to the college of my dreams. I collected so many awards during our awards ceremony that people wanted to rename it the Angela Awards. I accepted each award gracefully, and everyone appreciated it. Even some of the girls from Black Town applauded my accomplishments. I was the only person in the entire school to be awarded a four-year academic scholarship. Christ had showed up and showed out for me. It was no surprise to anyone when I was tapped to give the class valedictorian speech. It's funny why Satan decided that that would be the perfect time to tempt me.

My valedictorian speech was one of those situations when I just let God take the wheel. I spoke with poise and confidence. The normal boredom among the graduates was replaced with respect and admiration. I wanted my speech to be more than just another "good luck seniors," class speech. I wanted everyone to understand that I had a testimony. I wanted all those people who laughed at me on prom night to understand that Christ was greater than them, and that He was shining through me.

I looked around nervously not knowing how to start my speech, and then I heard a low voice say, "Just open your mouth and I will handle the rest."

Relying totally on my faith, I obeyed the voice, opened my mouth and witnessed a thing of beauty.

"Good afternoon graduating seniors. I had something written down on a piece of paper, but Christ is leading me another way. The one thing that I have learned over these past four years is that sometimes you just have to let go and let God."

I paused for split second to let the crowd feel the full effect of my words, and then I began again.

"In other words, sometimes you just have to let go and trust in God."

The audience erupted into loud cheers and applauses.

"There are times in our lives for a split second, we say, "*I can't take it anymore. I quit! I've had it!*In times like these, our mind tells us things like, "*You've got to trust God.*" But deep down in our heart, we're saying, "*Yeah, I've heard all that, but it's not working for me.* We might be 'going through the motions' and appear okay to everyone else, but on the inside, we've giving up and we are drifting further away from God."

Again, I paused for a split second and continued, "God is still God. Period! No matter what the prevailing conditions are, God can still do amazing things above all that we ask for."

Again the audience applauded and nodded in agreement as I continued.

"When you are disappointed, it is important to let the disappointment go, not look behind you, but move forward. I know it's hard trusting God at times like these. You're gonna have good days, but there will be really rough days too. I've learned that I can't focus on "this or that," or what I think I'm lacking. My focus must be on Christ! And Christ alone! Because if I'm not content with just Him, then He will not bring other things into my life."

The crowd grew silent.

"So! The secret to enduring a storm is not a man."

Again the crowd erupted as I spoke with greater emotional emphasis.

"But Christ!"

The crowd stood and started to cheer wildly as I continued to speak.

"The secret to weathering the storm is not getting that promotion that you wanted; it's Christ!"

The secret to withstanding the storm is not having that car that you've always dreamed about. "The secret is Christ!"

The audience was hanging onto every word I was saying, catching every syllable and gripping tightly onto every pause. I felt inspired, almost God like, as I looked out into the sea of people knowing these people were waiting, and listening to every word I was saying.

"It can be real tough letting go of a situation or person that has broken you or left you feeling betrayed. Why would God allow someone to feel this way or to be broken? You may never know why, but instead of asking God 'why', ask Him how you can learn from it and what it is that you need to do to change?Sometimes, God wants us to let things or people go so that He can do His work in us and even in them. If we don't let it go, we may end up slowing down our purpose. God's purpose is much greater than anything we can understand and it is good for us to walk away knowing this, full of faith and trusting Him."

The answer is knowing that Christ gives you strength to be content and to trust Him, even when you don't understand. So, whether it happens or not, be content with Christ. We must come to a place in our lives when we say, 'Lord, whether it happens or not, you are my portion, you are my strength, you are my joy. I trust you first, and Father you alone will provide all my needs in due season. In my current situation, it's a little harder to see the light at the end of the tunnel, but I'm choosing to trust in you. 'He is the same God who saved me, healed me, delivered me, set me free in the past, and He hasn't changed. If you are in one of those moments that didn't go the way you wanted, remember to look back and remind yourself of all the times you have seen God's goodness. If He did it before, He can do it again. I made a choice to Trust Him."

My speech ended with a thankful prayer to Christ for bringing me this far. It was followed by a thunderous standing ovation as people stared in adoration. I didn't walk off the stage egotistically; I left feeling blessed.

Everyone was clamoring to get a piece of the new and improved Angela. Both parents and classmates shook my hand and congratulated me. I was on an emotional high living in the moment when I felt someone touch my shoulder. I quickly turned around and saw Craig's bright smile. I smiled back at him. He surprised me when he leaned in to hug me.

He whispered, "Congratulations. I'm proud of you."

I glanced around nervously not knowing how to respond. I finally managed an uneasy "Thank you."

I felt more comfortable as other classmates approached excited about graduation and looking for pictures. I lost sight of Craig briefly and then he reappeared with a camera.

He held his arm out and asked, "How about one for old time's sake?"

There was something inside me screaming "no!" But I ignored it.

I didn't have feelings for him anymore, so it was like taking pictures with a friend. I agreed and he pulled me close to take a selfie. I should have listened to that little voice because my stomach started to twist and knot up. Being that close to Craig ignited feelings that I thought were buried.

Craig continued to hold me as he spoke. "All the seniors are going over to Max Dean Park for a cookout. Are you going?"

Again the little voice in my head started screaming, "No! No!" I spotted my father and brother headed in my direction. They looked like two burly bodyguards trying to protect a client.

My father interrupted our conversation. "Is everything okay?"

I smiled at my father and shook my head yes. My father and brother continued to glare at Craig. It was like they had unfinished business with him.

Craig felt the uncomforting stares and decided it was time to go.

He hugged me and spoke. "If you need a ride to the graduation party, let me know."

My father interrupted just as Craig was walking away. "What graduation party? I thought you were through with that knuckle head."

I responded in an almost pleading voice. "Dad, it's just a get together at Max Dean. I don't want Craig, I'm just catching a ride over there. I'll be in the car with five other people."

I really couldn't understand why I lied to my father. Craig and I hadn't spoken in almost a month, and yet I felt impelled to lie. My father finally agreed and hugged me with little hope written across his face.

He kissed my forehead and whispered, "Be careful."

It was almost like he was letting go, but also warning me not to do anything with Craig to mess up my life.

I heard my conscience speaking. "This is starting out bad. Maybe it's not such a good idea to go."

By the time I finished arguing with my conscience, we were at Max Dean. Craig made me feel so special. He complimented me and told all his friends that he and I would always be soul mates. I started to remember why I fell in love with Craig in the first place.

As the night drew to a close, I found myself alone with him. This was not what I had envisioned. I should have known it was wrong because I lied to my friends. I told them that I was going on a walk by myself, but actually I was meeting Craig far away from the cookout. When I arrived at the agreed upon spot, Craig already had a blanket spread out. I was nervous and I wanted to go home, but listening to Craig made me comfortable.

He held me tightly and spoke. "I'm sorry for hurting you like I did. We had something special together and I tossed it away for a moment of weakness. And now I'm finding out that Christy's not even pregnant with my child. She told all those lies to trap me with some other dude's baby. My mother has already given me the money for a DNA test. As soon as this baby is born, I'm going to prove it to you and everybody else that I'm not the father."

The words coming out of his mouth were everything that I had dreamed about. The more Craig talked, the more I blamed Christy for the situation. I leaned forward and kissed Craig. It felt like old times. He pulled me closer and I could feel the passion in his kisses. The thought of Christy trying to trap Craig angered me. I could feel revenge finally becoming a reality.

My voice of warning had been replaced with another voice asking, "Why not sleep with her, man? Not only sleep with him, but take him away from her."

I gently pushed Craig off me and looked deeply in his eyes. I saw his hunger for what he had been wanting, and tonight I was going to give it to him. I stood up and unloosened the bow of my sundress and allowed it to flutter softly to the ground. Craig immediately pulled up to his knees and started squeezing my breasts. His sudden grip on my breast made me cringe in pain. I softly pleaded with him to be gentle. He quickly wrestled me to the ground, and he was half naked before I could turn over. Craig gnawed at my neck like a vampire and fumbled with my bra strap. I wondered to myself what exactly was magical about this.

My dreams of a night filled with passion was turning into a nightmare. Craig was awkward as he poked and grabbed at my vulva with his fingers. Again, I asked him to be gentle, and he responded by yanking my panties off. He wedged his pants and underwear around his knee and jumped on top of me. Craig shoved his penis between my legs and began to hump. I felt bad for him because he was not even inside me.

I was paralyzed with fear as Craig continued to pull and tug at my leg so that he could get a better insert position. I started to think about my father's reaction and Christy's situation, and I just flat-out chickened out. I used all the strength I could muster and pushed Craig off of me. He fell back in anger leaking sperm on the blanket.

It was at that moment that the real Craig quickly surfaced. "What the fuck is wrong with you? You see, that's why I'm with Christy. She's a real woman who understands what I want in my life and you don't."

It was at that moment that I knew my life would never be the same again. I stood up and quickly dressed.

I could hear Craig screaming, "Where you going? Angela, Angela, hold up, here I come."

I continued to walk not waiting for him. As I got further away from Craig, I began to feel vindicated. I may have ignored God's signs at first, but I didn't ignore the most important one. When I arrived back at the cookout, I was praising God inside. I had defeated the devil. Craig arrived back at the cookout angry. He walked past us and went straight to his car. His friends looked at me suspiciously, but I didn't care. I got a lift from a friend and walked into my house singing.

My father looked at me uneasily and asked, "Are you okay?"

I hugged my father with excitement and responded, "Yes I'm fine! Whenever Christ fights your battle, you're always fine."

My father smiled back at me shaking his head yes. "That's right baby, you tell them." I would find that as my life progressed, God would always give me warnings and signs. I just had to obey them.

The rest of the summer blew by very fast, and I was looking forward to my freshmen year at Spelman. I hadn't seen Craig since the senior picnic, but in a small town like Baxley, it was hard avoiding the inevitable. My father thought that it would be a great idea to drive to Myrtle Beach for an end of the summer celebration. The whole family agreed to go, so my brother and his fiancé decided to drive down and ride with us.

My father stopped to fill up the car before getting on the road, and I decided to grab a few snacks. I was concentrating on which bag of chips had the least amount of calories when my awkward Craig moment arrived. I saw Craig and Christy trying on matching John Deere baseball caps. I was frozen with embarrassment and I tried to remain out of sight. Christy appeared to be six or seven months pregnant, and Craig was hugging and touching on her like he used to do with me.

I was trying my best to stay unnoticed when I heard a voice that reminded me of nails scrapping across a blackboard. It was Craig's mother.

"Hi, hummm hummm…. what's your name?" Ms. Harden asked with a smirk.

In my mind, I was screaming, "You know my name, bitch!"

But on the outside, I played it as cool as could be expected.

I smiled at her and spoke. "My name is Angela. Angela Anderson. How are you doing, Ms. Harden?"

I tried to walk away, but she was insistent. "Oh yeah, Ms. Angela. I'm doing fine, how about yourself."

Before I could answer, she blurted out, "Who you in here with, your man or something?"

The thing about country ghetto people is that when they talk, everybody knows what they're talking about.

This little encounter was no exception as she continued to scream, "There's Craig with his fiancée Christy over there. Hey Craig! Here go that one girl that you use to date."

I was saved and sanctified, but oh, how I wanted to punch that bitch. Craig and Christy quickly looked in my direction. I could have crawled under a rock because I was so embarrassed. Craig and Christy started walking towards me with smug looks on their faces. I looked around horrified, hoping that someone would save me from this nightmare coming to life.

I guess my older brother saw how the picture was unfolding, because I saw him headed in my direction like a superhero.

Craig and Christy arrived a few seconds ahead of my brother and Craig started speaking. "This is my fiancée, Christy."

I don't know if Craig was trying to hurt me or if he was just too dumb to understand what he was doing. I wanted to leave but my direction was blocked by them. Christy, Craig, and his mama stood in front of me like a bunch of arrogant farmhands. I just wanted to smash my cheese doodles in their faces.

I was about to start cursing when my brother approached and interrupted the uneasy silence. "Hey Hailey Mae and Leroy, it's been a long time!"

Ms. Harden looked at me and my brother confused and said, "My son's name is Craig, not Leroy, and this is his fiancée, Christy."

My brother replied, "Oh! Craig and Christy? I could have sworn someone told me that you live in the Pine Bluff trailer park."

Craig replied with a smirk, "We don't live in Pine Bluff yet, but our application is still under consideration."

I loved it when Steven played these roles because his wit and quick thinking always gave him an edge. Steven had the ability to humiliate you while having a civilized conversation with you.

When he made a statement like, "The sky is certainly dense," The victim would look at the sky and agree with him. In actuality, he was saying that the person was stupid. I felt so sorry for the Pine Bluff family because they were falling right into his trap.

My brother turned to me and asked in a serious voice, "Hey Angela, let's buy matching t-shirts for our trip. I bet nobody rocks it like that down in those back woods."

I did everything I could to avoid laughing in Craig's face. Craig reminded me of the road runner scratching his head and waiting for the next joke on him.

My brother glanced around the store with a look of pain on his face and continued to speak. "Seriously man, what's that smell?

Craig and company looked around uncomfortably as Steven continued, "It smells like ear backs and fresh baby milk. Hey Hailey Mae, ahh…I'm sorry, Christy, when is your baby due?"

Christy looked at Craig and his mother confused, and then responded, "In November."

Steven responded like Denzel Washington in *Training Day*. "Boom! I was thinking about buying some potted turkey meat for our family meal today."

The joke flew right over the heads of Christy and Craig's mother. But I almost pissed my pants. Craig and I knew exactly what Steven was talking about. The joke around town for years was that people who lived in trailer parks ate potted meat and corn starch gravy for Thanksgiving.

Craig shamefully scratched his head and pulled at Christy's arm as he spoke. "Come on mama, we got things to do."

Steven saluted Craig and his family as they walked away.

As if that wasn't funny enough, I heard him say, "Pine Bluff is in the mutha fucken house!"

Craig turned around as if he wanted to speak, but Christy grabbed his arm and pulled him toward the door.

Steven just continued, "A Leroy, keep it moving baby, keep it moving."

Craig's attempt to make me feel less than him backfired. I found out later that Craig's mother would not let the incident die.

In fact she was overheard telling co-workers, "Angela Anderson won't get far. I bet she will drop out of college and move in a trailer home next to Craig and Christy."

As I walked out of that 7-Eleven store, I felt like a million bucks. It would be a long time before I saw Craig again, but that day I was on top of the world. When we returned from the family vacation, I was energized. Christ was first in my life, my priorities were straight, and I was headed to Spelman College. My dream of moving to Atlanta had finally come and I was excited. What could possibly go wrong in my life?

Chapter 3

Shaquonda and I exited the plane, and after a short ride, we arrived at our hotel. In my room, I kicked off my heels and walked over to the window and gazed out reminiscing on how long it had been since I was in this area.

My first day at Spelman was nerve racking. My brother offered to let me stay with him and his wife, but I always knew that I would live on campus. There was something special about living on campus for the first time and being totally independent from my parents. I arrived on campus two weeks prior to my first day because I wanted to complete a walk-through of my classes.

When I arrived at my dorm, there were student ambassadors waiting to greet us. Deirdre Phillips greeted me and my family with a warm friendly smile. Deidre had smooth, brown skin with long, dark hair and a smile that could light up a room. Deirdre asked to see my dorm assignment and directed me towards Abby Hall. My father and I understood that a quick goodbye would be best for everyone. My mother had a harder time understanding that. My mother started crying first, and soon I was wiping tears also. After saying goodbye for what seemed like an eternity, she was dragged to the car by my father. Exhausted from the day's excitement, I slumped down on my bed and started to doze off.

My light sleep was interrupted when I heard Deidre scream, "Your roommate's here!"

Deidre came into the room and introduced me to a girl named Kayla Price. Kayla would eventually play a major part in my life, but that day we were just two geeky freshman.

I stood up and extended my hand and spoke. "Hello, my name is Angela Anderson. I'm pleased to make your acquaintance."

Kayla and Deidre looked at each other and started laughing.

Kayla shook my hand and responded, "Girl relax, this is not professor so and so time."

Kayla's older sister Donna walked into the room like she owned it. Donna looked like an older version of Kayla. She glared at me with suspicion and spoke to Deidre, "So this is the best we got?"

Deidre pushed Kayla near me and said, "Two pitiful crabs."

At first I felt offended, and then I heard Kayla respond in excitement, "Whatever, just wait till I cross over."

I looked at the three girls dumbfounded and responded, "Is there a basketball game tonight? Are you guys talking about dribbling a basketball?"

All three girls looked at me like I was from another planet and started laughing. They exited the room and then I heard Donna say to Kayla, "Come on girl, you have to coach her up. She can't be on campus like that."

I immediately called my brother hurt and confused. I told him that it might be a good idea if I stayed with him because my roommate was already being mean. I was surprised at my brother's reaction when he started laughing at me also.

After Steven caught his breath he spoke. "Angela, crab is another name for freshman, and crossing over is referring to her joining a sorority."

I felt really stupid as I hung the phone up. In small town Baxley I was the shit; I found out quickly in college that I was at the bottom of the food chain. Kayla and her sister came back in the room lugging three large suitcases and dropped them on the floor from exhaustion.

Kayla stretched out on the floor and asked, "Do you want to go to an AGA party?"

I was still unsure of what to say in this particular situation. I was raw and had no knowledge of Greek life. I was a member of the Senior Beta club in high school, but that was the extent of my Greek knowledge. I remember the freshman girls at my high school who had dreams of joining our Beta club. They would sit at Beta Club-designated tables at lunch wearing t-shirts that read, "I wanna be a Beta like (with some senior's name inserted on it)."

We felt like royalty because these poor freshmen girls were trying to be a part of us. The reality of it was that I had no clue to what Greek sororities and fraternities were about. My brother was interested in joining a fraternity until he saw people on the track team showing up to class beat up and branded.

My brother and I grew up watching the Cosby Show and School Daze, so both of our conclusions were already slightly skewed. I saw bits and pieces of Greek life when I worked as an intern at ESPN. Some of the older interns would let me tag along when they attended step shows. I enjoyed the step shows because all the steps were choreographed and in sync. I was always excluded from the meet-and-greets because I was still in high school. I remember wondering why they were so damn secretive.

When it came to sorority life, Kayla wanted to hit the ground running. Kayla made it perfectly clear that she planned to cross as an AGA as soon as she got the opportunity. Kayla said that she spent her entire high school years preparing herself to one day join an AGA chapter. I really didn't have a preference. My main objectives were the connections.

I finally gave in and agreed to go to the party with her. On our way to the party, Kayla made it clear that she would be busy. She encouraged me to get acquainted with different people because it would help me later. I didn't think much about it until we arrived at the party. As soon as we walked in, Kayla was whisked away to small, roped-off area of the room. All sororities and fraternities were separated by their distinct groups into long conga-like lines and they were twirling and jumping.

I thought I would eventually see Kayla dance with the AGAs, but she never did. All she did was stand in the little roped-off area and hold coats. I later found out that she was pledging underground. As a freshman, Kayla was not eligible for any sorority. It was like she was interning for their consideration. I never really understood why anyone in their right mind would choose to pledge underground because it was like a crap shoot. If you make it through the pledging process you are looked on favorably. If you are caught participating in this process, you are black-balled. You could never participate in the process again, in essence ruining your chance to ever being in the sorority. I have to give it to my girl Kayla; she was a champ for that cause.

The new freedom during my freshman year was intriguing. I studied hard but I also did some exploring. Most of my exploration consisted of hanging close to Kayla and a lot of Bible class. Kayla had a lot of connections through her sister, so she was always invited to a party on campus. I accompanied Kayla to a couple of parties, but I felt out of place. Sometimes I would go to church with Steven, but most of the time was spent in Bible class on campus. Most of the people in Bible class were just like me; new to the big city and loved Christ with all of their hearts. Kayla was a great friend during my freshman year, but nothing came before my faith.

The most embarrassing moment for me occurred when my father called one Saturday night.

I answered the phone while reading the Bible and my father spoke. "Hey baby girl, what are you doing?"

I responded with a bored yawn, "Nothing, just reading."

There was a long pause from my father and then he asked, "You ever thought about going out and having some fun?"

I giggled and responded, "Daddy what are you talking about? Are you calling me boring or something?"

My father laughed and than spoke. "No, I'm not calling you boring. I'm just saying you don't have to read the Bible 24-7. It's okay to get out and have a little fun."

I smiled to myself and responded, "Dad, I'm okay. I enjoy reading the Bible. I can't believe you called me boring."

My father and I laughed and talked about other things until he got of the phone. You know you have a boring life when a preacher tells you to get a life.

Even though family members encouraged me to go out and explore, I was afraid. The fear of God's wrath and my introverted personality always held me back. But that summer would change everything.

My freshman year flew by, and the day after finals, I excitedly packed my bags in anticipation of going home. I thought about all my high school friends and I even thought about Craig. I guess I was curious and wanted to see if he was still happy. I called my mother and reported that I was through with finals and ready to come home. I heard uneasiness in my mother's voice as she told me to talk to my father.

My father got on the phone and started the conversation by saying, "Baby girl, you know I love you, but you won't be coming home for the summer."

I tried to make sense of what my father was saying, but the whole conversation left me dazed and confused.

The last thing I heard my father say was, "Don't forget to call Steven, and we'll see you on Fourth of July weekend."

I immediately called Steven almost in tears and told him what had happened.

Steven consoled me and spoke. "They didn't mean any harm. They just want you to get the full experience of being anywhere except in Baxley. That's why they come here during the holidays. They don't want you to go back home and get comfortable. They did the exact same thing to me during my freshman year."

I thought back to my brother's freshman year, and remembered when my parents made him stay in Atlanta for summer break. Carson went back to Baxley and left Steven by himself. I remember Steven being so sad and miserable without Carson that summer. We piled in the car and drove to Atlanta to cheer him up. I remember my father took him out for lunch and he came back with a used car. Steven's whole attitude changed after getting that car and he never looked back.

Steven encouraged me to go outside. I walked out of my dorm thinking how nice that would be. I was halfway out the door when I saw Steven standing next to a car with a big bow on it.

People were crowded around the car taking pictures and wondering who the lucky person was. I heard a shriek of excitement bellowing from across the yard. I turned in time to see my roommate Kayla run past me. Kayla ran to my car and jumped in the driver's seat. Kayla seemed to be more excited for me than I was for myself.

Steven asked in a concerned voice, "What you don't like the color? We can exchange it for a red if you want."

I responded in a daze of excitement, "I love it but how did you buy this."

Steven responded, "Dad, Mom, and I pitched in and bought it for you." He wrapped his arms around me and continued, "Baby sis, I want you to stay in Atlanta and enjoy the summer like I did. There is nothing in Baxley for you. Always remember that."

Kayla and I were inseparable from that point forward. My cocoon full of self-doubt marred by years of Pentecostal Holiness guilt gave way to a butterfly in a new world. The church was the only thing I knew from when I was a baby to my senior year in high school. It was like being kept in a bubble in a very small town. My parents made sure that anything contrary to the church was quickly dismissed. I never had the opportunity to question my own beliefs. I wanted to try new things, I be dammed if I got it wrong!

During that summer, my confidence grew more and more. I was finally away from the watchful eye of my parents and the church. I started discovering new things that my parents and the church considered devil's work.

I loved being out of control and not having any boundaries. The church always gave me rules and guidelines that kept me from sinning. I may have tested those boundaries, but I never crossed them.

The church never allowed me to think without restrictions. The hell and brimstone sermons and the pain of regret had me paralyzed with fear. That summer was the first time in my life I had no rules. I had an abundance of curiosity with no rules for outlet.

I started sipping cranberry and tonic water, graduated to mojitos, and overdosed on Rosé. It was something about Satan's nectar that made me feel like I owned the world. The worse thing about it was the more devil's work I discovered, the more I wanted.

Instead of being attracted to guys in my Bible study group, I was attracted to guys like Malik Adams. Malik didn't follow anyone's rules and I loved it. Some of the guys in my Bible study class were cute. They were fun to be around, but they placed too many restrictions on themselves. The safe limits that they placed on themselves made them look almost infantile compared to Malik.

I met Malik while I was shopping at the West End Mall. The moment I saw him, I was attracted to him. His language was vulgar and he had bad manners. Malik was a piece of forbidden fruit that I could not resist. He allowed me to do and say what I wanted, without shaking a naughty finger in my face. Malik made me forget about my life of structure and pushed me towards disorder. And after Kayla left for that summer, he had total access to me.

Malik was raised in the crime-infested Bankhead Courts by a crack-addicted mother. He had done and seen too much in his life to ever believe that there was a future outside of Bankhead Courts. Zone 1, Westside Atlanta, was paradise to Malik. All of his friends grew up in the same area, sold drugs in the same area, got arrested in the same area, and were willing to die in the same area. Malik's motto was live life to the fullest because you only get one.

Kayla was my barrier between logic and mayhem. She only allowed me to have small doses of Malik. She had seen guys like Malik on the south side of Chicago and she knew he was trouble. Kayla warned me about Malik, but I just didn't care. I promised Kayla that I would limit my time with Malik, but I was lying. Now Satan controlled my voice of reasoning and I loved it.

Backsliding felt like a free fall of never-ending adventure. Malik introduced me to the gritty part of Atlanta, and I wanted to take in every ounce of it. During the day, I would dress in my business outfit and work my internship at ESPN. At night, I would let loose with Malik. I don't know what it was, but I just loved being around him. My father always taught me to put on the whole armor of God. I found out quickly that my armor was ill prepared for Satan's snares. I had always been stiff and straightedge. Malik taught me how to loosen up and be free.

I now considered my Bible class friends corny. Who the hell wanted to sit around all night discussing the Passion of Christ? I wanted to be in the club with Malik and the rest of the misfits. Along with drinking, I was introduced to marijuana. I found out very quickly that being that high scared me.

As usual, Malik and I were on our way to the club. I heard a lighter flick and then a strong aroma engulfed the car.

I looked at Malik and asked in a curious voice, "What is that?"

A slight grin crept across Malik's face as he responded, "Com'on now shawty, I know you curious, but you ain't ratty fo dis."

Malik's face looked relaxed as marijuana circulated throughout the car.

Again I insisted, "Come on, Malik let me try it."

Malik shook his head and pushed the long brown cigar in my direction. I placed the blunt to my lips and tried to inhale like Malik. I immediately started coughing like someone had cut my breath off. I handed the blunt back to a laughing Malik.

The initial feeling was of total relaxation spreading throughout my body. Then my ears popped and everything changed. The brake lights in front of us looked like little red dots in a curved tunnel. I shook my head to clear the imaginary cobwebs, but it just made the situation worse.

At the club, my legs felt like I was high stepping and couldn't control my direction. Malik escorted me to a booth and went to the bar to get me a bottle of water. Malik was making his way back from the bar and speaking to the usual crowd when I got the funny feeling of betrayal.

I saw Malik talking to one of his friends and I thought I heard him say, "Bet we can kill her tonight."

When Malik returned to the table I instantly flew off the handle and threatened to call 911.

Malik looked at me strange and said, "Gurrrl, wat wrong witchu?"

I pointed at Malik and responded, "I have friends in high places who will hunt you down like a rabbit dog if one hair on my head is harmed."

Malik doubled over and started laughing and said, "Gurrl you high, dat's dat hydro talking."

My mouth was dry and I found it hard to focus as I continued. "I think you should take me home. I can't trust anybody in here."

Malik helped me stagger to the car and we drove off. I still persisted and argued that he should take me home. The last thing I remember is sitting in the car with Malik and him laughing.

The next morning, Malik showed his friends and me a video of me from the night before. I was talking into my shoe to an imaginary 911 operator. I told the operator in my shoe that Malik was going to kill me at Turner Field. I would have to say that being that high was not cute at all. I was sweating and my wig was matted to my face.

I was mumbling incoherently into my shoe, "He got a knife, I'm dead." Malik's friends never allowed me to live it down and I never smoked weed again.

The best part about being around Malik was the way that he roughed me up sexually. Malik was the first guy to actually take my virginity. He had had other girlfriends and baby's mamas, but I just didn't care. When I got that itch between my legs, he knew how to scratch it and he could scratch it well.

My first sexual experience with Malik was not what I expected coming from a thug. Malik never pressured me into having sex with him, but I was curious. He could touch my body in a certain spot and I would just shiver with excitement. I especially loved when he would take off all his clothes and stand in front of me. He would let me touch every inch of his body.

The first thing you noticed about Malik was his brown, copper skin and freakish, green eyes. I had never seen a black man with such odd-colored eyes. When the sun reflected off of them, they almost looked like marbles. I would often catch both men and women second glancing into Malik's eyes because they almost looked unreal. He walked with a slow bounce as if moving to his own imaginary music. He had a long, slender body with broad shoulders and a muscular chest. The muscles on his body made him look like an action figure. Malik had spent time in a juvenile and adult prison. He talked grimy and acted every bit of it. After exploring Malik's body, I would always get excited. All I knew how to do was grind against him with my panties on, like I used to do with Craig. Malik would laugh at me not as a joke but in a "this is cute" kind of way.

He knew I had no idea of what I was doing, so he intensified the pleasure of my experience. He stripped me down to my bra and panties and leaned back in his chair. He pulled me on top of him and gently started rubbing my butt. I would grind against him until my body was convulsing and my panties were soaking wet. Unlike Craig, he never got overly excited to the point of sexual release. His dick would still be hard even after I was convulsing like a dope feign on the floor.

The day I lost my virginity was different. I arrived at Malik's apartment and he was already naked and smoking a joint. I quickly dropped all my belongings and stripped down to my bra and panties. I ran to Malik like a kid on Christmas morning and tried to jump in his lap. Malik laughed and stopped me in my tracks.

He gently tugged at my panties and said, "Go ahead baby and loosen them for me."

Malik leaned back in his chair and stared at me as if to say "your move." I was afraid because I was a virgin. I thought about all the times my father told me to wait because of all the bad things that could happen. I felt uncomfortable, but I still pulled my panties down. Malik's legs began to sway as his erect penis bobbed back and forth. He stood up and pulled me close. I nervously allowed his hard penis to slide between my thighs. I could feel my pulse race faster as he slowly moved back and forth. My stomach started vibrating with anticipation almost like the first hill on a rollercoaster ride.

Malik started kissing me as he slowly walked me to his bed.

He asked me if I was ready and I quietly replied yes. I took my bra off and laid it on his bed. I felt uncomfortable but excited at the same time. So many thoughts ran through my head that it was hard to catch one. Malik reached in his nightstand, pulled out a condom, and stretched it over his penis.

I sat on his bed trying to look sexy, but I felt myself shaking. I wanted to have sex with Malik but I was afraid of the unknown.

Malik moved my hair out of my face and spoke, "Baby, I know you're afraid, but you can trust me. I won't hurt you."

I felt a tear roll down my cheek as I shook my head okay. I didn't know why I was so emotional. Maybe it was from all the guilt of growing up in the church and all the excitement shooting through my body.

Malik pulled me near and again asked, "Are you sure about this?"

I wiped the tears from my eyes and responded, "Yes."

Malik inched toward me and kissed me while gently climbing on top of me. Malik hovered over me and waited patiently as I searched for courage. I slowly spread my legs open, and he carefully slid inside me. My body instantly froze with pain.

Malik gently pulled in and out of me and asked, "Are you okay?"

I quickly shook my head yes while wincing in pain. The pain was soon replaced with a feeling of pure pleasure as Malik guided my body into the unknown.

I always thought my first time would feel like a wild animal ripping me apart. I remember sitting in church and hearing horror stories about young virgins bleeding out. I really believed that I would have to go to hospital after my first experience. The reality was totally different. After my first time, I remember having a feeling of accomplishment. I felt empowered when I saw Malik struggling to stay in control. I could not believe that I was doing this to him. Seeing Malik in such a vulnerable state made me feel powerful. All of that tough talk was replaced with whimpers as he buried his face in the pillow and released inside of me.

For Malik, I was just another notch in his belt; the experience that he gave me that summer helped me grow as a person. I no longer feared the unknown; in fact, I embraced it. People in the church may not have agreed with my approach to freedom, but I never regretted it. Now when I look back, I almost laugh at who I was. It was like I was a small child in a woman's body. My only comprehension of the world had been taught to me by the church. That summer, I lived the experience and enjoyed it.

Being with Malik served its purpose at that time in my life. Malik gave me freedom from rules and God. I knew our relationship could never be more than what it was, and I was fine with that. I was kept in a glass snow globe my entire life and told what not to do. Malik helped me release by saying yes and satisfying my curiosity. That summer was a summer of great discovery for me. Everything that I was told not to do in New Heaven Pentecostal Church became a completed task for me. I finally was able to break free from the clutches of the church, and having sex was the ultimate freedom for me.

Malik was eventually arrested for armed robbery and parole violation. I guess I should have accepted that it was only a matter of time before Malik went back to prison. The strange thing about it was

I never saw it as something that could actually occur. Malik's lack of respect for rules was such an attractive characteristic, but it was also what destroyed him.

I guess I was selfish about the situation because I was angry at Malik for getting arrested. No matter how dangerous and twisted it seemed, Malik was the one person who really understood me. Every aspect of my life had always been controlled, and Malik's life was the total opposite. In Malik was a secret comfort zone that allowed me to be out of control without judgment. Now I was angry because that was taken from me, and I had no one to blame except Malik.

I ignored the collect calls and refused to visit him. I wanted him to suffer by himself the way he was making me suffer. Eventually I stopped being selfish and decided to attend his bond hearing, but I regretted doing so. Malik's bond hearing was just a formality because the judge had already made up his mind. There was no way the judge was letting Malik out of jail. Malik had just been in front of the same judge a month prior for violation of his parole. The judge promised Malik that his sentence would start at 8 years if he ever returned. Malik being himself did what I expected him to do. He lived for the moment no matter what the consequence.

Malik's green eyes widened when he saw me. He was escorted in the court and seated at the table with his public defender. He glanced back at me and waved and the corrections officer stepped in front of us. Malik was charged with four counts of armed robbery and parole violation. I never knew that robbing drug dealers of their drugs was a crime. Malik's public defender tried her best to reason with the judge, but it was of no use.

The judge leaned back in his swivel chair and growled at Malik, "What did I tell you last month?"

Malik opened his mouth to respond, but the judge slammed his gavel hard before any words could come out and snapped, "$250,000 cash bond no 10%."

Malik shook his head and flashed a crooked smile at the judge and responded, "Man, use an ol fuck boy."

The guards cranked Malik's arm until he screamed in pain. I could hear Malik cursing and kicking the wall as he was escorted back to the holding cell.

The judge leaned over to the court reporter and spoke. "Increase his bond to $500,000. I don't know who he thinks he is disrespecting my court like that."

I sat in shock trying to figure out what had just occurred. I tried to get the attention of the public defender, but she was busy sorting through a pile of folders and ignored me.

I was approached by young girl who spoke. "Hi my name is Diana Marshall, and I work with the public defender's office. Are you a family member?"

I responded with a lie. "No! That's my fiancé."

The girl smiled at me suspiciously and responded. "What happened today was a bond hearing for Malik. As you know, Malik has a long history of violent offenses. The judge placed the bond so high on him because he wants him to sit. Malik could have probably been sentenced straight to prison, but he disrespected the judge."

Malik had always told me that he would prefer to get his sentence over with instead of sitting and waiting in the county jail. Being in the county jail was dangerous for Malik because everyone knew each other. Everyone knew who sold drugs. Everyone knew who robbed banks. And in Malik's case, everyone knew who robbed drug dealers. Making Malik sit was like putting him in the eye of the storm.

I glanced around the quiet courtroom and spoke. "So tell me, what are his chances of getting out?"

Diana shook her head and responded, "Not good. If he beats the robbery charge he's still doing time on the parole violation."

Malik's case was problematic because some of the victim's clothes and jewelry was found in the car with Malik. I never understood why Malik didn't just rob for drugs and money. What sense did it make to strip the man naked and take his jewelry? I guess it was a power thing. I bet it gave him such a high just to see the reaction of a person when you strip him of everything including his dignity.

I felt bad for Malik and decided that I would at least try and cheer him up with a visit. I hated visiting Malik in jail because the guards treated everyone like prisoners.

The sheriffs at the door approached you and demanded, "Take that off! Put that on the X-ray belt! Sit over there and wait until I call your name!"

At college, I was treated like the future president. At the county jail, I was treated like an animal.

The guard would call your name along with others and shove a visitors badge toward you and point. "Go that way!"

We looked like cattle being herded through the hall. The further you walked down the cold, sterile hall, the more you realized that a jailbird relationship was hard.

I remember hearing two pregnant women complain about court delays and cases being continued for two and three years. There was no way I would be willing to put my life on hold for that long. That was something that I had not planned for.

Visitors were escorted to a row of small cubicles with tiny stools. Each cubicle had a dirty glass wall and a telephone receiver for talking. The cubicles were attached to the top tier of the cell pod. You could look down on the entire pod and see anxious inmates glaring back. They looked like little kids on Christmas morning looking for Santa. Only those guys were hoping someone would visit them. You could smell stale body funk mixed with whatever food was being served that day and it almost made you throw up.

A guard announced Malik's name over an intercom system and I could see him walk slowly towards me. Malik sat on the opposite side of the glass and smiled. I managed to flash a quick nervous grin, but it was obvious that I hated the experience.

Malik broke the awkward silence by speaking. "I spoke with my public defender the other day. They talking about pleading out for fifteen years." He shook his head in disgust and continued. "Damn shawty, I fucked up this time. They got all types of shit on me from that robbery. And my PO is on some bullshit. You know that motherfucker not even looking to drop the violation. He want me to do five years just on a violation. I guess I can write a letter to the judge and apologize. I think I can cut plea for around ten years. I can't have you going through this on an extra five."

Malik glanced at me to see if I had some type of reaction, but I had none. He looked bad! His normal wavy hair had grown into disgusting nappy dreads. His face was covered in a shabby unkempt beard and his normal bright eyes were filled with gloom. That was the day that both Malik and I knew that our time together was probably over.

Malik tapped the glass and called my name, "Angela."

I just sat there staring at the dirty table in front of me.

Again Malik spoke. "Angela, look at me."

I slowly glanced at him and my eyes filled with tears.

Malik continued, "Angela, I want you to go live your life. I mean, this is it for me. I can't ever offer you anything else except bars and glass. I would love for you to stay in my life, but that would be selfish of me. You have so much going for you and I love you too much to stop that."

I knew Malik was telling the truth, but it still hurt. Malik had been such a big part of my summer that I found it hard to let go. He was like a secret diary that only I knew about and now I was losing it. When the judge gave Malik fifteen to twenty years, he staggered backwards and looked at me for help, but there was nothing I could do but cry. It hurt so much to see Malik being taken away because I knew that chapter in my life was closing.

Malik going to prison was both a blessing and a curse. The blessing was that my life would not be as complicated as before.

Hiding Malik from my family and friends had become a task, and now that situation was gone. The curse was me missing Malik. No matter how wrong Malik was for me, I still loved him. The love I had for Malik was not a "future husband" type love. My love for Malik was like a best friend who truly understood me. Malik helped me experience "my first" with everything that intrigued me. Having sex with Malik was never about love; it was about the experience. My friends bragged about it in high school and during my freshmen year of college. I wanted that experience and Malik was my guide. Malik allowed me to grow from a church girl filled with guilt into a woman who was ready to make her on choices.

Chapter 4

My sophomore year of college started off with a bang. Kayla returned from Chicago and she instantly noticed the difference. I was more confident in myself and I had a little edge when provoked. My parents even noticed that church was no longer my priority, but they were happy with my grades.

Kayla and I finally had enough credit hours to be selected for a sorority line, and it was already understood that it would be AGA. We became experts at being in the right place at the right time.

We would invite Soros to brunch and treat them like Gods. "Is there anything you want? Are you sure you have enough? You weigh three hundred sixteen pounds; girl, you are so skinny."

The ass-kissing paid off because our names started circulating around the inner circle. We studied the history of the organization right down to the smallest detail. Kayla and I quizzed each other daily just to keep sharp and then finally we were selected for interviews. Kayla was so hyped about going to the interview that when we walked into the house, I could have sworn that she was ready to scream "Skeewee!" We mingled and talked with other prospective candidates, and overall I felt really comfortable with the organization when we left. The hardest part of the process was the wait. I remember sitting around the dorm asking other pledges if they had heard anything, and Kayla was no different.

Kayla would rush home every day in search of her acceptance letter and every day would end with more wait. I felt badly for Kayla because she really wanted to be an AGA. I also wanted to be an AGA, but I was certain that I would not get accepted. All the secret rendezvous with Malik and slumming in the ghetto probably had already sealed my fate. It had already gotten back to my parents that their sweet, innocent daughter was now serving the devil.

Over the summer, I ran into Craig while at Lenox Mall. He was visiting in Atlanta with two of his friends and he appeared to be stunned at my outfit. I had replaced the knee-length church skirt with tight, form-fitting shorts and a spaghetti-strap shirt that showed off every curve of my body. Craig tried to impress his friends by approaching me with a conceited look on his face as he extended his arms for a hug. I guess he was still under the impression I spent late nights obsessing over him. I quickly blocked his hug with my elbow and backed away, almost annoyed by his presence.

Embarrassed by my reaction, Craig tried to save face in front of his friends by grabbing my arm and speaking. "Oh! I get it, you're still mad because I broke up with you."

Visibly pissed at Craig, I yanked away from his grasp and pointed in his face, "Don't ever put your hands on me again, Bitch."

Craig glared back at me smiling and was about to answer when Malik approached us in a nervous manner.

Malik saw the anger on my face and instantly stepped in between me and Craig, saying, "Wass good homey, you got a problem wit my shawty?"

The goonish antics Malik exhibited caught Craig totally off guard. He backed up with a stupid grin on his face and glanced over at his friends from Baxley.

Malik, cool and composed, gazed back at the three-man crew from Baxley and again growled, "Nigga, do we got problems?"

Malik's raspy voice and sudden movement toward the gun tucked in his pants startled Craig. The overconfident smile plastered across his face earlier was replaced with fear.

Craig backed toward his friends with his hands out almost begging. "Naw man! We cool! I don't have any problems."

Terrified, he turned toward his friends and quickly headed for the mall exit. Three days later, I received a call from my parents. They told me that Craig was telling everybody that I had someone pull a gun on him. The more I thought about it, the more I realized it was no way Alpha Gamma Alpha Sorority was going to pick me up.

The waiting for Kayla was agonizing and I felt like telling her, "Three weeks. No answer, let's keep it moving."

The problem was that Kayla was stuck in a daze of uncertainty. She wanted to walk up to the AGA sisters and ask, "Why not me?" But she was scared her name was still in deliberation. Kayla was a legacy, but her GPA was right on the border. The GPA requirement was 3. 3 and Kayla was at a 3. 2 before semester finals. Kayla worked so hard to pull her grades up, and I felt so bad for her.

I was sure that joining AGA was just a dream, so I decided that I would attend another rush. I was in the process of mentioning it to Kayla when two envelopes slid under our dorm door. Kayla never saw the envelopes because she was in the kitchen cooking. I walked over to the envelopes and right away I noticed the pink and green AGA insignia. I opened the envelope addressed to me and silently read the first few sentences, when I saw the word "Congratulations," I have to say I was excited.

At the same time, I heard several excited shrieks in the hallway cumulating with a rush of several girls running into our dorm room screaming, "I got my letter! I got my letter! I got my letter!"

Kayla took a deep breath and walked over to the group of excited girls and forced a half-hearted smile on her.

She gently hugged me and whispered in my ear, "We can always apply through graduate chapter."

The evil side of me remembered how she laughed at me on the first day of college, so I decided to get even.

I yanked away from Kayla's loving grasp and looked at her with disgrace and said "I refuse to be in the same room with a person if they are not AGA."

The look on Kayla's face was priceless. It looked like she had gas but couldn't fart.

I held my acceptance letter high in the air and continued in a more hurtful voice. "Sorry girl! But you can always join Zeta."

The room went completely quiet and everybody waited for Kayla's response. Kayla looked at me with an intimidating glare, and just like that, she lost her temper.

The last thing that I clearly understood Kayla say was, "I'll tell you bitches what! Fuck you, Ethel Lyle, and the rest of you AGA motherfuckers."

Kayla's reaction made me fully understand that she was truly from the Southside of Chicago. I quickly grabbed Kayla in a bear hug just as she was turning her Southside venom towards the girls in our room and put her acceptance letter in her face. This new 5150 death to everyone Kayla was replaced by the sweet, loving kisses and hugs for everyone Kayla whom we all knew and loved.

Kayla and I had gone through so much as line sisters and friends. I was so happy that she had agreed to represent us. Any other person would have probably told us to get the hell on. Kayla arrived in my room shortly after we arrived and she was already in business mode. She ordered room service and flopped down on the bed besides me like we use to do in our dorm room. Kayla still looked the same from college and I complimented her on how well she had kept her shape. We both laughed because the last time we had this type of fun was during homecoming weekend after graduation.

During that particular homecoming weekend, all of my line sisters agreed to meet up on Friday and conduct a little session with the current pledges. There were already rumors going around amongst my line sisters that India Wheeler was in the house. The excitement flew into a high frenzy when everyone finally laid eyes on India. The first noticeable thing about India was that she had gained at least thirty pounds and she was wearing a line jacket with our crossover date.

Hold up stop the press! Is this the same girl who went paper?

When people thought of pledging, they thought singing songs and bonding with your fellow probates. Our process was a little different.

The entire pledge process lasted four months and the rules were very simple: Always show up for sessions on time, always answer the phone when a big sister called, and never wear pink and green. India had so much clout during our first line session that most of the big sisters were in agreement that she should simply walk through. Again I say MOST of our big sisters. Kayla's sister Deidre had a whole different approach planned for India.

India's mother had hit the lottery for twenty-eight million dollars and the rest was history. Their family went from the poor house to lifestyles of the rich and famous overnight. India's money gained her access to all the exclusive parties and she was a favorite among the older Soros. Her money excited the older sorority sisters because she was not afraid to spend it. Kayla's and my ass-kissing and fetching chocolate donuts could not compare to an all-expenses-paid trip to the day spa.

India was only twenty years old and already on the sorority's A list. Kayla's and Deidre's parents were wealthy, but they always reminded them how hard they worked to achieve their success. India, on the other hand, was spoiled rotten by mommy's new money. India was dog meat for the chewing even before our first pledge session started. Deidre was on India so fast that it made everybody's head spin.

Deidre first demanded that India take off her $30, 000 pink and green diamond Audemars watch.

I can still hear Deidre saying, "Who are you to wear my colors when you've done nothing to deserve them? Take that off and walk it back to your room. As a matter of fact, all of ya'll walk with her."

We learned a valuable lesson that day about wearing pink and green during the pledging process. We must have walked back and forth at least twenty times, ten times alone for each of her pink and green acrylic nails. I could definitely see that Deidre had it in for India from the start. The rest of us were just casualties of war. I found out quickly that no one had a pass, including Kayla. Session time and subject matter was at the discretion of our big sisters. Sessions consisted of everything from general study hall to washing dishes.

The hardest part of the sessions was the punishments. We became casualties often because of India's pride. If the big sisters said clean the house, India would make some type of comment about not being anyone's housekeeper. Deidre, being the Dean of Pledges, would smile and then make us clean the floor with toothbrushes.

Deidre enjoyed when India said no because it was an opportunity to turn her line sisters against her. There were many nights that we took wood for something that India did. Deidre made it plain to the other big sisters that she did not want India touched, but they made our lives miserable. Deidre's plan was working extremely well because our hate for India was growing with each session.

After a while, it became a test of wills between Deidre and India. If Deidre said right, India went left. Deidre would smile and then go down the line popping each of us with a rolled-up, wet towel. The feeling was like a knife slicing through your skin. If that didn't get the point, her slaps to the face did.

Slapping us in the face was degrading enough, but to saturate her hand in baby powder added to the humiliation. India would sit quietly in the corner as the abuse got worse for us, her line sisters. The long walk back to the dorm was always interesting. India would start out talking and try to explain her point of view. The conversation would almost always end with her being cursed at or threatened and her walking the rest of the way alone in tears. Deidre was wrong for driving a wedge between us, but India's attitude did not help the situation. India surprised all of us when she threw in the towel after four weeks and went paper.

That was what the big stink was about that particular homecoming weekend. The thing about being part of a line is that you have a common goal and you're willing to go through anything to achieve it. I know a lot of us hated her, but we still had her back. If she had just gutted out those four months, she would have earned all of our respect and no one could have taken that away. Under no circumstances do you ever go paper. Going paper is like being marked on your forehead with an "I am weak" sign.

Everyone was sitting around just mumbling about India when *Set it Off* broke through the loud speaker. There we were, professional women with careers, running toward the dance floor trying to keep step. At first I didn't notice the commotion until I saw AGA members dropping off the floor like flies. I crossed over with ten ladies of distinction, and two minutes into the song everybody was sitting except India. I felt sorry for India because she had been black-balled by my sisters. India embarrassingly strolled out the last few minutes of the song by herself with old alumnae members who smelled like bengay cream and cheap perfume.

Cooperate attorneys and school teachers were fighting to see who would take the poor girl's jacket. India exited the dance in a long walk of shame to courses of "Paper! Paper!" I turned around to see the expressions of my line sisters, who all showed satisfaction on their faces.

Those fun times in college also reminded me of the good times and bad with my first love, Patrick Jones.

Patrick was everything that I had imagined a man could be. He was handsome, caring, and loving. Patrick was the first person who had sole possession of my heart without boundaries. I met Patrick at a dance shortly after I crossed over. I was jumping around and strolling like an idiot. I noticed a tall man with flawless, brown skin and wavy hair looking in my direction. His full, sexy lips curled into a smile reveling perfectly white teeth. He reminded me of Shemar Moore with short, wavy hair. I could tell from the way that he was dressed that he was not a fraternity boy. The most popular boys on campus were the athletes and frat boys. Their wardrobes consisted of football jerseys and fraternity paraphernalia. The exotic skin shoes and matching jacket made Patrick stand out. Not like a clown, but like a real hustler.

He had all the signs of being from the streets, but his demeanor was controlled. The thing that stood out to me about Patrick was the way he carried himself. Most of the guys at the party were hounds trying to get as many phone numbers as possible or strolling with their fraternity.

Patrick looked as if the whole scene was beneath him. He danced with several women that night, but you could tell the attention from girls was nothing new to him. Patrick played it cool, but I could feel his eyes glued to my body. Hitting the club scene with Malik paid off because I could wobble-wobble and shake it-shake it with the best of them. A couple of times, I glanced over at Patrick and hit him with the shy smile just to let him know I was interested.

He would wet his sexy lips and hit me back with the "That ass is mine" look.

Toward the end of the night, I found myself strolling to one of my favorite songs when I felt someone gently touch my elbow. I turned around to find Patrick standing there smiling at me. Unbeknownst to him, he was being surrounded by some of my line sisters and fraternity brothers. Patrick looked so sweet and cute, but he definitely did not know the rules of Greek life. I felt sorry for him because it looked like he was about to catch a beat down.

Three of my brothers approached Patrick and asked, "Are you disrespecting my sister?"

Patrick responded in a perplexed voice, "No!"

One of the brothers inched closer to Patrick's face and responded in a merciless tone, "I didn't think so, because you know where this was going."

There was a short period of silence and then I saw Patrick respond in a low, direct voice. "My man, let's get two things perfectly clear. One, I don't disrespect women, especially when she's beautiful. Two, if you ever jump in my face like that again, I will kill you."

Sometimes when people say things like that, you don't believe them. Patrick said it in a way that was believable. He didn't say it as a threat, but almost like a promise. People eased away from him like he had a bad disease.

Patrick handed me a business card and spoke. "When you get a little free time, call me." He waved his hand and fifteen other goons followed him out of the party. There was something dangerous about him that attracted me to him. I loved that bad boy demeanor with a touch of sophistication.

Calling Patrick was not on the top of my list, especially after Malik. I was attracted to Patrick, but I had no time for the drama. I was done with jail visits and gangsters. My mind was occupied with bonding with my line sisters. Fall semester ended in December and I was excited because my hard work had paid off. I made the dean's list and I was in the mood to celebrate. I decided to attend a party with Kayla. Attending a party in Buckhead is about as exclusive as it gets when it comes to partying in Atlanta.

We arrived at the address on Tuxedo Road and I was in awe. The large, black gate and long, winding, cobblestone driveway made me understand the meaning of true wealth. Kayla was accustomed to this type of wealth because her circle of friends had parents who were wealthy. I was used to my parents struggling paycheck to paycheck in our middle-class household. I wanted to ask Kayla about the wealth of her friend, but I didn't want to seem nosy.

We entered the mansion and were greeted by servers with champagne. Kayla was instantly swept away by her rich friends and I was left to explore. I mingled in the crowd and flirted with a couple of guys. But mostly I celebrated my success at school.

I was in the middle of sampling a sushi platter when I heard a deep, baritone voice break my concentration. "I just know you're not about to eat that whole platter?"

I quickly turned my head and saw Patrick's perfectly white teeth gleaming at me. Patrick, catching me with my face stuffed, made me giggle. I turned away in embarrassment trying to compose myself. I could not stop giggling and my face was starting to change colors. Patrick leaned forward and gave me a warm hug and I reciprocated.

Patrick looked a lot different from the last time I saw him. It had to be the suit.

The last time I saw Patrick, he had on jeans and an ostrich wind jacket. He was cute at the college party, but wow did his suit make him more attractive.

Patrick and I entered the sunroom and we both were amazed at the beauty. The beach-inspired sunroom reminded me of a Myrtle Beach. Patrick motioned for a server and offered me a drink. I flashed a quick smile at Patrick and accepted. The conversation was not forced and I enjoyed how he gave me his undivided attention when I talked.

Patrick spent most of the night making me laugh, but I was also impressed with his intellect. Patrick had graduated from the University of Cincinnati with a Bachelor's degree in Financing. I enjoyed hearing him talk and engage in conversation with other people because he expressed himself in an intelligent manner. I don't know if I was more impressed with his making me feel comfortable or with his knowledge for business.

Patrick had moved to Atlanta after he graduated because he wanted to get a true urban feeling, and in just a short period of time, he was a business owner. At twenty-five years old, he already owned four climate-controlled storage companies and was looking to buy two more. Instead of a street thug, he turned out to be a successful businessman. Any woman would be happy to show him off, and here he was with me.

The night ended with Patrick and me exchanging numbers. This time I made sure I called him. I ran for the phone as soon as I got in the dorm.

Kayla looked at me jumping over the couch for the phone and commented. "Damn girl, you acting real thirsty right about now."

I blushed and started laughing. I nervously dialed his number and he immediately answered. Patrick commented on how surprised he was that I had called. The butterflies in my stomach were itching for release as our conversation continued into the night. I knew something was special about Patrick because I had never stayed on the phone with a man for almost five hours. I found myself dozing off because I was so sleepy, but neither one of us was willing to hang the phone up first.

Patrick would speak just as I was dozing off. "Angela, if you're tired, go to sleep. I'll call you tomorrow."

I would perk up and respond. "No! No! Patrick, I'm fine. I was just reaching for something and the phone fell."

This routine continued until finally, sunlight penetrated the windows of my dorm room and we both agreed to call each other later. The thing that impressed me most about Patrick is that he did not have me waiting for him to call. I hated when Malik would say "I'll call you" and then call two or three days later. I hated waiting by the phone for Malik. I hated myself more when I finally called him out of frustration.

Patrick took the awkwardness out of the equation by calling me as soon as he woke up. We talked about having dinner and I hung up the phone excited. Kayla sat on my bed, and I eagerly told her about Patrick.

Kayla jokingly commented, "Be careful not to fall on his dick after that first date." I laughed and playfully tossed a pillow in her direction and walked toward the bathroom. I filled the tub with warm water and added some scented bubbles. I climbed in, turned on my MP3 player, and prepared myself for total relaxation.

Just as the mellow mood was starting to take effect, I heard my stranger ring tone blaring. I paused for a second wondering if it was Patrick, then I decided that he was probably still sleep. I glanced at my phone after hearing the voicemail notification chime, and to my surprise, it was Patrick. I nervously listened to the voicemail and screamed with excitement when he offered to take me to dinner at 7:00pm. Kayla burst through the door thinking I was being attacked and then laughed as I stood their naked listening to Patrick's voicemail again.

Kayla shook her head and again commented, "Yep! You'll find a way to slip and fall on his dick."

Again I laughed, and then pushed the door shut as she left.

Being around Patrick became intoxicating, and I wanted to spend every free moment with him. My line sisters would comment about me spending so much time with him, but I just didn't care. When I was away from him, I ached to be around him, and when I was around him, the time seemed to go way to fast. Everything about him was so alluring. He would call me at the drop of a dime and ask to fly with him out of town. When he invited me to dinner, it was always at the best restaurants. The most attractive quality about him was how protected I felt around him.

No matter how threatening the situation appeared to be, it just didn't bother him. Once we attended a listening party for a local rapper and ran into one of Malik's friends. Malik's old acquaintances approached the table and spoke to me. I spoke back and tried to introduce Patrick as my boyfriend.

I guess Malik's friend wanted to test the heart of Patrick so he interrupted my introduction. "Yea, yea, yea, whatever, I'm just trying to find out wus up wit you."

There was a short uncomfortable silence and then Patrick stood up and responded sternly with a calm demeanor, "I don't know who or what you're relationship is with Angela, but don't ever disrespect me like that again."

Maybe it was the way Patrick said it or maybe it was the uneasy silence that filtered throughout the crowd.

Malik's friend smiled and responded, "Oh we going to the streets with this."

Patrick's lips curled in the corner as he glared back as if to say, "I believe that would be the best option to solve this."

Malik's friend walked away from the table shaking his head and responded, "Okay, we'll see!

I saw him congregate in the corner for a short time with his friends. Patrick was smiling back at them as if taunting. I took a deep breath and prepared for the worst as the goon hurried back to our table. The first thought that entered my mind was that this is going to be ugly.

Malik's friend arrived at the table and clumsily searched for the correct way to apologize, "My fault! I mean, I'm sorry for disrespecting you. I mean, we cool, right?"

Patrick glared at Malik's friend as if to say, "Go and sin no more." Patrick accepted his apology and Malik's friend offered to cover our bar tab for the evening. Malik's friend quickly retreated to the comfort of the corner with his friends and continued to gaze in awe at Patrick. I spent the rest of the evening wondering who this man was and what exactly made him so powerful.

Regardless of the setting, Patrick could adapt to it. No matter whether he was talking to company executives or cut-throat gangsters, he knew their language. When Patrick walked into an establishment, he was met with respect and admiration, and I enjoyed being part of it. Not just any twenty-five-year-old was invited to the Mayor's Inauguration Dinner, but Patrick was. Not just any twenty-five-year-old owned a townhome in Buckhead, but Patrick did. And not just any twenty-five-year-old could charter a jet and party in South Beach when he wanted, but Patrick could.

The closer we got to each other, the more I found myself falling for him. Patrick never pressured me for sex, but my God, every time he came around, my body caught fire. Sometimes I would just lie in my bed naked wrapped in his shirt just to be close to him and dream about making love to him. My line sisters would tell me to be careful; that I was moving way too fast. I would just write it off as jealousy. Patrick was everything that I had ever wanted in a man and I was not going to let those jealous hoes come between us.

Patrick was not a trick or a sugar daddy, but he made sure that I had everything. My father was worried that I was being pimped out, so he caught a plane to Atlanta. I was so embarrassed when my father showed up at the Sun Dial Restaurant.

Patrick and I were dining and slowly rotating when I rotated toward the door and saw my father and brother. I was mortified, but it never made Patrick uncomfortable. He simply invited my father and brother over to the table to have dinner and paid for it. My father grilled Patrick about his job, family, and intentions with me for what seemed like an eternity. Patrick smiled and replied with respect. He invited my father to come see his business if that would make him feel more comfortable. Seeing Patrick's storage facilities appeared to satisfy my father's curiosity. He seemed impressed by Patrick. My brother seemed more concerned about how Patrick made his money than my father.

My father and Patrick were having a spirited conversation about the latest news when my brother leaned over and whispered, "I'm just saying sis, there's no way you can own a condo in Buckhead just by renting out storage units. What other illegal shit is he into?"

I looked at my brother in disbelief because he was always the one who supported me. "Steven, how can you ask me that? Patrick is a successful businessman who has his life together. Why can't you just be happy for me?"

Steven just shook his head as if he was watching a tennis match in overdrive and responded, "Something's just not right about this."

I have to admit that I thought about Patrick possibly being involved in something illegal, but I always found a way to push that thought out of my mind. Everything about Patrick seemed perfect in my eyes and I wanted it to stay that way.

The more time I spent with Patrick, the more I wanted him. Patrick and I would spend many nights just talking about our thoughts and dreams. Most nights we would go from talking and touching to nearly nude grinding. I could tell Patrick wanted to go further, but I would always pull back. Maybe I was afraid of eventually losing him to prison like I did Malik, or maybe I was just afraid that he would hurt me. I was tired of ending up with the short end of the stick. I wanted more then just a summer fling. I wanted a long-term commitment.

This game of cat and mouse lasted for four months until I was convinced that Patrick was everything that he was portraying. If Patrick wasn't the person that he claimed to be, he sure was a damn good actor. Everything about Patrick indicated that he was everything that I had dreamed of.

One night, I just decided to throw caution to the wind and go with what I was feeling. I was sitting in the chair and he was on the floor watching TV. I always enjoyed messaging Patrick's shoulders while he sat between my legs with his arms draped across my thighs. I loved when he would lean back between my thighs while watching TV because it made me feel so protected. That night, I was gently messaging his shoulders when I found myself wondering how it would feel to have Patrick inside of me. Patrick was telling me about his day and I leaned forward, pulled his body close to mine, and just held him tight.

Patrick rubbed my leg gently and asked, "What's wrong, baby? You okay?"

I responded by whispering in his ear, "I want you inside of me tonight"

I proceeded to pepper his neck with gentle kisses.

My aggressiveness must have caught Patrick by surprise because he turned around and looked at me as if warning me not to start something I couldn't finish.

There had been many nights that I had teased Patrick with my body but had not followed through. Tonight was different. I wanted to go further. I wanted the beast to come out of Patrick.

I slowly pushed Patrick to the floor and slithered up his body. I continued to kiss his soft lips and grind against his body until his hard penis was begging to be unleashed. I slowly unzipped his pants and gently massaged his dick until it was throbbing with anticipation.

I nibbled at his neck and ear until I felt his massive hands start gliding up and down my thighs. He could sense I was nervous because I was trembling as I curled around his sculptured body.

Patrick gently kissed me on the cheek, brushed my hair away from my eyes, and asked me, "Are you okay?"

I responded yes and bashfully glanced into his eyes.

I helped Patrick pull his t-shirt and boxers off and instantly I saw the body of a God appear before my eyes. His body was chiseled like granite from his strong chin to his pubic bone. Both Craig and Malik had nice bodies, but damn! Patrick's body was sick. Every line of his sculptured body was separated by 3-D muscles ending at the tip of his penis. Patrick unbuttoned my shirt and let it fall to the floor exposing my perky nipples.

Patrick smiled at me and said, "Mm Mm mmm! I never knew you were hiding all of this under that shirt."

I stood there in my sexy panties smiling as if I were a bikini model. Patrick gently pulled my body close to his and traced my panty lines with his fingers. He kissed my neck softly and then pulled me down. I felt his hard penis slide between my thighs and I froze with anticipation. I tried to look as sexy as possible but I was trembling with eagerness. The man of my dreams was about to make love to me, and I was shaking like a virgin on her wedding night.

Patrick kissed me passionately and laid me on my back. He pulled himself upright and hovered over me as if he were completing his last set of pushups. Patrick's tongue slowly drifted from my neckline and stopped at my breast. My body was tingling and I felt a slight chill that caused my body to shake inadvertently. Patrick gently sucked my nipples until they were on the verge of eruption. His tongue continued a blissful march down my body. I enjoyed it.

This level of pleasure was something that I had never experienced. What separated Patrick from Craig and Malik was the level of his sexual IQ. He understood what my body wanted almost like we were in sync with each other. The gentle way he messaged the back of my neck while kissing me. The way he touched my body full of passion made me feel special. I felt like I was the only woman that he had ever touched in this way. I felt guilty for giving my virginity away to a person like Malik because he didn't deserve it. The man who was making my body feel like this deserved to be the first.

Patrick continued to tease my body with his tongue until I was about to burst open with anticipation. Like a skilled marksman, his tongue plunged deep inside me, filling my body with pleasure. Patrick's tongue caressed and teased my pussy until I could feel my body shivering uncontrollably. He placed his hand on my stomach and I instantly felt a relaxing buzz throughout my body. I could feel my body trembling uncontrollably, but in my mind, it felt like a warm, soothing, spring shower. Patrick's eyes beamed with excitement as my body curled up shivering and fighting to recover.

I felt Patrick's hand on my thigh and I quickly grabbed him because his touch was like an electric charge. I pulled Patrick close and I hung on for dear life as he carried me to his bedroom. He gently laid me on the bed and soothingly rubbed my knee as I lay there shivering for more. Now I understood why Patrick had glanced at me as if warning me not to start anything. Patrick smiled at me as if to say, "We're just getting started."

I was eager and also afraid of what else he could do to my body. Patrick slowly parted my trembling thighs and amazed me with his love-making skills.

There was no comparing to Patrick's love-making skills. Making love to Malik reminded me of an exam on a cold, sterile table. Making love to Patrick reminded me of a cozy night in front of a fireplace. It was as if my body and mind were in two separate universes. My body, aching from orgasms, was screaming for mercy. My mind, high from the pleasure, wanted to experience more. The type of satisfaction

Patrick gave me made me feel exclusive. I truly felt like no other woman had been touched like me.

The biggest pleasure that I got from Patrick was when we finished making love. Instead of falling asleep, he pulled me close and held me tight. Being in Patrick's arms only intensified the experience. Visions of a big wedding with family and friends in admiration flooded my mind. Patrick was twice the man of Craig, and Malik's dreams were confined to his tiny neighborhood. Patrick lying beside me made me proud of him. He was everything I had ever wanted and he was with me. I drifted off to sleep in Patrick's arms smiling because of the endless possibilities.

Being with Patrick was like a burden finally lifted off me. Malik only understood the world from a street mentality while Patrick's view was that of a successful businessman. Malik being around my friends was always an awkward moment. He would call them bougie or they would call him an ignorant asshole. Regardless of who was right, I was always left apologizing to the other side. The only time that Malik really felt comfortable was when he was in his neighborhood around his friends. After a while, I just stopped bringing him around because I was so ashamed of what he would do or say.

Patrick was the total opposite. I was proud of who Patrick was. When Patrick came to gatherings with my friends, I never was embarrassed about him. When I took him to Baxley during spring break, my parents allowed him to stay at their house. Patrick knew how overly protective my parents were, so he made them feel comfortable around him. He carried himself like a strong gentleman who had his shit together. My parents were proud to have their daughter dating a person with such promise.

The highlight of my relationship was that summer when Patrick chartered a jet and flew the whole family to Aruba for a week. I lounged on the beach with Patrick and my family and thought about how perfect my life was.

Chapter 5

Everything was going great for me. It was my senior year of college, I was on the Dean's List, and I had the man of my dreams in my life. Everything was perfect until that cold November night. I still remember the phone call as if it were yesterday. I had just finished popping up some popcorn when my cell phone rang. I was not familiar with the number blinking on my caller ID, so I put the phone down and continued to relax.

I grabbed the remote and punched the play button when I heard the familiar sound of my favorite assigned ring tone. I grabbed the phone with anticipation of hearing Patrick's voice and was shocked to her someone else's voice.

The voice on the phone asked for Angela Anderson.

I replied in an apprehensive voice, "This is Angela Anderson. Who is this?"

The voice on the phone responded, "This is Monte Stephens. Patrick and I are friends." I listened intently as Monte continued to speak. "It's nothing to be alarmed about; Patrick just wanted me to let you know that he was arrested this evening."

I was frozen with fear and disbelief as I tried to understand what Monte was telling me. Monte continued talking. "He was arrested on a warrant for possession of drugs. It was probably for something a long time ago. I'm really not sure about what's going on, but it should be cleared up soon."

No matter how articulately Monte spoke, I did not believe him. I had received these types of calls far too many times from Malik.

Monte continued to talk in a supportive manner. "Patrick will call you as soon as he is processed. It shouldn't take anymore than a couple of hours."

Once again, my alert antenna was buzzing. Processing at the Fulton County Jail in two hours? Who was this guy fooling?

Monte assured me once again that everything was okay before hanging up the phone. I waited for what seemed like an eternity, and finally, I received a collect call from Patrick. As soon as I heard Patrick's voice, I started arguing and demanding answers.

Patrick responded in a calming manner, "Angela relax, everything is okay."

I responded with a smirk, "Okay! What do you mean by okay? You're sitting in jail on charges for God knows what, and you seem to think everything is okay? I don't know who you think you're talking to, but it's not a fool. I been down this road before, and I'm not about to go down it again. Drugs! Drugs! That's what you're sitting in jail for, Patrick. Drugs. Or at least that's what you're little flunky told me. Are you saying that he's lying?"

I continued to scream, argue, and threaten to leave until Patrick shouted back. "If you would shut the fuck up for half a second, I could tell you what the fuck is going on."

I instantly stopped talking because this side of Patrick scared the hell out of me. This was the first time that I had ever heard Patrick go off, and it was scary. Patrick had spoiled me with his calm demeanor, and now I was seeing the opposite. The intelligent, sophisticated man whom I had fallen in love with was turning into someone else.

Patrick took a deep breath and started talking. "Look, I'm sorry for screaming at you, but you were not listening. You were going off on me before even knowing any off the facts. You have to listen at what I'm trying to say. This is all a mistake! A client left some drugs in a storage unit. It has absolutely nothing to do with me. His drugs are his problem. I run a legitimate business, and I had no idea that this was going on. Just give it chance; everything will be cleared up at my bond hearing."

I inquired about the time of his bond hearing and Patrick responded, "Angela, I don't want you there! It's my job to keep you safe from this type of stuff, not put you in the middle of it."

Patrick was in the process of saying I love you when I slammed the phone down. I paced the floor angrily. I felt deceived by Patrick, but I really was angry with myself. The signs had been there, I just chose to ignore them. I stayed up all night wondering how I had gotten involved in something like this. My father had always told me to ask more questions, but that's hard to do when you really don't want to know the truth. All I cared about was the fairytale that Patrick was giving me. Now I had to face the music. Patrick's bond hearing was held three days later and Monte was right. I definitely got a clarification.

I needed a lot of support because my life was failing apart. Kayla and my brother offered to come to the bail hearing. I already knew that bringing them was like a double-edged sword. Sure they would support me, but I knew they would also give me their frank opinion about the situation.

When I arrived in the courtroom, it was crowded with spectators and local reporters. We found a seat in the rear of the courtroom and waited for the hearing to start. Patrick was brought in with five other people chained at the wrist and ankle. As soon as Patrick's named was called, the cameras started flashing. Patrick was charged with four counts of money laundering and conspiracy to distribute cocaine.

Shocked would be an understatement; traumatized would be what happened next. The district attorney's case sounded like a slam dunk until I heard Patrick's lawyer start talking about search and seizure, Fifth Amendment rights, and motions to suppress.

I was thinking to myself that Patrick had a very good attorney until Steven leaned over and whispered in my ear, "Why the hell is Lazarus Goldstein representing Patrick?He only represents drug dealers. Angela, are you sure you know everything about Patrick?"

I slowly shook my head yes, but in my mind, I was questioning what I actually knew about Patrick. I started thinking about all of the five-star restaurants, trips to Las Vegas, and respect from Malik's low-life friends. The more questions I asked myself, the more I feared the answers.

Patrick glanced around the courtroom and smiled when he saw me. He mouthed, "Everything is okay."

My mind started flipping as I screamed to myself, "No baby, everything is not okay. That judge just said conspiracy to distribute cocaine. What part of this is okay?"

I was on the verge of collapsing when I heard the judge ask, "What is the state's recommendation for bond?"

The lady from the DA's table stood and responded, "Your honor we strongly recommend that Patrick Jones, AGA Cashmere, be held.

I was thinking, "Who the hell is Cashmere?" when, my brother quickly excused himself from the courtroom. The attorneys argued back and forth for what seemed like hours. The DA was concerned about Patrick being a flight risk. Patrick's attorney argued that there had been enough evidence presented to hold him.

The judge quickly brought the arguments to an end after he ruled in both parties' best interest. The judge agreed that the state had enough evidence to move forward on the case; however, he also believed that Patrick was entitled to a bond. The judge gave Patrick a $120,000 bond and he had to prove that the 10% raised was not through any type of illegal funding.

Patrick looked around the courtroom as if to find the person who could pull off such an extraordinary feat and come forth with $12,000. I felt sorry for Patrick because I knew his situation was critical.

I was about to leave and find Steven when I noticed a man walking toward Patrick and his attorney.

Mr. Goldstein stood up and spoke. "Your honor! This is my client's business partner, Mr. Monte Stephens. He has agreed to the terms of the bond."

Monte was a short, dark-skinned man with a stocky build, sort of like a black Joe Pesci from *Goodfellas*. He talked with a heavy Haitian accent and he always seemed serious about everything. On this particular day, he appeared to have all the answers for Patrick. Patrick's demeanor reminded me of John Gotti on trial. He showed no signs of fear and his confidence couldn't have been higher.

Patrick looked back at me and flashed his million-dollar smile and then winked at me. There were so many thoughts going through my mind at that time and I had no answers. Kayla and I walked out of the courtroom in a smoke-like daze as we tried to digest everything we had just witnessed. Steven was on the phone talking and quickly hung up when he saw me. I assumed he had been talking to my father because my phone started buzzing as soon as he hung up. I looked at my caller ID and saw my mother's number. I simply looked at Steven and rolled my eyes.

Steven normally would just smile and give me that "I'm sorry, but I had to" look, but it was different that day.

Steven looked at me with fear in his eyes. I hadn't seen that look since my grandmother's funeral. It was a shock to everyone when my grandmother died, but it wasnothing compared to the shock at the funeral. We walked in the small church and saw our grandmother's entire coffin standing vertical. It looked like my grandmother was standing and smiling with her eyes closed. Steven stayed outside during the service because he was so afraid. I could see that same fear as he walked over to me.

He hugged me like we were best friends and spoke. "Let's get out of here, I'll tell you what's going on later."

Patrick was granted bail, but it would be hours before he was processed. Monte rushed through the courtroom doors and headed in my direction.

Monte looked at Steven suspiciously and spoke. "Patrick wants you to come over to the house later."

I tried to say okay, but the words would not come out of my mouth.

Steven noticed that I was having problems responding and spoke. "Excuse me, hey ahhh what's your name, Monte. My name is Steven, and Angela is my sister. She's not coming over tonight because we got a family dinner scheduled."

Monte glared at Steven and then at me as if to say, "Bitch, stop lying."

Patrick's attorney came out of the courtroom and called for Monte.

Monte turned to walk away and I started pulling at Steven's and Kayla's arms. We quickly walked to the elevator and jumped on just as Monte called my name.

All three of us quickly exited the building and lost ourselves in the crowd of pedestrians bustling back and forth.

Steven was right about having dinner with the family at his house because my mother and father were probably doing a hundred miles an hour up 75 by now. The long ride to Steven's house was agonizing because everybody had opinions, but no one wanted to express them. I laid my head on Kayla's shoulder and she rubbed my back as to soothe the pain. Steven would look back at me periodically through the rearview mirror, but he never showed any emotion or said anything. When we arrived at Steven's house, I knew that things were worse then expected. My parents were already at there and I knew my father was biting at the chops to talk to me.

My mother must have heard the car pull up because she bounced out of the house just as my father was about to go off. Steven pulled at my father's arm and escorted him to the house. My mother hugged me tight and asked me if I felt like walking and talking. The last time my mother and I had a walking and talking conversation, it was about me eventually finding a better boyfriend than Craig. My mother started the conversation about school and my friends, and then the conversation slowly shifted to Patrick. I had always felt comfortable talking to my mother about my personal life because she never passed judgment on me. I was completely honest with my mother about my relationship with Patrick. I told her that I had been completely in love with him, and this new information about him had caught me by surprise.

My mother asked me if I believed what the police were saying, and I responded no. My mother looked in my eyes with what appeared to be a love for all mankind and told me to talk to Steven when we got back to the house. The walk back cheered me up because we talked about what was going on in Baxley. When we arrived back at the house, I heard my father laughing as Steven's kids and Kayla put on a makeshift talent show. Steven grabbed my arm and quickly escorted me into the guest room and told me to stay put until he came back. I curled up on the bed and turned the TV on to watch the news.

I felt myself dozing off as I heard a reporter say, "A local business man bonds out of jail on a drug and conspiracy charges."

I woke up the next morning to the smell of freshly cooked bacon and toast. I walked toward the kitchen and heard Steven and his wife talking about the upcoming holidays. With all the drama in my life, I had forgotten that Thanksgiving was only a week away. Steven commented on how quickly I had fallen asleep last night and how we never had a chance to talk. I encouraged Steven to speak now or forever hold his peace because the conversation seemed important. It was at that time that Steven told me the truth about who Patrick really was. Steven told me that Patrick is known in the streets as "Cashmere," or the dry cleaner. Steven went on to tell me that Cashmere cleans high-level drug dealers' money by investing it in small, cash-only businesses in Atlanta. His storage units were used as drug and money stash depots.

Steven continued on about the man that I thought I knew, but I was finding out that he was some mythological street thug. My phone had been vibrating continuously all morning, but I refused to answer because I knew it was Patrick. I remember not wanting to feel anything. My life was crashing all around me and all I felt was numb.

I decided to take a short nap during lunch, but I was abruptly awakened by commotion downstairs. I looked out the window and saw Patrick's Range Rover outside. I could hear my father getting loud with Patrick and my brother was asking him nicely to leave. Patrick saw me peeping through the curtains and waved. I quickly moved back so that I did not have to acknowledge him. At that moment, I hated Patrick. I don't know if I hated him more for being a drug dealer like Malik or for embarrassing me in front of my family.

The next few days leading up to Thanksgiving were pretty much the same. I would go to bed early and wake up late. My father tried to talk to me a couple of times, but my mother would always override his attempts. My mother understood that I was hurt and I needed my space. We had always been taught that family was important, especially during a crisis. My mother knew that this type of crisis was the exception. This was the kind of crisis that required alone time and healing. Hearing a bunch of people say "I told you so" was definitely not going to make me feel better. This was something I needed to process by myself.

On Thanksgiving, I decided to venture out of my room and see what was going on. My father was the first to see me and he commented on the weight I had gained since he last saw me. I admit that I had put on a couple of pounds, but was it really that noticeable?

My mother heard all the commotion and encouraged me to go back upstairs and freshen up for dinner. I allowed the warm shower water to roll down my face and thought nothing could be as embarrassing as this. I came back downstairs and attempted to eat some of my mother's famous dressing, but it felt like my stomach was twisted in knots.

My father looked at me in fear and spoke. "Are you okay?"

I shook my head yes, but I felt like I was going to throw up.

I saw a pale expression come over my mother's face as she spoke. "Angela, can you please come in the kitchen for a minute?"

I followed my mother into the kitchen and saw her and my sister-in-law already deep in conversation.

The next words that came out of my mother's mouth were even more shocking, "Are you pregnant?"

The thought of being pregnant never really crossed my mind. I mean I may have missed taken my pills a couple of days here and there, but I was normally careful.

I responded to my mother with embarrassment, "No! Why would you say something like that? I'm fine, I'm just a little stressed that's all."

The more I tried to convince my mother, the more she doubted me. She instructed Steven's wife to go to the drugstore and pick up a pregnancy test.

I walked back into the living room and my father noticed me upset and mumbling.

My father glanced at me quickly and asked, "What's wrong with you?

My mother stuck her head in the door and spoke. "Ronald, leave that girl alone and watch TV."

My father rolled his eyes at my mother and continued watching TV. Steven's wife returned from the store twenty minutes later and we all convened in the upstairs bathroom. The five-minute wait for the results of the test were agonizing. I thought about all the times Patrick and I made love. I thought about how my father would react. Most of all I thought about how I would tell Patrick.

My thoughts were interrupted by the loud booming voice of my father. "What are y'all doing in there? Since when did it take three women to pee?"

My mother's normal response would be something sharp and witty when telling him to be quiet. When I looked at my mother this time, all I saw was fear and panic as she showed me the pregnancy results.

Chapter 6

I pulled up in front of Patrick's house and rested my head on the headrest in a feeble attempt to gather my emotions. Three weeks earlier, I had just found out that I was three months pregnant with Patrick's baby. My father absolutely blew his stack because he felt like I ruined my life. The family's Thanksgiving meal normally attended by aunts, uncles, cousins, and close family friends turned into a big argument. The dinner turned into what's best for Angela. The family was still arguing when Steven handed me his car keys and mercifully allowed me to sneak away. I ended up spending the rest of Thanksgiving weekend in my dorm room alone. Kayla eventually talked me into going to the doctor just to make sure it was not a false test. It wasn't. So there I was sitting in front of Patrick's house contemplating my next step.

When I finally gathered up enough courage to ring Patrick's doorbell, I quickly leaned over the rail because I felt like throwing up. I saw two hands slowly divide the curtains and then the face of Patrick. Patrick quickly opened the door and wrapped his arms around me, as if to say, "I'm here." I've always considered myself to be emotionally strong, but I guess it was the gravity of the situation. I felt my legs go limp as I fell into Patrick's chest and cried. Patrick finally calmed me down, at least to a point that we could talk. The first subject up for conversation was obviously the elephant in the room.

Patrick held my hand and spoke. "Baby, I'm sorry for the things that I have put you through. I never wanted you to see this side of me. I wanted this part of me dead because I saw a future with you."

I was shocked because I thought Patrick was going to say everything was a lie. This was the time to say I was framed. Everything that I believed about Patrick should have been confirmed at that moment. Instead, he said the opposite. Patrick took a deep breath and slowly opened up about who he really was.

"Monte and I started a lawn company called Perfect Picture Lawns. We allowed lower-level drug dealers to pay a flat fee of $2000 to invest, or should I say launder, $8000 in dirty drug money. The dirty money made from drugs would be placed into Perfect Picture Lawns bank accounts and redistributed to drug dealers through pay checks."

The more Patrick talked, the greater the weight seemed on my chest.

Patrick continued with his story. "The plan was working well at first, and then it just got to big. We needed other business to invest in because to the IRS, it looked like we were making $500,000 a month cutting grass. We started investing in anything that was a cash-heavy business. We invested in carwashes, hair salons, discount malls, and the prize possession storage units. The storage units allowed drug dealers to store money and drugs for long periods of time without drawing attention to them or their customers. We eventually scaled back because it looked like their storage companies were hiring more people than a Wal-Mart. We scaled our operation back to only dealing with high-level dealers and finally only dealing with one kingpin and his crew. This crew was eventually busted and it was just a matter of time before all the dominos started falling. I got busted because all those small businesses were in my name and not Monte's."

I leaned back in disbelief because I could not believe what he was telling me. I asked Patrick, "What are you going to do about the charges?"

He hunched his shoulders and responded, "I don't know the outcome, but my lawyers are working on it."

I stared at the floor in search of answers and started cry. I knew that was the wrong time to tell Patrick about the baby, but he had to know.

Patrick rubbed my back gently and asked, "What's wrong?"

I opened my mouth to tell him about the pregnancy when there was a knock at the door.

Patrick quickly rushed to the door and pulled the curtains back. I heard Patrick curse under his breath and shake his head as if something was troubling him.

I walked towards Patrick and asked, "What's wrong?"

I pulled the curtains back and heard Patrick mumble, "We need to talk."

I could hear Patrick but my attention was on the women standing at the door. The woman looked old for her age and she had a bad hairpiece that was light brown with dirty blonde streaks.

I turned to Patrick asked, "Who is that?

He was pale and looked as if he was going to faint. Patrick opened the door slowly and stood by the door in silence as the woman entered the house and put her purse on the counter. The scene was almost comical because the woman was popping her chewing gum loudly and dragging her feet across Patrick's pristine woodened floor. The expression on Patrick's face made me believe that he was going to faint from embarrassment.

Patrick slowly walked over to me and spoke. "Angela, this is my friend Sha'quonda."

I looked at Patrick as if to say, "Okay! Is there anything else I need to know?"

Before Patrick could speak, I was startled by Sha'quonda's voice. She sounded like a country version of Shana-nay from the Martin show when she spoke. "I knows her, dat gurrl goes to school wit my antee's daughter. How you know my baby's daddy."

I looked at Patrick shocked and in amazement because the surprises from him just kept coming,

I tried to take the high moral ground in the conversation when I spoke. "Hi Sha'quonda, This is not a good time right now! I need to speak with Patrick about a pressing matter, so would you mind excusing us?"

Ms. Sha'quonda froze like I had called her a bitch and spoke. "Uumm Ms. What ever your name is! I understand you trying to get back to your little date night, but I need to pick up lil Pa'trika."

And with that I heard a loud shriek bellow out of the bedroom. Sha'quonda snapped her chewing gum, rolled her eyes and then clumped off towards the shrieking baby sound. I don't know, maybe it was the way I glared at Patrick and spoke. "Lil Pa'Trika, hum? I'm sorry, do you need a little time to get Lil Paprika and that bitch situated?"

Patrick quickly walked in Sha'quonda's direction and screamed, "Would you hurry the fuck up? I told your stupid ass that I would bring her home later. Hurry up, and get the fuck out."

I heard Sha'quonda respond with aggression, "Hold up motherfucker, don't be acting all brand new now. That bitch can wait patiently for me or she can leave, I don't give a fuck. But what you ain't going to do is come in this motherfucker like you running shit boo boo, because you ain't."

Sha'quonda came from the bedroom carrying a seven-year-old girl in her arms. I've never been one to call a child ugly, but this little girl looked like a giant blob fish.

Sha'quonda looked at me and then at her daughter with pride as she spoke, "Dis is Pat's lil baby girl."

Without thinking, I looked at Sha'quonda and exploded. "Shananay or Sha'quino or whatever your name is, this is not a good time."

Patrick placed his hand around me and whispered, "Sha'quonda. Her name is Sha'quonda baby, or you can just call her Wanda."

I quickly turned toward Patrick in anger, placed my hand on my hip, and pointed my finger in his face.

Patrick tried to hug me and that's when I exploded, "You probably want to hold on to that thought, because I'm about to put my foot in everybody's ass starting with yours."

Sha'quonda rolled her eyes at me and grunted, "You betta git your girl, Pat."

I glared at Patrick and responded, "Yes Pat, please get your girl."

Patrick quickly escorted Sha'quonda out of the house and reluctantly returned to the living room. Patrick sat beside me and tried to calm me down but I was already full of rage.

All the things that I was feeling for the past few months came out like a volcano. "Where do I start? How about the fact that I came over here to tell you that I was three months pregnant? Or how about the fact that I was willing to turn my back on my family to be with the person I love? Or the even bigger fact that I've been with you almost a year and I'm just finding out who the fuck you really are!"

I headed toward the door and Patrick reacted by blocking the door. "Angela, you need to give me a chance and listen, please."

I swung at his face and he quickly ducked out of the way. He pulled me close and locked his arms around me. I screamed at the top of my lungs for him to get off me, but he refused. The more I fought the tighter he held me. Patrick and I staggered over to couch and he continued to hold me while I cried profusely.

Finally, his grip loosened and he spoke softly to me. "I'm so sorry! I never meant to hurt you. The first time I saw you at that college party, I knew you were meant for me."

I just listened and cried quietly as Patrick continued to talk. "I was trying to put the drugs and baby mama drama behind me because I wanted better. I know I don't deserve you because you deserve so much better. I know I was wrong to deceive you, but I just didn't want to lose you."

The words coming out of Patrick were sincere and soothing. Patrick always had a way of comforting me when I was out of control. He was holding me close to his heart, and whispered in my ear. No matter how angry I got with him, I was silly putty once in his arms.

I remember once when I caught Patrick at a club dancing with another girl. I blew through the club like a tornado and practically ripped his head off. He simply pulled me to the side and gently kissed my cheek and put my fears to rest. That day was no different. The only thing that I regretted about that day was allowing him to make love to me. My rule had always been three days. Any fight, with any man, was a three-day punishment. I never wanted a man to think he could bring me back just by giving me dick.

That day, Patrick took advantage of my emotional state. His passion was so strong that it overpowered my will to hate him. I remember scraping my nails across his back because I hated what he was doing to me. I hated him for embarrassing me. I hated him for lying to me. And I hated loving him so much. The rage inside me only intensified the sex. I fucked him like I wanted to punish him. He made love to me like he wanted total possession of my mind and body.

I remember lying in his arms afterward and it felt like paradise. That was the place I wanted to be no matter what. I didn't care what obstacle was placed in front of us. I wanted to be with him.

That night, Patrick painted me the perfect picture of our family. The apex of that evening came when he returned from the kitchen with a cupcake.

Patrick smiled at me and spoke. "Here baby, this is for you. I was waiting until graduation to surprise you, but now is even better."

Patrick reached in his pocket and gave me a promise ring.

I remember being a little disappointed because I though it was an engagement ring.

Patrick saw the disappointment in my face and spoke. "Angela, we will eventually get engaged. But right now is just a bad time. Fighting this court case is bad enough, and now you're pregnant! Can you imagine how this will play out with your family? Just think of this promise ring as a pre-engagement ring."

I was young and blinded by love, so I caved in to Patrick's argument. I accepted Patrick's promise ring. Excuse me? Can you please repeat that? Yes, ladies, I accepted a pre-engagement ring that would show Patrick's commitment to a monogamous relationship. Kayla and I still laugh about how retarded I must have been to buy into that line.

My father's plan was for me to have an abortion immediately, but he found out that it is highly illegal to have an abortion after three months. My father invited Patrick over for Christmas dinner just to clear the air and find out his intentions. The Christmas dinner turned into a question-and-answer session that was clearly not in Patrick's favor. My father expected Patrick to step up and do the right thing by marrying me. He almost popped a blood vessel when Patrick explained to him that he had already given me a promise ring. My father's face turned beet-red as he stared at me. I tried to keep my eyes focused on the little snowmen on the tablecloth, but I could feel his eyes burning a hole in my head.

My father lost his composure and blurted out, "What the fuck is a promise ring? Who the hell gets engaged, just to get engaged to be married? Why not just get married? What kind of stupid-ass shit is that?"

My mother must have noticed the venom starting to spew out of my father because she quickly chimed in with her always calm demeanor. "Look Patrick, you have to understand that you two are asking us to take in a lot of information that we just don't agree with. My husband and I are having a hard time understanding how our daughter could have been so irresponsible. And it sounds like my daughter is not in your future plans."

Patrick's response only worsened the situation. "I want to marry your daughter, but right now is not a good time. Fighting this court case is going to take up a lot of time, so right now, I'm just asking everyone to be patient."

My father glared at Patrick and responded, "Be patient? See, that's something that I don't have a lot of. And babies have no concept of time or money. I think it's best if we look at other options for the baby like adoption.

Patrick quickly cut in. "No disrespect, Mr. Anderson, but I plan on keeping my child."

My father quickly fired back while looking in my direction, "It's not your decision."

I nervously played with my fingers until my parents stormed out of the room mumbling. My parents' anger was justified. Patrick's immediate future was in question because of his legal situation. If Patrick went to jail, what would happen? Being three months pregnant was problematic for me because the baby was due near my graduation date. The thing about being young and in love is that decisions are made without thinking clearly. Deep in my heart, I knew that my parents were right. Keeping the baby would probably be a bad decision, but in my mind I could only see a positive scenario.

I made things worse by moving in with Patrick.

I was starting to hear the rumors on campus, "Girl, have you heard, Ms. Goody Two-Shoes is pregnant by a drug dealer!" "Girl, have you heard, she was offered a full scholarship to law school and turned it down to have a drug dealers baby!"

Eventually, I just got fed up and moved of campus. The only person who stayed in my corner during that period was Kayla. I mean Steven was there, but his allegiance was to my parents. Kayla had every right to move on and forget about me, but she stood strong with any decision I made. When my line sisters would question her about my situation, she would refer them to me. She didn't believe in getting messy with people's business, and I appreciated that.

The rift between my parents and me was widening because everybody in the family knew that I was keeping the baby. My mother was angry because she felt I was making a mistake, and my father was just plain angry at the entire situation. The biggest heartbreak for my parents occurred during my college graduation. My mother and father flew in from Baxley excited about my graduation, and I was excited because finally something was going good in my life. On the morning of my graduation, everybody was rushing to get ready for the ceremony. Steven agreed to stay back and throw some food on the grill. I was busy getting my hair and makeup together when I received a call. Patrick called me sounding subdued and worried.

I asked him, "Baby, what's wrong? Is everything okay?"

Patrick hesitated at first and then responded, "I got some bad news baby. I received a call from the bondsman, and they told me that my bail was being revoked. I'm scheduled to appear in front of a judge this afternoon."

The thought of screaming came to my mind because this could not have come at a more inconvenient time.

I questioned Patrick, "Why? What happened?"

Patrick responded in a low voice filled with guilt, "Monte had a little get together last night and I stopped by. I lost track of time and violated my curfew. I have to be in court at 10 am."

When I calculated the time in my head, I thought I could be at both places. His hearing was scheduled at 10 am. I figured I could run down to the courthouse and support my man, and then quickly get to my graduation ceremony. Reality destroyed that timeline in a matter of seconds.

When I arrived at Patrick's hearing, I knew there would be problems. Patrick's lawyer arrived forty-five minutes late, which really pissed the judge off. On the positive side, it appeared the decision would go Patrick's way. Instead of rendering his decision, he informed the court that he would take a recess until after lunch. This caused a dilemma for me because either I would stay and support my man or go to graduation.

I did what any girl in love would do. I chose to stay and support Patrick, and then rush over in time to walk across the stage for my degree. At the time it sounded like a good plan. I called Kayla and told her the situation and she reluctantly agreed to help me. I told her to call me as soon as the guest of honor started their speech.

I guess the Gods must have been against me because the judge took an extra hour, and unbeknownst to me, my cell phone went dead. The bail hearing finally concluded and Patrick was allowed to remain in the community. By the time we arrived at my graduation, it was over. Everyone was mingling about and congratulating one another.

Kayla ran up to me in a mad dash and screamed, "Girl, what happened? You need to get the fuck out of here, because your family is on a war path."

I can't remember if I was leaving or if I was frozen with fear. I just remember my family surrounding me at the same time.

My father was livid and my mother was crying uncontrollably. Patrick tried to pull me close, but that was probably the wrong thing to do at that time.

My father blurted out in the most condescending way he could, "So let me understand this; you missed your graduation to attend another court hearing." He turned to Patrick and asked, "Young man, exactly how many people did you kill, eat, and sell drugs to, so that I can understand? I need to understand what the fuck was so important that she had to miss her graduation."

I looked at my mother as if to say, "Hey Mom, this is the time that you usually step in." But all she did was look past Patrick as if we were statues and ask, "How could you?"

In her mind, I had chosen Patrick over a very personal family moment. Patrick tried to explain what had happened, but my father wanted no part of it.

He continued his attack on me, "I just don't understand what's going through your head. Do you see anybody else here missing their graduation over a dope dealer?"

Again Patrick tried to intervene. "Sir, I'm sorry you feel like that, but I am not a dope dealer."

My father stared at Patrick and fired back. "Jailbird, worry about your own life and get the fuck out of ours."

At that moment, I felt Kayla move forward and try to defuse the situation because people were starting to stare. Kayla kissed my mother on her cheek and asked my parents to take a picture with her. I could still see utter contempt in my father's eyes, but he agreed to take the picture. That gave me a chance to pull Patrick to the side and ask him to leave. Patrick really wanted to stay and support me, but I knew that the situation would only get worse.

We arrived at my brother's house, but no one was in a mood for a celebration. Instead of family and friends screaming "Congratulations!" or "Surprise!" I received silence and cold stares.

Steven pulled me to the side and said, "I heard what went down at the graduation. Do you think it's wise to have this thing?"

I smiled nervously at Steven and shook my head yes.

Again, Steven yanked at my arm and spoke. "I don't think you're getting what I'm saying. I invited Patrick over here before I knew what had happened. He's probably on his way over here right now!"

That was the last thing that I needed. I franticly tried to call Patrick's phone, but all I kept getting was his voicemail. And like clockwork, Patrick walked into the backyard.

Patrick walked past me and headed straight for my father. All I could do was cringe because I knew WWIII was commencing. The argument between my father and Patrick was unlike any other argument that I seen before.

Patrick started by asking my father, "What type of preacher are you to ask his daughter to get an abortion? I bet the white side of you must really hate having a black grandchild."

Ever since I was small, I remember my father having issues with his race. He was too light to be in the black crowdand too dark to fit in with the white crowd. My father grew angry and confused because he did not fit in. He dropped out of school in the ninth grade and became a street hoodlum. He ran the streets causing all types of problems until my mother introduced him to God. Now here was a young punk questioning weather he was black enough.

My father exploded when he spoke. "This has nothing to do with if I hate black grandkids. The issue is I don't want your low-life, salad-tossing ass to be the father. You're nothing but a sorry excuse for a man. What type of man would try to keep another man's daughter from him? I can tell you never had a father because you don't have respect for hers."

Patrick immediately responded, "Father! What type of father are you? Your idea of a good father is to keep his daughter's head buried in the Bible all day. The moment she doesn't agree with you and your God, you disown her. You're nothing but a bully who hides behind the church."

My father and Patrick inched closer to each other ready to fight when my mother stepped between them and spoke. "Okay, that's enough!"

Steven grabbed my father and nudged him toward the house. Patrick walked to a far-off corner of the yard and started sulking.

My friends stared silently at me afraid to interfere. They had come to have a good time and ended up in a crazy situation. Most of them slowly exited the party whispering about what had just occurred. I was still trying to put on a happy face until Kayla came over and hugged me. It was at that moment that I started to cry uncontrollably.

Patrick and my mother began to walk towards me from opposite ends of the yard. But I was content with crying on the shoulder of my best friend. My mother slowly retreated back into the house and Patrick sat alone in the corner. The expression on his face showed that he was sorry, but I knew he would never apologize to my father. My father came back outside and apologized to me and turned towards Patrick.

Patrick pulled himself out of the chair and exited the backyard before anything could be said. I wanted to go after Patrick, but under the circumstances, I thought it would be best if I let him go.

I went in the house and freshened up, and by the time I returned, Kayla was ready to leave. Kayla and I hugged and she told me that she wished I were going with her on the seven-day cruise we had been planning since we were freshman. Pregnant and weeks away from delivery, those dreams seemed like they were years old. I watched

Kayla leave the yard to live her life, leaving me sad and alone with my reality.

My parents asked me to sit with them, and it was at that moment I realized that my actions could never be corrected.

My mother spoke. "We're sorry for what we did earlier. I don't know what it was! We were just so hurt and embarrassed. Can you imagine hearing your child's name called and no one walks across the stage? Your name was the only one called where nobody showed. That absolutely crushed us!"

I was looking down at the ground when I heard my father almost whisper, "Angela, what are you doing? I mean, what are you really going to do about your future?"

I gave my father some bullshit story about my future plans, but the reality was I had no idea. I had a BA in Business, but my dream had always been to become an attorney. But with everything on my plate now, that was just a distant dream. My parents and I talked for little while longer, and then I received a text message from Patrick asking when I was coming home. I ignored the text message and turned my phone off.

When I finally got around to calling Patrick, it was around 1:15 a. m. and the call went directly to voicemail. I woke up the next morning at around 6:30 a. m. to the sound of my cellphone ringing. It was Patrick. I decided to ignore the phone call and see my parents off instead. After my mother and father left, I decided to surprise Patrick with breakfast. I stopped at IHOP, grabbed a couple of breakfast omelets, and drove to Patrick's house.

When I arrived at Patrick's house, I was surprised to see him getting out of his car dressed up.

I smiled at Patrick and asked, "Where are you coming from all dressed up so early in the morning?"

Patrick looked at me and shrugged, "I'm just coming home like you."

I could tell Patrick was still angry at me for being so insensitive, but I figured he of all people should understand. After all I missed walking on graduation day because of his stupid court hearing.

I responded to his comment, "Come on Patrick don't be like that. You know it was a crazy day. Baby, I'm sorry."

Patrick shot back in a condescending manner, "Whatever, spoiled brat! Go home to your daddy and grow up."

I was shocked at what I was hearing from Patrick. I knew Patrick and my father went at it, but he was just being nasty that day. What's worse is that I suddenly saw movement in the passenger's seat of his car. I took a closer look and saw Sha'quonda emerge from the car with a pleased look on her face. I looked at Patrick enraged, eyes full of jealously, and quickly turned to walk away. Patrick knew I was hurt because he ran after me and started apologizing. I continued to walk and he grabbed my arm. I quickly whirled around and swung at Patrick's face in an attempt to slap him. The initial miss must have made something snap inside me, because I lost it and started swinging wildly at Patrick.

Patrick avoided the blows the best he could, but my onslaught was just too overwhelming. I punched and scratched him without mercy until he was able to pin both arms to my body. Not able to release any more rage towards Patrick, my body went limp and I started crying uncontrollably. Patrick held me tightly and pleaded with me to calm down for the baby's sake. In my fit of rage, I had forgotten that I was nearly eight months pregnant and stress was not good for the baby.

I leaned my head against Patrick's chest and he started talking. "Baby, this is not what it looks like. This is innocent. Sha'quonda brought my daughter over this morning and invited me to breakfast. She saw I was hurting from yesterday and she was trying to make me feel better. This is nothing, I swear!"

I was about two sentences away from believing Patrick when I heard Sha'quonda say, "Whatever, Patrick! If that's what makes you feel better."

I looked at Sha'quonda and then back at Patrick.

Patrick intervened by screaming, "Shut the fuck up, Wanda! Stop playing these silly-ass games."

Sha'quonda froze in place as if somebody had walked past her with bad breath. Then she exploded. "Hold up motherfucker! No you didn't! Ummm, mizz whatcha call it, you needs to know everything. You see the problem is don't nobody care about you walking round her what no college degree. Pat was fine until your stuck-up ass got in the picture."

Patrick pointed at Sha'quonda and threatened her. "Shut the fuck up, Sha'quonda, before I slap your silly ass. I told you this ain't the time! Now go home!"

Sha'quonda responded as if not to care about his threats. "Whatever. The poor girl needs to know the truth. Pat is not only fucking me, but he fucking his other baby mama too. If you really want to know the truth, bitch, you third in line for that dick."

Patrick rushed towards Sha'quonda and shoved her towards the car. Sha'quonda threw a bottle of water at Patrick striking him in the head.

Patrick pointed at Sha'quonda and screamed, "I'm not telling you, no more! Get the fuck in the car!"

Patrick walked slowly towards me and he looked guilty. The expression on his face made him look as if somebody had taken an x-ray shot of his heart.

I gently grabbed Patrick's hand, looked him in the eye, and asked him, "Are you cheating on me?"

Instead of Patrick responding with the word no, he started making excuses. "What we have is special, and I don't ever want to lose it. People like your family can hate on us all they want, but it won't change our love. My relationship with my baby's mama is different from ours. Besides, that stuff happened a long time ago, not now."

I stared into Patrick's eyes and shook my head in disbelief because I knew he was trying too hard to convince me. If Patrick had just said, "No, I'm not cheating," I would have probably believed him, because I loved him too much to ever think he would cheat on me. As soon as he started being specific and giving too much information, I knew he was not being truthful. Frustrated by the situation and my life, I turned to leave.

I heard Sha'quonda still chirping in the background with that annoying voice. "Pat, Pat, let that stuck-up bitch go. You don't have to kiss her ass. I don't know who the fuck she thinks she is."

My first instinct was to go punch the bitch, but a pregnant girl fighting just seemed too ghetto. I picked the bag of IHOP food up and tossed it in her direction. Most of the food landed on Patrick's car, but a nice portion splashed in Sha'quonda's face.

Sha'quonda went crazy and started going off, "Holup, holup. No dis bitch didn't. I know dis bitch didn't just throw this shit at me. Bitch, I will beat your ass. Naw! Fuck that shit. Pat, get off me."

Patrick grabbed Sha'quonda just as she was running in my direction. I walked to my car and gunned the engine as I sped off. I could hear Patrick screaming my name, but there was no way I was going back. I felt so stupid for sacrificing so much for someone who didn't give a shit about me. That was one of the times in my life that I felt alone. I ended up at a park just outside of Atlanta, and all I could do was stare at the pond and cry.

I couldn't talk to any of my family or friends because all they would say is, "I told you so!" That was the last thing I wanted to hear from my parents. So I just sat and suffered in silence. Thoughts of suicide raced through my mind, but I knew I didn't want to hurt the baby. I hated Patrick, but not enough to kill the baby. Although the sun was shinning brightly, I had a dark cloud over my head.

The next few weeks went by slowly. As my due date got closer, I started to realize that Patrick and I were better off apart. I never thought of myself as being a baby's mother. I had dreams of marriage and a family with Patrick. All those nights we spent together talking about our life had became a nightmare.

Steven allowed me to stay with him and his family until I was able to figure things out, and of course, my mother stayed in Atlanta to help provide moral support. As the long hours turned into days, I started to understand what my family had been saying. Having a baby by Patrick was the worst mistake I could have made. Patrick would call me periodically, but things were not the same. When we did talk on the phone, it ended up in arguments. He blamed my family for pushing him to cheat, and I blamed him. After a while, we just stopped talking altogether.

Having an abortion was not an option, so my mind immediately switched to adoption. In my mind, I had called an emergency adoption agency, but the reality was I never did. I could not bring myself to call because I guess somewhere in the back of my mind, I was hoping that Patrick and I could work it out.

On the morning of June 25th, I jumped up to a strange feeling around my pelvic area. I felt an uncontrollable, stronger-than-normal urge to pee. I started toward the bathroom and then the water started poring out of me like the Niagara Falls. Steven's wife must have heard the terrified scream because she rushed in the room to see what was going on. She instantly took control. She started shouting demands, first at Steven and then at me.

I was scared and nervous, so the only thing that I could muster up to say was, "I'm sorry your carpet got wet."

It must be something in the Anderson genes that makes us panic because Steven was screaming, "The hospital's phone is disconnected!" Steven's wife directed him to get my hospital bag and my mother quickly escorted me to the car.

The short ride to the hospital seemed like an eternity because Steven kept looking back every second asking me, "Is it coming yet?"

We arrived at the hospital just in time for me to throw up the remaining portion of my rice pudding all over the hospital's sidewalk. I was placed in a wheelchair and taken to a private room. Steven agreed to call Patrick. I don't know what Steven said to get Patrick to the hospital so quickly, but he arrived twenty minutes later.

Patrick walked in my room and there was an eerie silence between him and my mother. Patrick took the initiative and spoke to my mother. My mother forced a pleasant smile on her face and responded, "Hi."

Patrick walked over to me and asked, "How are you feeling?"

I responded, "Okay."

Patrick placed his hand on mine and I quickly pulled it back as tears started to stream down my cheek.

Steven walked in the room just in time to see the uneasy exchange of body language, and spoke. "Patrick, come with me and let's get some coffee."

Patrick followed my brother out of the room. My mother tried to calm me down, but she couldn't. I thought about all the sacrifices that I had made in my relationship with Patrick and I guess a part of me still loved him. The nurse entered the room and notified me that I needed to calm down for the sake of the baby. She showed me the baby's heart rate and it was racing. This was not the first time that I had heard this. My doctor had been telling me for weeks that the baby's stress levels where way too high. Patrick and Steven came back to the room just as the nurse was adjusting my pillow. My mother looked at me and then back at Patrick. I guess she decided that she had been silent long enough.

My mother pointed at Patrick and spoke. "Can't you see what you're doing to my daughter? Can you please wait outside until she has the baby?"

Patrick fired back at my mother, "You wait outside! I'm not missing my child's birth just because you have a problem with me. I've never missed the birth of any of my children, and I'm not starting now."

That comment infuriated my mother even more because she fired back, "Are you serious? You're the same person who made my daughter miss her graduation, sells drugs for a living, has God knows how many other baby's mamas, and now all of sudden you want to be father of the year?"

My mother turned to the nurse and demanded that she contact security.

I had been so accustomed to defending Patrick that I found myself defending him again. "Come on mama, don't you think you're being kind of hard on him?"

Steven, who never pokes his nose in other people's business, finally spoke up with surprising anger. "Patrick, I understand that you and my sister have history together, but this shit has got to stop. You and I have run into each other plenty of times out on the town, and you were with other women. I never once said anything because I felt it was not my business. Now I'm making it my business and asking you nicely to leave."

An uneasy silence fell over the room as Patrick and Steven stood face to face, nose to nose in the middle of the room, neither willing to back down.

The uneasy silence was broken when the always jovial Dr. Smith entered the room and spoke, "So who's ready to have a baby?"

There were forced smiles coming from all parties in the room, including the nurse. Dr. Smith broke the tension by speaking. "Who's staying in the room for the birth?"

My mother and sister-in-law quickly volunteered as Patrick raised his hand in an attempt to stay.

Steven whirled around as quickly as Patrick's hand went up and shouted, "My man, we already had this conversation; you are not staying in this room."

Dr. Smith noticed the building tension and abruptly held his hands in the air and asked everyone to please calm down. If the mood had not been so serious, I probably would have laughed.

Dr. Smith looked in my direction and spoke. "Ms. Anderson, you have to make a choice between these guys. This is not a Jerry Springer show. We will not be trying to find out who the baby's daddy is today."

My mother took offense to Dr. Smith's comment and proceeded to admonish him. "Excuse me sir! I think there's a misunderstanding. First off, that comment was offensive to me and my family. This is her brother and not her baby's daddy. I'm not sure why you just assume there were multiple daddies involved, but for clarity there are not."

Dr. Smith's face turned red as he began to backtrack and apologize. I saw Steven looking at me as though he was about to fall on the floor laughing.

Dr. Smith again asked, "Ms. Anderson do you want the father in the room when you have your baby."

A part of me still wanted Patrick in the room even after everything he had put me through. I wanted to say, "Patrick please stay with me and let's live out our dreams together." The reality of the matter was that Patrick's hearing was in two days and although his attorney was sure that he would get off, nothing was promised. Even after all of the baby mama drama and court hearings, I still had strong feelings for Patrick. A small part of me still felt we could be family. I had grown up with two parents and I wanted my son to have the same experience.

The answer that I gave to Dr. Smith all but ended those dreams. "Dr. Smith, I will feel much more comfortable if my mother and sister-in-law stay with me."

Patrick looked at me as if he had just caught me cheating and lashed out. "Oh, it's like that! I tell you what, Ms. Prissy. You have the baby with your mother, but please don't come to me when it needs shit. As a matter of fact, I bet that little motherfucker ain't even mine."

Patrick's ranting was interrupted by Steven as he stood between Patrick and my bed. "Look! I'm telling you for the last time, stop disrespecting my sister. If you say one more thing about my sister, you're going to have a serious problem."

It was like Patrick's street mentality kicked in as he glared at Steven and walked in his direction and spoke. "Well, step that shit up, bitch! You talking real grimy, but I don't see your bitch ass moving."

Poor Steven. I love him for trying to protect my honor, but his going against Patrick would be like watching Mike Tyson and Manny Pacquiao. Don't get me wrong, Steven would give anybody a good fight. But when it came to the streets, Patrick was in a class all by himself. I knew it, my mother knew it, and worst of all, Steven knew it.

I quickly grabbed Patrick's hand and spoke just as security arrived. "Just let it go, please. If you've ever had any feelings for me at all, just let it go. It's over!"

The pride in Patrick wanted to keep arguing, but he knew deep in his heart that the relationship was over. Patrick turned and quickly exited the room. The last time that I ever saw Patrick was on the day his son, Ronald Clancy Anderson III, was born.

Chapter 7

Patrick was sentenced to twelve years in federal prison. After all those promises from his attorney, the evidence was just too overwhelming. Patrick refused to cooperate with the state and he paid the price. Ten years for distributing drugs and an additional two for tax evasion. When I heard about Patrick, I really didn't know what to feel. Knowing that he was in prison gave me some closure, but I still had feelings for him.

I stayed with Steven for short time after I was released from the hospital. I never thought I would be a single parent, but I had to adjust quickly. Being a new mother and not knowing anything about a baby was frustrating. Steven's wife helped as much as she could, but the majority of the childcare fell on me. If my family had not had mercy on me and helped, I would have gone crazy. I found myself at my doctor's office more than I wanted because I was suffering from depression. I felt like I was going crazy at times because I would look at my son and see Patrick's face. Patrick had called my parents' house a couple of times asking if someone could bring my son to prison and see him, but all I could do was send him a picture and keep it moving. For the first time in a long time, I found that I was calling on God to help me more and more.

The longer I stayed at Steven's house, the more I felt like I was a burden on his family. Steven and his wife assured me that I was not a burden, but I felt otherwise, and made preparations to move. I found a job at the W Hotel as an accounting clerk. Little RC and I found a small apartment in Decatur. There was nothing special about my new place. It was a two-family-side-by-side-split house. The owner lived on one side and RC and I on the other. The neighborhood had a mixture of low- and middle-income families.

Mr. Turner, the owner of the house, was a comedy show all by himself, from his little pot belly to his huge eyes. He reminded me of the comedian Robin Williams. He talked with a strong southern accent and he walked fast like he was always in a hurry. Mr. Turner had several rental properties throughout Decatur, and he worked hard to make sure they were in good shape. On the weekends, he would sit out on the step with his little handyman buddies. They would listen to old-school music and reminisce about what they use to do.

The handymen's club would sometimes get a little rowdy when Mrs. Turner was at bingo, but nothing serious. Women cute or ugly were fair game.

You could hear their comments as women passed by. "Good God, almighty look at them dumplings," or "Looks like a truck done ran over her face."

I was even the victim sometimes. "Ms. Angela, lawd have mercy. It's got to be jelly cause jam don't shake like that."

Sometimes I would make them old men pee on themselves. I would come to the mailbox with booty shorts and a tight tee and stand bowlegged.

The fellows would have a fit. "Oh God! Ms. Angela, you gonna make my hernia act up."

One Sunday, Mrs. Turner knocked on my door. I was surprised when she invited me to church. At first I was hesitant, and then I felt something inside me urging me to go. The truth of the matter is that something had been urging me to go to church that entire week. An incident had occurred that week that I could not explain. The incident scared me to the point of seriously seeking God for the first time since I left home for college.

I was giving RC a bath and I heard a voice repeating over and over, "Look what Patrick did to you. He left you burdened with a baby and everybody including your family thinks you're stupid for keeping it. Go ahead and kill little RC. All your problems will go away."

At first, I ignored the voice and laughed it off. But then I found myself listening to the voice. I felt my hands tighten around RC's little shoulders and start pushing his head toward the water. I could feel RC fighting, but something was almost forcing me to push harder. Consciously, I knew I could never hurt my son, but this feeling was like a nightmare that I could not wake up from. For some strange reason, my son had turned into my enemy and I wanted to rid my life of him. Just as little RC's face was about to go under the water, my doorbell rang, snapping me back to reality.

I quickly released RC and ran toward the door as if a horrific spirit was chasing me. I could hear RC screaming with fear as I quickly opened the door and saw Mrs. Turner.

Mrs. Turner smiled and asked, "Baby, is everything okay?"

I was afraid to answer because I didn't know if I was okay. Mrs. Turner looked into my frightened eyes and quickly pushed her way into my apartment. She ran towards RC's screaming voice in the bathroom almost as if she knew something was wrong. She gently plucked my frightened son from the water and held him closely. I stood in the corner of the living room crying, afraid to tell her what had happened. Mrs. Turner smiled with apprehension and walked towards me with RC as if to say, "Would you actually hurt your own flesh and blood?"

I held my hands out to hold RC and he tightened his hold on Mrs. Turner and looked at me nervously. Mrs. Turner stared at me closely and then glanced at my son, afraid and clinging to her for dear life.

My thoughts were interrupted by Mrs. Turner's voice. "Sweetheart, you need a little break."

I gently rubbed my son's face and tears started to roll down my face as I shook my head yes.

Mrs. Turner asked me to bow my head in prayer and then she spoke. "Christ, only you know what this daughter is going through. I break the power of every principality of darkness. I rebuke any evil spirit working to claim Sister Angela in the name of Jesus Christ.

Father, you told me that greater is he that is in me, than he that is in the world. Satan, you and your minions have no authority over her soul. I bind you from hurting anyone in this house. In the name of Jesus Christ, Amen."

Mrs. Turner quickly walked out of the house. I could her RC next door playing and laughing like nothing had ever happened. That night was the first time I had a peaceful night's sleep in weeks. I was literally at the end of my last string that day, and Mrs. Turner saved me.

When Mrs. Turner asked me to go to church that Sunday, I felt like I was still battling with that same evil spirit. Thoughts of suicide had become more common and I was afraid to reach out to anyone. I asked my parents to keep RC for a couple of weeks just to make sure I was okay. Mrs. Turner asking me to go to church that day felt like a life jacket being thrown to me while I was drowning in an ocean filled with evil spirits.

The spiritual side of me had died a long time ago. It had been so long since I last attended church for the right reasons, and I felt uncomfortable when I walked in. Jesus had long been forgotten between running the streets with Malik and all the drama with Patrick. I felt ashamed as I walked in the church. I followed behind Mrs. Turner like a lost puppy searching for its mother. I stayed close to Mrs. Turner and barely made eye contact with people who were welcoming me to the church. Thoughts of death and suicide continued to filter throughout my mind as I sat with my head lowered in shame. I was about to scream for help when I heard an angelic voice singing an inspiring rendition of *God's Grace* by Trin-i-Tee 5-7.

The angelic voice brought tears to my eyes as my anxious feelings began to subside, and I nodded my head to the sound of the music.

I was still sitting in the pew with my head lowered when I heard a voice explode through the building. "Hold your head up because God still loves you."

107

Mrs. Turner quickly jumped to her feet and started praising God along with other church members. I strained to see who was speaking. The voice speaking and the saints praising God reminded me of New Heaven Church of God. The voice continued to proclaim that Jesus's blood will wash away all your sins. It felt like something was punching me in the chest as warm tears began to flow down my face.

I was already walking towards the voice when I heard, "God can take away all that pain and heal your heart. Is there anyone who wants to accept Jesus as their personal savior?"

I don't know what it was, but I just felt like something was pulling me towards the voice. When I finally arrived at the voice, I was surprised. The woman was short and pudgy with patchy, bad skin. Her voice didn't match her appearance, but she was sending shock waves through the crowded church. A pudgy Flavor Flav with a wig would have been the best way to describe her. There was nothing beautiful about her except the words coming from her mouth. Every word that came out her mouth felt like a hard punch to my chest.

The women locked her arms around me and whispered in my ear, "God has loved you since you were a child. God has even loved you when you hated yourself. It's time to come home."

I tried hard to fight the tears back, but it was of no use. I felt weak from all the stress with a new baby, Patrick, and living my life wrong. The more I cried on Linda's shoulder, the better I felt. Linda stepped back and kneeled down and an invisible force made me kneel also. I remember smelling the strong aroma of cinnamon as consecrated oil was smeared across my forehead. I remember a strong, warm force rushing through my body and me sprawling on the floor. The feeling was so euphoric as every stressful nerve appeared to relax and the pain of heartbreak disappeared.

Something unknown crashed against me, knocking me on my back. I stared at the ceiling of the church in a comatose state, unable to move. I remember the old saints in Baxley calling it "being in the spirit." I had never felt that type of joy and relief before. I felt like I was floating towards the ceiling, but my body was still lying on the floor. I felt my body climb higher and higher as I felt God's spirit forgive me of every evil deed that I had committed. I slowly began to regain consciousness, and eventually I felt people helping me to my feet. I remember being saved when I was younger, but this feeling was different. This time it was more real for me. It felt like I was saved for a reason and not because it was expected.

The lady asked if I had a testimony. I proudly proclaimed that I had been touched by God and saved. The church erupted into loud praises to God, and I felt my feet begin to slide forwards and then backwards to the rhythm of the music. That was the first time that I had ever "shouted" in church, and I don't mean screaming. My mother used to tell me that God would give me a holy dance once I was saved, and on that night, I received my holy dance. My holy dance and shouting turned into a full twenty-minute workout because I would not sit down.

The sisters in the church would escort me to my seat and I would bounce up like a jack-in-the-box. There was happiness in my soul that day that just could not be contained. Giving my life to Christ that day felt like a two-hundred-pound weight had been lifted off my chest. All I wanted to do was praise God for delivering me. I left church that day feeling excited about my new life as a Christian, and I was willing to do anything to hold on to that joy.

Solid Foundation Cathedral became my life. I joined several committees and started attending church services on Wednesday and Friday nights. I was so involved in the church that Mrs. Turner could no longer keep up with me. I signed up for the transport shuttle instead of waiting for Mrs. Turner. I became very close with the van driver, Linda Stanford—the same pudgy lady who had brought me back to Christ. I truly believed that God had placed Linda in my life. Linda attended theology school and used the money from driving the church's van to help offset school costs. We would often discuss our past relationships. I found out that Linda and I had a lot in common.

She grew up in Jessup, GA and attended Wayne County High School, which was about thirty miles from Baxley. We were both raised in a Pentecostal holiness churches, and we both had backslid.

Linda's testimony about her past made mine look like a fairytale in comparison. Linda stopped attending church because she wanted to experience life without all of the guilty feelings. Her mother kicked her out of the house at age fifteen after giving her an ultimatum about attending church. She moved in with a girlfriend, started partying, and eventually was taken advantage of by several men. She eventually returned to the church at age nineteen with a four-year-old daughter.

Linda sounded hurt when she talked about how her mother would introduce her to up-and-coming ministers in the church, trying to get her married off. Linda's voice cracked as she explained how one up-and-coming minister fooled everyone. He said all the right things to get her to the altar after only a couple of weeks of church dating. I was curious about the church dating, so I asked her to explain. Linda explained that young people in the church would go to the movies and different functions as a group to avoid being tempted by Satan. You never really spent intimate time getting to know each other because all that time was controlled by the church. Your one-on-one time was normally after morning service. Those meetings were normally under the watchful eyes of the church mothers, who made sure no inappropriate touching was going on under or above the table. Talking on the phone without supervision was scorned upon because it gave Satan an opportunity to put "nasty" thoughts in your mind. She was grateful at the time because she thought she had finally met a man who was God-fearing and who accepted her daughter.

After they were married, she began to see a different side of him. He was very controlling and often had bizarre sexual urges. He was not sexually aroused unless he was tied up or she talked to him in a little girl's voice. She never put it together until she came home one day and found her five-year-old daughter half naked sitting on his lap.

Linda told her mother, the police, and most importantly, the church, and everyone accused her of lying, including her mother.

Her husband was well respected in the small town of Jessup, and when he told everyone that the house was hot and they were just trying to cool off, everyone believed him. Her mother somehow convinced her granddaughter that it was just a hot day. The small town's police never followed up on the complaint, and eventually the case went away. Linda hated her mother because she had sided with that man. She took her daughter and moved as far away from Jessup as possible. Linda had to be one of the strongest people I had ever met. I don't know what I would have done without my mother's support.

Linda and I were inseparable. RC and her daughter were close in age, so we watched each other's kids. Almost everything we did was centered on church activities. There were a lot of really cute guys at church, but we were focused on our salvation. The one thing that I truly loved about Linda was the way she hustled for Christ and the church. Linda was energetic with a beautiful smile and she was not afraid to witness about Jesus Christ to anyone. Linda's hustle for Christ soon rubbed off on me. The new power given to me by God started to show in my life.

My parents were so excited when I told them I was saved and sanctified. My brother Steven was happy for me, but he was concerned about the amount of time I was spending at church. He was even more concerned because of my dedication to paying my tithes. No matter how small my check was, I made sure 10% went to the church. When the church asked me to give more because of the new church being built, I gave it happily. Steven would argue sometimes because I had to borrow money, but that was just something I had to endure. God and Solid Foundation came first and there was nothing going to ever change that.

The men near my apartment had been accustomed to seeing me in tight booty shorts. Now they had to adjust to seeing me in knee-length dresses. The guys would just shake their heads and say, "Here comes that old church lady."

I would just laugh and praise God for allowing my light to shine through. The more I read the scripture, the more I felt like Jesus was really doing great things for me. I joined a youth group in the church called SOFC (Sold Out for Christ). We were like little interns for the church. We gave our free time and energy all for the betterment of the church. Our mission was to witness about Christ and invite people to our church.

After a while, it just became part of our speech: "Hello, my name is such and such. Do you want more in your life? Well come on over to Solid Foundation and worship with us."

Bishop Calvin Tyler Sr. was bishop and overseer at Solid Foundation Cathedral. I didn't consider the church to be a mega church, but it had definitely grown. When I first started attending Solid Foundation, it had approximately two hundred members. But thanks to SOFC, it now had well over sixteen thousand members and millions more watching weekly.

We would ride the MARTA train all over Atlanta recruiting souls and the church would repay us with a cookout or movie tickets. We were given little bracelets and bandannas that we wore proudly, almost like little gangsters for Christ. Most of the people in the group were single moms who took advantage of the discount daycare service offered at that time. I found it hard to understand how Solid Foundation's best community outreach program eventually evolved into a lucrative private school.

Most of single mothers in the church were head over heels in love with the Bishop's son, Calvin Tyler Jr. Calvin was the unofficial leader of SOFC. Calvin Jr. was like a general in his father's growing army. Calvin Sr. would consult with other high-ranking officials in the church. They would give the game plan to his son, and Calvin Jr. would pass it on to us. We would arrive early Saturday morning, get our marching orders from Calvin Jr. , and then blanket the city like a swarm of bees. They awarded us with train tokens for the week. Whoever had the most converts was awarded movie passes or Six Flags tickets.

Linda and I always worked as a team, and we always seemed to bring in the most converts on Sundays. Linda's "overcoming the odds" story always attracted single mothers. My copper, brown skin, long, flowing hair and hips that begged for a fucking had men approaching by droves. One time I received Six Flags tickets for three weeks straight. Bishop Tyler found out that I had convinced two professional football players and a record producer to attend Solid Foundation.

Most of the men I convinced to come to Solid Foundation always thought they were getting more than what I was offering. I would bat my big, brown eyes, flirt a little, and play the innocent church girl, and they would fall for it. I didn't know it at the time, but Solid Foundation was actually training me to be the person I was today. I truly believed that God was using my looks to bring people to Solid Foundation, and for added satisfaction, I was rewarded. By the time those poor men had figured out that I was just recruiting them, they were being dunked in the baptismal and signing direct deposit slips. If they approached me at church about a date, I would politely refuse. To me, I had accomplished what God had wanted, and there was no need for a further relationship. I knew that God would eventually send me a God-fearing man, but a new recruit was not him. New recruits were still learning about Christ Jesus and I needed a man who was strongly planted in God's word.

Most of the single moms in SOFC believed that Calvin Jr. was their God-fearing man. Sure he was cute, but a little scrawny for me. Calvin was tall and lanky and I teased him because he was bow-legged. Calvin Jr. and I would flirt, but we both knew that God was in control of our lives.

Sometimes he would tease me like, "Angela, when are we getting married? God wants us to procreate as son as possible."

I would respond, "Boy please! You better run along and play before you get your feelings hurt."

He would respond with a huge grin on his face, "Hurt me? Well then hurt me, Ms. Anderson. If you think you got it like that, please hurt me."

I would push him and respond, "Calvin, there is nothing about that scrawny little body that says you can handle this. I'm too much woman for you."

Calvin would playfully shove me, and we would go our separate ways laughing. Calvin and I, like every member of in SOFC, were taught to be born-again virgins.

Being a born-again virgin was a weird concept. If you really think about it, it's almost ridiculous. There was no way I could go back and change all those passion-filled nights, when Patrick's dick was sliding in and out of me. The concept was even more baffling because I had a two-year old son. But as a loyal servant at Solid Foundation, I abided by the rules given to us by the church elders.

The born-again virgin ceremony was a ritual conducted on the first Saturday of each month. The male's ritual was conducted separately from ours, so it was always a mystery. The girls in SOFC often joked that the men were taken into the woods and beaten until their whorish behavior changed. The ritual for the girls reminded me of when I crossed over as an AGA. When you entered the church sanctuary, all the lights were off and white candles illuminated in the darkness. We wore black dresses in the beginning of the ceremony to represent our old promiscuous life style. Then we switched to white dresses to represent our new life as born-again virgins. The whole ceremony was almost believable, except I still had penises on my mind.

Getting it good from Patrick on regular basis was a feeling not easily forgotten. An alcoholic's greatest weakness is manifested when they are around alcohol. My greatest weakness was apparent when I was around penises, especially big ones.

I remember being at work one time when Marquis Potter came into my office. Marquis worked in the housekeeping department and he came in my office to dump the trash. We were talking, and I just happened to look down.

I saw a large bulge near his front pocket so I grabbed at it, and without thinking, I said, "Give me some of that money man."

As soon as I hit the bulge, my face flushed from embarrassment. Marquis's penis was coiled up near his pocket like a sleeping python snake. I guess the touch must have excited him because it began to swell until it was fully erect. Embarrassed, he started giggling and quickly exited my office. I was amazed at the size of Marquis's penis. I just stood there embarrassed and speechless, shaking my head in astonishment. It took me a week and half to get over having wet dreams about Marquis. I would wake up in the middle of the night sweating thinking about Marquis and his dick. I would shove a pillow between my legs and ask Jesus to take away those evil thoughts. Every time I saw him in the hallway, I would just shake my head and say, "Umm umm umm!" Marquis would laugh and quickly walk away, still embarrassed about the encounter.

Some of girls in SOFC would talk about how easy it was being a born-again virgin. I would just shake my head and say to myself, "You just didn't have a nigga like Patrick in between your thighs."

My sexual urges would come and go depending on whom I was around. Lately, the urges were pounding between my legs. And the reason was Desmond Hubbard.

Desmond was nothing more then a slick-talking thug who cleaned up part time around church. He had every negative quality from all my past relationships, except his were supersized. He was not a member at Solid Foundation, but he often attended church functions. Every girl in SOFC except me ran the opposite way when Desmond came around. Even though I already knew where that ride was headed, I was still curious about the ride.

Desmond was tall and muscular with golden, brown skin. His eyes always looked sleepy hidden behind his wood-framed designer shades. When he smiled, he flashed two gold caps attached to his two upper canine teeth. He had a tattoo of the name "Imani" on his neck. Desmond told me that the name Imani was his daughter's. Really I didn't care whose name it was. It was sexy. He would give me a respectable holy hug and my vagina would buzz with excitement. I would pull Desmond close and imagine him on top of me. I couldn't tell by our interactions if Desmond was attracted to me, but I made sure to throw my hips extra hard when I walked away from him. The older sisters in the church called it being hot. Whatever they wanted to call it, that's what I was. No matter how much prayer and Bible reading I was asked to do, I was "hot."

My attraction to him was noticeable by everyone in SOFC and I was teased relentlessly with Linda leading the insults. "Angela, why is that when Desmond comes to church functions you're all teeth and gums, and when he doesn't come you sit in the corner like you've lost your puppy?"

I always managed a half-hearted laugh and shrugged off the comments, but there was some truth to what she said. I was feeling Desmond in the worst way, and it was only a matter of time before the God in me was tested. One Saturday, my temptation presented itself, and I failed miserably.

I was riding MARTA with Desmond on my way home from church. The train was packed, and I found myself standing in front of Desmond. He was talking to me and his sweet honey breath was tickling the hairs on the back of my neck. The train came to a sudden stop and my butt mistakenly brushed against his penis. He leaned in close to my ear and apologized, but I was already aroused.

Desmond continued to talk to me, but my mind was on something else. I placed my hand behind my back and slowly extended my finger until it brushed against his penis. Desmond quickly looked at my hand to see if it was a mistake.

I swallowed hard as he pushed his body near mine. I extended my ass out as far as I could and pushed backwards. Desmond gently pulled me backwards allowing my butt to rest on his erect penis.

I felt his soft lips nudge my ear as he spoke. "Hummm! This feels good."

My body exploded with lust. With all the people crowded around us, it was even more exhilarating. It felt like I was getting away with committing a nasty act without God seeing me. I quickly turned my body so that we were face to face, grabbed his hands, and placed them on my butt. His hands gently caressed my ass as his penis grew harder. I could feel my chest breathing in and out deeply as my whole body trembled for a more intimate touch. The gentle breeze coming from Desmond's nostrils bounced off my forehead causing shivers down my body.

The God in me wanted to push away, but his hard dick kept my body stationary. He traced the panty lines on my butt with his finger and then gently squeezed it, causing my legs to buckle. Deep in my heart I knew I was wrong, but my body had been aching for this type of touch for so long. The train conductor's voice startled me as he announced the next stop and I pushed away from Desmond. The train quickly cleared and I made my escape and took an empty seat in the next car. I heard the door open after a short time and saw Desmond staring at me confused. I quickly turned away and lowered my head in shame. Desmond must have got the hint because he sat in a chair far from me. I glanced in Desmond's direction and he smiled at me as if to say this was our secret. I quickly opened my Bible for strength, but all I could see was Desmond and all I could feel was my body hot with passion.

When my stop came, I quickly exited the train trying to avoid Desmond. Desmond quickly gave pursuit and grabbed my arm.

I turned to look at him and he had a concerned look on his face as he asked, "Angela, what's wrong? Did I do something to hurt you or something?"

I stared at the ground in silence unable to give Desmond an answer that made sense. I couldn't exactly tell him the truth without giving him an open invitation to fuck.

I responded with the best answer I could think of. "Desmond, I'm sorry about what happened on the train. I had a moment of weakness and committed a selfish act."

Desmond looked at me like I was a comic on stage telling a joke with a delayed reaction and then started laughing as he responded. "Ha ha ha! Did you say you committed a selfish act? Ha ha ha! You sound like a Wall Street banker on trial for stealing money. Girl, you are crazy."

I had to laugh myself after seeing Desmond almost in tears from laughter. I playfully slapped Desmond on his arm while telling him, "Shut up! Oh my God, you make me so sick."

I pretended to walk fast in an attempt to get away from him but he trotted behind me and playfully bear hugged me while saying, "If you promise not to commit another selfish act, I will make sure you get home safely."

I broke loose from Desmond's bear hug and playfully swung at his face as he ducked and dodged my blows. I could not help but laugh with Desmond as we walked down the long street to my apartment.

When we arrived at my door, I was still apprehensive but comfortable. Desmond sat on the steps and I joined him. The fall breeze was nippy, but I felt cozy with Desmond's leather jacket on.

I apologized again for shamelessly throwing myself at him when we were on the train and he responded, "Forget about it, Angela! I didn't let anything happen that I didn't want to happen."

I leaned over and nudged Desmond with my shoulder and he responded by smiling at me and brushing my hair out of my eyes. I would have been safe with just a smile, but that damn touch sent shock waves through my body. Desmond noticed my response from the touch, because I was shyly staring at the ground and smiling from ear to ear.

Desmond saw me smiling and inquired, "So what's got you so happy?"

Still smiling, I nervously glanced at Desmond and responded, "You!"

Desmond wrapped his arm around me and pulled me close to him and gently rocked back and forth. A calm stillness surrounded us as we sat snuggled together on my front porch.

That goofy boyfriend-girlfriend feeling flooded my body as my mouth opened, and I spoke. "Would you like to come inside for some coffee?"

As soon as the words were out of my mouth, I regretted saying them. What the hell was I thinking?

I was still regretting it when Desmond responded, "Sure, I'll come in for a little while. But I want to try and catch that last train going back downtown."

I felt an uneasy spirit come over me as my key unlocked the door and we went in.

The God in me was saying, "Kick him out now."

But my flesh was weak and willing to compromise by saying, "It's just a cup of coffee. What's the worse that can happen?"

I went through all the possible scenarios in my head looking for something positive, but they all turned out bad. As soon as I turned the key to my door and we walked in, I knew I was in trouble. The one love seat in my small living room didn't give a lot of options for seating. Desmond sat down and stretched his arm out along the back the love seat, like he was in a movie theater. I turned on the TV and quickly made my way to the kitchen.

I placed a pot of water on the fire and returned to the living room still nervous. I stood in the middle of the room with my arms folded, watching TV as if I was interested in the six o'clock news. I was hoping that Desmond wouldn't notice. I thought that if I could quickly make his coffee and get him out of the house, everything would be okay.

Desmond broke the uneasy silence in the room by motioning for me to sit beside him.

I gave Desmond a quick glance and said, "No thank you, I'm fine."

I quickly turned back toward the TV and pretended to be interested in the latest news about brown bears in their natural habitat. I could feel Desmond's eyes slowly working their way up and down my body.

I nervously stood in one spot afraid to move when I heard Desmond say in a somber voice, "Angela, you don't have to be afraid of me. I'm not going to hurt you. Come and sit next to me."

Again, I glanced at Desmond and responded in a nervous voice, "I know you're not going to do anything. I'm just waiting for the water to get hot then I'll sit down."

Before I could finish my sentence, Desmond was off the couch and standing in front of me. Uneasy by his sudden presence, I took a step backwards, but he gently grabbed my hand and pulled me closer.

Desmond leaned forward and spoke to me in a calming voice, "Look at you! You're so afraid of me that you're shaking. Why are you so afraid of letting me see who the real Angela is? When we were back on that train, I felt like you were searching for something, and if you're still looking, it's right here."

Desmond wrapped his arms around me and started swaying back and forth, almost comforting me. My body started trembling as I wrapped my arms around his muscular back and pulled him closer. Desmond tilted my head back and stared into my eyes, causing me to tap his back anxiously. I was so afraid of what was going to happen next. When I heard the water starting to boil, I bolted from his arms to the kitchen. I turned the water off and nervously searched the cupboard for a cup. Desmond came behind me and wrapped his arms around me, causing my body to paralyze.

I stared nervously at my cupboard as Desmond gently kissed my ear. Relaxed by his grip of seduction, I leaned my head back on his chest and allowed him to gently nibble on my neck. I could feel Desmond's hands slowly working their way up my body towards my breasts. If I was going to stop him, that would have been the time.

I could hear a small voice inside me saying, "Stop now, Angela," but it was too late. Desmond's hands cupped my breast and gently squeezed. My eyes rolled back in my head as my hunger for him grew. I spun around and faced Desmond and gave one last half-hearted attempt to push away. But he responded like I thought he would by pulling me closer and kissing me passionately.

My arms were still wrapped around Desmond's neck when I felt his hands tugging at the zipper on my jeans. The small voice normally telling me to stop had been replaced with a voice asking for more. I allowed Desmond to unbutton my jeans and then I took him by the hand and led him to my bedroom. Desmond took his shirt off and sat on the side of the bed and watched as I undressed. He placed both hands behind his head and leaned back on the bed smiling. His legs slowly swayed back and forth as I pulled my panties off. I could tell he was turned on because his dick was fully erect when I pulled his pants and underwear off. Desmond continued to play it cool and keep his hands behind his head in a reclining mood. I slowly slid up his body, kissing him as he slowly guided me on top of him. I felt his penis enter inside me, causing my body to tingle with pleasure. I felt Desmond tense up and then embrace me tighter as we made love.

To say that Desmond was good at what he did was an understatement. His touches were sensual and he amazed me with feats of lovemaking that my body had longed for. Although my body was deeply satisfied, my mind was far away. I could feel the guilty feelings of backsliding gnawing at my conscience.

The feelings from backsliding can run the gamut of your emotions. They can be as simple as a guilty afterthoughts, or like mine, as severe as an attack of depression. The first thought is why? Why would I sacrifice all my progress in God for simple taste of lust? All I could think about was what God thought of me, or if I could ever go back to Him. God had brought me back from the brink of losing my mind and this is how I repaid Him. I thought back to when my father preached about Satan always tempting you when things were going well. I stared at Desmond sleeping peacefully in my bed and wondered why I felt so miserable.

The next morning was a carryover from the previous night. Desmond tried to pull me close, but I was cold and distant.

He sensed that there was something wrong and asked, "Baby, what's wrong? Did I do something? Come on, you can talk to me."

I pushed Desmond away irritated and lashed out at him. "Look Desmond, I'm fine! I just have a lot of things on my mind. Can you please stop bugging me? I'm fine."

Desmond quietly walked away from me toward the bathroom. I wanted to tell him what I was feeling, but it would have been useless. Desmond was just being a man; he pursued and conquered me. My conscience was admonishing me for being so weak. I should have stopped with all the flirting weeks ago. I regretted the day that I first saw Desmond. Desmond took a shower and proceeded to dress without saying anything else to me.

He stared at me strangely and I could only imagine what was going through his mind.

"Damn! I know I waxed that ass pretty good, and she's acting all cold towards me. What the fuck is wrong with her?"

I wanted to put Desmond's mind to rest, so I grabbed his hand as he was walking out the door and spoke. "Desmond, let me first tell you that it's not youI really enjoyed our time together, but I was wrong for doing that. After we got finished making love last night, I just felt guilty. I was cold towards you this morning because I blamed you, which was wrong. I'm taking responsibility for me because I should have never placed myself in that position. If this was any other situation, I would probably see were this would lead us. But I can't right now. Right now I need to get back right with God."

Desmond shook his head as though he understood and kissed me on the cheek. As he walked down my steps, I felt some relief. Desmond may not have understood my entire situation, but he had been around enough church folks to know when enough is enough.

Sometimes I think back on Desmond and I wonder "What if?"Sometimes the church has your mind so screwed up that you don't know if you're coming or going. I was burdened with so much guilt about that day that I never gave Desmond a chance. The only thing on my mind was finding the best way to get right with God.

Two weeks passed, and I decided to finally speak with someone. I spoke with Linda about what had happened. I didn't tell her all the particulars like who, what, when and where. But she still seemed to understand the situation. We talked on the phone all night and I finally began to feel better. Linda instructed me to come to church that morning because she believed my blessing was waiting.

When I arrived at church that morning, I was shocked to see Desmond. My normal bronze shade of skin turned pale as my mind tried to figure out what was going on. Did Desmond show up to church to bust me out, or was he there on some stalker shit?

Linda was concerned about the sudden dazed look on my face, so she asked, "Girl, what's going on? I haven't seen you at church in a couple of weeks. You called me last night about backsliding, and now you're looking like you've seen a ghost. Is everything okay?"

I knew I had to come clean with what was going on, but I had just hoped that names could have been left out. Desmond smiled at me and waved, and just like that I started yearning for all that good dick hanging between his legs. Here I was trying to get right with God, and that motherfucker was looking like a male centerfold model.

I quickly turned away from Desmond and responded to Linda, "I was having personal problems and wanted to try and figure things out myself."

There was a long pause between us and I glanced in Desmond's direction and smiled back. Linda looked into my eyes and saw that my thoughts were clearly absorbed with Desmond.

Finally, Linda just blurted out, "It's Desmond, isn't it?"

I played it off and tried to play coy, but Linda had my number.

I finally took a deep breath and just told Linda everything. I told her about our encounter on the train, and how we had made love that night. I also explained how my lust for Desmond was getting stronger. I explained to Linda that backsliding was the last thing I wanted to do, but that I had just been too weak.

I continued talking. "Girl, I just don't know what's going on in my head. I came to church to try to find my way back to God and there was Desmond. There is no way I can continue to keep my salvation with Desmond at the same church."

Linda laughed at me and spoke. "Now Angela, stop panicking! I know Desmond is fine, but Christ is greater than your lust for him."

Linda walked away still laughing as I stood there getting angry because she was not taking me seriously. I turned and saw Desmond making his way toward me, so I quickly walked to the last seat available in the front row. Desmond found a vacant seat three rows behind me as devotion service started.

Finding a solution was easier said than done. The problem that I was facing was the battle between God's will and the flesh. On the night that Jesus saved me, I swore that I would serve him forever. Everything that I had done over the past few months was for the glory of God. Any temptation that had come my way was always ignored, but for some reason, Desmond was stuck in my mind.

I was still thinking about my dilemma when Linda stood in front of the church and halted service. Linda glanced over at Calvin Jr. , and I saw him slowly walk to the front of the church. Calvin Jr. lowered his head in shame as Linda held out her hand and told me to join her. Already knowing what was about to happen, I stayed seated.

Once again, Linda held out her hand and said, "God wants you to come back home."

Embarrassed by what was occurring, I stood and slowly walked toward Linda.

Linda hugged me tightly and whispered, "It's going to be okay."

Next, Linda held her hand toward Desmond and asked him to come forward. If I could have had one wish, it would have been for the roof of the church to fall on me, because I was so embarrassed. Linda was a great friend to have, but she had no idea when it came to discretion. I could tell that Desmond was just as embarrassed as I was. He walked forward with his head lowered and staring at the floor. I guess he thought it was going to hide him. That's the funny thing about Christians like Linda. They always want you to confess your sins in front of other people, almost like they want to embarrass you.

Linda glanced at me and must have realized that I was feeling embarrassed because she quickly opened her Bible to James Chapter five and the sixteenth verse and started speaking. "The Bible says that if you confess your sins one to another you will be healed."

I shook my head in disbelief hoping that this moment of shame would end, but I already knew that it was just starting. Linda continued to quote verse after verse from the Bible about public confession until it was clear as to what she expected. Linda glanced over at Calvin Jr. and he reluctantly shook his head in agreement.

Linda turned toward Bishop Tyler and spoke. "Bishop Tyler, God has brought it to my attention that these two souls need deliverance from the clutches of Satan. I quickly turned away from Linda rolling my eyes in disgust.

Linda continued to speak, "Angela, you know that the only way that your sins will be forgiving is through public confession. Not only have you sinned against God, but you have also sinned against the church. You have to make this right with God before you can continue this Christian journey. And Desmond, this goes for you as well. You haven't accepted Jesus as your personal savior, but you have an understanding of Christ. That makes you just as guilty as Angela."

I glanced over at Desmond and his face was twisted like he was eating raw cheese as he responded, "What's up with all of this, Linda? This is not cool! I thought we were friends, and you turn around and embarrass me like this!"

Linda responded, "This is not about our friendship. This is about doing what's right in God's sight."

Bishop Tyler quickly shook his head in agreement and interrupted the conversation.

"Desmond, this is a way of life for us."

Linda held the Bible high over her head and continued to talk to Desmond as if she were scolding him. "This life of Christianity is not a game. When God condemns us with the power of his word, we must obey. Sister Angela understands this, and it's imperative that you also understand this. The only option available to you and Angela is a public confession."

I lowered my head in shame because I knew deep down in my soul that she was right. Confessing my sins in front of church was nothing new to me. I remember once when I was a child at New Heaven, Elder Timothy Hill and Sister Diane Crawford were having an affair. It became a big deal at the church because both were married to other members of the church. Nobody really knows how the shit hit the fan; just one Sunday out of the blue, Elder Hill and Sister Crawford were called to the front of the church.

As a kid at New Heaven, it was like TMZ meets Jesus. Craig and I, along with the other kids in the church, stared at Elder Hill and Sister Crawford standing in front of the church looking guilty.

My father stood at the podium and laid out all the evidence like a Perry Mason novel, and then asked in a demanding voice, "Do either one of you have anything to confess before this church?"

There was an eerie silence and then both Elder Hill and Sister Crawford fell to their knees, begging for forgiveness. My father, along with the other ministers in the church, gathered around them and started praying. As a child growing up in the church, I really didn't understand what was going on, but now here I was in the same situation.

I could tell that Desmond was not feeling the situation because he blurted out,

"Man you motherfuckers are crazy! I'm not about to stand in front of a bunch of strangers begging for forgiveness."

And with that, he exited the church leaving me to face the music by myself.

Bishop Tyler walked to the podium and started reading James Chapter five and the sixteenth verse. "Therefore confess your sins to each other and pray for each other so that you may be healed. The prayer of the righteous person is powerful and effective."

Then he said in a loud, demanding voice, "If there is a confession to be made, now is the time. Don't loose your soul over something that you can get right today."

Linda stared at me with a look of delight. I stood before the church alone and afraid and nervously spoke. "I. . . I…would first like to give honor and praise to God. I also would like to give honor and praise to the Bishop, and the first wife of the church. I would like the church to know that my lust for a certain person in this church led to me backsliding."

I tried to leave it at that but Linda interrupted, "Sister Angela, you have to confess everything. You can't just admit to a little sin, you have to own all of your sin."

The church erupted with hand claps and cheers of amen.

Anger and embarrassment collided as I lowered my head in shame and spoke. "I sinned against God and the church by lusting after Desmond Hubbard. My lust pushed me to sleep with him two weeks ago, and now I'm asking Christ and the church for forgiveness."

The little kids giggling reminded me of how we did back at New Heaven.

I broke down and began to cry as the church stared at me and whispered amongst each other. Bishop Tyler moved from the podium towards me and wrapped his arms around me. I felt like my father was comforting me after I had fallen of my bike. The longer he hugged me, the more I cried. The elders, ministers, and mothers of the church crowded around me and started to pray. I kneeled and prayed for what seemed like an hour seeking that euphoric feeling that I once had felt, but it never came. When I finally got to my feet, I lied to the church by telling them that Jesus was back in my life. The reality was that I didn't have the same feeling or respect for the church that I had before. Linda looked at Bishop Tyler with a smirk on her face, and he smiled back at her, almost like he was thanking her for the TV ratings. She hugged me and rocked back and forth speaking in tongues like the Holy Spirit was moving her.

She kept repeating over and over again, "God is married to the backslider."

The only thing that came to my mind was "Bitch, fuck you!"

I sat in my seat the rest of the service fuming about what had just happened. I wanted to get right with God, but not at the expense of my dignity.

Bishop Tyler's started his sermon by saying, "You shall not bring the fee of a prostitute or the wages of a dog into the house of the Lord your God, in payment for any vow, for both of these are an abomination to the Lord your God."

As Bishop Tyler preached, the cameraman turned towards my direction and my face was instantly plastered on the big screen. Bishop Tyler instructed the church to repeat the words from the passage, and the congregation complied. I felt like an idiot as the word "prostitute" slowly scrolled across my face on the big screen. When church service was over, I headed to the door as quickly as possible.

I heard Linda scream my name, but I was already in my car. I just wanted to get as far away from Solid Foundation as I could. I was hurt and embarrassed by what had just occurred, and I just wanted to be alone. When I arrived home, I just sat in the house and stared blankly at the wall. I wondered if Elder Hill and Sister Crawford had felt like I did. I remember them looking relieved, almost like a weight had been lifted off their chest. I was angry! I was angry at Linda for calling me out in front of the whole church and TV audience. I felt that as a friend, she should have treated my situation with more respect.

As I continued to seethe with anger, I heard the phone ring. I looked at my phone and saw Linda's picture pop up. My initial reaction was to throw the phone at the wall, but I was curious about what she would say.

I mean really! How do you apologize to someone when you embarrass the shit out of them? "I'm sorry for making you look like a fucking idiot. Did I hurt your feelings? Oh well, God still loves you, and so do I."

I had an attitude and I wanted Ms. Goody Two-Shoes to know. I answered the phone angrily with one word. "What?"

Linda started the conversation off by saying, "Angela, I know you're mad at me right now, but I did it for your own good."

I wanted to say, "Bitch, how the fuck was that for my own good?" But I didn't.

I just sat and listened as Linda continued to talk. "Sometimes we need a push to get back to God. I invited Desmond to church because I wanted to show you what type of man he was. Desmond is not a God-fearing man. If he had been a God-fearing man, he would have obeyed and not stormed out. When he stormed out of the church, I said, 'Praise God. ' I praised God because God reveled to the church and the TV audience that Desmond was full of the devil. Desmond would have always been there to tempt you because he was full of Satan. God told me to call you out so that he could run Satan out. Satan acting as Desmond defiled your body. I know it is hard to accept, but your embarrassment was worth it."

Linda finished by asking me to pray with her, but I declined. I still loved God, but it was time for me to find a new church. There was no way she was going to convince me that God gave her the green light to embarrass me like that. And if God gave her the green light, I was in the wrong religion.

The next few weeks were a miserable time for me. Just thinking about Linda and Solid Foundation made me bitter, but I still longed for that happiness when I was around church members. I visited a couple of churches, but none ever measured up to Solid Foundation. I felt like a child on punishment. All of the other kids were out playing at Solid Foundation, and all I could do was watch from a distance. I felt tempted to go back a few times, but I would always remember that smirk on Linda's face.

Linda never called me back, which hurt me more because I was expecting her to at least try to talk, even if I wasn't listening. Mrs. Turner stopped pressuring me to come back after the first couple weeks. Mrs. Turner could see the hurt and embarrassment in my eyes whenever I discussed the incident. My mother and father felt like I should have taken my medicine and stayed in the church. But they also believed that broadcasting my indiscretions on TV was wrong. What I hated most about that experience was that no one showed me any compassion. All Linda and Bishop Tyler wanted me to do was beg for mercy on TV because it was good for ratings. Once that happened, it seemed like I was expendable.

Four weeks after leaving the church, I was still sulking around the house, but I was feeling better. I heard a knock at the door and I was shocked to see Calvin Jr. standing there. He smiled at me nervously and said hello. I responded with a suspicious grin and said hello.

Calvin took in a deep breath and started to speak, "Hey Angela, I was just dropping off some things for Mr. and Mrs. Turner, and I thought I'd just drop by and see how you're doing."

I remember seeing Calvin Jr. 's face during the church incident and he looked visibly shaken. I remember him looking shocked as Linda carried on in front of the church and camera. When Calvin Jr. glanced at his father, it looked like Bishop Tyler was disgusted with him. I guess he was shocked at the way his son appeared to bitch up when it came to doing dirty work.

Calvin Jr. continued to speak in a low apologetic voice. "Angela, I'm sorry for any hurt that my father caused you. I want to assure you that I had nothing to do with that fiasco. I knew Linda and my dad spoke about you confessing your sins in front of the church, but I never thought it would turn into a three-ring circus for TV. I'm sorry, and I hope we can still be friends. We have been good friends for the past two years, and I would like to at least hold on to our friendship."

I almost felt sorry for Calvin Jr. as he stood there apologizing for his father's indiscretion.

Calvin would have probably rambled on and on if I had not interrupted him and spoke. "Calvin, Calvin, relax! I don't blame you for what happened. We're cool. First, I should have never put myself in that situation by messing around with Desmond. And I definitely should have had both eyes open when it came to Linda."

I was about to call Linda a short, dumpty, fat bitch when Mrs. Turner interrupted our conversation and opened her door. She started watering the plants on the steps humming a gospel tune.

Calvin looked at me and shook his head saying, "Ear hustling. Man, that will never go out of style."

We both started laughing, and Mrs. Turner stared at us like we were talking loudly in Sunday school class. I opened my door and invited Calvin in, but he declined. I gave him a quick hug and thanked him for being concerned, and he turned to leave.

The following Monday, I was surprised to see Calvin again. It had been a long time since I had been to my favorite coffee spot. The Green Room was a nice, laidback spot where you could surf the web and enjoy a good cup of coffee. Yes, there was Starbucks and other coffee shops, but there were none quite like the Green Room. This was a place I could relax, and in my case, meet with like-minded people. I started meeting with people who were spiritual and not wrapped up in religious beliefs. We studied the Bible and discussed different points of view without criticizing each other. My small group was a refreshing take on my faith. I didn't have to worry about people calling me out for my sins, and I slowly lost my guilty conscience for backsliding. I finally was able to enjoy my faith again without being a slave to the church. That afternoon, I walked in the door, and imagine my surprise when I saw Calvin. He was sitting at a table by himself surfing the web.

I walked behind Calvin and tapped him on the shoulder and asked, "Is this your way of saying that you're stalking me?"

Calvin turned around surprised to see me. He responded, "Hey you, what are you doing here?"

I told him the short version of how I discovered the Green Room. I really didn't feel comfortable telling him that his punk-ass daddy drove me to find peace at the Green Room. Calvin Jr. invited me to sit with him and I agreed. I may not have had a lot of respect for Calvin's father at that moment, but Calvin Jr. was cool. He had always been an easygoing type person, and that day was no different.

He was easy to talk to and he kept me laughing with his off-brand humor. Calvin confessed that he had left the church for a short time, but he eventually found his way back to Christ. Even though I was angry at his father, I felt totally comfortable talking to him about backsliding. Calvin never passed judgment on me for backsliding. He just listened to me and understood from experience what I was feeling.

I enjoyed talking to Calvin that day because he was such a breath of fresh air. He reminded me of my brother Steven when it came to humor. It was dry and little condescending, but still funny. I told Calvin that it had been a while since I had laughed and really enjoyed myself without being afraid of retaliation or feeling guilty.

Linda was the type of friend who only allowed you to have fun on her terms. Whenever someone in the group said an inappropriate joke or talked about someone in church, she would be the first to chastise them. If she said a dirty joke or talked about somebody, it was always okay. There were a couple of people who called her out about her behavior. She always found a scripture to justify it or found a way to condemn them for calling her out. Linda would glare angrily at them as if she had the power of life and death in her hand. Most people in the group would instantly stop and change the conversation after receiving one of those angry glares. Everyone knew the consequences if they continued talking, because she knew everyone's dirty little secretes. Linda was an expert at acquiring information on people and holding it against them.

Linda had befriended 90% of the people in SOFC when they were at the lowest point in their life. When you befriend a person who is burdened with personal issues, you become a life raft for that person. They feel comfortable exposing there darkest secrets to you because they trust you. Those long conversations on the bus with Linda were like therapy for me. Not only did she convince me, but she also convinced others in the group that their secrets or indiscretions would always be safe with her. No one really gave a second thought about telling their secrets to her until she started using information like ammunition.

Members of SOFC learned quickly that backing Linda into a corner or embarrassing her was a mistake that you would never forget. Calvin admitted that he had been on the receiving end of one of Linda's vindictive tirades.

Calvin held his head down in shame as he talked about his experience with Linda. "I confided in Linda by telling her that I got my girlfriend pregnant when I was sixteen and that my parents helped pay for the abortion. One time she got angry at me when we were having a Bible discussion and just blurted out in front of the entire group, 'Every child deserves to live. ' The Bible discussion had nothing to do with a child dying, so everyone was confused. No one in the group knew what she was talking about, but I sure as hell knew. She glared at me as if she were daring me to challenge her further. Linda has been holding that over my head ever since."

Now I understood why he looked so hurt during my ordeal. I don't think Calvin ever wanted to intentionally hurt me, he was just afraid of the consequences. Both Calvin and I had been backed into a corner at Solid Foundation. The difference between Calvin and me was that I decided to leave. I felt sorry for Calvin because he was placed in situation over which he had no control. He was expected to eventually take over the reigns of Solid Foundation, but he could never be as heartless as his father.

Bishop Calvin Tyler had built a multimillion dollar enterprise on illusions. Calvin Jr. would spoil all of that with his caring attitude for others. I learned that night that Calvin was torn between doing the right thing and feeling good about himself and continuing to victimize the less fortunate like his father.

Talking with Calvin showed me just how intelligent and funny he was. I never really thought of Calvin in terms of a relationship because he was not my type. His long, gangly body and duck feet reminded me of Goofy, the cartoon character. The most adorable trait about Calvin Jr. was his large, koala bear eyes. Those eyes would have me saying yes to him for the next couple of years. Calvin was adorable, but at that chance meeting, I only saw him as a fun friend.

Calvin and I began to hang out as friends. The next few months were filled with lots of fun stuff that I had never experienced before. We went white water rafting, attended wine tasting events, and flew to Vegas and saw a boxing match. The most exciting activity of them all was entering karaoke contest. Calvin and I had to be the most intimidating contestants to ever grace the karaoke scene in Atlanta. We had stage presence and energy and the crowd loved us. Most people in the crowd thought we were actually a couple because we complemented each other so well. One time, Calvin and I won three karaoke competitions in one night. The look on our competitors' faces was all the satisfaction we needed. We were unstoppable and they knew it. When I think back to all of the fun we had during that year, it made me sick what our relationship turned into.

Calvin and I became such good friends during that year that it was inevitable that the rumors would start. I never had proof, but I was sure that the rumors started with Mrs. Turner. I was so comfortable with Calvin that I gave him a key to my place. There was nothing going on between us, but it was clear that Mrs. Turner had an issue with our friendship. She would glare at us when we stumbled up the steps tipsy from the late nights out on the town or make sly comments about me when she thought she was alone with him on the porch.

One evening, I overheard her talking to Calvin. "Calvin, do you think it's appropriate for the Bishop's son to be carrying on like that with a backslider?" When I heard Mrs. Turner say that about me, I was truly hurt. Mrs. Turner had been there for me when I was at my weakest point. And now here she was speaking about me as if I were some two-dollar whore. I felt my anger rising as I walked toward the porch.

I was about to kick the screen door open and check the bitch when I heard Calvin speak. "Mrs. Turner, I don't think it's appropriate for you as a Christian to be spreading lies about me and my friend. Angela is a good friend of mine, and I will continue to be around her."

I could tell that Calvin was angry and frustrated because the tone of his voice was more direct and spiteful. "Never once have you seen me or Angela doing anything inappropriate. All you ever do is peep out your window and go back to the church and spread lies. I'll give you a rumor to spread if you want."

As I was opening the screen door, Calvin grabbed my arm and yanked me toward him. Caught off guard by the sudden pull from Calvin, I stumbled toward him and he caught me in his arms. Not knowing what was going on, I was even more surprised when he pulled me closer to him and kissed me. I didn't know whether to push away or wrap my arms around him. The kiss was rough and demanding while at the same time soft and sensual.

I heard Mrs. Turner gasp and then storm off slamming the door behind her.

Calvin abruptly pulled away from the kiss and started laughing as he spoke. "I bet that will show that old nosey bitch."

I felt silly standing there with my eyes closed, head still tilted sideways, with my tongue slightly hanging out my mouth, kissing the air. I quickly composed myself as Calvin continued talking as he bounced down the steps.

He looked back at me and spoke. "Angela, you just don't know how long I wanted to do that."

Confused about what he was talking about I inquired, "What, you mean kiss me?"

Calvin looked at me befuddled and responded, "What are you talking about?"

Puzzled, I decided to let him finish talking. "Angela, I've waited so long just so that I could give them something to talk about. Sometimes I just get so tired of people always watching and waiting for me to do something wrong. And if I don't do something wrong, they make up stuff. I just want the freedom to live my life the way I want, without being judged. I can't understand why it's so hard for people to understand that I may not want to follow in my dad's footsteps."

I walked over to Calvin and hugged him. I felt so sorry for him because I understood what he was going through. Preachers' kids spend their whole lives chasing after the dreams of their parents. People expect you to be this perfect person destined to be the next generation's savior. I broke under the pressure, Craig broke under the pressure, and now Calvin appeared to be breaking under the pressure. Calvin's cloud-nine high had been replaced with a look of dread and doom as the realization of what had just happened would get back to his father.

I could see Calvin fighting back tears as he continued to speak. "I just wish I could have a small space to myself where I could be free to do what I want without judgment."

I pulled Calvin close and hugged him. I placed my hands on his cheeks and stared into his big dark eyes as I spoke. "Calvin, you will always have a special place with me. No matter what you eventually become, you will always be free to be yourself around me. I love you because you are a special person to me."

Calvin's facial expression went from sadness to surprise as he looked into my eyes. I leaned forward and gave Calvin a quick kiss on his cheek as I walked back into my house. The evening sun gave way to dusk as Calvin opened the screen door and came in.

He closed the door and sat silently beside me. I could tell that he was still thinking about the repercussions of what he had done earlier.

I moved closer to him and started talking. "Calvin, you have to let that go. You are a grown man who's sitting over here worried about nothing. If she wants to go back and tell on you like some little school girl, then so be it. You deserve to be happy."

Calvin smiled at me and responded, "You know what? You're right. Whatever happens happens! I'm not going to sit over here angry and all stressed out about it. At least not while my beautiful friend is offering to cook me a hot meal."

I frowned at Calvin and responded as he sat there smiling from ear to ear, "Boy, please! I ain't cooking you no meals. I don't give a damn how you feel."

I looked at him out the side of my eye and tried to hold my frown, but I couldn't. I broke out into a hearty laugh as he grabbed me and started tickling me. I tried to break free from his playful grasp, but I couldn't. He fell backwards onto the couch and jokingly pulled me down on top of him. It was at that moment that our relationship would change forever.

The lively laughter that once had filled the room was replaced with an intense silence. The playful smiles on our faces were gone as we gazed into each other's eyes. Calvin slowly leaned forward and whispered, "Angela."

The warmth of his breath ignited a flame of passion that had been dormant for the past year. There was warmth of excitement that started in my chest and slowly spread throughout my body. I could feel his eyes watching my every move, from the nervous twitch in my lips to the intensity of my breathing. Calvin slowly leaned forward, his hand brushing the hair out of my face, and in an instant, his lips melted inside mine. Tilting my head, I deepened the kiss and traced my tongue against his lips. Calvin's lips parted and I could taste the sweetness of his tongue.

I could hear the low murmur of the radio, but I was fixated on his hard penis pressing against me. With our lips still intertwined, I half-heartedly attempted to push away from him. Calvin wrapped his arms around my waist and pulled me closer. His hands massaged and gently squeezed my butt until my body was completely relaxed on top of him. He softly nibbled at my neck, causing a chill of excitement to engulf my body. Every voice inside of me was screaming, "Don't do this!" But my body was trembling from excitement as his hands caressed my thighs and pulled me closer.

Calvin continued to gently massage the back of my neck as he whispered in my ear, "Angela, if you don't want to do this, I will understand. I don't want you to do this if you'll wake up with regrets tomorrow."

This is the part where I should have told him, "You're right, Calvin. This is wrong. We have a great friendship, and I don't want to fuck that up with sex."

The excitement rushing through me caused by Calvin's electric touches of passion instead made me mumble, "Calvin, don't stop. This is what I want."

My answer must have help to kindle the flames already burning between us because he quickly pulled his t-shirt over his head, allowing his warm body to engulf me.

What Calvin lacked in attractive features was made up in the passionate way he tore into my body. He made love to me like he was angry at me. It excited me as he cursed at me under his breath. He was angry at me because he was backsliding. He was angry at the church for making him feel guilty. Most of all, he was angry at God for making him weak.

Calvin and I made angry, passionate love until we were exhausted. I gazed into Calvin's eyes and I could see the regret already setting in. Calvin pulled me close and buried his face into my body, almost as if he were attempting to hide from God. I gently rubbed his back and I stared off into the quiet darkness knowing what he was feeling.

Calvin was already an ordained minister at Solid Foundation. Everyone in the church knew that once he finished his course work at Divinity School, he would be groomed to take over his father's church. I could feel Calvin's breathing growing more intense as if he were having a panic attack.

I whispered in his ear, "Calvin, calm down. You'll be okay." But I felt like a hypocrite saying it because I knew I was lying. How would Calvin ever be okay? If he stood in front of the church and confessed, he would be disgraced. If he never told anyone and lived with the degradation, he would be destroyed by the guilt.

As Calvin lay helpless in my arms, I felt like a modern-day Delilah. The strength of Calvin had been his connection with God. He had given his life to God at the age of eighteen and never once had he wavered until now. Calvin had always been the good soldier marching for Christ. Even when the whole church treated me like a disease, Calvin fought for me.

There had been many instances over the past year when church members saw Calvin with me. They would smile at Calvin and congratulate him on the success of the youth ministry and then ignore me like I didn't exist. Calvin could see the hurt in me and he always made sure I was okay. I could feel Calvin's body tense against mine, but there was nothing I could do to help with his conscience.

Calvin pulled me closer and I heard him mumble, "I'm sorry," and then he drifted off to sleep.

I didn't know if he was apologizing to me or if he was apologizing to God for his indiscretion. I wanted to tell him that it was okay, but I already knew it would get worse. Calvin cuddled up next to me tightly as if I were his mother protecting him from danger. I didn't have the heart to tell him that those painful feelings of guilt were only going to get worse in the morning.

The worst feeling in the world is the morning after you backslide. You regret everything that had occurred the night before. You lie there motionless, staring at the ceiling, thinking how you got to this point. When I backslid, I hated Desmond. I remember looking at Desmond the next morning, hoping he was a bad dream. That morning I felt Calvin waking up, and I braced myself for the same reaction. I pulled the covers over my head and pretended to be sleep as Calvin yawned and slowly tip-toed toward the bathroom.

I heard the shower water slowly gain force, so I peeked out from under the covers. I was surprised when I saw Calvin leaning against the bathroom entrance way with a bath towel wrapped around his waist. I have to be honest, Calvin looked really sexy. The gangly body had turned into a tall, athletic body, the receding hair line now looked distinguished, and those long, goofy feet were kind of sexy in just a bath towel. I waited for the inevitable comment that would lead to me kicking Calvin out. I had already prepared a speech that would allow both of us to feel comfortable. I had no problem with Calvin blaming me for backsliding, but he was not going to disrespect me. I was prepared to sacrifice our friendship because the most important thing for him was probably getting right with God.

I prepared myself for the blame game speech, but that moment never came.

In fact, Calvin looked happy and spoke in an upbeat tone, "Good morning, beautiful. How are you feeling?"

I stared at Calvin with a weird look on my face and responded, "I'm good, are you ok?"

Calvin still upbeat responded, "Sure, I'm fine. I was trying to get showered and dressed before you woke so that I could cook up a quick breakfast. The weatherman said it was going to be sunny today. What do you think about renting a couple jet skis and hitting Lake Lanier?"

Calvin was still bouncing around the room happy when I abruptly stopped him and asked, "Calvin, what's going on? You do remember us sleeping together last night? Why are you acting like nothing happened?"

Calvin looked at me with a confused look and walked over to the bed. He sat down beside me and placed his hand on my leg as he spoke, "Angela I'm not sure what you're getting at, but I'm cool with what happened last night. I mean, you definitely satisfied me, and I hope I satisfied you also."

Calvin paused and looked at me for a reaction. I looked back at Calvin with a "you stink" look on my face and then mumbled, "Hmm. . . the experience could have been better."

Calvin looked at me half smiling and responded, "Oh, you got jokes."

I tried my best not to laugh as I spoke, but the laughter forced its way through. "I'm just playing, I'm just playing."

I held Calvin's hand and I smiled at him shyly as I spoke. "Yes, Calvin Tyler, you satisfied me. I was just concerned about you feeling guilty about us making love. I was prepared for our friendship to be over."

Calvin glanced at me suspiciously and asked, "Why would I be feeling guilty?"

I was searching for the right words to say when he said, "Oh, you're concerned about me backsliding?"

I continued to stare at his hand as I shook my head yes.

Calvin continued to speak, "Ahh, that's so sweet, you're concerned about my spiritual well being! Well trust me, I'm okay, and my God is okay.

I exhaled a huge sigh of relief as he continued to talk. "I would be lying if I didn't wish we were married and in the church, but we're not. I have to believe that God placed me in this unique situation for a reason, and I'm glad you're in it with me. You're my best friend, and I wouldn't want this experience with anyone except you. I crossed over our friendship line with both feet last night, and I'm staying right here beside you until you get tired of me. I guess the appropriate question would be how do you feel about us?"

I tried to respond, but there was a lump in my throat that kept me from talking. I kept my head lowered and played nervously with his finger as thoughts about us flooded my mind. Over that past year Calvin, became my best friend. The loyalty that he showed toward me surpassed anything that I had ever felt before. I still had close friends from college and my sorority, but none had ever showed that the type of loyalty that Calvin did. Calvin never paid attention to the nasty rumors being spread about us. The only thing he ever cared about was if I was okay.

Calvin just didn't know me as a person; he knew me from the inside out. If I was happy, Calvin was happy. If I was sad, Calvin was sad. Calvin knew how to respond to my mood without even asking. If I was sad or stressed out about something, he would grab a blanket and just cuddle with me. Calvin felt comfortable letting me cry my eyes out until he had the opportunity to cheer me up. A friend who drops everything to be with you is a true friend. No matter if he was on a date or if he was in the middle of a church function, he made me feel like I was first on his list. As I thought more and more about our friendship, I felt warm tears clouding my vision.

Calvin leaned forward, gently tilted my chin up, and asked, "Angela, what's wrong? Come here, come here."

He pulled me close to him and held me tight. Any reservation of not having Calvin in my life quickly dissolved. Warm tears trickled down my face onto his neck. Calvin knew me almost as well as I knew myself. He knew I was crying not because I was sad or upset, but because I was happy.

Calvin softly pulled away and looked into my eyes and spoke. "I see all these tears, but I'm still waiting on an answer. Are we going to be just buddies, or are we going to be BUDDIES?"

Calvin tilted his head sideways and made his eyebrows dance as he slowly pulled the covers exposing my nude body. I quickly snatched the covers back up and playfully punched him. Calvin made a weird karate squeal and jokingly dove on top of me, then he proceeded to tickle me until I was once again crying from enjoyment.

Our impromptu wrestling match suddenly ended as Calvin suddenly got serious. He held my hand tightly and asked, "So do you think we should move forward and be more than just friends?"

I nervously swung my leg back and forth, tightly held Calvin's hand and responded, "Yes."

Chapter 8

My relationship with Calvin proved to be challenging from the start. Calvin and I felt comfortable with each other, but I could tell that it annoyed others. Calvin really wanted me to come back to the church, particularly Solid Foundation. I think he actually believed that if I came back to Solid Foundation, our relationship would be accepted. I already knew that our relationship being accepted by the powers that be in that church was just a pipe dream. In fact, when I did finally give into Calvin's relentless pleading, Solid Foundation quickly proved me right.

Calvin and I decided to make our relationship public on Easter Sunday. Calvin was certain that when we walked through the doors, flocks of people would run towards us and praise and adore the cute couple. Their reaction was not only the total opposite, but ruder than I imagined.

Devotion service was in full swing when the ushers escorted us down the long aisle hand in hand. People who were shouting and screaming "Jesus!" Instantly stopped and stared at us. The closer we got to the front of the church, the more people started whispering. Linda caught a glimpse of us and immediately stood up and signaled to Bishop Tyler's nurse. The Bishop's nurse leaned in as an animated Linda painted a picture of what was going on. Bishop Tyler's nurse quickly exited the sanctuary as Calvin and I managed to find a seat in the crowded church.

Calvin sensed that I was uncomfortable from all the pointing and whispering, so he put his arm around me and pulled me close. I had to give credit to Calvin because he displayed me like a diamond despite what people were saying. I tried my best to ignore all of the eyes fixated on us, but there was one pair of eyes that almost looked obsessed when staring at us. Those eyes belonged to Linda.

Linda appeared to be fuming as she stared at Calvin and rolled her eyes. I looked at Calvin and than back at Linda, who was still incensed by what she was seeing.

Calvin leaned in my ear and whispered, "My father had been trying to get me and Linda together for the longest time. Don't worry about it."

I leaned back toward Calvin and replied in a smug manner, "Oh, I'm not worried about it."

And with that said, I softly kissed Calvin on his lips and wiped the lipstick with my finger. I looked back in Linda's direction and she appeared to be angry enough to burst.

I was enjoying my small moment of victory over Linda when I saw Bishop Tyler's nurse walking toward us.

She leaned over and whispered in Calvin's ear and Calvin whispered to me, "I'll be back. My dad wants to see me."

As Calvin walked closely behind the Bishop's nurse, I remember feeling unprotected. I could feel the evil glares of people looking at me as Calvin disappeared through the closing door. I tried my best to look relaxed, but an uneasy feeling was slowly creeping over me as I noticed Linda stand and walk towards the podium. I had seen this same scenario play out almost two years ago when she embarrassed the hell out of me. I vowed that I would never allow anyone to make me feel like that again. My leg began to shake with nervous anticipation as Linda opened her mouth to speak. I was comfortable with resorting to any means necessary not to be embarrassed, including violence. I felt like Dirty Harry that day. I was hoping that the bitch would say something stupid so that I could get my revenge in the way that I had dreamed.

Linda started to speak and I leaned forward and clutched the pew in front of me as if I were a jack-in-the-box. "Good morning, church."

The people in the audience responded to Linda with choruses of "good mornings" and "praise the Lord."

Linda nervously shuffled a pile of papers on the podium and then looked in my direction and spoke. "I've learned in my walk with God that sometimes you have to be the bigger person in a dispute."

The bright lights of the TV camera beamed off Linda's shinny forehead as she continued, "God has revealed to me that sometimes even my best efforts fall short of God. I want to stand here and confess to everyone that the green eye of envy tried to find its way in my heart, and I fought it. I want everyone in the church to know that the devil is a liar, and I won't let him take my soul."

The church erupted into joyful cheers as Linda's eyes quickly darted around the church and finally rested on me. The roar in the church came to a low buzz of excitement as Linda held up her hands to speak. I have to admit that I was even in awe of the way Linda commended the crowd.

Linda's stock had risen dramatically since I had first met her on the back of that church van. Linda had turned into the unofficial mascot for Solid Foundation. The single mother who had escaped an abusive marriage was now known around the county as Prophetess Stanford. Many people felt that God was so connected to Linda that she could reveal the future. I remember watching Solid Foundation on TV and seeing the show that sprung her into the national spotlight.

When Solid Foundation first started out on TV, people recognized Linda as the burly looking cheerleader with bad skin.

Linda would sit in the corner and scream, "That's right, Bishop!" or "Teach, Bishop!"

As time went on, she gained more recognition as a person who could rebuke the devil. In another words, if she found out that you had sinned, she would destroy you on TV. Bishop Tyler loved Linda because the ratings would spike anytime he gave her the stage, which led to a nationally syndicated show.

The show that gave her international prominence occurred during a guest appearance on the Trinity Broadcasting Network.

Linda stepped forward and the show erupted as she demanded members to move when God is speaking. Linda's voice went up two octaves as she began to preach about how she trusted God when she left her abusive husband and how she had prayed day and night for the devil to flee. I could have sworn she stole the sermon straight from Shirley Caesar. She sounded like her and walked around the stage jerking in and out of the spirit like her.

Linda demanded that church members show faith and bring forward seed money to help grow the show. She staggered around the church in a trance-like state, stopping at selected members in the audience and requesting money.

The demands were for different amounts, but I was shocked at how the church members reacted. They would sprint full speed to the pulpit steps and toss their money. I was even more surprised when she staggered up to a well-known boxer at that time and requested a seed of twenty thousand dollars. A quiet hush came over the audience as Linda stood directly in front of the boxer, pointed her finger in his face, and spoke in tongues. The boxer appeared to be nervous, almost childlike, as Linda continued to point at him and speak in tongues.

After around thirty seconds of an intense face-to-face interaction with the boxer, she blew her breath on him and the boxer fell backwards to the floor. He lay on the floor and mumbled incoherently as Linda wiped his body with a hand towel like she was painting him. The audience grew silent and everyone stared at the intense scene between Linda and the boxer. Linda raised her hand, and on cue, an usher brought her a microphone.

Linda began to speak and the sound of her voice startled everyone, including me, because it sounded like Vincent Price in Thriller. "God is not asking you to give the money. He is commanding you to give the money."

Linda sat next to the boxer still lying on the floor and held both her hands up high as she stared at the ceiling and continued to speak. "Do you think you could have been as successful as you are today without God's help? He has shown you undeserved favor, and all he is asking for is a tiny portion back."

Linda's voice changed into almost warning the boxer as she helped him to his feet. She glared at him and then said, "God has spoken to you today! Don't ignore him or you will be cursed. God not only punishes you when you're cursed, he punishes the children, and their children, for the sins of their fathers to the third and fourth generation."

The crowd grew extremely quiet as everyone waited for the boxer to make a decision. He played with his fingers nervously, not knowing whether to leave or pay the money. Linda moved back from the boxer and he reluctantly walked to the pulpit and deposited five thousand dollars in cash on the steps and wrote a check for fifteen thousand more. The crowd erupted into cheers and loud applauses as the boxer sheepishly walked back to his seat. I was still staring at the TV mesmerized by what I had just seen as the ending credits began to roll across the screen.

Prophetess Stanford's status became internationally known as people tuned in week after week hoping to get a glance at her antics.

As I sat perched in my pew ready to attack, I wondered what the backlash would be when I busted the bitch in the face for talking slick. Every eye in the church followed Linda's sight of direction as she stared directly at me. I prepared myself by rising from my seat and moving to the aisle.

Linda opened her mouth and shocked everyone in church by saying. "I want to first apologize to you and then the rest of the church."

Every eye in the church turned towards me as I stood ready to attack. I wasn't prepared for this, so it made me look kind of crazy. I didn't know if I should smile or stay on alert. I knew what she was apologizing for, but it didn't seem obvious to the rest of the church. The low sound of restless chatter filled the sanctuary as Linda held her hand out and asked me to come forward. Her soft, gentle smile lit up the church as the crowd screamed with excitement and encouraged me to move forward. I slowly moved forward with apprehension until Linda met me at the steps of the pulpit and hugged me.

The hug from Linda appeared to be genuine until we separated. I turned to walk toward my seat, and I felt the hot light of the TV camera point in my direction. I heard Linda start mumbling, and within seconds, she was speaking in tongues and staggering towards me.

My mind drifted and I remembered a saying that said, "Everyone has a plan until they get hit." And that's exactly how I felt as the church cheers turned into quiet whispers.

Linda continued to speak in tongue until she was directly in my face. She opened her eyes and I saw the same look that I had had nightmares about.

Linda pointed her finger in my face and started to talk. "God wants you to go." I was embarrassed to the point of no movement as she spoke again, but this time she spoke much more harshly, as if to humiliate. "God said, you go! You are not of him and he is not of you. The Bible says, 'God hates sin and loves the sinner.' I love you because that's what God requires us to do. I hate the sin you live in because God hates it."

Linda nudged my arm and turned to walk away, and that's when I snapped out of my frozen state of embarrassment. I sprung towards her like a caged tiger and threw a punch towards her head. The punch landed squarely on the back of her neck and knocked her forwards. Linda stumbled to the floor, and I moved in to finish her.

I straddled Linda and threw another punch at her face as she struggled to fight back. I felt a strong grasp jerk my body and then lift me up. I continued to kick in anger, swing wildly, and curse at Linda as I was taken out of the church. I heard Calvin's voice encouraging me to calm down, but my mind was flipping from anger. Calvin quickly put me in his car and drove me out of the parking lot as people exited the church looking shocked and confused.

Calvin touched my hand and asked me if I was okay. I pushed Calvin's hand away and mumbled that I was fine. Calvin glanced at me and must have decided to leave the situation alone. He could tell that I was still angry, and he probably thought I blamed him. After all, it was his idea to go to Solid Foundation and make our relationship public. Social media was on fire that night as headlines talked about Prophetess Linda Stanford being assaulted on TV.

Bishop Tyler and Linda still found a way to profit from the situation. By the time the church's production team got finished editing and adding sound bites, I looked like Linda Blair in the Exorcist. If you had not seen the original footage, you would have sworn that I ran in the church growling like a wild animal and attacked Linda for no reason. Bishop Tyler played it up by saying the devil had launched an attack on him, and it was thwarted by Prophetess Linda Stanford. The whole situation was crazy because Solid Foundation's ratings actually skyrocketed after I beat Linda's ass. The weird part about the whole scenario was that no one ever pursued charges against me. I guess it was an even trade and ass whooping for ratings.

Calvin and I continued to date, but I could tell things were slowly changing. As the weeks and months passed, I could tell Calvin was being influenced by his father.

I could only imagine what Bishop Tyler was saying about me. "Calvin, you have to leave that girl alone. This is not good for the church or the family. You have two semesters left and you will take over the church. How could I in good consciousness give you control of this church when you're spending your free time laid up with a whore? Think, son! Think!

And trust me, Calvin was thinking. I would ask Calvin to tell me what was wrong but he always laughed it off or say, "Babe I'm fine! I don't know why you keep asking me the same question. I'm fine, we're fine, and I love you."

I wanted to believe him, but I could tell that Calvin was starting to listen to his family. Calvin appeared to be torn between living for God and being with me. The reality was that he was afraid of losing his status in the church. I believe he really loved me, but the limelight of Solid Foundation appeared stronger. When we first started dating, it was like Calvin was living a double life. Calvin was a God-fearing minister who was struggling to do the right thing and he was risking everything to be with me. Calvin and I would often talk about all the expectations that had been placed on him as a man of God.

He was expected to be above reproach and flee from sexual immorality. I remembered all those times when I would go to church with no panties on after a hoe- bath feeling guilty. I could only imagine what an heir to a spiritual throne was going through. Calvin would come to my house after church and talk about all the guilt he was feeling, and then end up in my bed. I respected him and felt for his situation, but there was no way I was going to give him up. Every time Calvin started feeling guilty about his faith and torn whether to stay or go, I'd let him slide between my thighs and give him a real coming-to-Jesus moment. I knew it was wrong, but God had probably given up on me a long time ago.

Then there was the little situation with Linda. Calvin and Linda often attended Student Ministry classes at Solid Foundation.

Calvin would call me and I would hear her in the background. "Hurry up, Calvin! We have to go to class." Linda wanted Calvin so badly that I could hear it in her voice. She wanted Calvin but was afraid to act on it because of her belief. Calvin told me that everybody at Solid Foundation was probably praying that he and Linda get together, but then he would melt my heart by saying that he only loved me.

Both Linda and Calvin were up and coming in the church and everyone just assumed they would eventually get together. Hell, it only seemed logical, the prince and princess of Solid Foundation coming together as one. Linda probably already had Calvin married to her with the dog and white picket fence in her dreams, but I had that dream stopper right between my legs. While she was connecting spiritually with him during Ministerial Preparation Class, I was satisfying that sexual beast. No matter how many times Prophetess Linda prayed for Calvin to be surrounded by Christ's presence, he ended up in my bedroom.

Linda hated the fact that Calvin could be so strong and unwavering in God's presence and drop all of that to come be with me. Jesus may have controlled his soul, but I had his mind and body. The only thing that she could do was call his daddy. I remember early one morning when she called Calvin's phone while he was sleep. As soon as I saw the name Prophetess Stanford pop up on Calvin's phone, I answered it. There was a long pause at the other end of the line, so I helped her out by saying, "Yes, can I help you Linda?"

Linda stammered to find the words to say and then finally spoke. "Oh! I was just looking for Calvin, and I thought I dialed his apartment phone. I guess I dialed his cell number."

I responded with a short quick shot to the gut. "This is his apartment, but he's asleep in bed right now. Do you want me to wake him up?"

I heard the word "no" come out of her mouth, but I was already three steps ahead of her.

I shook Calvin and continued to speak while on the phone. "Babe, babe someone wants to speak with you on the phone."

Calvin, still half asleep, responded, "Who is it? Tell them I'll call them back. I'm tired."

A deceitful smile crossed my face as I spoke into the receiver and told Linda, "Hold on" and promptly laid the receiver on the table. I snuggled up next to Calvin and began to massage his penis. I gently stroked it until he was moaning. I quickened the pace and softly tugged at it until it was fully erect. Calvin yanked the covers off me and pulled me on top of him. He quickly slid his penis inside me and started pumping. I faked an orgasm as if I were a trained porn star. I glanced at the phone on the table and saw that Linda had hung up. There was nothing sensual about what I did. I just wanted Linda to know that Calvin was fucking me.

I wanted her to understand that what I was doing to him couldn't be satisfied through reading the Bible or with prayer. I knew it ate at her because she told Calvin's father. Bishop Tyler called Calvin the next day and scolded him for hurting Linda's feelings.

Calvin got off the phone with his father and was furious at me. "Angela, what did you do?"

I looked at Calvin innocently and responded, "What do you mean, baby? Did something happen?"

Calvin shook his head still upset and responded, "You know what you did. Why did you answer my phone knowing Linda was on the other line?"

I answered Calvin in a sarcastic manner, "I didn't know I had to ask permission to answer your phone."

Calvin responded even more upset. "Angela, you know what you did. Prophetess Stanford was offended when she heard another woman answer the phone of a man of God. The Prophetess was offended to the point of not being able to deliver the word for the TV show, cutting into the ratings."

Calvin questioned me about what had happened and I innocently responded, "Babe, the only thing I did was lay the phone down after you told me that you would call them back."

Calvin shouted back angrily, "You didn't hang it up?!"

I shook my head no as if confused and responded, "Most phones automatically shut off when you lay them down."

Calvin shook his head and stared at the ground frustrated as he spoke. "Angela, we have to be more careful with our relationship. This type of situation could ruin a lot of lives."

I pretended to be sorry and remorseful about making such a big mistake, but inside I was ecstatic.

I had tears in my eyes as I begged for Calvin's forgiveness. Inside I was saying, "Bitch, that's what you get. Calling my man's house and trying to slither into my territory. I bet you'll think before you call the next time."

Calvin thought it would be best if we were more discrete with our relationship. Truthfully it probably was best, but that decision still angered me. Why should we be ashamed of our relationship because of what Linda was feeling? If Calvin loved me like I loved him, it really didn't matter. Keeping our relationship quiet benefited Calvin the most. I mean, how could Calvin explain to daddy that his golden goose, Prophetess Linda, left his church because junior was skipping preaching class so that he could come over and knock the linen out of this coochie?

Calvin and I continued to keep the relationship secret for close to a year. Calvin's reputation in the church continued to grow as his father gave him more responsibility. No longer was Calvin just a junior minister. He was now a fully ordained elder in the church and one of three assistant pastors. You could tell that Bishop Tyler was preparing Calvin to take over as senior pastor. The stars appeared to be lining up for Calvin until a few weeks before his graduation from divinity school.

The problem started after I missed my period. I had missed my period before, but not for two weeks. I scheduled an appointment with my doctor, and he confirmed that I was, indeed, pregnant again. Calvin looked like he was in a daze as we left the doctor's office. I think he wanted to ask me how, but that probably would have been a stupid question. The reality of the situation was that I had planned the pregnancy without Calvin's knowledge.

When we first started dating, we both used protection. For whatever reason, Calvin decided to stop. I think he was comfortable because I continued to use protection. Once I started seeing a change in our relationship, I decided to stop using protection. I loved Calvin, and in my mind, a baby was the best way to keep him. It sounds crazy to me now, but back then I was convinced this was the best way. I was up against Calvin's father, the church, Linda, and most of all, Calvin's confused mind. We had always talked about getting married and having kids, but I thought it was best to speed up the process because of the circumstances.

Calvin's reaction to the unplanned pregnancy was not at all what I expected. He was angry and he felt like I had trapped him. Although that was true, I honestly did not think he would react like that. Saying that I trapped him was a bit harsh. I admit that I wanted us to be together, but I always thought that's what he wanted. In my mind, all he needed was a little push to help make his mind up for him. The truth of the matter was that Calvin's father already had big plans for him, and I was not included. Bishop Tyler wanted his son and Prophetess Linda Stanford together. Who cared if they were compatible? He saw a financial opportunity. Calvin would be bishop over the biggest church in Atlanta. And beside him would be arguably the most anointed Prophetess in the world. To Bishop Tyler, it was a match made in heaven.

I tried to explain how I felt, but Calvin disagreed. He spent the next few weeks trying to convince me that our having a baby at that time would be a mistake. He argued that Linda or his father had nothing to do with what was going on. He kept harping on the idea that I was trying to trap him. I never looked at the pregnancy as a trap. In my mind, having a child with Calvin evened out the scales for me. No matter how much pull the church and his faith had, he would never abandon us. Calvin countered my argument with a move that would forever change the course of both our destinies.

Chapter 9

Calvin arrived at my house late one Sunday and I invited him in. I could tell he was still troubled about the pregnancy when he asked me to sit beside him. Calvin nervously fumbled in his pants and retrieved his wallet. He opened the wallet and showed me a calendar with a circle around a date in two weeks.

Calvin stared deep and into my eyes and spoke in a low concerned voice. "Angela, do you see this date? On that date, I was planning to ask you to marry me."

I could feel my heart thumping in anticipation as he continued to talk. "That date is the date that I graduate from Divinity School. I wanted that date to be the date when I would finally propose to you and break free from my father's church. I wanted to start my own church and finally feel free to serve God, the way I wanted. I wanted to be free to show my love for you without being afraid of what would happen. Do you understand how hard it's going to be trying to open a church in the middle of a scandal? I can see the headlines now: 'Prominent bishop's son has child out of wedlock. ' I'd be disgraced!"

The more Calvin continued to talk, the more guilt I felt. I wanted to marry Calvin and have a life with him, but not at the expense of destroying him. For the first time in a long time, Calvin and I just talked. I felt that old connection with him from when we were just friends; when it was just him and me against the world. I had missed that Calvin so much. The Calvin of late was always rushing to go back to church or go to class. Instead of the usual wham bam, thank you ma'am, I had that gentle man who didn't care about time back. Calvin wanted to spend as much time as possible with me to solve the problem.

I lay on Calvin's chest and allowed him to wrap his body around mine. I could feel his heart crashing against my face as his hands glided up and down my body. There was nothing sexual about the touches, but my body was shivering from the excitement. Being in Calvin's arms made me feel protected again. Those past few months had me questioning if I could really deal with being involved with a man of God. My happy-go-lucky Calvin started showing up to the house torn apart with guilt. Making love to him never was the issue, it was the after-effects—refusing to hold me or immediately getting up to leave.

But that night was different. His comforting voice assured me that no one would ever take my place.

The way he spoke to me made me feel loved once again. "Angela, I know I haven't been doing the things I needed to make you feel secure, and I apologize for that. My mind was to busy battling with the church and my love for you. You can't imagine all the pressure I've been under to break up with you. Everybody thinks you're wrong for me. People feel that you have led me down a path of iniquity, but I know otherwise."

Calvin hugged me tighter and gently kissed my forehead as he continued. "Angela, I love you more than life. Everything I have done, all the love I have for you, is my freewill. You have always supported me even when I struggled with my feelings. When the doctor told us about the baby, I almost had a nervous breakdown. You can't imagine being pulled in ten different directions by the church and then being hit with that type of news. Angela, I want you in my life, but not like this. I want to be free to tell the church my decision and move on with you without looking as if I was forced. The only thing that I'm asking is that you give me the opportunity to do this the right way. Give me the opportunity to open my own church without a scandal attached. Please, baby, can you do this for me?

I knew what Calvin was asking me to do. No matter how many ways he tried to sugarcoat it, I knew he was asking me to get an abortion. There are so many thoughts that go through your mind when the person you love most asks you to get an abortion. The first thought is, "Where is the love and compassion?" He wanted me to go through all the pain and psychological effects so he could be free. Granted, the pregnancy was not planned, but I expected more. Should a person who claimed to have loved me really be asking me to kill something so special? I couldn't even imagine having a life without my son RC, and here I was considering an abortion. Against my better judgment, I once again chose a man over my feelings.

Calvin was still in the middle of talking when I abruptly cut him off. I pulled myself up and placed Calvin's face in my hands as I spoke. "Calvin, you know this is going to be one of the hardest things that I've ever done. I'm going to literally trust you with my life."

I could feel tears forming in my eyes as I continued to speak. "It's hard for me to trust people with my heart, especially when you've been hurt before. I hope that I'm doing the right thing, and I hope that you will be there to support me."

Calvin pulled me closer and swore that I would never have to make a sacrifice like this again. Calvin opened his Bible and began to read, "Then God said, 'Take your son, your only son, whom you love – Isaac – and go to the region of Moriah and Sacrifice him there as a burnt offering on a mountain I will show you. '"

Calvin began to speak as tears poured from his eyes. "Angela, it's like this is a sign. You gave me my life back for a reason. I will never put our relationship in a situation like this again. You can't imagine how stressful these past few weeks have been. My father would have never understood the concept of my destroying his plans because I love you. You have shown me what true sacrifice is, and now I'm ready to take on the world."

Looking back at that night, I've often wondered why I let my guard down so easily. I knew I should have been more careful, but I was too far gone. Was it the way that he whispered "I love you"? Or was it the way he made my body feel? When he started softly kissing me on my neck, I should have fought harder. When I felt his hands undressing me, I should have pushed him away. But I didn't! I simply lay there trembling, wanting him to go further. Calvin pulled himself up and lifted me into his arms. A slight chill crossed my nude body causing an inadvertent shiver.

Calvin glanced at my naked body in the dim light and smiled as he spoke. "Mmm-hmmm, Mmm-hmmm."

It sounded like a combination of invitation and satisfaction. I buried my face in his neck and nervously played with his chest as he lifted me. Calvin slowly walked toward his bedroom and I nervously giggled as he stumbled over a shoe. Calvin sat me on the bed and I waited with anticipation as he removed his shirt and pants. He pulled me close and I could feel his penis swell with excitement. He placed his dick between my thighs and I slowly began to move my hips. Calvin moaned and wrapped his arms tightly around my waist, pulling me closer.

I could feel the warmth of Calvin's body and I felt protected. Calvin lifted me and tossed me on the bed. As he mounted the bed, he looked like a savage lion slowly stalking his prey. He nudged me backwards with his chest and I slowly opened my thighs. Calvin nibbled at my neck causing me to laugh nervously and I playfully slapped his shoulder, telling him to stop. Calvin positioned himself inside me and my body trembled with eagerness. Calvin and I had made love many times before, but this time was different.

It was like he wanted that night to be special for me. He wanted any fear that I was feeling to fade into the night as he satisfied me with his passion. That night he was relentless. I opened my thighs wider in anticipation of his explosion, but it didn't happen. He grabbed the bed post for leverage and began to stroke me with more intensity and passion. Each time I thought my body would recover from an orgasm, he would have me trembling and on the brink of another. What he did to me that night and the following days would have my mind confused for the next year and lead us both down a path of destruction.

Calvin held me close the rest of the night and I felt special. My body simply melted as his hands slowly caressed me. We laughed and talked until we fell asleep and I woke the next morning with joy in my heart.

That week was one of the happiest times in my life. I took a vacation from my job and dropped little RC off over Steven's house. Calvin finished up his final exams and then called me. He was excited about graduating, but I was excited about just spending time with him. Calvin and I flew to South Beach, and for the first time since we started dating, I felt free. We walked on the beach hand and hand without caring if someone would see us. He held me close and showed affection towards me in the middle of the Lincoln Rd. Mall. The highlight of that week was when we went from jewelry store to jewelry store and we looked at engagement rings. I found the ring of my dreams and was fitted for it. By the end of the week, I was convinced that Calvin Tyler Jr. and I would be married within the next year.

When we arrived back in Atlanta, I was floating on cloud nine. I finally had the man of my dreams and we were only days away from making it official. I played stupid, but I was convinced that Calvin had bought my engagement ring. Whenever I looked at Calvin, he would glance back at me with guilt written all over his face.

I wanted to look through his bags just to see the ring again, but I didn't want to spoil the surprise. I dreamed of him asking me in front of his father, Linda, and the church. I wanted everyone to choke in shock because I had finally won. I wondered how his family and the church would take it. They spent so much time devising ways to break us up, but I would have the last laugh. We grabbed a quick lunch at the airport and then headed to my house. My appointment for the abortion was scheduled that next morning, and Calvin's father was throwing him a big bash at the church later that night.

I really wanted to go with Calvin, but I understood the situation. Calvin was going to destroy a lot of people's dreams and he didn't want any backlash towards me. He promised to come to the house early so that we could drive the two hours to Macon. Calvin pulled me close and kissed me, then he whispered, "Angela, whatever happens in the next few days, always remember that I love you and only you. I don't want you to ever think that I didn't love you because I do. One day you'll look back at this day and laugh because this is the beginning of our lives."

The conversation was weird, but my head was stuck so far up his ass that I didn't read between the lines. Calvin jumped into his car and sped off into the night, and I closed the door and raced to my bedroom. I called my parents and told them about Calvin buying me a secret engagement ring, and they both seemed happy for me. My parents always told me that they were proud of me, but secretly I knew they wanted more for me. My father was especially concerned for me because of RC.

He saw the things that I didn't see. He knew how hard it could be for another man to take on another man's child. He never expressed his opinions to me, but I could tell by his facial expression that he was concerned. My father probably put himself in the place of Bishop Tyler and tried to understand why Calvin and I were together. Everybody knew that Calvin was in line to take over the reins of the most powerful church in Atlanta. Why in the world would he sacrifice all of that for an already-made family?

I never understood why my father asked me that night if I wanted RC to live with them permanently. Did my father know something was going to happen, or was he just trying to protect RC?

I told my father, "RC will be fine with us."

My father hesitated and then mumbled something.

I did not want to argue with him, so I told him I loved him, and then he responded with an eerie comment that I hadn't heard in years. "Angela, be careful"

The last time my father said that to me was when Craig and I went to prom.

I hung the phone up, but I couldn't go to sleep. I was anxious because it was past 12:00am and still I hadn't heard from Calvin. I wondered if he had followed through with his plan.

I could see Linda hearing the news and storming off mad. She would probably pray to God and then demand that Bishop Tyler take action, like she always did. Different scenarios continued to run through my mind as I dozed off to sleep.

The next morning, my sleep was interrupted by the buzz of my cell phone. I picked up my phone and saw that I had two missed calls from Calvin. Just as I was about to call Calvin, I glanced at the time and immediately started running towards the bathroom, because I was late. Calvin would probably be angry with me when he arrived because he hated being late. I took a quick shower and grabbed some clothes just as I heard a loud knock at the door. I rushed to the door expecting Calvin but was shocked when I saw Deacon Bruce Langley.

Deacon Langley was an imposing figure who appeared to be about business all the time. At first glance, Deacon Langley reminded you of Suge Knight, the former CEO of Death Row Records. He stood approximately 6'5" with a linebacker frame, bald head, and menacing beard. When he smiled at people, his lips would curl up into a sinister scowl. Anytime there was a money discrepancy at Solid Foundation, Deacon Langley was the point of contact. Deacon Langley would move swiftly towards you with a menacing glare and demand to know what the problem was. People would question him about receiving the wrong amount of change, but they looked really uncomfortable when doing so.

I tried to be silent and peek out the window, but all I saw was the intimidating deacon staring back at me.

Embarrassed because I was discovered, I tried to play the situation off by speaking.

"Good morning, Deacon Langley. Is there something I can help you with?"

Deacon Langley responded in a loud, unapologetic manner, "We need to get moving because were running late."

Confused about what he was saying, I responded, "I don't understand. Is there a reason why you're at my house?"

Frustrated, Deacon Langley turned and looked in the direction of a black Mercedes Benz. Then he held out his arms as if he were asking, "What the fuck is going on?"

I saw a hand extend from the window of the car and motion Deacon Langley to come over.

Deacon Langley started down the steps and turned back and screamed, "I'll be back."

Unsettled by the situation unfolding in front of my house, I immediately called Calvin.

Calvin quickly answered the phone and started talking before me. "Are you on your way yet?"

Still puzzled, I responded, "Calvin, what the fuck is going on? I got this crazy-ass deacon beating on my door, and you're asking me stupid shit about me being on my way."

Calvin responded with a smirk and then he asked, "You didn't check your voicemail, did you?"

Still confused, I asked, "No. Was there a reason that I should have checked it?"

Calvin explained to me, "I'm not going to be able to take you to the clinic this morning." He paused for a few seconds and then continued, "That's the reason I called you last night, because something came up and I couldn't get away. Deacon Langley will take you to the clinic and bring you back home. I'll meet you at your house later tonight."

Angry at what I was hearing, I shouted back, "Are you fucking kidding me? This is something that you should be going through with me, not the fucking church deacon. What type of sorry motherfucker calls the church deacon to take his fiancée to an abortion clinic?"

Calvin cut me off in the middle of my rant. "Fiancée?! What are you talking about?"

Calvin was in the middle of his sentence when I angrily hung the phone up. Calvin immediately called me back, but I was too embarrassed to answer.

How could I have been so stupid? I did not want him to know that I saw the engagement ring.

Calvin continued to call me as I peeked out the window and saw Deacon Langley walking toward the door.

Deacon Langley pounded on the door and yelled, "Someone needs to speak with you."

Still angry about what was going on, I responded, "You need to leave my house before I call the police. I don't know what Calvin told you, but I'm not going anywhere with you."

Clearly frustrated about what was going on, Deacon Langley put his face in his hands and shook his head. He walked back to the car and I saw him speak to someone in the back seat. I could tell that Deacon Langley was annoyed because his gestures were getting more animated, and the person in the car was arguing back.

I was about to call Calvin to find out what was going on when I saw the back door of the car open. The familiar face of Calvin's father, Bishop Calvin Tyler Sr. , uncoiled out of the back seat. Calvin Jr. was the spitting image of his father. The long, slender body and long duck feet were a dead give away. Bishop Tyler slowly walked to the door with an uneasy look on his face.

He knocked on the door softly and spoke. "Sister Angela, can I speak with you briefly?"

Every fiber in me wanted to say, "Fuck you, old man. Get away from my house."

But my respect for a man of God would not allow me. I opened the door and Bishop Tyler smiled at me. He greeted me with a warm hug and said that he had missed my energetic spirit around the church. I was shocked that he remembered who I was because we rarely come into contact with each other. Bishop Tyler had the gift of gab. When he spoke, he sounded like Martin Luther King Jr. making a passionate plea. He made you feel all warm and fuzzy inside. I could see why he had such a powerful hold over his church members.

The commotion of having the bishop outside my door must have gotten the best of Mrs. Turner.

She opened her door with a fake surprised Macaulay Culkin expression on her face and started stammering, "Bishop, is that you? I was just watching your service on TV. Wha. . . what are you doing here?"

The bishop managed an uneasy smile and then turned towards me. Bishop Tyler looked like a shocked deer in headlights. His facial expression made it look as if he were begging for help.

I informed Mrs. Turner that Bishop Tyler had come by for spiritual consultation. A part of me wanted to laugh because I sounded ridiculous. My picture was still circulating around social media networks for knocking Linda's ass out, and here I was talking about spiritual consultation.

I motioned for Bishop Tyler and Deacon Langley to come in. Bishop Tyler quickly entered my apartment like it was the last lifeboat going to shore. Bishop Tyler thanked me and then quickly scanned the apartment.

He froze when he saw RC's toys, then he glanced at Deacon Langley as if to say, "This hoe is a hood rat."

Bishop Tyler quickly turned his attention back towards me and started speaking. "Angela, I want to apologize for meeting under these circumstances. Had I known that you and my son were this serious about each other, I would have intervened a long time ago."

The bishop smiled at me nervously and glanced at Deacon Langley. Then he tried to clean up his last statement. "What I meant to say is, ahh, well, I think this situation came as a surprise to everyone. Had I known that you and he were so serious, I would have made arrangements for some type of marriage situation. As you can see, this is an embarrassment for all parties involved. I have plans for my son, and he can't move forward until this is resolved."

Bishop Tyler glanced at RC's toys and continued to talk. "And it clearly looks like it would be added pressure to your current situation."

I wanted to speak and say that Calvin and I had already made plans and that his plans for his son were not included. I really wanted to tell Bishop Tyler the truth about his son. I meant to really shove it in his smug-ass face that his son was in love with me. I wanted to tell him that all those plans that he had made for Linda Stanford to be the chosen one had died. I wanted Calvin beside me at that moment so that we both could tell him to go to hell. But I was in shock. I was shocked that Calvin had told his father about the baby, I was shocked at what was going on that morning, but most of all I was shocked that Calvin was not there.

Calvin's father continued to speak to me as if he were preaching a Sunday sermon. "If my son had a baby now, it would hurt him as well as the church, because it was conceived out of wedlock. I think the best solution for all parties involved would be to terminate this pregnancy because the baby was conceived out of wedlock."

At first, I was a little confused because the bishop was encouraging me to go against the beliefs of the church. The bishop must have noticed the questions running through my mind because he asked me to pray with him. After prayer, he opened his Bible and handed it to me.

"Sister, sometimes abortion is encouraged in Bible when the situation is wrong. Will you please read Numbers 5:21?"

I read the verse and started to cry because it talked about my thighs being rotten and a curse into my bowels. Bishop Tyler gently touched my face and encouraged me to read verses 27-28, which said I would be free if I was not defiled.

I asked the bishop about the verse and he spoke. "Sister Angela, don't you understand that by sleeping with Calvin it curses you? You

166

cannot seduce an anointed man of God without there being consequences."

I thought to myself, "Seduce?! I don't remember your son's dick saying no when he was screwing me."

My thoughts were interrupted by warm oil that smelled like cinnamon being smeared across my forehead. The bishop started praying, speaking in tongues, and sprinkling holy oil around my apartment. I hated cinnamon because my brother had once shoved a handful in my mouth and it burned like hell. Now my whole apartment smelled like cinnamon.

I had always been taught that abortions were against the church, but I wanted the best for Calvin and me. I assured the bishop that it was not my intention to hurt Calvin, but that I was just afraid. Bishop Tyler could see that I was afraid, but he was not willing to compromise his family's name. This was a delicate situation that could potentially turn into a nightmare for him. Bishop Tyler explained that he and his son could not accompany me to the clinic because of the potential fallout. He promised that everyone's best interest was being looked out for. But to me, it appeared that he was only looking out for his family's interest.

Bishop Tyler offered to have Deacon Langley accompany me to the clinic to make sure I was treated fairly.

I glanced over at Deacon Langley and he was staring back at me with a "Bitch, I wish you would" look.

Deacon Langley looked like he was perfect for knocking heads and hiding dead bodies. But dealing with a delicate situations like this did not appear to be him.

Reluctantly, I accepted Bishop Tyler's offer. When I accepted, the bishop looked like he had just hit the lottery. He grabbed me and hugged me like a lost son. Then he held his hand towards Deacon Langley, and the deacon placed a large, brown bag in his hand.

Bishop Tyler smiled at me and then handed it to me. He did not appear to be uncomfortable when he gave it to me; it was like he was familiar with doing something like this.

I opened the bag and saw nothing but hundred-dollar bills, which from my calculations appeared to be around fifteen or twenty thousand dollars.

The bishop looked at me sheepishly and said, "Calvin Jr. wanted you to have this for all the past trouble that I had caused."

I wanted to give the money back and say, "Like really, motherfucker! Do you actually think you can pay me a little money and I'll go away?"

But the angry and frustrated side of me was saying, "Girl, you better take this money. You deserve it."

Bishop Tyler stared at me suspiciously and then glanced at Deacon Langley. I guess my taking the money must have confirmed to him that I was not worthy of his son. The way I looked at, it was like this was a down payment on my new life with Calvin. Besides, Calvin and I were going to need a little extra money after he was cut off.

Bishop Tyler hugged me and slowly backed towards the door staring at me.

I guess he thought that I was going to change my mind about the money, but that thought never entered my mind. I was investing in Calvin long term. Getting an abortion would help Calvin now, but I was his future.

Bishop Tyler turned towards Deacon Langley and told him, "After you leave the clinic make sure you get her whatever she needs."

Those comments would later come back to haunt him, but that morning he walked away as if he had pulled off a million-dollar heist.

Deacon Langley offered to wait in the car as I gathered up my things. Bishop Tyler motioned toward his car, but a white Jaguar pulled up behind the Mercedes instead. Bishop Tyler handed Deacon Langley a set of keys, climbed into the passenger seat of the Jaguar, and drove off. Deacon Langley pulled the Mercedes to the curb and opened the door for me to get in.

I climbed into the car and stared out the window shaking my head in disbelief. I mean, damn, shit happens, but in my life, it seemed like shit just kept happening over and over again.

The forty-five-minute drive to Rome was relatively short considering the circumstances. I spent most of the ride trying to contact Calvin. The closer we got to the clinic, the more nervous I got. I wished Calvin would pick up the phone but he never did.

Deacon Langley must have noticed the fear in me as we pulled into the clinic's parking lot, so he spoke. "Ms. Anderson! Is there anything I can do for you or somebody I can call for you?"

I quickly glanced out the window hoping that Deacon Langley could not see the tears in my eyes. I opened my purse and found a pair of dark sunglasses.

I placed the glasses on my face and responded to Deacon Langley. "I was hoping that I could talk to Calvin before my appointment. He sent me a text message earlier saying good luck and that he loved me. But he never answered his phone when I called him. Is there a number that I can reach him at?"

Deacon Langley reached for his phone and then paused as if he had remembered something.

"Ah, I'm sorry, Ms. Anderson, but I was instructed not to disturb the Tylers today. I think they're throwing a big party for Calvin. You know, with him graduating and all."

I glanced out the window and tried to look strong, but deep down inside, I was crying. This was something that I was doing for both of us, and instead of supporting me, he was somewhere partying his ass off. I felt like calling the whole thing off and waiting until he had time to support me. But deep down in my heart, I knew he was probably just as miserable as I was. We both were making sacrifices. I was making sacrifice by getting an abortion, and he was sacrificing his entire family.

169

Deacon Langley opened the door and extended his hand to help me. He quickly turned away and sheepishly asked, "Do you want me to come inside with you?"

I smiled at him and shook my head yes. I quickly skimmed the face of this intimidating mountain of a man that everyone feared and noticed how gentle he really was. I had heard rumors around the church about Deacon Langley being in prison for killing people, and that wasn't including the bodies of those who had never had been found. Deacon Langley reminded me of a throwback gangster who intimidated you before killing you. He just carried himself like that. And now, here he was fumbling with car locks and stumbling to open the door for me. I thought it was so cute because he reminded me of a big, dumb Tarzan protecting his Jane. Deacon Langley hugged me and promised that he would wait until I was finished.

The nurse asked him if he was the father, and Deacon Langley glared back at the nurse as if she had offended me. "No, this is my favorite niece, and I don't give two shits about the father."

I glanced at Deacon Langley as if to say, "Okay, that's my man you're talking about. Don't disrespect him like that."

Deacon Langley softened his glare and apologized to me as I took a deep breath and followed the nurse down the hallway.

A nurse took my weight and temperature and then I was escorted into a small room. The smell of medicine and disinfectant had my stomach in knots. The nurse gave me a small gown and told me to undress as she left the room. I quickly started undressing because I didn't want the doctor to catch me half undressed. There's nothing more embarrassing then having your bare ass out when a cheerful doctor comes in. "Whoa! You almost got me there! Sorry about that! I'll be back when you finished." My doctor always caught me because I was such a slow dresser, but not today. I was out of my clothes and in the gown within sixty seconds. I sat on the table just as I was instructed to by the nurse and I thought about all the other patients before me. Did everything go well for them? Would there be any complications this time? What the hell was I doing there?

My mind was starting to run wild again just as I heard a knock at the door. The door slowly opened and I saw an older man dressed in surgical scrubs. The man greeted me with a cold smile and said his name was Dr. Tucker. He quickly explained the procedure to me and then he told me to lie on my back and place my feet in the stirrups. He assisted me by grabbing my legs and helping me to scoot into place. I could feel myself panicking as the doctor applied some gel inside me. He tried to make me as comfortable as possible by making small talk, but he could tell I was tense. Pretty soon, his finger was inside me and he was feeling my stomach at the same time. He said he was examining my uterus, but it just felt plain disgusting. This doctor was rough and business-like, unlike my doctor who made me feel comfortable. The doctor seemed like he was getting agitated because he was struggling inside of my vagina. I wanted to tell the doctor that my vagina was tight because I was afraid."Hey smart guy, the reason I was having a hard time relaxing was because you're preparing for an abortion." My poor vagina fought with the doctor for as long as it could before it finally let him finish doing what he was going to do.

The abortion process took less than fifteen minutes, but the aftershock was more painful. I felt alone, scared, and guilty. I could not believe that I was still putting the wants of a man before me. I was angry, and I wanted to tell Calvin how I felt.

The nurse led me back down the hallway and I saw Deacon Langley staring at me. I wanted that mean Deacon Langley back, because this new one was breaking my heart.

As soon as Deacon Langley saw me, he rushed toward me and gently pulled me towards him in a protective manner. "Ms. Anderson, are you okay? Here, sit down and I'll take care of the paperwork."

The tears trickling down my face had now turned into a stream. Deacon Langley looked so adorable running back and forth trying to make me comfortable. He reminded me of a worried father determined to find out what was going on with his daughter.

I was happy that at least someone was in my corner. But the more pain I felt, the more I wanted to hold Calvin accountable. Deacon Langley escorted me to the car and made sure I was comfortable for the ride back. I immediately dialed Calvin's number ready to spew venom and fire. What type of man would send not only his father, but a church deacon, to take care of his responsibility?

I tried to reach Calvin not once, not twice, but three times, and he never answered. Deacon Langley glanced at me in the rearview mirror, but said nothing. It was at that moment I started really questioning things. Calvin started changing for all the wrong reasons the day after Linda called his house. It was as if he met with God and his father and grew a conscience. He no longer placed me on a pedestal and he felt guilty about being in public with me. Could it be that he made up a bunch of bullshit just to get what he wanted?

I leaned forward and gently nudged Deacon Langley and asked in an almost begging voice, "Would it be okay if I please borrowed your phone? My phone battery is dead and I know my parents are worried sick about me."

Deacon Langley shook his head and replied at me almost frustrated. "This is why I asked you before if you needed to call somebody. You should not be going through this type of situation by yourself."

I replied to Deacon Langley by repeating his words, "Going through this situation by myself? Why makes you think that I'm going through this by myself?"

Deacon Langley glared at me in the rearview mirror with a puzzled look on my face, then he responded, "Never mind. Here, take my phone."

I wanted to go further with the conversation, but I decided to hold off. Deacon Langley stared out the window mumbling obscenities while I dialed Calvin's number. Deacon Langley would have probably spilled the beans that day if I had pushed. But I just didn't feel comfortable putting him in that situation.

As soon as I dialed Calvin's number, he answered. He sounded out of breath and a little panicky. "Man, what took you so long? Is everything cool?"

I felt like that would be my only chance to find out the truth, so I replied in the deepest voice I could muster, "Mmm hmm."

Calvin took a deep breath and responded, "Cool, do me a favor? When you get Angela home, make sure you call me, because I'm going to need you to pick us up."

Again, I responded in a deep voice, "Mmm hmm."

Calvin continued to talk. "Man, this shit is crazy, did she ask you any questions or anything?

I managed a deep mumble and Calvin responded, "Oh yeah, my fault. She in the car probably listening, right?"

I responded with another "Mmm hmm."

"If everything works out like it should, we'll be out of here before any problems are caused. So hurry up and get back."

Again, I responded, "Mmm hmm."

I ended the call and quickly dialed my parent's number just as Deacon Langley was glancing in rearview mirror. I pressed the end call button, but I pretended to have a deep conversation with my mother. I quickly erased Calvin's dialed number and handed the phone back to Deacon Langley.

Deacon Langley asked me if everything was okay and I said fine. If Deacon Langley had only bothered to look at me, he probably would have saved a lot of people a lot of heartache. But he never bothered to look at me. He never saw me seething with anger, and he definitely never saw me dial Calvin's number again with my phone.

Calvin's phone went straight to voicemail again, which further pushed me towards the edge. By the time Deacon Langley pulled in front of my house, I was in full meltdown. Whatever Calvin was planning, good or bad, was going down that evening with me in attendance.

Deacon Langley exited the car and opened the door for me. I played the damsel in distress and insisted that Deacon Langley escort me to me door. He glanced at his watch with impatience and then agreed. I slowly walked to my door as if I were on death's doorstop. I occasionally would stop and take a deep breath, mostly for the appearance. I needed time to get to my car and follow Deacon Langley without over-exerting myself.

Deacon Langley did as expected. He walked me to my door, and then made sure I was comfortable on my couch. He fetched my favorite blanket and grabbed an ice-cold glass of water so I could take my medication. By the time Deacon Langley was sneaking out my house, I had convinced him that I was sound asleep, cuddled up with my favorite stuffed animal.

Deacon Langley slowly pulled off and I moved toward my car as fast as possible. I could feel pain ripping through my body, but I was determined to catch Deacon Langley. I tore down the street like a bat out of hell, hoping that Deacon Langley was still driving slowly. I got even luckier because he was stuck in traffic. Deacon Langley was four cars ahead of me, but I could clearly tell he was frustrated. Atlanta traffic has a tendency to do that to people. Don't get me wrong, I hate Atlanta traffic, but I was thanking God for it on that day.

I followed Deacon Langley on 285 W and then he merged onto 400 S until we reached the Lennox Rd. /Buckhead exit. I thought to myself, "Wow! Calvin is really doing it big. While I was at the clinic getting rid off his indiscretions, he was in Buckhead munching on jumbo shrimp, not taking my calls."

Deacon Langley came to a sudden stop and turned on his signal light. I was surprised as I followed him into the parking garage of my job. I immediately saw a huge sign across the entrance of the W Hotel that read, "Congratulations Bishop Calvin Tyler Jr."My mind instantly went into implode mode. Why was this motherfucker being congratulated if he had just told his father about us? And why the fuck was I seeing a sign with the word Bishop in front his name? The mind can play a lot of tricks on you when you don't have all the facts, and this was one of those times.

I smiled at the security guard and flashed my badge as I entered the building through the employee's entrance. My bladder felt like it was about to explode as I exited the elevator on the main floor. I knew I was headed in the right direction because I started to see familiar faces from Solid Foundation. I hid myself in the crowd and slowly made my way toward a huge sign with a picture of Calvin and Linda. I felt like fucking Nipper the Dog staring into an Edison Bell cylinder phonograph as I passed by the sign.

Calvin and Linda were in separate frames holding a Bible in one hand and a gold cross in the other. The words "The Future is Now" were in big bold letters across the top of the sign. An arrow pointing to Great Room B directed the crowd to the festivities. I continued to follow the crowd towards the entrance, but I was stopped by a church usher who was dressed as a banquet hostess.

She immediately asked me if I had an invitation. I looked at her in a confused manner and responded, "I'm sorry, I didn't know this was an invitation-only event. Calvin and I went to the same college, and I thought he was having a graduation party."

The lady smiled at me and responded, "This is a graduation party for Calvin Tyler, but you still need an invitation."

I thanked the lady and she continued to scan the growing crowd for invitations. I walked away and quickly gained access through the service entrance on the balcony level. I quickly scanned the crowd and saw Calvin seated in the front of the banquet hall talking with his father. Calvin looked incredibly sexy with his three-piece cream and chocolate suit. Calvin's bright engaging smile and slender build made him look like a number-one draft choice in any woman's book. I felt a smile creep across my face as I gazed at my baby looking so dapper and working the crowd.

I was about to stand up on the balcony rail and scream at the top of my lungs, "I love you, Calvin Tyler."

I heard Calvin's father ask for everyone's attention by barking it through the microphone. Bishop Tyler demanded that everyone gather around because his son had an announcement. I felt my throat instantly go dry as Calvin approached the microphone. His engaging smile had been replaced with solemn look of despair. I could tell that Calvin was about to reveal something big. I had seen that serious, stone-faced look before. The day he found out that I was pregnant was the last time I saw that look. The same night that he had cried in my arms and told me that he loved me and wanted to marry me. That same look was now being used to break his father's heart.

I can't say that I was ecstatic because I felt sorry for Calvin. Calvin's father had prepared his son for the takeover for so long that he had lost sight of what he was feeling. Calvin's father only saw Calvin as a puppet to carry on his name. He never saw the Calvin who loved me and was willing to do anything for us to be together. No one could have known the love I felt for Calvin as he embraced his father and took the microphone and spoke. "First, I would like to give honor and praise to God, who is the head of my life. I want to give honor and thanks to my parents, who have successfully guided me through life, and made me into the man I am today."

I felt so proud to be in Calvin's life as he continued to talk and hold the crowd hostage with his words of encouragement and thankfulness. Again, I wanted to leap on the balcony rail and scream, "I love you, Calvin Tyler" when I heard words coming out of Calvin's mouth that destroyed my world.

"And in closing, I would like to bring forth the most beautiful woman in the world and make it official."

Instead of the crowd turning to look at me, the crowd turned toward Linda. I could feel my heart pounding against my chest as Linda walked towards Calvin. She was beaming with pride as Calvin pulled her close and they embraced. Calvin playfully spun Linda around and dipped her as if they were newlyweds. Linda giggled like a silly church girl as Calvin pulled her closer and then kissed her on the lips. I heard choruses of "Ahhh, they make such a cute couple" as she blushed and he smiled.

It felt like I was watching a nightmare in slow motion as Calvin kneeled and presented my engagement ring to Linda. The same ring that I had tried on three days ago was being placed on Linda's finger. I could see Calvin's lips moving, everyone cheering, and Linda passionately kissing Calvin after accepting the ring. But all I heard was a loud buzzing in my ear. It felt like someone was pouring acid on my head and I was melting. I was sweating but my hands were cold and clammy. My stomach muscles kept clenching painfully and I lost feeling in my arms and legs. Walking back to my car felt like an eternity as I struggled to keep my balance. I felt like I was walking in quicksand and the hole kept getting deeper. I finally made it back to my car, but I couldn't move my fingers. They felt frozen as if I was in the middle of a blizzard storm. I could feel that same dark spirit that wanted me to murder my son coming back. The same dark spirit that had frightened me so long ago now felt warm and confronting as I sat shivering in my car. I tried to start my car, but my hands were shaking too hard. I glanced at the exit door and hoped that Calvin and Linda would walk through that door. I wanted them to come skipping through that door so that I could kill both of them at the same time. I wanted their bones to grind beneath my tires as they begged for God's mercy. I wanted Bishop Tyler to come into the garage and hold his dying son's hand, beg for Jesus to help him, just as I put a bullet in his head.

I finally started my car and raced out of the garage. My intentions were to go home, but thoughts of murder and suicide directed me to Calvin's apartment. I parked my car in front of Calvin's apartment and waited. I waited for the opportunity to end his life. All I could hear were the sounds of crickets chirping as I plotted Calvin's murder.

The minutes turned into hours, and the hours turned into the next day, and then that day turned into the next day. For two days I sat outside Calvin's apartment perched at my steering wheel waiting to end his life, but it never came.

Maybe it was God saving me from myself again, or maybe it was the fact that I looked like a lunatic. Whatever the case, one of Calvin's neighbors thought that it was odd that a crazy-looking lady had been sitting in her car, babbling to herself for the past two days. By the time the police arrived, there was a crowd of people surrounding my car. I could see the concerned looks on their faces, but my mind was not processing.

Everything looked like an out-of-body experience. I saw one of the police officers slowly move towards my car and repeatedly ask if I was okay. All I could manage to do was stare off into space as if my mind was blank. I sat frozen with my hands tightly gripped around the steering wheel. The police officer slowly opened my door and quickly turned away in horror. The stench of blood, urine, and human feces seeped out of the hot car and I continued to stare off into space as if possessed.

By the time other emergency vehicles had arrived, I was sitting on the curb with a blanket around me. People walking passed me would glance in my direction and quickly turn away. My body had developed an infection from the abortion, and I guess it didn't help that I was sitting in my own piss and shit for two days.

I was rushed to the hospital and immediately placed under a 1013 hold. I remember hearing about a 1013 hold when I was dating Malik. Malik would commit some wild-ass crime and then start acting crazy when he got arrested. He confessed to me that the only reason that he acted crazy was because he preferred doing his time at Georgia Regional instead of the county jail. Now here I was on a 1013 hold at Central State Hospital.

The whole scene was like a nightmare out of some movie. There were some who sat staring at the wall mumbling, while others screamed at the top of their lungs for hours. I guess I got lucky, because all my roommate did was cut her wrist. At first, my roommate and I rarely communicated. Ironically, all Olivia did was spend the day listening to gospel music and praying. The poor girl spent hours on her knees crying and begging God to forgive her.

I wondered if she had gone through the same thing that I had. I wondered if she was a person like me who was tired of being hurt. Was she pushed to a point that she lashed out at the only person who truly mattered—herself? Those demons were doing everything they could to keep her in that cold, damp darkness. All she could do was pray and play gospel music, hoping things would get back to normal.

I could always pick the backsliders out of a crowd, because we were cut from the same cloth. When life was good, we never thought about Christ, but when the waters got murky, you could find us begging him for deliverance. The hardest part of being around Olivia was her collection of old Shirley Caesar songs. Those songs reminded me of when my life was innocent. I could see my father dressed for Sunday school, impatiently sitting at the dinner table sipping coffee. Every time Olivia played "Mama I Remember," I would break down and cry. I had put my parents through so much and this was just another coal in the fire.

The first time I saw my parents at the hospital, I turned my head and buried my face in my pillow. No matter how hard I tried, I simply could not stop crying. Although both my parents assured me that everything was going to be okay, I felt like such a failure. It seemed like any decision that I made backfired.

My father comforted me by holding my hand and encouraging me to be strong. My mother simply stared at me quietly as if she was holding in what she wanted to say. I wanted my mother to pull me close and hold my face in her warm hands. I wanted my mother to make me feel like I was still that nine-year-old, innocent girl in Baxley. My mother managed a quick smile, but I could tell it was forced.

The only thing going through her mind was questions. "What in God's name is wrong with my daughter? Why would she go get pregnant when she's always dumping this one on us? What do I tell her son when he asks for mommy?"

My mother continued to stare at me as if I were a stranger until she finally got the courage to speak. Her voice shook with emotions as she began to speak slowly in a barely audible voice. "Angela, you know we love you, but this shit has got to stop."

I heard my mother curse before, but that was the first time she had ever cursed at me. I stared at her in shock as she continued to speak. "I can't allow you to keep doing this to your son. Little RC is almost four years old, and you're treating him like he's a doll baby. You drop him off at Steven's house as if he's their child. You don't think RC sees this? It's almost like you don't want him."

I wanted to tell my mother, "You're right. I blame RC for destroying my dreams. I hate that RC looks like his sorry-ass daddy. I blame RC for destroying me and Calvin. Above all, I blame RC because this made my mother a prophet."

My mother told me not to have RC, but I was blinded by love. I stared at my mother fighting back tears as she continued to tear into me. "You really thought that this man had your best interest in mind when he asked you to get an abortion. This man asked you to risk your life for his family, and you did. Just for once, did you think about how your family would feel? The police said they found you in a car damn near dead while your son was at his uncle's house crying for you."

The more my mother spoke, the more it hurt. My mother was right, but it hurt to hear it from her. I was always used to being my mother's baby girl, and there I was being put on blast by her. There was a steady stream of tears flowing down my face, but my mother was set for another round of reality check. She opened her mouth to add more insult to injury when I saw my father gently nudge my mother's arm. My mother glared at my father's hand as if annoyed that he had interrupted her.

My father matched my mother with a defiant stare of his own and said, "That's enough."

My mother looked at my father wanting to say more, but decided not to go further.

My father's temper was legendary in Baxley. He told you what he felt and really didn't care how you took it. But this day was different.

He could have piggy-backed off of what my mother was saying and destroyed me even more. But he didn't. My father slowly walked toward me and simply pulled me close to his chest.

I could feel his heart pounding as he started to speak. "Angela, we love you so much. We're not trying to be mean. We're just trying to understand what happened. Your son is worried about you. We're worried about you! I understand that sometimes we have problems and go through things, but your problems are affecting your son."

Normally I had a response if someone was hurting my feelings, but that day I had none. The only thing I could do was stare silently at my food tray. Even as my father finished by telling me that they were taking temporary custody of RC, I just sat there unresponsive.

Deep in my heart, I knew that it was the right thing for RC, but it still hurt. My son never asked to be born. RC was the result of a stubborn young girl who wanted to prove people wrong. He deserved better than what he was given. I was hurt by what my parents were doing, but I finally agreed because it was best for RC.

My father wiped my tears from my eyes, and for the first time that day, I felt the warmth of my mother's love. She pulled me close and hugged me as if we had not seen each other in years.

She held my face in her hands and finally spoke. "You will always be RC's mother. You can see him whenever you want, and when you get better, he can come and live with you. Right now I want you to concentrate on getting your life together. Do what you need to do to get healthy and be the mother you're supposed to be."

By the time my mother got finished talking to me that day, I felt like I could conquer the world. Although my mind was still mush from all the evil thoughts, I felt rejuvenated. I wanted my son and parents to be proud of me, and I was going to do everything I could to make sure it happened.

The next few weeks was all about getting my life together. I was diagnosed with having a psychotic break. The way my doctor explained it, all the stress from Calvin, the church, and the abortion overloaded me mentally. My mind just shut down because the pressure was too much. My doctor warned me about staying away from those stressors because they could lead to a relapse.

Being around people who had issues like me helped. Olivia started using headphones with her gospel music, and she always made sure to watch Solid Foundation when I was asleep or in the dayroom. I came to really appreciate Olivia because she was one of the sweetest persons you would ever want to meet.

What I enjoyed most about Central State was the group activity. No one seemed comfortable standing in the middle of the floor telling their story, but it was refreshing. Each person was given the opportunity to release and it felt good. I found out quickly that we all had a story to tell. Most of our stories were similar except for Olivia's. Olivia's case was so different because it was so extreme. Her case involved an abusive husband. When you think of an abusive man, you think of a drunk, burly man slapping his girlfriend around. Her situation was even worse. She was in a relationship with a man who abused her mentally.

Imagine being told nobody else wanted you on a daily basis. Wouldn't you eventually snap? Wouldn't you snap if you did everything your man asked of you and he still wasn't happy? Wouldn't you snap if he cheated over and over and you took him back every time? I wondered what was going through her mind when she took a butcher knife and stabbed him to death and then slashed her own wrist.

When Olivia told her story, you could hear a pin drop. Her story made all of us think about just how far a person was willing to go when hurt. I could understand why she kept her side of the room decorated in pure white linen. Why she kept spiritual music and TV evangelist on 24 hours a day. And why she prayed every hour as if the world were coming to an end. She never wanted to go back to that cold, dark place where demons convinced her to destroy her life.

No matter how many treatment plans Olivia finished, she would never be able to go home. Her life would either end in prison or at Central State Hospital. It was hard seeing her trapped in that situation, but I truly believe she wanted me to live for my family because her family was gone.

My discharge date was scheduled in two days and I wanted to do something special with Olivia. Olivia had always begged me to attend church with her, but I had always declined. That Sunday, I decided to surprise Olivia and attend church. When Olivia came back from her group I was dressed and ready to go. I stood in her area looking at her with a stupid smirk on my face.

Olivia squinted at me and then asked, "Why are you standing there with that stupid look on your face?"

I smiled back at Olivia and responded, "You remember all those times you wanted me to go to church with you? Well I've decided that I will grace you with my lovely presence. Sort of like a going-away present."

What I thought would be a fun moment between Olivia and I turned sad quickly as she placed her hands on her face and started tearing up. Before I knew it, we were both crying like babies as we hugged each other.

Olivia was excited for me, but at the same time, she was hurt too. Going home was not an option for Olivia and her seeing me about to leave added to that sadness. Olivia seemed happy that I was finally going to church with her. We walked hand-in-hand to the hospital chapel like two little girls going to Sunday school. I felt Olivia's joy and I knew she felt my love for her. That day would also be the day that I remember, because my eyes would finally be open to the truth.

That day in church started like any other service I had been to. People sang songs of joy and testified about God's greatness. I was enjoying the service when I saw a familiar person being led into the chapel. My body tensed up in horror as I saw Linda and her entourage being led to the front of the chapel.

Olivia noticed the change in my body language almost immediately. She nudged my arm and asked, "What's wrong?"

I quickly turned away and started looking around the room as if I were panicking. My mind started racing as I thought of worse case scenarios.

I looked at Olivia terrified, thinking to myself, "This is the worse-case scenario, being seen by Calvin and Linda at a mental hospital."

I heard a voice introduce Linda, "I know many of you already know who this amazing woman is."

The room erupted in loud applauses and cheers, and the speaker continued to talk. "Prophetess Stanford has ministered to millions of people all over the world. She has healed and delivered thousands from their debilitating diseases. And she has also taken time out of her busy schedule to set demons free here at Central State Hospital."

The crowd continued to clap and cheer as Linda walked toward the podium. She leaned forward and whispered something to the speaker, and the speaker quickly grabbed the microphone and started speaking nervously. "I'm sorry, but Prophetess Stafford also wanted me to let you know that she also had time to be engaged to the dynamic Assistant Bishop at Solid Foundation Cathedral, Calvin Tyler Jr."

Roars of laughter filled the room as the speaker continued. "I'm sorry, Prophetess. We don't get social media much in Central State."

Linda flashed a huge smile across her face and the crowd exploded with adoration for her. As the crowd continued to stand and applaud, I quickly made a dash for the door. Olivia must have noticed the panicked look on my face because she was right behind me. She had heard my story of betrayal by a well-known bishop, but it was not until that day that she actually knew who I was talking about.

Olivia escorted me back to our room and closed the door. I sat on my bed quietly and stared out the window as if contemplating something. Olivia closed my curtains and began apologizing as if I were an abused house wife. I wanted to be mad at Olivia, but how could I? There was no way she could have known that the two people that I blamed for my predicament may have been in the same building with me. Olivia rubbed my back in a comforting manner and continued to apologize.

I stared at the floor nervously and tried to find the words to express myself. But the only thing to come out was, "I just couldn't stay there! Especially like this."

I held my hands out displaying the dingy blue jump suite with Central State Hospital written on the back.

"Can you imagine the fun she would have had knowing that I was in a mental hospital?"

I climbed on my bed and buried my head in my pillow not wanting to speak to anyone. Olivia noticed that I was hurt so she laid my blanket on me and tugged at the curtains that separated the room. She turned on her TV and plugged in her headphones. For a few seconds, I heard Linda hooting and hollering on the TV. It sounded like fingernails on the chalkboard. I briefly raised my head and peeked at Olivia. She was shaking her head and praising God as Linda preached on TV. I shook my head in disbelief because even after all the stories I told Olivia about Linda, she still believed that she was her connection to God.

I had to admit, Linda had become an overnight sensation in the TV evangelist word. Her story as an abused woman left to care for her child as a single mother connected well with the bishop's core audience—single females. Calvin's father saw a void in the game and capitalized on it. Linda was a breath of fresh air from the normally sophisticated, grammatically correct TV evangelist. The short, pudgy woman with two gold fang teeth could hold her audience captive. She could touch your heart by being overwhelmed with joy and crying. And the next minute she would demand that a woman leave her abusive husband.

If women stood up and testified about having problems at home, Linda would bristle up like a cat ready to attack and shout, "Devil you're a liar! I rebuke that devil who you call your husband. If a man is cheating on you, abusing you, and holding you back from your blessing, leave that rotten, no-good demon. God will give you a new one."

The single women who were going through that pain would jump up and testify, "I put that sorry demon out because he cheated on me. I know God will help me get through this pain."

Calvin's father really saw the profit margins grow after he elevated her to the position of a prophetess at Solid Foundation. Linda would get on TV and make broad predictions, like "There's someone out there who is struggling to hang on after going through trials and tribulation."

No shit, Dick Tracy. That sounds like 90% of the world. People would call in, especially young, single women bawling and asking God to strengthen them, and Prophetess Stafford would mail them a video tape and a bar of soap for a $30 love offering.

Olivia once sent in a $30 love offering. She got a bar of Irish Spring soap with "healing time" wrote on it. The directions instructed her to pray and bathe three times a day for a week. The soap was supposed to wash away all the sin and bad spirits from her life. There were a lot of people who swore that their lives had changed and gladly testified about it during the televised church service. From what I saw, nothing really changed for Olivia. She eventually went to prison for life. I guess in some twisted way it was worth it to her, because she would gladly do life in prison knowing that all the evil had been washed away. It was like a win-win situation for all parties. The church's bottom line exploded with Linda as the main attraction, and people actually believed they were being delivered.

All that time in Central State Hospital opened my eyes to Bishop Tyler. He was pimping his son out because he knew that Calvin could never connect with his female audience like Linda could. Linda was the main attraction in a three ring circus. Calvin's father gave him every opportunity to shine by giving him total control of the 10am Sunday service. Linda still outshined him during the 7:30pm services on Wednesday.

As member of Sold Out for Christ, Linda would go anywhere to hustle for souls. Calvin's primary duties were to stay back at the church and relay messages from the top. When we got back from a long day of hustling for souls, all he did was collect the money. We would come back all stinky and sweaty from a long day and he would be waiting for us in an air conditioned office sipping ice tea. He was afraid to go where Linda hustled for souls. That punk bitch wouldn't come off the porch to hustle if his life depended on it.

Linda was built for this type of game and it showed. No matter how much screeching and hollering Calvin mustered up, it didn't compare to Linda. Linda came off authentic. She made common people feel like she was struggling with them. Calvin's privileged ass made you feel like you were lacking something. Calvin's father saw his son's inadequacies and made the changes like a Hall of Fame coach.

As soon as he saw the short, pudgy woman, he saw dollar signs. Her bad, clumpy skin, curly perm, gold teeth, and broken English made the average woman feel comfortable. Calvin's privileged life, provided by Bishop Tyler, showed through like an ink stain on a white shirt. He tried to word his sermons like Linda's, but it would end up sounding like an educated preppy talking to Leroy the drug dealer.

As soon as Linda started sharing the main stage with Calvin, profits doubled. After Linda and Calvin got engaged, profits quadrupled. Everyone wanted a piece of Calvin and Linda from TV sponsors to heads of state. Calvin was the shinny red Lamborghini that everybody wanted and Linda was the million dollar engine. Bishop Tyler was keeping all the eggs in one golden basket and Linda was the goose. The only problem was that there was a crazy, jealous woman filled with aspirations to derail Bishop Tyler's plans.

Chapter 10

The money that the Bishop Tyler gave me turned out to thirty thousand dollars. I spent most of it on a car and a new apartment. The new apartment was located just off highway 400 near Sandy Springs. The area was quieter and I finally could breathe without Mrs. Turner sticking her head out the window every five minutes. My parents asked questions about how I could afford the new place and I just flat out lied. I could never tell my parents that I killed my unborn baby for thirty thousand dollars.

Just as I was getting used to my new surroundings, I received a call. It was Calvin. The first time I heard Calvin's voice, I could feel my blood boiling. The nerve of this motherfucker calling me like everything was cool.

He gave me some lame duck story about being pressured by his father to end our relationship and not knowing how. He kept going on and on about how he missed what we had and bla, bla, bla.

I knew what Calvin was missing and it definitely wasn't our conversation. Linda might have known how to bring souls to Christ, but she had no idea how to keep her man satisfied sexually. I knew it was just a matter of time before he would come back around sniffing for some pussy, and I was already ten steps ahead of him.

Those ninety days at Central State not only gave me insight about Calvin and his father, it also gave me a lust for revenge. I spent countless nights thinking of ways to make that family suffer. I had an entire notebook dedicated to getting even with the Tylers. The bishop's son became public enemy number one in my book because of the way he betrayed me. He not only destroyed what little faith I had in men, but he also placed my life in danger. Killing the Tylers and Linda would have been too easy. I wanted to destroy everything they built, and Calvin was first in line.

I agreed to meet with Calvin not because I was still in love with him, but because I wanted to hurt Linda. I was going to show her that no matter how much faith she had in Christ, it was no match for the hatred I felt for her. I was going to fuck Calvin anytime I wanted, and there would be absolutely nothing she could do about it. I wanted to destroy their fake-ass marriage and publically humiliate her in front of the world.

I wanted people to say, "You mean to tell me that with all that power given to her by God, she couldn't keep her man from fucking another woman?"

Destroying Solid Foundation and making Linda look like an idiot at the same time—what could be better?

Calvin arrived at my house on a Sunday at 2:45pm. He smelled like Linda's cheap Walmart perfume and he could barely look me in the eye.

I played along with his pitiful apology game as he tearfully told his side of the story. "Angela, you have no idea what it's like to be literally forced to do something against your will. I begged my father to accept you, but he just would not listen. He knows that I love you, but still he insisted on me joining forces with Linda. I just don't know. Sometimes I wake up in the middle of the night and wonder about what I've gotten myself into. I just want to make things right between us, you know, with all the things that we went through with the baby and all."

For a split second I paused because I could not believe he was claiming to have gone through the abortion with me.

I bit my tongue and stayed in character as I replied, "Baby, are you sure you're okay?"He pretended to still be stressed as he sighed and quickly shook his head yes.

He glanced in my direction and finally noticed me sitting in the chair across from him. I had on an oversized t-shirt and no panties. I smiled at Calvin and told him that I had really missed him. I slowly leaned back and started rocking my legs back and forth so that he could get quick flashes of my vulva. Calvin tried to play it cool, but I could see that his penis was already erect in his pants.

I continued to rock my legs back and forth as Calvin glared at me. Calvin's leg was shaking nervously as he fought to control his inner beast. I could see that he wanted me, but he just did not know how to ask.

I walked over to Calvin and stood in between his legs. Calvin quickly lunged forward and started rubbing my thighs and butt.

He closed his eyes and rested his head on my stomach as he rubbed his hand between my thighs. Calvin mumbled, "Oh my God, I've missed you so much."

He leaped from the chair as if he was possessed and shoved me towards the wall face-first. He was aggressive, vulgar, and acted like he was pressed for time. He quickly pulled his pants down and fumbled to rip the rubber package open. He bent me over and staggered to keep his balance as he jammed his penis inside of me.

Calvin cursed, grunted, and growled until he finally unlocked and stumbled backwards onto the sofa.

I followed Calvin to the sofa and slid to my knees. I gently removed the rubber from his penis and smiled up at him.

Calvin coldly nudged me out of the way with his leg and stumbled off to the bathroom. In a way, I was happy that Calvin treated me like that, because it made it easier for me not to feel guilty about what I was doing. I honestly don't know what I would have done if the Calvin that I had fallen in love with had shown up. It would have been harder for me to deceive him because I loved him so much. This new Calvin who only wanted to make booty calls in between sermons deserved everything I was doing and more.

I heard the shower water come on and I rushed the condom to my bedroom and plunged the needle into it. Then I unloaded the sperm into a small vial and placed it in the freezer. The thing about revenge is that you have to be willing to destroy something or a person. I could have destroyed Calvin ten times over, but the thought of him betraying me had never entered my mind. I could have never used any of the sleazy tactics that I had learned from the streets on Calvin. But now it was different. And his humming in my shower like everything was fine made it worse. I was willing to open up my arsenal and destroy him at any cost, and stealing his sperm was the first attack.

Stealing sperm was a little trick I learned from one of my sorority sisters, Tawana. According to ghetto standards, Tawana had to be one of the luckiest persons in the world. She had four children by four different men, which would have been a tragedy in any circle except the streets. Hood girls thought Tawana was so lucky because three of her baby fathers played professional basketball and the fourth was a college quarterback expected to be chosen in the top five of the upcoming NFL draft.

When we were in college, Tawana always talked about marrying a professional athlete, but it never happened. She came close once, but it ended like a train wreck. Tawana and her professional football fiancé planned a huge wedding and invited all of their family, friends, and enemies. Tawana pranced down the aisle in her $30,000 wedding dress only to be stood up when her man caught cold feet. The Cincinnati String Quartet just stared at each other not knowing if they should play the wedding march or hit the road jack. The upscale affair turned into a mess with family members arguing, her enemies laughing, and people trying to take back presents. I felt bad for Tawana as we escorted her to her dressing room. She cried for what seemed like hours, embarrassed about what had occurred. Tawana fell off the face of the earth after that fiasco and resurfaced at a homecoming dance on the arm of a hoop star, her first child's baby daddy. Tawana still had the same old showboat mentality, but her agenda for love and marriage had changed. There were rumors floating around the line sisters that she was trying to trap men by freezing their dirty condoms.

Some of my line sisters asked her if this was true and she didn't try to hide it. She made it perfectly clear that the only love in her dictionary was for money and she planned on obtaining it by any means necessary.

Tawana knew every trick in the book. She would insist on having unprotected sex and usually use lines like, "I can't feel it with the condom on. Just take it off for a second and pull it out."

Or she used guilt trips on men like, "If you love me, why do you need a condom?" She would intentionally stop using her birth control without the man knowing and even go as far as sticking pins through her boyfriend's condom package. The men never suspected a thing until he pulled his penis out, and the condom was ripped to pieces.

Most of my line the sisters stopped hanging with her and made damn sure that their husbands and boyfriends stayed far away. While my line sisters ran in the opposite direction, I found myself intrigued by her. I was fascinated at the way she investigated men. By the time Tawana "supposedly" bumped into a man by chance, she had already investigated him. She knew his family, she knew what his scoring average, was and most importantly, she knew his money-making potential. How many women can actually say that they attended four NBA drafts and watched their baby's daddy chosen in the first round?

By the time the man finally saw who the real Tawana was, he was standing in a delivery room angry as the golden child was being born. After going through all that bullshit with Patrick, I wanted to be like Tawana. Tawana taught me how to control my emotions and only get out of the relationship what I wanted. She showed me how to be cold and calculating but also replicate love at the same time. I buried those powers of destruction deep inside because I fell in love. Dealing with a creep like Calvin now made me anxious to use those same tactics.

I called Tawana and she was more than happy to give me a refresher course on collecting sperm from a condom. I never told her who I was setting up, but she had enough sense to know that it would not be "little pistol starter" from Bankhead Courts. She walked me through the procedure step by step, from collecting, unthawing, and inserting the sperm with a syringe.

Calvin came out of the bathroom, looked at me suspiciously and asked, "Who are you on the phone with?"

I immediately became defensive and responded, "Who the fuck are you talking too? I don't answer to you, or any other man."

Calvin glared at me and then smiled. I could tell that my comment had caught him off guard and that he was angry.

I fell in love with Calvin because he gave me freedom, something I needed at the time. As time went on, I saw him morph into a control freak. He wanted to know where I was at all times. It was like I was on call only for him. He probably started treating me like that because he was screwing around so much.

Calvin walked behind me and pulled me close, "Come on baby, you know I was just playing."

The hug felt cold, almost scripted as a means to pacify me. I quickly pulled away and asked him if he could take me out to dinner.

Calvin glanced at his watch with an "oh shit" look on his face and started stammering, "Uhh! Well uhh! I would really like to take you, but I had already made plans. Would it be okay if I got a rain check?"

I looked at Calvin with a fake worried expression and asked him if everything was okay. Calvin shook his head and quickly moved toward my door.

I followed behind him, and just as he was opening the door, I said, "You're running off like you have to get home to your fiancée or something."

Calvin froze as if he was looking at a ghost in the breeze way and started speaking. "Wha! Wha what are you talking about? I have to go back to a special service at church."

It felt good making Calvin nervous, so I continued, "Can I go? And I mean, it's been so long since I've been to church. Who knows? I might come back to Christ."

194

There was an uncomfortable silence as Calvin tried to think of something to keep me from going to "church." Calvin's arms were moving, but nothing was coming from his mouth.

I laughed to break the tension, but you could still see a panicked look on his face. Calvin quickly walked away and waved at me awkwardly. I closed my door and started laughing. I glanced out my window and saw Calvin looking back at my window and fumbling with his keys. Knowing Calvin, he wanted nothing to do with me except a slide-by every now and again for a quick screw. Calvin knew I could destroy everything his father had built by simply showing up for Sunday service. He probably thought he could just use me for sex and then slither back to dinner with Evangelist Stanford. Calvin called me later that night to see if I was serious about coming to church. I played the role of love-struck puppy willing to do anything for my man.

I started sneaking back to church just to see how my adversary was playing. I would dress in a wig and some dark shades and nestle in the rear of the overflow room. Calvin would deliver the word at the 7am, Calvin Sr. would preach during the 9am service, and then Linda would deliver the showstopper at 11am. The three headed-monster had the ability to attack your emotions like a tidal wave. By the time Linda stepped to the pulpit, eighty-four-year-old Sister Betty was ready to give her light bill money away. Poor Sister Betty would wobble out the church on her cane praising Jesus and go home to a dark house with no lights. I have to admit they were good. Sometimes I even found myself in the back of the overflow room praising Jesus, and flushing money down the fifty-gallon barrel.

The income groups in Solid Foundation ran the gamut and the powers made sure everyone knew. People would stand in line for hours just to get a glimpse of the professional athletes, entertainers, and corporate CEOs. These Solid Foundation dignitaries were treated like royalty. They had access to valet parking service while the rest of the peons huddled together in the massive parking lot and waited for the shuttle. Their seating area was like a V. I. P. lounge at a club. The roped-off area had plush white leather seats, private security, and a bottle service of freshly squeezed fruit juices. The other poor souls in the congregation stared jealously in the restricted area, hoping to be included one day.

Calvin and his father played off of the crowd's envy through contest. A white bench was placed near the V. I. P. section. The bench was reserved for the first eight tithe givers who gave $2000 dollars or more that Sunday. Calvin's father would call these members to the front of the church and praise them for all their hard work, almost like an impromptu ceremony. You should have seen how the saints of God hustled for money just to sit on that bench. During tax season, the Tylers would add two more benches just to accommodate the $2000 club.

The young and poor people in Solid Foundation gave back to the church through hours of hustle and grunt work. They never received money for their tireless work, just trinkets and more promises from the Bible. You would have thought that these people would get tired of hearing about their reward in heaven for doing God's work. Bishop Tyler praised them for bringing souls to Christ, but make no mistake, nothing was more important than the almighty dollar.

Calvin and his father were idolized almost like Gods. The church would be in the middle of a good old Pentecostal service with the organ blaring, drums booming, and people shouting. Then all of sudden you would see the bishop and his confidants gathering in the back of the church. The church would grow silent and then the bishop would make his grand entrance. Everybody had to stand in perfect silence until they sat down. Then the church would break back into a wild hysteria and continue praising God.

The best performance came when Calvin would sneak over to my apartment. He always arrived in a rental car, which he always parked several doors down from my apartment. He would sit outside and call to make sure I was alone. Then he would quickly exit the car and jog to my apartment. The fake mustache, baseball cap, and sunglasses made the good reverend look like a pervert.

Calvin would arrive at my house and immediately pull his pants down looking for sex. He always insisted that we use condoms, which made collecting the sperm easier for me.

Setting up Calvin was like cheating off of a first grader's test. All he wanted from me was the animalistic, no-feelings-attached fuck. He enjoyed putting Linda on a pedestal, but he came to me so that I would do all the things that she wouldn't.

I could hear him apologizing for an inappropriate touch when he was with Linda. "Oh my, I'm so sorry! Did my hand mistakenly touch your hip? Let's pray so that Jesus forgives us."

But when he got to my apartment, all I heard was, "Suck that" and "Give me this, bitch."

Calvin hated any type of intimate touching. All he wanted to do was act on any sexual desires which came to his imagination. Sometimes in church, I would see him staring off into space. Then I would receive a dirty text message from him begging to come over. Sometimes he would exit the pulpit and send a text message showing his penis. If only the good old church folks knew what their beloved son was doing in his free time.

Sneaking back and forth to Solid Foundation was bringing back old memories. I was starting to have fun again and the atmosphere in the overflow room was truly uplifting. Most of the people in the overflow room were God-fearing Christians just looking for a little spiritual push. The church was their outlet for all of the frustration.

If your man was cheating on you, give it to God. If your job was shitty, give it to God. If you had money issues, give it to God.

Any problem in your life could be left with God at the church. And the overflow room became that special place for them at the church. There were no V. I. P or church dignitaries in that room, only poor people searching for a blessing from God. The spirit in that crowded overflow room felt real. If I didn't know the truth, I would have probably convinced myself to give Solid Foundation another chance.

The truth of the matter was that I was on a mission to be paid or destroy Solid Foundation. Calvin and his father owed me, and I was going to get my revenge and reward at the same time.

The first part of my plan was to find the trusted money man and work him for information. I narrowed it down to Deacon Langley and Deacon Berry. Deacon Langley was the same bear of a man who was initially given marching orders to take me to the abortion clinic. His sole objective was to collect the money at the church without any issues. If there were issues with the church's money, he dealt with them quickly. Rumors about Deacon Langley asking people to step outside the sanctuary and roughing them up were just rumors. I never saw him threaten anyone, it was just the way he carried himself. You never wanted to be on the opposite side of him during a money discrepancy. On the other hand, Deacon Berry appeared to be more brains than brawn.

Deacon Marlon Berry was quiet and very reserved when he was around people at church. His mannerisms reminded me of Steve Urkel, but he had the looks of a young Louis Gossett Jr. He had a bright, engaging smile, but he always sounded aloof and disorganized when he spoke. My surveillance of Deacon Berry was like watching paint dry every day for two weeks.

He always left the house at 7:30am and taught at a small community college in Gwinnett County. He finished class at 11:30am and had lunch by himself on campus. The highlight of Deacon Berry's day appeared to be the multiple hours spent at the library just reading and researching things. At 5:30pm, he would return to the confines of his home with his wife, dog, and white picket fence.

His wife was one of the most overbearing nags that you would ever care to encounter. Most people at Solid Foundation went the other way when they saw her coming. She was short and portly with an outdated wig from the 70s. When she talked or laughed, it was always loud and annoying. If there was any gossip floating around the church, she was the cause.

On Sunday mornings, she would eat a huge breakfast at Waffle House and then come to church and belch like an ill-mannered sailor. Deacon Berry would shake his head in disgust and shrink with embarrassment. The bright glimmer of love and happiness in Deacon Berry's eyes had all but gone out. The only thing that kept him sane was the occasional glimpse at his neighbor's daughter in her underwear.

Deacon Berry was rarely seen around the church for the actual service, but when it came time to collect the offering, he was front and center. He would be in the front of the church pointing and directing as his army of deacons collected the money in large buckets. The deacons would exit the sanctuary and line up in a single file line organized by Deacon Langley's and the bishop's security team. The money would be dispensed into five sixty-four-gallon trash cans and wheeled away. Deacon Berry, the money, and the security team would disappear into the bowels of the church for the remainder of the service. This elaborate display of power would be orchestrated by Deacon Berry at each service. I had never seen him not perform it. If Deacon Berry was the blueprint to my plan, then the person who I considered to be my most hated enemy would be the missing piece to my puzzle.

Chapter 11

Kayla's phone seemed like it was ringing every five minutes. She would get on the phone, mutter some legal terminology, and slam the phone back down. I stared at Kayla like she was a strange person from another planet.

Kayla looked at me with mistrust and ask, "What the hell is wrong with you?"

Seeing that expression on Kayla's face made me burst out in laughter because she always knew when I was up to mischief. Kayla and I graduated from college together but our paths in life were totally different. Although I liked working as an Accountant at the W Hotel, it was nothing like the big show. Kayla was working the big show. Kayla Price graduated from Spellman College Summa Cum Laude that June and enrolled at Emory Law School that fall. While I was dealing with Patrick, having babies, and all the other bullshit, she was keeping her eyes on the prize. Everybody, including her parents, thought Kayla was crazy because she wanted to be an entertainment lawyer instead of practicing criminal law. I have to admit that I thought she was crazy too because it's so competitive, and most law firms only bring you aboard if you already have well-established contacts. Kayla was already ten steps ahead of everybody else and their opinions. She started making contacts in the entertainment business by working with unsigned artist pro bono. Several prestigious law firms began to seek her service as an intern because she was literally closing million-dollar deals for basically nothing. When it came time to negotiate her contract with the top law firms, she had all of them by the balls. Kayla came in the door making almost six figures with a top law firm in Los Angeles because of her contacts and savvy business sense. The law firm gave her a car, condo, and *paid off her law school tuition. As Kayla stared at me with mistrust, I smiled and shook my head in disbelief because she was doing the damm thang, and now she was working her magic on Calvin's shiesty ass. Calvin's punk ass had ducked and dodged my demands for long enough, and now I had my dream team in place. I was about to ask Kayla about the latest high profile client she was representing when I heard Sha'quonda stumble out of the bathroom cursing about being hungry.*

Sha'quonda Elise Patterson, or Patrick's baby mama, became the MVP on my team of destruction. Running into Sha'quonda was a chance encounter that occurred while I was spying at Solid Foundation. I arrived late that Sunday, and to my surprise, I was escorted into the sanctuary. My black Farrah Fawcett wig and oversized sunglasses was not the best disguise, but it was enough to keep me unnoticed. I was instructed to quickly sit down because Bishop Tyler Jr. was preparing to come to the pulpit. The church was in the middle of a powerfully moving song about God's greatness. The music was blaring and people were shouting. All of a sudden, there was silence. The entire church stood on their feet in unity and waited quietly for Calvin's entrance. The whole scene looked like a sick movie about programmed robots. Ushers and church nurses surrounded Calvin like a God as he began to walk. No one made any sudden moves or dared to talk as the bishop's court slowly walked to the pulpit. The church was crowded and everyone was clamoring to get a better vantage point. Calvin started speaking and I could just feel all of the hatred starting to melt away. Calvin preached about forgiveness and redemption and how we should strive to understand one another's feelings. The sermon was so good that I felt myself agreeing with his message.

Maybe I had been wrong about Calvin. The church erupted into beautiful choruses of praise. I actually found myself on the brink of walking to the alter when I saw Calvin motion to Deacon Langley. Calvin requested that all heads be bowed for prayer. At first, I bowed my head out of respect for God along with the crowd. Then a heard an irritating country-ass accent from past demons.

I turned around with a, "what the fuck expression" on my face and saw Sha'quonda's country ass. Deacon Langley was leading Sha'quonda toward the back of the church.

I sort of chuckled to myself because Deacon Langley had a grip on Sha'quonda like "Bitch, why yo ass didn't come home last night?"

Wanting to see Deacon Langley beat the shit out of Sha'quonda made me curious. I quickly followed the duo out of the sanctuary just in time to see Deacon Langley standing with Sha'quonda at a private access door. Deacon Langley was having problems with the door's code and Sha'quonda started complaining.

She let out an irritated sigh and nudged him out of the way. "Fo da last time, the code is eight foe foe two."

And with that, I heard the door latch give. Sha'quonda was quickly hustled in the door and Deacon Langley walked back toward the sanctuary cursing. I smiled to myself because I understood how nerve wrecking that bitch could be.

My prying mind started chanting eight foe foe two over and over again. And before I knew it, I was punching the numbers into the door. I heard the latch pop, and I quickly walked inside.

The area behind the door looked nothing like the beautiful splendor of the sanctuary. I could still her muffled music blaring and people shouting overhead as I walked down a long, dimly lit corridor. There were rooms on both sides of the hall without doors.

I almost made it to the end of the corridor when I heard Sha'quonda say, "You like dat don't you."

I heard a slight moan and then a familiar voice. I dropped to one knee and peered into the dimly lit room. I saw Calvin sitting in a large office chair slumped sideways. I looked closer into the room, and I saw Sha'quonda nude on her knees. She was giving Calvin some of the best head that he had ever had.

Calvin's eyes were closed and his body was tense like he was riding a rollercoaster. I thought I was pretty good at oral sex until I saw Sha'quonda. The way she twisted her head back and forth as if she enjoyed what she was doing. I heard Calvin shriek as Sha'quonda nibbled at the tip his penis, causing him to jerk uncontrollably. Calvin held on as long as humanly possible, and then I saw his body go limp. He remained motionless in the chair as Sha'quonda continued to tug at his penis with her lips.

Calvin suddenly launched the chair backwards as if trying to escape and screamed, "Stop! Stop! Shit! Damn, girl, you trying to kill me?"

A look of satisfaction came across Sha'quonda's face as she wiped her mouth and walked to the sink. She turned the water on and spit Calvin's semen down the drain.

Calvin glared at Sha'quonda's naked butt and smiled as he began to talk. "Sha'quonda, would it be okay if I came over later."

Sha'quonda smiled at Calvin as if she were taking her first school picture. It was almost like she thrived off being the church tramp. She was excited that she was sucking the bishop's penis while the choir was singing.

Sha'quonda bent over and grabbed her ankles and asked, "Is this what you want later tonight?"

Calvin's face broke out into a wide grin as he marveled at what he was making Sha'quonda do. He was pretending to beg for more sexual goodies when Sha'quonda suddenly got educated.

"You know Calvin, I really enjoy pleasing you, but I just can't keep getting by with $500 here and there. I got all this shit going on like rent and daycare, and it's just not enough."

Calvin started talking in his happy, I-been-sucked-and-fucked voice. "How much do you need, baby?"

Sha'quonda responded, "Well to be honest, I need at least $1000 more."

Calvin glared at Sha'quonda suspiciously and then smiled at her.

203

I had seen that look on the face of Calvin's father when he gave me the $30,000. It was a look of arrogance mixed with disgust. In his mind, no woman was worth helping, but he enjoyed making them into charity cases.

I quickly walked back down the long corridor and exited the church shaking my head in disbelief. I thought to myself, "At least Sha'quonda was getting a little money from Calvin's punk ass. All I got from him was a ride to the free clinic."

And just like that, a light went on in my head. The best way to get what I wanted was to use Calvin's weakness to destroy him.

My initial plan to get just a few thousand dollars was out the window. The more surveillance I did, the more I believed more money was at stake.

The Tylers' trusted money man always made the church's money deposits on Monday morning. Who would have thought that the geekish-looking man driving in a 2006 Chevy Malibu was depositing at least $60,000 a week? Deacon Berry was the perfect man for the job. He brought no attention to himself and he kept his demons to a minimum. Finding out what made Deacon Berry tick took a while, but eventually I figured it out. His tendency to be voyeuristic was his Achilles heel.

Deacon Berry enjoyed watching people during their most intimate moments. Not only did he enjoy watching his neighbor's daughter get undressed, but he also enjoyed watching people having sex. Deacon Berry's favorite pastime was driving to prostitution areas in Atlanta and watching tricks get satisfied. It was almost like he was addicted to the thrill of it. He would sit for hours waiting for the right prostitute and the right john to meet. There were videos of pro athletes, government officials, and regular everyday Joes on Deacon Berry's cell phone. He probably could have made a nice piece of change if he had chosen to blackmail people. But the movie collection was not for sale. It was for his private viewing.

I knew that if I could catch him in a just by chance meet, I could get what I needed.

My first chance meeting with the deacon didn't go so well. I followed him while he was making a drop and it spooked him. His alerts went up and he lost me in no time flat. I needed a more subtle approach so that I would not scare him. A month later, I found it.

The annual Praise for Christ Conference was the place that I drew first blood from the Tylers. The conference was set up at a place where all the local churches came together to celebrate the greatness of Christ. In actuality, it only benefited the bishops and pastors invited. The four-day event was attended by thousands of people, and even better it brought in millions of dollars. Deacon Berry was always present when it pertained to the Tylers' money, so his attendance would have been no surprise.

The shock occurred when the W Hotel in Midtown was announced as the meeting place. Imagine an opportunity like this dropping in my lap. My security clearance with the W Hotel allowed me to quickly find his name in the system. I convinced the reservations manager to give the deacon his rooms for the weekend free as part of a promotion. I was taking a big chance hoping it would pay off, and it did. Deacon Berry accepted the room and never told his wife. By the time Deacon Berry had checked in and was settling in for the night, I was already waiting in the adjoined room.

As Sun Tzu stated, "Know your enemy."

I knew my enemy like the back of my hand, so I waited for the perfect time to attack. I listened as Deacon Berry ordered dinner and I pulled out a bottle of cheap liquor. I unlatched the adjoining doors and peeked through the crack. The deacon was completely nude and watching a porno movie. He was stroking himself and moaning as his hand became an imaginary vagina. I left the door cracked between our rooms, so if Deacon Berry opened his door, he could see into my room. The plan worked beautifully.

I pretended to be singing to the music of my iPod and he quietly cracked his door and began to watch me. I slowly undressed and lay on my bed in the buff singing. I saw the door move as if the deacon was opening my door so that he could get a better view. I quickly turned around and looked at the door, just as Deacon Berry was pulling his hand back. I acted like I had been startled and pulled my headphones off. Deacon Berry started apologizing quickly as he tried to close his door.

I walked over to the adjoining door and quickly gained his trust by engaging in a conversation as I put a robe on. "I'm sorry sir, but I had no idea anyone had checked into your room."

I offered him a drink and he quickly accepted. We both unlocked the adjoining door chains and Deacon Berry cautiously entered the room. Deacon Berry seemed detached as I continued the conversation about this being the first time my parents had allowed me to stay in a hotel by myself. The deacon asked if my parents would be coming back tonight, and I said no. Deacon Berry must have had a vision of fucking a young girl because I could see his crotch area swell up. I caught Deacon Berry off guard by switching the conversation to sex. I giggled like a silly school girl and asked him why his dick was on hard.

The deacon, embarrassed by the question, put his hand over it and laughed. I giggled again and shyly asked if he would show it to me. The deacon responded that he would show me his if I showed mine first. Again, I giggled and then slowly opened my legs so that he could see the smooth, brown skin around my vagina. The deacon quickly unzipped his pants exposing his hard, uncircumcised penis. I held in the laughter played like a silly school girl, asking if I could touch it.

The deacon quickly took off his clothes and allowed me to fondle and play with it. He trembled with anticipation as I gently caressed it, and I made silly school girl comments like, "Wow, I've never seen anything as big as this."

The pride in Deacon Berry made him ask if I wanted to put it in my mouth. Acting like I was nervous about the question, I told him that I had never given a blow job before. Deacons Berry's penis started leaking fluid as he asked me to try it with him.

 Again, I acted hesitant as I kneeled in front of him and said, "Don't hate me if I do it wrong."

Acting like a wide-eyed girl eager to learn, I gently massaged it and placed it in my mouth. Deacon Berry appeared to be very nervous because it was over before he got started. Poor Deacon Berry slowly sat down on the bed and apologized from embarrassment.

 I guess he was so excited that somebody else was touching him that he was caught off guard. I rubbed his leg and promised to fulfill all of his dreams later.

I could tell he had never been in this situation before. He looked uncomfortable, not knowing what to say or do next.

I smiled at him and asked if he would mind getting me some ice, and he quickly grabbed the bucket and headed for the door.

Just as he was about to leave, he said, "You know, I had a lot of fun tonight, and I wouldn't mind getting together with you some other time."

I cut him off mid-sentence and asked, "How would you like to grab breakfast in the morning?" knowing full-well that the answer would be no.

He nervously scanned the room to try to find the right response. "Well, I uh. . . have a lot of business to take care off in the morning."

I quickly responded, "Doing what? What time will you be done? Who are you going with?

I could see the deacon's mind spinning faster and faster as he wondered why I was asking so many questions.

He glared at me and responded in an agitated voice, "Look, I'm not really into a lot of questions and personal talk. I enjoyed what we did, but I have to be perfectly honest with you about any further interaction. We may have to hold off."

My face showed disappointment, but I was doing summersaults inside. I had to throw Deacon Berry a curve ball to keep him discombobulated. Having any future interaction with him would derail the whole plan. I needed everything to happen tonight, right now, and as soon as possible.

The deacon asked if I still wanted some ice and I rolled my eyes and responded as if I hated him. "Yes, and if it's not asking too much, could you get me something adult to drink from the bar downstairs? After all I'm only eighteen, and certain people don't believe I'm grown yet."

The deacon looked at me and shook his head almost as if he were saying, "What the fuck have I gotten myself into?"

Deacon Berry smiled at me and agreed to get me a drink. As he spoke in an appeasing manner. "I will gladly get you a mixed drink. Would a strawberry daiquiri be okay?"

I responded as if I were disgusted. "Strawberry daiquiri? Man, what are you talking about? Can you please get me something stronger, like a sour apple ciroc? Damn!"

The deacon glanced back at me as if he were shocked and walked at the door. He was probably thinking to himself, "This bitch is an alcoholic, first-class psycho. Man I have to hurry up and get out of this situation."

I opened the door just as the deacon was getting on the elevator and screamed at the top of my lungs, "And don't forget the ice!"

The deacon looked embarrassed as he hung his head low and boarded the elevator.

As soon as the elevator started descending, I ran to Deacon Berry's room. My plan would have totally been destroyed if Berry had used the in-room safe, but he didn't. As soon as I entered the room, I saw his leather brief case open on the table. I carefully searched the case and found a brown bank deposit bag. The bag was closed and marked with the number 80. I carefully opened the brown bag and it was loaded with stacks of hundred-, twenty-, and ten-dollar bills.

The everyday untrained hood rat would have only seen the money and taken that. On the other hand, I saw something far more important. As soon as I moved the deposit bag, I saw an electronic tablet. I turned the tablet on and quickly glanced at the files. I saw files filed with porno and hundreds of videos of him watching people. I scanned further and eventually found the church's account ledger with bank security codes. I ran to my room and retrieved my external hard drive and quickly downloaded the information.

I placed everything back in position and quickly exited his room. By the time the deacon returned, I was deep in thought. What I was doing was beyond shady. The stuff I was doing landed people in prison for years. Was getting revenge really worth everything I was doing?

I heard a soft tap at the door and I responded, "Who is it?"

Deacon Berry responded softly, "It's me. Open the door."

I quickly got back into character and opened the door with an attitude. He handed me a mixed drink and I took a long sip. Deacon Berry looked as if he wanted to comment, but he remained silent. I walked over to the bed and pulled the covers over my head.

Deacon Berry was standing near the door that connected our rooms. He was probably looking for an easy way out, but he didn't want to seem tacky.

Marlon broke the silence by asking me, "Are you okay? Is there something I can do for you?"

I uncovered my face and rudely interrupted him by saying, "Can you please leave? I don't think we have any thing else to talk about. I got it! You don't think I'm mature enough to handle a relationship with you, so let's just end it now."

Marlon placed his face in both hands and shook his head as he responded, "Relationship, what are you talking about?"

He wanted to explore the situation further but decided just too leave it alone.

He broke the awkward silence in the room by speaking. "You know what? I can't do this. I'm sorry that I hurt you, but I thought it was understood that this was just something casual. I would have avoided this situation if I had known you were looking for something else."

I glared at Marlon and responded, "That's funny, you didn't say that when you had your dick in my mouth."

Marlon shook his head as if frustrated with the conversation. I purposefully made the conversation petty.

He was probably thinking, "I'm having a conversation with a certified nut."

Marlon turned to walk away and I gave him parting comments. "Please pull my door up and lock it, and please don't ever speak to me again. Thank you."

Marlon tried to take the higher ground with his response, "I'm sorry you feel that way, and again, I apologize for hurting you."

I walked over to the adjoining door and locked it as he was locking his side. I stood quietly by the door and held my breath, hoping that nothing seemed out of place. I listened until I heard Marlon pick up the phone and mumble something. I quickly manufactured a story in my head just in case something went wrong. I would accuse the deacon of being a peeping Tom, and demand that the authorities search his tablet and phone.

I prepared for the worst, but it never came. Deacon Berry had notified the hotel that he was checking out. Ten minutes later, I heard movement in the next room as a bell hop helped him with his bags. Marlon was probably scared shitless. He never thought that a quickie would end up being a meeting with a psycho. I peered through my peep hole as Marlon anxiously waited for the elevator to come. When the elevator finally came, I heard him release a loud sigh of relief. I returned to my bed and sat thinking about my perfect plan.

I glanced at my hard drive and decided that my curiosity was too much. I had to know exactly what I was dealing with, so I opened the ledger on my laptop. My mouth almost dropped to the floor as I scrolled down the screen. Not only was the church bringing in almost $90,000 a week in tithes and offerings, but it also had side deals with financial and mortgage firms. Calvin and his father were using church members' homes as collateral to secure loans from financial firms. They had deals with charity organizations in poor countries. Ninety-nine percent of the funds went to the church while these organizations got one percent. Would an organization really complain if they got one percent of ten million dollars?

The church was making so much money in so many different ways that Deacon Berry's amounts and descriptions were color-coded. And there I was sitting with the master code in my hand.

Things were going to start moving faster, and I needed to have my game plan ready. All of the work I had done would have been worthless if I couldn't get Sha'quonda. She was so important because of her information. There was no way I could go into a hostile situation and bluff. I needed an ace in my hand, and she was it.

Chapter 12

I could tell that Kayla was a little suspicious about me being with Sha'quonda. Sha'quonda's belly was sticking out to the point that she was starting to waddle from her six-month pregnancy, and my makeshift baby bump looked irregular in comparison. I couldn't tell if Kayla was looking at me out of anger or if she was starting to figure things out. Kayla whispered to me, "We need to talk," and I simply smiled at Kayla and encouraged her to wait until after room service left.

The first time I attempted to make contact with Sha'quonda was a mistake. She was returning from her usual hoe spot in the church basement when I spoke to her as pleasantly as possible. "Hey girl, how are you doing?"

Sha'quonda glanced in my direction and rolled her eyes as she responded, "Whatever."

The only thing I could do was shake my head and laugh as we passed each other. I knew our history would probably be a problem, but I had to keep trying. There was no telling how much information Sha'quonda had on Calvin.

The next Sunday I saw Sha'quonda, I approached her and spoke again. "Sha'quonda, look! I know me and you are not the best of friends, but we have a lot in common. We both did a lot of things to hurt each other in the past. But let's just leave it were it's at, in the past."

Sha'quonda paused and looked at me suspiciously as she responded, "I agree, I never had anything against you. You were the one who was pressing the issue about Patrick. I already knew he was a dog. He was screwing everything that moved, but you didn't want to see it."

I smiled and shook my head in agreement, "You're right! What can I say? I was young and dumb. He had my mind so screwed up that I couldn't see any wrong in him."

Sha'quonda laughed and extended her arms to hug me and said, "Girl, I forgive you. He had my dumb ass the same way."

We both laughed and then she asked, "What are you doing here?"

I wanted to tell her that I was on a mission to destroy the motherfucker whose dick she sucked, but it would have probably came out wrong.

I responded, "Well, I just started dating this guy, and a friend told me he attends this church. I don't know why she insisted that I come see him at church."

I could see the gears churning in her head as she contemplated asking me his name.

In my mind I was screaming, "Dumb bitch ask, dumb bitch ask."

There was an uneasy silence and finally Sha'quonda said, "Do you mind if I ask who he is?"

I turned toward her and responded in the clearest voice I could muster, "Calvin Tyler Jr."

She didn't have to know all the details, but I wanted her to know that Calvin and I had fucked.

Sha'quonda stepped backed and glared at me almost as if she were saying, "I know this bitch didn't say what I thought she said."

She placed her hands on her hip, and I braced for that old ghetto Sha'quonda. I could just imagine her going crazy, screaming and hollering. Security getting involved and my getting exposed. I was glad that it was the total opposite.

She scratched her forehead and repeated what I had just said. "Did you say Calvin Tyler, the bishop's son?"

I shook my head yes and she quickly grabbed my hand and led me out of the church.

As soon as we were clear of the church, she spun around and started talking. "We need to talk."

I played stupid and stared into her eyes as if confused.

Sha'quonda grabbed my hand and spoke. "Angela, this man is foul. He supposed to be engaged, but he worse than Patrick."

I stared at Sha'quonda and responded, "How so?"

She glanced back at the church to make sure no one was coming and then continued, "Don't be mad or anything, but I've been fooling around with him for almost four months."

She stared at me waiting for a reaction, but I just shook my head and said, "Hmm, that's interesting."

I took my hand away from Sha'quonda and folded my arms.

She quickly asked, "Are you angry?"

I shook my head no and responded, "Girl, I'm not angry at you, I know these trifling men can be dogs. I'm just glad you were woman enough to let me know."

Sha'quonda sighed as if weight had been lifted off her. She looked almost ashamed as she gave me detail after detail about the Tylers, Linda, and Solid Foundation. The poor girl looked as if she were purging herself of something evil. I thought about my time I had spent at Central State Hospital. What if I had had somebody to talk to? Instead of bottling all that anger and resentment inside, what if I had just let it out? Would I still have ended up in a mental hospital?

That day was the start of something special between Sha'quonda and me. Whether I liked it or not, Sha'quonda and I were of the same kindred spirit. Our situations were similar, our kids were brother and sister, and we fell for the same old sorry-ass men. As she continued to talk, my eyes drifted slowly down her body to her stomach. It was that moment that my plan was finalized. That was the day that I decided that Sha'quonda would be my human vessel. Calvin's frozen sperm inside Sha'quonda was more valuable than those little trinkets of information she had. A big goofy smile crossed my face as my plan became clearer.

A look of concern crossed Sha'quonda's face as she spoke. "What's wrong with you? Why are you looking at me all crazy?"

My head slowly moved from side to side as I responded, "Nothing, I just can't believe all of this stuff that your telling me."

Sha'quonda shook her head and responded, "Yep! It's true, girl. Everything I just said."

I stared at Sha'quonda with an amazed look on my face and wondered if she even knew what I had planned for her.

Sha'quonda and I started talking over the phone daily and soon became fast friends. Two people could have never been more opposites of each other. I was college-educated and she dropped out of high school. I was taught to work hard for what I wanted and she was content with living off the state. Sha'quonda's idea of revenge was slicing tires or putting sugar in gas tanks. My idea for revenge was more complex and needed more planning. That's why I found it necessary to bring Sha'quonda on board gradually. I had to start with what she knew best—cash money.

Three weeks after we had made contact, I started laying the seeds for deceit. I asked Sha'quonda as politely as possible how long she had been involved with Calvin. Sha'quonda was hesitant at first, but then she revealed that she had been seeing Calvin off and on for almost a year.

She stared off into the distance before continuing her story. "I first met Calvin at the library. I was attending GED class and he was a volunteer teacher. I thought it was so sweet that he was volunteering his time. The first time I saw those big, brown eyes, it was over. I started doing everything I could do to seduce him. I have to give it to him, he held strong. That was until I started asking him for extra help after class. The after-class tutoring sessions led to innocent flirting. I knew he wanted more when I invited him over to my place and he accepted. As soon as he came in my apartment, he started talking about how he was engaged. At the time, I really didn't care, because I felt like he wouldn't have been at my place if he was getting what he needed at home. It really didn't take much convincing. As long as I was comfortable with being a side chick, he was happy."

Sha'quonda started bragging about getting her $1000 monthly stiffen.

I shook my head and blurted out, "You do know that you can get more money, right?"

Sha'quonda looked as if she were hurt by my comment and then tried to save face by retracting. "I know I can get more money out of him because he's offered it. I just didn't want to mess up a good thing, plus he told me that he was falling in love with me."

I glanced at her with that "Bitch, please!" look on my face and she quickly changed the subject.

I left Sha'quonda alone that day, but was back at it a few days later. I knew I had to keep the pressure on her to get the best results. Sha'quonda and I were having our weekly brunch when I casually brought up the subject again.

"Sha'quonda, can I be honest about something?"

The tone of my voice appeared to scare her, but she shook her head yes.

"What if I told you that Calvin paid his other side chicks more money?"

A look of disbelief came across the face of Sha'quonda as she inquired who the other person was. I told Sha'quonda about the abortion, which angered her even more because she also revealed that she had had an abortion. What angered her more was the fact that Calvin's father had only given her $400. I could see Sha'quonda was angry almost to the point that she wanted to confront Calvin. I calmed her down and offered to help her get even.

I assured Sha'quonda that he would pay for everything that he did, but we needed to play our cards right.

The next few days were spent convincing Sha'quonda that being on board with my plan equaled benefits. The church's account numbers and Deacon Berry's security codes gave me unlimited access to money. I connected a dummy account to Bishop Tyler's accounts and started moving small increments of money over. If the bishop got paid, so did Sha'quonda. I was never greedy when I withdrew cash, but I made sure Sha'quonda was comfortable. She was the most important cog in the wheel, and I had to get her accustomed to living the good life.

I was shocked at how easily Sha'quonda adapted to a life of not needing and only wanting. Sha'quonda went from a $1,000 a month Reebok bandit to a $10,000 a month Dolce & Gabbana bitch. She quit wasting her time at the value mall and started shopping at Phillips Mall. She gave up her diet of Ramen noodles and started dinning out. After three months and $30,000 dollars worth of clothes, she decided that she wanted a new home. Knowing Sha'quonda, she probably was eyeing a brand new SUV.

Imagine her parking an $80,000 Range Rover in front of a $350-monthly apartment. She couldn't care less about a house in a better community. Her little ghetto ass was perfectly content living in Zone 3. All she wanted was to be ghetto fabulous in those South West Atlanta projects. Thirty-thousand dollars in clothes, a Range Rover, and some jewelry was the extent of her dreams.

Sha'quonda's greed was foolish, but this is what I wanted. I wanted her ill-advised dreams to be within reach so that I could reprogram her thinking. I wanted Sha'quonda hungry for more money or prepared to be cut off. As Sha'quonda sat in front of me running her game, I pulled out my computer. I slowly inserted the hard drive and shook my head. I was half listening to what Sha'quonda's was saying, so I interrupted her and motioned for her to sit beside me.

I pointed at the computer screen, but she continued blabbering on about needing more money. Once again, I pointed at the screen, and finally, she paid attention. The numbers tumbled down the page like an out-of-control waterfall ending with a grand total of 18. 4 million dollars. I looked in Sha'quonda's direction and saw her counting on her fingers. Her little pea brain was probably trying to calculate how many pairs of Jimmy Choos she could buy.

After getting a reasonable assessment of what she was seeing, she opened her mouth and spoke. "Can you withdraw around $100,000 without them knowing? I would be cool with that."

I looked at Sha'quonda in amazement and laughed, "Sha'quonda, that's 18. 4 million dollars, and you talking about just getting enough for a few months."

Sha'quonda stared blankly at me as if she was confused. I pulled her chair closer to me and started talking. "When you see 18. 4 million dollars, you start plotting on how you can be set for life. I'm tired of getting a little change here and there, I want to crack the piggy bank open."

Sha'quonda started laughing as if she had heard a joke, and then she spoke. "Angela, are you serious? We are getting 10,000 dollars a month, and you want to screw that up? I think your being a bit greedy."

I started getting angry with Sha'quonda because she was not seeing the big picture. The Tylers were worth 18 million dollars apiece, and she was still trying to hold onto her shoe money. Sha'quonda was still giggling and I became annoyed. I angrily kicked her chair and glared at her. I wanted this bitch to focus, and she was acting like this was a joke. I felt like a desperate pimp at the bus station talking to a silly runaway girl. I had to somehow convince Sha'quonda that I was her only life line.

I highlighted Calvin's name to show Sha'quonda how much money was being transferred to his personal account weekly.

When $180,000 popped on the screen, I glanced at Sha'quonda and asked in a sarcastic voice, "Can you please tell me again how much money he was giving you before I came along"

I could tell that Sha'quonda felt a little used because she whispered back, "One thousand dollars a month."

Still annoyed at Sha'quonda, I started pressuring her to see things my way. "This motherfucker built a 1. 5 million dollar home for a woman that he's never screwed. And here you are being used weekly for a measly $1,000 a month. You could probably make more money at UPS. At least you would have benefits."

I could tell I was hurting Sha'quonda's feelings, but I was not finished. I wanted her to understand that her options were now limited.

I continued to speak to Sha'quonda in a scolding voice. "I'm going to be really real with you. I put my neck on the line for you. I wanted you to have better because I know how Calvin treats people. I gave you $30,000, half of which was mine."

Sha'quonda's forehead wrinkled up as if to say, "What the hell are you talking about?"

I repeated what I said with emphasis, "That's right, half of that belongs to me. I gave you my $15, 000 because I had a bigger plan. Now here you are thinking about living like this for life. I hate to bust your bubble, but I definitely didn't go through all this to be owed $15,000 by you."

Sha'quonda nervously looked around as my voice became louder and more deliberate. "Let me tell you like this. If you don't want to move forward, I can pull the plug now. That $15,000 that you owe me can be your severance pay."

The poor girl just sat looking at me as if I had killed her favorite puppy. Sha'quonda quietly evaluated her options. That old saying about the "eyes being the window to the soul" could not have been truer that day. Sha'quonda was familiar with being screwed over, but this was catastrophic. The past three months had been full of exciting new things for her, and now she was on the verge of losing it all.

I silently stared at Sha'quonda until she felt uneasy and asked me what I was thinking. I responded in a serious sisterly tone, "You ever thought about getting pregnant again."

Sha'quonda stared back at me as if I had said something unreal. I repeated my question in a way that left her no option and appealed to her greed. "How would you feel about getting pregnant again if I could assure you that it was worth six figures?"

Sha'quonda looked hesitant and was about to answer when I chimed in again to sweeten the pot.

"Karin Stanford fucked a baby out of Jessie Jackson and got $4,000 a month in child support and a $365,000 home. What do you think nine million dollars is equal to in child support? Even better, how much money do you think an 18. 9-million-dollar business would pay to keep you silent?"

I could see that Sha'quonda was apprehensive, but the money made her want to learn more. I laid out my entire plan to her as if I were pitching and ad to a Fortune 500 company. After I finished laying out my plan, I still felt like she was sitting on the fence. I needed something in a hurry that would push her over the edge. That opportunity would come two weeks later while I was at work.

I was going about my daily tasks when I saw Calvin in full disguise. He was looking around nervously as he headed toward the front desk. The front desk attendant smiled at Calvin and gave him a room key to 1102. Calvin walked to the elevator and stood as if waiting for someone. Two minutes later, I saw Edna approach Calvin and speak. Edna Smalls was a maid who gave the guest turndown service. Basically, she pulled the bed linen at night, and placed chocolate candy on the pillow. Calvin and Edna may have had the rest of the staff fooled, but I knew. As soon as Calvin saw Edna, I saw it in his eyes. I called it the Tyler glance. It was a look of lust mixed with guilt. Calvin smiled back at her and quickly boarded the elevator.

Edna nervously looked around and boarded the next elevator. I watched as the elevator slowly ascended and stopped on Calvin's floor. I shook my head in disbelief and walked toward the front desk. Edna's reputation as an easy-come-easy-go girl was only proceeded by her looks. Edna had a body like a video girl and a face like Whoopi Goldberg.

The men around the hotel always joked about having a brown bag handy just in case she gave them some. Edna was happy with her role as a "clean up women" as long as she got paid. The rumors about her screwing everyone from the Assistant General Manger down to the Security Supervisor were probably true. Edna didn't care who talked about her as long as she got paid. If sucking a security guard's dick got her ugly ass money, she was on all fours. Sha'quonda knew of her reputation because they were from the same area of Atlanta. But she definitely didn't know that Calvin was screwing her. I knew this would rattle Sha'quonda, but I was unsure of just how bad.

I approached the front desk attendant and asked, "Girl, who was that man that just checked in? Oh my God, he was fine."

The attendant laughed and replied, "That's Daniel Price, but he's married. He always meets up with his wife this time of the day. They come around every two weeks to get it in. Personally I think it's cute, two people keeping the romance alive in their marriage. It's just funny that I've never seen him with his wife"

I smiled at the attendant and shook my head thinking, "And you never will."

I walked toward the entrance door and immediately dialed Sha'quonda's number and screamed into the receiver, "Sha'quonda, you'll never believe who I just saw!"

Sha'quonda responded as if she were bored, "Girl, who? I'm trying to get some sleep."

I eagerly responded, "Calvin."

There was a short period of silence and then I heard Sha'quonda say, "Stop lying."

I quickly shouted back, "That's right! Calvin Tyler. And he's with your girl Edna from down your way."

I heard the phone loudly shift from one hand to the next as Sha'quonda adjusted it to hear better. "What did you just say?"

I placed my hand on the receiver and tried not to laugh. Once I got my breath back, I continued, "Edna. Edna Smalls. I just saw your girl get off on his floor."

Sha'quonda was already halfway out the door as she responded, "Hold up. Keep the bitch there. I'm on my way."

I could hardly contain my joy as I heard the phone line go dead.

This was exactly what I wanted. I wanted that old, mad-at-the-world Sha'quonda. I was getting sick of the dizzy, scared-to-make-a-decision Sha'quonda. I wanted her mad so that she would be willing to go all out and destroy Calvin.

Sha'quonda came through the front door of the W Hotel puffing mad. She was cursing at the Midtown traffic and she was angry because she was checking on a man. The thing about ghetto girls is they know their men cheat; they just don't want it to be with someone they know.

I spoke to Sha'quonda and she mumbled back, "Yeah, yeah, so where that bitch at?"

I turned and walked toward the elevator and smiled. Sha'quonda was so mad that I could hear her discussing options on who to hurt first. We exited the elevator and I pointed toward room 1102. That was all Sha'quonda needed. The rest was ghetto autopilot as she bolted toward the door and started banging and screaming, "Calvin! Calvin! Get your bitch ass out here."

I turned and quickly walked toward the stairs as Sha'quonda continued to scream obscenities and bang on the door. I wanted her mad, but I didn't want to lose my job because of her. I quickly opened the door to stairway just as guest doors started to open.

I walked to the eighth floor and entered the elevator. As I neared my office, I saw hotel security staff rushing to the elevator. I later overheard two of my coworkers say that Sha'quonda was escorted out of the hotel and Edna was suspended. What was even more hilarious about the situation was what Calvin told security. Calvin pulled the Jesus card by telling security that Edna was in his room for prayer and that he did not know who Sha'quonda was.

Later when I arrived home, I saw Sha'quonda waiting outside my apartment with a big grin on her face.

"I'm glad you called me about that bitch. I was just waiting for the right time to get in her ass."

Sha'quonda told me that Edna had screwed Patrick in a nightclub bathroom while she was pregnant with Patrick's baby. Patrick, Sha'quonda, and Edna went to the same high school and grew up in the same neighborhood, so they were always talking to or screwing each other one way or the other.

Sha'quonda continued to talk. "I can't believe he was screwing that tramp. Do you know that motherfucker ran out of the hotel with a bathrobe on looking like a pervert?"

We both laughed. I could just imagine how ridiculous he looked running out of a five-star hotel in a bathrobe with a crazy woman chasing him. Sha'qounda was smiling, but I could see the anger building inside of her.

I felt sorry for Sha'quonda because I probably destroyed any feelings that she had for him. I never wanted to hurt Sha'quonda's feelings that way, but it was necessary. No matter how hard I tried to convince Sha'qounda that Calvin was foul, she had to see it for herself. She may have wanted to believe that Calvin still cared, but my plans had no room for doubts. I needed Sha'qounda focused on destruction like me, and that was the only way to get it done.

I turned toward Sha'quonda and asked, "So what are you going to do?"

There was a short pause, and then I saw a deceitful grin creep across her face as she opened her mouth to speak.

"You know what? Let's take this motherfucker for everything he got."

I held my head back and breathed a sigh of relief. That was what I had been waiting for. I wanted her angry enough to do anything, and the time had finally come. People could have said that Sha'qounda was just a pawn in my sick, twisted game against Calvin. Deep down, I probably would have to agree with them. Sha'quonda trusted me totally, which she probably should have never done. I may have smiled in her face and told her that I cared. The reality was that she was just a means to an end. My motivation to befriend Sha'quonda was to get my revenge on Calvin and his father, not have a BFF at the end of the day.

My plan was multilayered and complex, and at times I was making it up as I went. I found the right puppet for my show. Now it was time to accomplish my goal.

Chapter 13

I have to give it to Calvin because he had been a good boy. The final few weeks leading up to his wedding had been hard for gaining access to him. No matter how many times Sha'quonda texted him, he ignored them. I could tell that Sha'quonda was getting frustrated, but I knew we had to be persistent. No matter how many times Calvin said no, it was just a matter of time before he broke.

I called Sha'quonda a couple of weeks later to find out if she had called him. I could tell she was back to her lazy role when she spoke. "For what? Why should I keep calling and texting him? It's obvious that he's trying to be faithful."

This was not what I wanted to hear from my star player. She was about to give up and it was my job to coach her up. We agreed to meet early on Sunday and try to make contact with Calvin. My plans were to catch Calvin before church.

I handed Sha'quonda my phone and encouraged her to call him.

"Come on, girl! Call him one last time from a different number."

She rolled her eyes at me and loudly banged her fingers against the phone.

The phone rang a couple of times and then she heard a familiar voice. "Hello."

Sha'qounda's facial expression went from upset to cheesy as she started talking. "Hey baby, how are you doing?"

I could hear Calvin sigh loudly as if irritated as he responded, "Yeah, how you doing? Whas' up, what's up with all these phone games? You don't have anything else to do?" I looked at Sha'quonda as she turned into a love sick puppy begging for affection. "I'm sorry for calling you like this, but it's just I miss you so much. I know I was wrong for coming at you crazy at the hotel, but I was hurt when I saw you with Edna."

Now either Sha'quonda was the best actor in the world or I could have sworn that that bitch was about to cry as she continued to talk.

"I can't understand how you can just hurt a person's feelings who you claim to love. Boo, you hurt me every way possible, and I still gave you everything. Can't we just get together and talk about it?"

Listening at all that "I love you boo boo" shit was annoying the hell out of me.

Calvin responded by cutting Sah'qounda's whining short. "Well look, I'm sorry you feeling some type of way about this, but I really got to go. I got a lot of things that I got to get done before church, so I'll call you later."

The phone went dead, and Sha'quonda stared at the phone as if shocked he had hung up.

I glared at Sha'quonda and slowly spoke. "What the fuck... are you doing?"

She glanced back at me as if not understanding, so I tore into her like a disgusted pimp.

"Aint nobody trying to hear that oh baby, baby bullshit. We need this nigga to be at your door with his tongue hanging out. Your stupid ass is sounding like a bride on the eve of her wedding. This motherfucker does not give a shit about you. He has a hard penis and that's all you need to know. Now get back on the phone and get his ass over here."

The expression on Sha'quonda's face was like she bit into a ghost pepper as she angrily dialed Calvin's number.

Calvin answered the phone with frustration in his voice. "Sha'quonda, what the fuck do you want? I just told you I'm busy."

Calvin was about to blow her off again until Sha'quonda interrupted him and said, "I need you to come fuck the shit out of me."

Calvin screamed back at Sha'quonda angrily as he stammered to find the words to say. "I didn't hear you. What did you just say? I didn't hear, I didn't hear what you just said, because you were talking low. Don't be afraid, say what you just said."

Sha'quonda repeated what she said, and it was so raw that even I blushed. "Motherfucker, you heard what I said. You need to stop playing and come get some of this hot pussy. All you do is sit over that bitch's house and kiss and rub her arms. Then you go home mad and frustrated because your dick is still on hard. You can have all the pussy you want right now if you come to my house. Why don't you stop acting like a pussy-whipped bitch and do what makes you happy?"

Calvin responded in a sarcastic manner. "Why are you talking all crazy at 7:00 in the morning? I mean, you must really miss good dick, because you calling me like you hurting for it."

I was proud of Sha'quonda because she stayed in character with her response. "You right, I do miss good dick. So why don't you come over and show me what I need. Unless your daddy won't allow you to get it up no more."

Calvin responded with cynical laughter and then his voice got serious."Oh, okay, so that's how you feel, huh? You're really talking a lot of shit for some bitch that's hard up for some sex. I'll tell you what I'm going to do. I'm going to slide through and show you what you've been missing."

I didn't know if Sha'quonda was still in character or if she really meant what she was saying. She responded with the same fire and piss that he had. "Yeah right, motherfucker! Whatever! Say it while you driving, bitch."

And with that, she ended the conversation with an abrupt hang up.

I stared at Sha'quonda and then at the phone. She was still mumbling obscenities and I was praying that Calvin would call back.

Sha'quonda's phone buzzed once and she glanced at her incoming messages.

She immediately started laughing as she handed me the phone and said, "Look what this silly motherfucker wrote."

I scrolled through the message and it read, "Look bitch! Don't be hanging up on me like you running shit. You the one calling me for sex, cause bitch I gets mine. I can't wait to show you why I'm not to be screwed with."

I handed the phone back to Sha'quonda and she was still laughing hysterically. But I took the message seriously. Calvin was just like his father. He hated to be showed up. Calvin's pride would not allow Sha'qounda to get away with insulting him. He had a very charming and charismatic personality. But he could also be very mean and vindictive if you angered him. I remembered one time when I was teasing him about being afraid of a rollercoaster.

We were standing in the line waiting, and I playfully said, "What would your daddy think if he saw your punk ass shivering at the sight of a rollercoaster?"

Calvin glared at me and then smiled as if to say, "Okay, I'll show you!"

We boarded the rollercoaster and I quickly forgot about our conversation. As soon as we reached the top of the first hill, he tossed my purse over the side of the rollercoaster.

I looked at Calvin in shock and screamed, "Why the hell did you do that?"

He calmly glanced at me and said, "I guess my daddy didn't like the way my punk ass was shivering."

Luckily I found my purse intact after the ride. Calvin stared at me with a look of satisfaction as park officials retrieved my belongings. I just found it odd that he would do something so extreme to prove a point.

I quickly learned that Calvin hated being compared to or being perceived as a yes- boy to his father. I wanted Calvin challenged, but not to the point of him being spiteful. The last thing that I wanted for Sha'quonda was for Calvin to arrive angry because he was insulted.

I warned her as best I could when I spoke. "Sha'quonda, you need to be ready for anything because something just doesn't feel right with that text."

Sha'quonda responded with the same unconcerned disregard as always. "Ain't nobody thinking about his precious little feelings. He should have thought about all of that before he started playing games with people."

My conversation was interrupted by another message buzz from the phone, and Sha'quonda cheerfully announced that he would be there in forty-five minutes.

I looked at Sha'quonda and felt a sense a pride and fear for her. I was proud because she was becoming the person I wanted her to become. It was like watching your son or daughter go from the amateurs to the pros.

On the other hand I was fearful of what Calvin had in store for her. I just couldn't see him allowing her to get away with clowning him.

Sha'quonda quickly ran through the house preparing it for her secret rendezvous. She changed the bed linen, lit some scented candles, and dimmed the lights. She really looked like she was preparing a romantic evening with her husband. Sha'quonda probably was thinking along those lines, but in my mind, I knew better.

This was the result of months of planning. I dreamed about this day when I was medicated in Central State Hospital. Sha'quonda was looking to convince Calvin that she was the woman for him. I was looking to destroy him and his daddy. I sat on the edge of the couch with my leg shaking in anticipation. My iPad was fully charged and I was waiting for the actors to take the stage. I glanced at Sha'quonda, who was making last-minute adjustments to her floral arrangement on the table. I had to admit that she actually looked like a virgin bride.

My thoughts were broken up by the sound of a weak knock at the door. I quickly ran toward closet and hid inside. I left the door partially cracked so that I could see. From my vantage point, I had the perfect angle when I pointed my camera toward the couch.

Calvin arrived at Sha'quonda's house looking like he was in a hurry. Sha'quonda offered him a drink and he quickly declined. He complained about being on a tight schedule because he had to meet with his father at 10:30am. He was mumbling about not wanting to be late for his meeting. Calvin was really dropping hints because he wanted Sha'quonda to stop talking and get down to business. Calvin had on a track suit with no underwear, and his demeanor was rude. Every question Sha'quonda asked was answered with an abrasive one- or two-word sentence. I could tell that he only came for one thing and Sha'quonda was taking way too long to give it up. Sha'quonda finally realized that the bishop was getting irritated by the questions and quickly switched to freak mode.

Sha'quonda tried to kiss Calvin, but he seemed to turn his head in disgust as if to say, "You are not even worthy of a kiss."

I kept the camera focused on their faces and saw that Sha'quonda was starting to get annoyed. Sha'quonda probably thought that if she could sweet talk Calvin long enough, he would eventually be nice to her.

Personally, I had been long over that dream. And I think Sha'quonda was finally realizing it too because of the way he was treating her.

Calvin grabbed Sha'quonda, yanked her toward him, and growled, "You were talking a lot of shit earlier, huh, but you real quiet now."

Calvin grabbed her by the back of her hair and tugged until she fell backwards on the couch. The person who said a smile is worth a thousands words could have won the lottery with Calvin's. There was something almost wicked about Calvin as he clenched her shoulders and shoved her to her knees. Sha'quonda acted happy with the treatment, but I could tell she was surprised. She waited patiently on her knees as Calvin pulled down his pants.

He continued to talk to her in sadistic way. "I give you sluts a couple of dollars and you think you can say whatever. I bet your ass learns today."

Sha'quonda had a partial smile on her face, but I could tell she was offended by what he was saying. She was probably remembering how Calvin used to be. When Calvin was romantic and when he made her feel loved. When he made her feel like nothing else in the world mattered except her. To go from feeling that special to being reduced to a two-dollar whore had to be degrading.

Calvin ripped her shirt off and exposed her breast. His abrasive demeanor continued as he laughed and roughly squeezed them. I focused the camera on Sha'quonda and I could see her eyes glisten with tears. I could see that she never wanted this. She probably thought that if she could just reason with Calvin, she would prove me wrong. Now she understood that there was no reasoning with him. The same assistant bishop who uplifted thousands with his message was dragging her through the mud for kicks.

Sha'quonda nervously rocked back and forth on her knees waiting for Calvin to finish pulling his pants. After he had finished, she pulled Calvin's penis close to her mouth. Calvin abruptly stopped her and pointed his finger in her face.

Calvin glared at Sha'quonda like he despised her and said, "Hold up, I got to take a shit."

Calvin chuckled as he walked toward the bathroom. He opened the door and turned back toward Sha'quonda. Then he screamed in a sarcastic manner, "Stay on your knees, hoe. I'll be right back."

Calvin continued to laugh as if he were the star of some horror movie. I shook my head in disbelief because I could not believe he was being so vulgar. I turned the camera off and hurried over to Sha'quonda. I could tell that Calvin's behavior was hurting her. He was being nasty to Sha'quonda on purpose, and it was killing her.

I gently cupped Sha'quonda face in my hands and spoke. "Sha'quonda, you have to be strong. He's acting like this because he is a dirty motherfucker. He wants to hurt you because you offended him. If you don't feel comfortable going any further, I will understand. I knew he was coming here with some bullshit, but this is ridiculous."

Sha'quonda's big, brown eyes turned black with anger as the wheels in her head started moving. It was like she finally realized that I was using her too. She pulled away from my hands and quickly ran toward Calvin's track suit. Sha'quonda rifled through his pockets and came out with a freshly sealed magnum condom. I saw satisfaction in her eyes as she repeatedly plunged a needle in the center of it.

I wanted Sha'quonda angry, but not to that extent.

I quickly ran toward Sha'quonda flailing my arms in an attempt to stop her from destroying the condom. She stared back at me blankly and placed the condom back in his pants.

Both Sha'quonda and I could hear Calvin on the phone talking to Linda. "Hey baby, what are you doing? Nothing, I'm just finishing up at the gym. Yeah, I should be there in time for 11:00 service. You know I'm counting down! Forty-five days and counting! Yes, you are the most important person in my life. Well, other than God. You know my salvation will always be first. Okay, baby, I love you too. I'll see you in a few."

The whole conversation almost made me barf. The sound of Calvin's voice made Sha'quonda even more determined to break him as she paced nervously back and forth.

I scurried back into the closet, just as I heard the toilet flush. Calvin opened the door and let out a loud, disgusting burp.

He looked at Sha'quonda walking around in the nude and seemed upset as he spoke. "I thought I told you to stay on your knees."

Any hot lust for lovemaking that Sha'quonda had vaporized in the fowl stench coming from the bathroom. The paint was literally melting off the walls. The smell of rotting eggs aging inside of a rhinoceros cage seeped from the bathroom. Calvin whistled and walked toward his pants as if fabreeze was spouting from his butt. He retrieved the condom from his pocket and roughly pulled it on. Both Sha'qounda and I prayed the rubber would hold.

Sha'quonda was still staring strangely at the condom when Calvin screamed, "Damn! What the fuck are you waiting for? I don't have all day! Come on."

He guided her to the arm of the couch and forced her to bend over. There was nothing sensual or romantic about what Calvin was doing to Sha'quonda. There was a sinister smile painted across his face as he roughly pulled her hair. He grunted and growled like an untamed animal. Calvin made no attempt to pleasure or be gentle with Sha'quonda. He pulled, tugged, slapped, and cursed at Sha'quonda just to be spiteful.

Sha'quonda had both hands on the sofa's arm as if she were getting a paddling. The dreamy look of delight had been replaced with a glare of revenge. She stared directly at the closet almost as if she knew where the camera lens was at.

She looked bored but she stayed in character as she encouraged Calvin. "Come on baby, give it all to me."

Calvin began to look awkward as he fought to control himself. He was probably thinking that he had used a condom hundreds of times before, and it had never felt this good. He eyes started to glaze over and his body began to shake uncontrollably.

The angel on his right side was screaming, "Pull out! Pull out! This feels way too good."

The demon on the opposite side was telling him, "Stay in! You're good! You got a rubber on. Besides, you just haven't had any in a while."

I was praying that he would listen to the demon. Calvin began to swallow hard as if his mouth was dry. He started babbling incoherently as he released inside her.

Sha'quonda hissed with enjoyment as she felt Calvin's stream penetrate through her. Calvin tried to free himself because he knew something was not right. Sha'quonda grabbed his butt and forced him further in.

She began to quickly glide back and forth until Calvin's face was distorted and his body was hunched over in pain. Panic-stricken sounds replaced his words as he continued to unknowingly inseminate Sha'quonda. Calvin finally was able to push her off and fall clumsily toward the sofa. His breathing was ridged as he stared down at his penis and confirmed what he thought. The mangled condom hung from his penis like shredded tissue. All the bravado of before had been replaced with a look of terror.

Sha'quonda added fuel to the fire by saying, "We should be okay, baby. I only missed a couple of days with my birth control."

Calvin slumped down even further on the couch as he tried to make sense of the situation. I focused the camera on Calvin's face. He froze. I knew what he was thinking."What if this tramp is pregnant? How am I going to explain this mess to my father? Even better, what would the church think?" Calvin closed his eyes and began to pray silently as I continued to record his misery.

Calvin slowly pulled his pants up and mumbled goodbye to Sha'quonda. The earlier disappointment on Sha'quonda's face had been replaced with joy. She looked revived as she floated across the room and slammed the door behind Calvin. In her mind, she had just gotten her revenge. To see Calvin stagger down the steps uncertain about his future was payback enough for her.

I turned the camera off and ran towards Sha'quonda with open arms screaming, "We did it, girl! We did it!"

Sha'quonda responded in a low threatening voice, "That piece of shit is gonna pay. All those things he did to me tonight are gonna come back to bite him in the ass."

In all honesty, I never thought of it like that, but she was right. I mean really, how could the next bishop of one of the most influential churches in the nation explain his behavior? Sha'quonda getting pregnant, great! Calvin acting like an asshole, and treating her like shit, priceless! A big smile crossed my face because finally I was in the driver's seat.

I grabbed Sha'quonda and hugged her like a long-lost sister. Then I whispered in her ear, "You have to be the bravest person that I have ever met. I love you."

Sha'quonda's head lifted with pride as her eyes began to water. She had probably been looking for this type of sisterly love for a long time. Sha'quonda's life had been full of mistakes, but mostly regrets. That day she seemed happy because she was finally contributing. I was genuinely proud of Sha'quonda for what she had done because it took a lot of heart. If I had been in the same situation, the camera scene would have ended with Calvin's murder. Sha'quonda stood firm and never cracked under Calvin's sadistic antics. I had a newfound respect for Sha'quonda, but it only tied to what she was willing to do. She passed my first loyalty test with flying colors; now it was time to push her to the limit. With a little luck and good timing, we could make a splash that would be talked about for years.

Chapter 14

My initial plan was to be pregnant along with Sha'quonda. I had a couple of vials of Calvin's sperm left over, so I injected myself. I took a couple of home pregnancies, but it never panned out. I guess that served me right because I could have never loved that baby. Looking back at that time in my life, I was consumed with revenge. If I could have used baby Jesus as a pawn in my sick game, I would have. I was in Central State Mental Hospital for a reason, and those issues just didn't go away over night.

I have to admit that it was a delicate time for me and my plan. Sha'quonda had just started showing signs of her pregnancy and I did not want to discourage her. After her doctor confirmed that she was four weeks pregnant, I did the only sane thing I could think of at the time. I bought myself a padded stomach and promised myself to tell her the truth later. I knew it was wrong, but I was focused on the end result. When I told Sha'quonda that I was pregnant, it looked like the weight of the world was lifted off her shoulders.

She stared at me with tears in her eyes and spoke. "Oh my God, I'm so happy. I was afraid that I would have to go through this by myself."

I looked at Sha'quonda concerned and responded, "Why would you think that you were going to have to go through this by yourself? I already told you that we were in this together."

Sha'quonda glanced at the floor and nervously played with her fingers as she spoke. "Don't get me wrong! I'm not saying that you're not in my corner. It just felt like I was being used sometimes. You know what I mean?"

I frowned at Sha'quonda and shook my head no. Sha'quonda responded with a frustrated sigh and continued to speak. "I just don't think I would have been able to get through this by myself."

Sha'quonda rubbed her stomach and a look of regret drifted across her face.

Sha'quonda's response scared me more than anything. The remorseful look and tone of despair signaled to me that she had considered a plan B. The option for an abortion or adoption was not what Sha'qounda should have been thinking about. As the ring master of this three-ring circus, I needed to keep my star encouraged. Sha'quonda had to believe that no matter if we sunk or swam it would be together.

I extended my hand and gently placed it on her stomach and spoke. "Girl, I feel the same way sometimes. Sometimes I feel like I made a mistake dragging you in to this. Calvin is a low, down, dirty snake, and he deserves everything coming to him. Sometimes I just feel like we're just not strong enough to finish our plan. I don't know, Sha'quonda! Do you think we should just throw in the towel after coming so far?"

I pulled Sha'quonda near and allowed her to touch my stomach. Sha'quonda stared deep into my eyes and I forced myself to look fragile and pathetic.

It was like a bolt of strength tore through Sha'quonda as she pulled me close and spoke, "Angela don't you ever think like that! We are two of the strongest women walking this earth. We are strong because we have taken our destinies in our own hands. There is no way I will allow this sorry motherfucker to beat us. We've come too far, and I refuse to go back. We're gonna have these babies and get what's coming to us."

Sha'quonda locked her arms around my neck and hugged me tightly. A feeling of delight rushed through me as we held each. I knew it was despicable of me to play on her emotions, but I had promised myself a long time ago that absolutely nothing was going to derail my plan. Sha'quonda slowly became the person who I had envisioned she would become. She accepted my word as the Holy Grail and she stopped questioning my intentions. If I told Sha'quonda the sky was red, her response would have been light or dark? It was imperative that she remain in an almost infantile state. Not to say that I was better than her, but it was important that she did not ask questions.

To say things were going according to plan was an understatement. I used money from the church accounts to help keep Sha'quonda financially stable. I was never greedy with the money, but I wanted her to be stress free. I gave her some pocket money and bought her a nice cash car. I even splurged a little and surprised her with living room furniture. The added financial security gave Sha'quonda less reason to complain. Once she believed we were in the same boat together, I found that she was easy to control.

Rumors about the super couple's marriage date was circulating around social media. The wedding of Bishop Calvin Tyler Jr. and Evangelist Linda Stanford became the talk in Atlanta. Of course, Sha'quonda and I were in no mood for festivities because our main objective was revenge. We were happy that social media was giving the marriage a larger stage, because that meant that Calvin had more to loose. Calvin and Linda finally decided on a late July wedding date, which only gave Sha'quonda and me an extra two months to finalize our plan.

A week after they announced there wedding date, I received a frantic call from Sha'quonda. She sounded out of breath and she was screaming, "Angela! Angela! Turn on Fox 5 News!"

Sah'quonda continued to talk loudly, but I could barely hear her because her phone was going in and out. I hung my phone up and flipped the TV to News 5. Bishop Tyler was talking to a local reporter named Diane James, who was also a member at Solid Foundation. She was known for interviewing famous and fabulous people around Atlanta. Diane always pretended to be impartial, but trust me, she always had an agenda. She could destroy you with a hard interview and make you look perfect with a positive one. Bishop Tyler was a regular on Diane's show and his interviews were always biased. The Diane James show was nothing more than a propaganda machine for Bishop Tyler and Solid Foundation.

Bishop Tyler appeared to be happy as he spoke about Linda and Calvin. "My son and Linda have made me proud. Not only as a natural father should be, but also as a spiritual parent."

I could tell the show was one big fluff piece, but the more Bishop Tyler spoke, I found myself getting angry.

Calvin's father stared in the camera and spoke. "Linda has been the best thing to happen to Calvin. My son having Linda in his life is proof that God will eventually send you the right person. My son was involved with a woman who was full of a Jezebel's spirit. This particular woman attended our church, but she was only there to seek out and destroy a spiritual man. I saw this demon go from man to man in my church until it finally chose my beloved son. I saw my son battling with this Jezebel demon, and there was absolutely nothing I could do."

I could feel the anger growing inside me. I didn't really care if Bishop Tyler was talking about me. What angered me most was the way he was painting me.

Calvin's father became more animated as he continued to talk into the camera. "I wanted to help my son by destroying that wretched beast, but God would not allow it. God was testing my son's faith to see if he was fit to be bishop. That's why I was so happy when Christ placed Prophetess Stanford in my son's life. Linda interceded on behalf of my son to God for mercy. If Linda had not intervened for Calvin, I believe that demon would have killed my son. God finally revealed to Calvin that that Jezebel demon also had a son. The Christ living inside of Calvin still wanted to take care of the child, but The Prophetess received a vision from God and told Calvin. Prophetess Stanford told him, 'God said Uh-uh-uh! No sir-ee! I will never have my servant support a child full of evil demons. '"

The reporter was fixated on Bishop Tyler as if he was really saying something powerful. My phone immediately started ringing as Sha'quonda tried to contact me. Everything was moving in slow motion as my anger reached its apex. I could have dealt with the Jezebel bullshit, but calling my son a demon had me seething. I finally calmed down enough to answer the phone.

As soon as I answered the phone, I heard Sha'quonda screaming. "Angela! Can you believe this motherfucker? All the times I sucked and fucked this nigga, and this is how he repays me. Did you hear what he said about my daughter?"

I stared at the phone confused. I was about to tell Sha'quonda that he was actually referring to me and my son when I came up with a brilliant idea.

I pulled the phone close to my mouth and exploded. "That motherfucker ain't shit! Oh my God! That is so mean! I can't believe he said that about you."

You guessed it! I allowed Sha'quonda to think that he was talking about her so that I could capitalize from it. Bishop Tyler's interview made Sha'quonda feel like she was being attacked and I just became the colorful commentator.

Each time Sha'quonda calmed down, I would make a comment like, "If he talked about my child like that, I would make sure he never said it again. I can't believe you are letting him get away with that."

I would brace myself as she responded with explicit language full of threats of violence. "I can't wait until I catch that motherfucker without his security. I'm gonna fuck his bitch ass up."

Sha'quonda was still in the middle of one of her rants when I saw Bishop Tyler speak. "Yes Diane, Calvin and Linda will have their wedding shower this Saturday at 4pm at the W Hotel."

In an attempt to charm Ms. James he continued to speak. "And you, Diane, will be my VIP guest."

Diane James giggled like a teenager talking to her first crush. She leaned forward still laughing and gently touched Bishop Tyler's knee.

Bishop Tyler responded by grasping Diane's hand and kissing the back of it. Diane gushed with approval as they ended the show still laughing and talking. The whole scene looked staged, but I didn't care. I gained valuable information. I would use the wedding shower as a testing ground for my battle. The setting would be intimate enough to make contact with Calvin and public enough to avoid any type of embarrassment. My plan was simple enough—pull Calvin to the side and see if he was willing to make a deal.

I found out that Calvin had reserved the Whisky Blue Bar. The Whisky Blue is located on the rooftop of W Hotel. The party was an exclusive invitation only. The main entrance was only accessible by elevator, so Sha'quonda and I entered the party through the service elevator. Getting to Calvin was a task in itself because people were already staring at us. Since we did not get an official invitation we looked out of place. My kiwi lace dress and Sha'quonda's sky-blue brocade skirt were not the authorized dress code for and all white party. Sha'quonda and I took two steps towards Calvin, and we were quickly approached by two security guards requesting invitations.

I was content with accepting defeat and living to fight another day. Sha'quonda's was determined to speak with Calvin, but his security would not allow it.

She made the situation worse when she started getting loud and causing a scene. "Watcha mean do I have an invitation? You ain't asking nobody else. Go that way, motherfucker! Get the fuck out of my face."

I quickly retreated to the service elevator and exited near the lobby. I blended in with the crowd and watched as Sha'quonda's was escorted out of the hotel. Bishop Tyler quickly gathered his security team together and placed a guard at every possible entrance. There was nothing more I could do but leave, because the situation had gotten out of hand.

I turned to walk out the lobby door and I was startled by a deep but familiar voice, "Hey Angela, I didn't know you were scheduled to work today."

I turned around and saw the pale face of Mr. Bell, a security officer. Mr. Bell was an easygoing, middle-aged man who really didn't care about the hotel rules. His main concern was completing his eight-hour shift with the least amount of trouble.

I responded with my professional voice, "No, I'm not scheduled today. I was just picking up a few things from my office. I was nosy, so I decided to look in on the wedding shower of the year."

Mr. Bell responded by saying, "This is crazy, huh? Just think about all this money being spent this weekend. It will probably be double that in a couple of months. At this rate, they will pay our wages for the year.

I smiled at Mr. Bell and questioned him, "So they're having their wedding here too?"

Mr. Bell nodded his head yes and responded, "Yep! I just found out today. Bishop Tyler reserved the main ballroom for their wedding today. Man, I can't believe how much money Bishop Tyler is spending on his son. And he's not even the head of the church yet. Just wait until his father makes him bishop. He'll really be into the money."

I stared at Officer Bell like he was the guiding light. My plan gained clarification at that moment. The truth of the matter was that we were holding all the cards. We had Calvin on tape screwing, and the ace up the sleeve was that we were pregnant. Well, at least one of us was. I walked through the garage feeling reinvigorated. Why rush and blow our chance on some personal stuff. We could have an even bigger payday once he became bishop and took over the church. I unlocked my car door smiling because my plan was taking a new, bold approach.

My happy thoughts were interrupted by the crude shrieking of Sha'quonda's voice. "That was just so ugly."

Startled by the voice, I glared at Sha'quonda as she walked angrily toward me still speaking. "I mean, how you gonna leave me looking all dumb and shit? We suppose to be in this together trying to get paid, and you dipped out on me."

I looked at Sha'quonda like I smelled sour milk and responded. "Sha'quonda if I hadn't left, you would have blown the whole plan. How many times do I have to keep telling you that we are not targeting some thug from around the way! We are going after very wealthy and influential men. The last thing I want Calvin or his father to do is go on the offensive before we get a chance to strike first. I don't understand why you started acting all crazy in the party anyway. That was really dumb because now we have to come up with a different approach. You should have just let me take the lead."

Sha'quonda's greed was in the right place, but her tact was almost none existed. She appeared to be offended by what I said, but the truth had to be told. This bitch was going to screw up everything before we even had a chance. Sha'quonda was focused on getting paid on or before his wedding day. I was under no such illusion. By the time the lawyers got involved, we would be happy to get something in two years.

My plan was to string Sha'quonda along until I could figure out everything. My plan was a work in progress, and it was changing almost daily. As long as she believed we were close to a payday, I could control her. Sha'quonda may not have liked what I said, but she had no intentions of going anywhere. She rode silently in the car and sulked as she stared out the window.

I nudged her arm and spoke, "Guess what?"

Sha'quonda turned toward me still pouting and responded, "What?"

I smiled at Sha'quonda and said, "How about me a you crash their wedding for old time's sake. I feel like making somebody squirm."

I could tell that Sha'quonda was still upset, but what I said put an apprehensive smile on her face as she spoke. "So when are they having the wedding?"

I glanced at Sha'quonda and back at the road and spoke, "In a couple of months. Hotel security told me about it today. We can sneak in and crash it, but we have to do it my way, okay?"

Sha'quonda eagerly shook her head yes and quickly changed the subject to what she should wear. I started at Sha'quonda as she happily babbled on. I shook my head thinking how naïve she could be sometimes. If sneaking into a wedding made her happy and not ask questions, then I had to make it happen. I had no idea of what I was going to do, but I knew that in two months, I would find a way.

The day of the wedding started off badly. My plan was to go to the wedding early and make contact with Calvin and his family. I wanted to rattle them but not screw up anything. Our approach had to be delicate but also aggressive. Sha'quonda and I arrived at the hotel and security was heavy as expected. My employee badge allowed us into garage, but Sha'quonda was not permitted because she did not have an employee ID. Things were not going according to my plans, so again I had to improvise.

I thought about calling Calvin, but he had disconnected his phone after his wedding shower fiasco. He wanted nothing more to do with us, and hell, I didn't blame him. Calvin had to marry Linda to keep the Tylers' money growing, and avoiding me and Sha'quonda was imperative. His father probably had so much security around him that he almost certainly had trouble going to the bathroom by himself.

The wedding was covered by local and national news media. Calvin Tyler Jr. , the heir apparent to his father's 24,000-member church was to wed prophetess Linda Stanford. Sha'quonda and I finally decided that we would take a chance and call the groom's room. I gained access to the hotel and opened a side door attached to the Whisky Bar. I gave Sha'quonda a waitress t-shirt and apron and she blended right in. After I retrieved the room number, we met in the main lobby. I had Sha'quonda dial his room and try to make contact with him. I wrote down everything I wanted Sha'quonda to say because she was known to go a little off script.

Sha'quonda called Calvin's room, and the phone was answered by one of his college friends. Sha'quonda asked to speak to Calvin and she was placed on hold. Calvin answered the phone a short time later, and hung up as soon as he heard Sha'quonda's voice. I would have probably hung up on her ass also. I instructed Sha'quonda to call him back again, and this time, the phone was answered by Deacon Langley. Deacon Langley warned Sha'quonda that he would call the police and place a restraining order on her if she did not stop calling. We decided that it was time to shake the bishop's team up a little.

I looked at Sha'quonda and smiled as the words slowly rolled off her lips.

"You need to let the bishop's son know that I'm four months pregnant with his baby."

She slammed the phone down with such aggression that the receiver almost cracked. Sha'quonda's cell phone started ringing thirty seconds later from a phone number that was blocked. Sha'quonda answered the phone and I could hear Calvin cursing and swearing.

"Why the fuck are you playing these childish games on my wedding day? You really need to get a fucking life and grow up. I swear to God if you ruin this day for me I'll…"

Sha'quonda, known for dancing on people's last nerve, cut Calvin off mid-sentence and responded, "Bitch, you'll what? The only thing that you'll be doing is explaining to the media how you got me pregnant. Now keep fucking with me and see what happens."

Calvin took a calmer approach and tried to rationalize with Sha'quonda. "Think about it, Sha'quonda. It's been a while since we were together. And the times when we were together, I used a condom. You really need to be smart, and think before you make false allegations."

Sha'quonda laughed out loud and continued to provoke him. "You know what, Calvin? You are really stupid. We've been plotting on your silly ass for months."

Calvin appeared to be paranoid by Sha'quonda's comment when he responded, "What do you mean by 'us'? Who's been plotting on me for months?"

I began to frantically wave my hands and motion for her to be quite. The last thing that I wanted was for Sha'quonda to show all our cards.

Thankfully, she listened and pulled back when she responded, "Anyway dummy, you'll be hearing from me soon."

Sha'quonda hung up and we both started laughing. This was exactly what I wanted. I wanted to give the Tylers something, but I did not want to cause a major commotion. We were walking toward my car when Sha'quonda's phone began to ring.

The number was blocked again so Sha'quonda answered the phone thinking it was Calvin. "What, stupid? What do you want? I'm busy, so hurry up."

There was a long pause and then I heard the familiar voice of Calvin's father bellowing out of the speaker. "Ms. Patterson! Is this a good time to talk?"

Bishop Tyler's voice was a gift from God. No matter how angry or upset you were, that voice was always calming. Bishop Tyler could disagree with you and still make you feel like you were right.

Bishop Tyler continued, "Would it be possible for you to take me of speaker phone and allow me to speak to you about a delicate situation?"

Sha'quonda took the phone of speaker and held the phone so we could both hear.

"My son revealed to me that you might be pregnant with his child. Is this true?"

Sha'quonda placed her hand on her hip and responded, "Yes."

Bishop Tyler continued, "Well, I want you to be the first to know that we have every intention of dealing with your situation as soon as possible. I know my son can be a little stubborn at times, but he was just stressed with the timing. I mean, with it being his wedding day and all, you have to admit that it was alarming. Honestly, I'm still trying to wrap my mind around how my son could have been so careless. I mean, don't get me wrong, not to say that there is anything wrong with you. I'm sure you're a good, God-fearing woman. It's that this could be bad for all parties involved."

As I listened at Bishop Tyler talk, his speech started to sound really familiar. Bishop Tyler was the type of person who made problems disappear. No matter how big the crisis was for Calvin, Bishop Tyler had the power to make it go away. Calvin had probably been stepping in shit for years, and daddy was always there to clean it up.

Bishop Tyler finished talking by asking Sha'quonda sarcastically, "Are you certain that the baby is Calvin's? I mean, honestly, I can't tell which person is with whom nowadays. One minute you young people love each other, and the next time you've broken up."

Sha'quonda responded in an unemotional way that made even me cringe. "Yeah, I'm sure it's him. Your son came harder inside of me than he had ever came before. It was like he was sowing his final seeds before he got married."

There was an eerie silence on the other end of the phone, and then I heard Bishop Tyler clear his voice and speak. "Well, I don't know about all of that, but you understand that we have to be certain."

Sha'quonda chimed in cutting him off, "Oh, naw, I'm very certain your son is my baby's father."

I had to do everything I could not to laugh. Sha'quonda had a serious look on her face and her heavy southeast Atlanta accent was on full display.

Bishop Tyler promised to sit down with Sha'quonda and handle the situation as discreetly as possible as soon as the wedding was over.

Instead of getting the particulars of the meeting, Sha'quonda's dumb ass asked Bishop Tyler, "How much did you think discretion was worth?"

I heard a gasp on the other line and Bishop Tyler responded by saying, "Young lady, I don't think you're pregnant by my son." and hung up the phone.

Sha'quonda slammed the phone down and started cursing not understanding what happened.

I started laughing as I explained to Sha'quonda what happened. "Do you actually think he was going to talk about money over the phone? Sha'quonda, you have to slow waltz this process. This family has probably been through this before. Trust me when I say they know what they're doing. But that's okay! We'll see him face to face in a few hours. He can't just push us off to the side like that. It's time to step up the pressure."

Sha'quonda and I decided to grab a quick bite to eat, and by the time we arrived back at the hotel, the wedding was almost over. I knew we were cutting it close at the restaurant, but I thought we had more time to spare. I jumped out of my car and darted through the parking garage like Carl Lewis, searching for the newlyweds. I could hear Sha'quonda's footsteps fading as she tried to keep up with me, but I was focused. I had to make contact with the first family to at least show them I meant business.

As I came out of the garage, I saw Deacon Langley directing a gauntlet of security as Calvin and Linda exited the building. Loud cheers echoed off the entrance of the garage as the family's entourage moved toward their car. Linda appeared to be happy, but I was not there to wish them good luck. Calvin glanced in my direction as he was getting into his limousine, and I responded by rubbing my belly. He looked as if he were confused, so I pretended to have a baby in my hands, slowly rocking it back and forth.

The gesture turned Calvin pale as Linda pulled him into the car. The car sped off just as Bishop Tyler was approaching. Deacon Berry and Deacon Langley followed closely behind him. As soon as both deacons saw me, they froze. Deacon Berry looked like he wanted to dive under a car because he was so embarrassed about our encounter.

I smiled at him and spoke, "Hi Marlon, how are you doing? It's been a long time."

Deacon Berry stared at the ground as Bishop Tyler glared at him confused. Deacon Langley approached me and spoke as if I were a wounded animal. "Hey, Ms. Anderson, are you okay?"

I must have looked bat-ass crazy because he held both hands in front of him as if he were calming me down.

I responded to Deacon Langley in a pleasant manor, "Mr. Langley, I'm fine. I just came down here to conduct a little business with the Tylers."

Deacon Langley sighed heavily and turned toward Bishop Tyler as if to say, "What next?"

Deacon Langley saw how the Tylers had treated me, and he wanted no more of it. I just think Deacon Langley was tired of covering for them. No matter how much trouble he covered up for them, they just got into more.

Deacon Langley backed away from me just as Sha'quonda arrived.

She smiled at the Bishop and extended her hand and introduced herself. "Hi, I'm Sha'quonda. We spoke on the phone earlier today about Calvin's unborn child."

Bishop Tyler turned toward Deacon Langley as if asking for help. Deacon Langley shook his head as if to say, "Uh huh, I'm not touching this one. Leave me out of it."

I could tell that Bishop Tyler was irritated as he opened his mouth and exploded. "This is ridiculous! Not only are you making a fool of yourselves, you are harassing my son. Ms. Patterson, you will never get anything accomplished by playing these silly games with this woman."

Bishop Tyler pointing in my direction was all I needed to get going. I thought about all the things that he put me through and just snapped. "First off, old man, you need to keep my name out of your mouth. You're mad because somebody finally got your ass. Your son was a hoe when I dated him, and he's still a hoe. The only difference is now he's gonna pay. Trick, you haven't seen harassment yet."

The bishop's entourage appeared shocked at my comment and demanded that I apologized.

I smiled at the party and agreed, "You know what? You're right, that was a terrible thing to say to such a holy man of God."

Sha'quonda was pacing back and fourth like a little poodle anxious to jump into the conversation. But I would not allow it. This was something that I wanted to do. I wanted Bishop Tyler to feel that same burn of embarrassment that I had felt when I backslid. I remember standing in front of that church looking for someone to help me, and all I saw was an arrogant smirk on his face.

I continued my sarcastic attack on Bishop Tyler. "You got all these people around you thinking you Jesus in the flesh. Bitch, you ain't nothing but a two-dollar pimp. All of that garbage that you preach about applies to everyone except the Tylers. What, are you too high and mighty that you can't listen to your own sermons?"

Bishop Tyler was upset to the point of shaking as he responded, "Now you listen here, young lady! I am a man of God, and you are blaspheming against me. God will not stand idly by and watch you desecrate his servant's name."

I glared back at Bishop Tyler as if his breath was stinking and responded. "Bitch, please! All that bullshit that you're shoveling should go in that direction." I pointed at the large crowd of members starting to form around us and continued talking. "They believe that bull, not me. I know what type of low, down, disgusting person you are. And that poor excuse for a son is following right behind you."

Church members began to give hints to Bishop Tyler and tried and help him. "She's possessed by Satan. Only a person who is possessed would try and defile men of God."

Sha'quonda heard the small audience rumbling and decided to speak. "Defile? Ain't nobody trying to ruin these motherfuckers. If anything, his son has been doing all the defiling."

Sha'quonda handed the bishop two Father's Day cards and continued to talk. "Give those to your son. Tell him that he has two trick hoes pregnant, Oh! And Happy Father's Day, grandpa."

Sha'quonda pulled me and started walking away. I glanced back at the bishop's party and tried to contain my laughter. Deacon Berry and Deacon Langley were escorting Bishop Tyler through the crowd. He looked like a drunken soldier with weak ankles. Both deacons were struggling to keep him upright. He glanced in our direction for a final time and stumbled into the limousine. Sha'quonda and I wiggled back into the garage excited as the crowed watched in shock. Little did they know that this was only the beginning.

Chapter 15

The next week was fairly quiet. Sha'quonda and I met for dinner a couple of times, but we mostly talked on the phone. I could tell that Sha'quonda was starting to panic. By that following Friday, she was calling me every hour. Sha'quonda was starting to show and she was becoming more agitated. I was trying to stay patient, but it was getting hard. My biggest fear was that the Tylers would take a "wait and see" approach. Maybe they wanted to see if the babies were really Calvin's. It would be smart of them to do that, but could they really afford the bad press.

By that Monday, I had turned my phone off. Sha'quonda was becoming unbearable. As usual, she was arguing about money and threatening to put the baby up for adoption. I turned my phone on silent and went to work.

At lunch, I noticed a voice message on my phone. I pushed play and the voice said, "This is the law firm of McCoy, Schroder and Mills; please contact our firm as soon as possible in regards to a very pressing matter."

I didn't think twice about it because no one said my name. I turned my phone on silent and put it back in my purse. At the end of the day I noticed a call from Sha'quonda.

I reluctantly returned her call expecting to hear a bunch of threats. Sha'quonda was breathing hard, and sounded panicky as she spoke. "Did you get a call from a law firm?"

I remembered the message and responded, "Yes, but I don't think it was for me."

There was a long pause and then she spoke, "I also got a strange call from Calvin asking to meet with me."

I placed Sha'quonda on hold and quickly glanced at my phone. I had several missed calls. I checked my voicemail and heard Calvin asking me to call him as soon as possible. I told Sha'quonda to meet me at my house and we would call Calvin together.

I knew things would eventually start moving, but I had no idea it would happen this fast. Sha'quonda was waiting outside my apartment when I arrived. Neither one of us had a lot to say because we were concerned about the phone call. Both of us agreed that Calvin sounded happy, almost excited. Which was bad news for us, especially me. My only ace in the hole was Sha'quonda. If she had caved in to shoe money, I was screwed.

When I called Calvin, I could hear fine china clinking together in the background.

I could hear Linda asking who was on the phone. Calvin lied to her and said it was his father and then he excused himself from Linda.

He got back on the phone and started cursing, "Why are you two hoes playing games and telling people that you're pregnant by me? I mean just because I don't want your ghetto ass, don't mean you have to go around playing fucking games and lying!"

I must have been around Sha'quonda too long because I quickly went southeast Atlanta on him. "Hold up, motherfucka. Just because your dumb ass got caught slipping does not mean we're lying. You know you fucked Sha'quonda raw. And as for me, let's just say never trust a bitch to throw away your dirty condoms, dumb ass!"

Sha'quonda started pushing and shoving me like I had just made the winning basket. Calvin immediately calmed his voice trying to play the victim. "This is wrong what y'all are doing. I mean, why are y'all doing this to me? I never meant to hurt either one of you, and you know that. People have bad break ups all the time, but you don't ruin their lives over it. This shit is crazy! You're doing all of this because you still want me."

I responded with feelings and emotions that had been buried in me for a long time. "You know what, Calvin? I really loved you. I would have done anything for you. And what did you do? Use me. I mean, all that time you were coming over to my apartment and fucking me, it was just to tide you over. All you wanted was a piece of ass to tide you over for the next bitch. That was your whole plan all the time. I never meant anything to you. The only thing that matters to you is what your daddy wants. Your daddy wants you to marry that bitch Linda, and your dumb ass did it. You know what? I'm not even going to talk about Linda like that, because she never knew what you were doing."

I could hear Calvin trying to interrupt, but I was on a roll. "Your sorry ass is sneaking over to my apartment to screw me. And when you get me pregnant, you don't know me anymore. Then you started screwing Sha'quonda in the church dungeon. Nigga, you ain't shit."

Calvin responded, "Sha'quonda? What church dungeon? Who is Sha'quonda?"

Sha'quonda quickly grabbed the phone and started screaming. "Oh you don't know me now! You know what, Calvin? You so stupid. You caught and you still lying, but that's okay. You're gonna do right by us, you can bet that."

I took the phone back from Sha'qounda and I could hear Calvin laughing as if he were trying to play the situation off. "Okay, Angela! You got me. So how do you want to handle this? I'm not paying any money to anybody if those babies ain't mine. As a matter of fact, I don't think they are mine."

I responded to Calvin by asking, "Do you really want to take that type of chance? More to the point, does your daddy want to take that chance?"

Calvin quickly revaluated the situation and blurted out, "$Ninety thousand dollars! I'll give you both $90,000 to terminate the pregnancies."

Disgusted with Calvin I quickly hung the phone up.

Sha'quonda went into a rage and started screaming at me. "Why you didn't take the money?"

I tried to explain my reasoning behind it, but it fell on deaf ears. Sha'quonda wanted to take the money and run. I was the one who was obsessed with revenge. Sha'quonda made a good point about the money. I had family helping to take care of RC and I had a decent job to help tide me over. Sha'quonda was desperate and struggling with two kids, one with Patrick and pregnant with Calvin's, and no help. I wanted to help Sha'quonda, but dipping into the church's account would raise suspicion. I felt for Sha'quonda, but she was in this for the long haul, weather she like it or not. She glared at me as if finally understanding what I was doing. She probably figured out that I had been stringing her along, and she was thinking about going solo. I was trying to paint a picture of a better day, but she was not buying. She wanted money at that moment and I had nothing to give her. I was about to give into Sha'quonda's nagging and moaning by dipping into my account when the phone rang.

I answered it thinking it was Calvin, but it was a lawyer from McCoy, Schroder and Mills. Through all the commotion, I had forgotten that they left a voicemail that morning.

I quickly motioned for Sha'quonda to come to me. I voice sounding like Regis began to talk. "I want to apologize for calling you so late in the day, but we really have a pressing matter to discuss."

Sha'quonda and I listened at the voice like little lost children speaking to a mother.

"I'm representing Calvin Tyler Sr. in possible negotiations about a delicate matter involving Angela Anderson and Sha'quonda Patterson."

I pushed the button to speaker and allowed Sha'quonda to listen as the lawyer continued.

"Bishop Tyler is willing to negotiate a settlement with both ladies if you are willing to sit down with us as soon as possible."

I told the lawyer that we had received an offer from Calvin and thought it was insulting.

Sha'quonda looked at me and rolled her eyes.

I continued to talk. "But we are willing to sit down and listen."

The voice responded, "Mr. Calvin Tyler Jr. may have made an offer but it had not been authorized by Bishop Tyler. Bishop Tyler is willing to weigh all the evidence and make a substantial offer that will satisfy all parties."

Just like a ghetto prom queen, I heard Sha'quonda chirp in, "How substantial."

I mean, really, Sha'quonda!

The voice continued. "We are sure that the offer would be at least six figures or more."

Sha'quonda nodded her head yes like a starving Somalian looking at a plate of food.

Before I could respond, she snatched the phone from me and screamed, "Yes we can meet. Just give us the day and time, and we'll be there."

The voice responded by saying, "Is 10 am tomorrow fine?"

Again, before I could make any gestures, she screamed, "Yes!"

I wanted to talk to Sha'quonda about a possible number that would make us happy, but I knew we were miles apart. Sha'quonda wanted the quick hit and I wanted the long dollar. I fell back in my chair thinking of a way to bring the subject up to Sha'quonda when I saw Calvin, Linda, and Bishop Tyler on TV.

Their arms were interlocked as they stood in front of a cheering audience.

I told Sha'quonda to turn the TV up just as Bishop Tyler started speaking. "Brothers and sisters of the word, God has revealed to me that it is time for me to step down as senior pastor at Solid Foundation Cathedral. God has blessed me beyond my wildest dreams and now it's time to retire. God instructed me to appoint my son, Calvin Jr. as senior pastor and bishop here at Solid Foundation Cathedral.

The crowd erupted into loud cheers as he continued to talk.

"His beautiful wife, Prophetess Linda Stanford-Tyler, will be assigned as senior pastor at our new beautiful auditorium in Savannah, GA. And I will install myself as overseer of both churches."

My mouth dropped to the floor in astonishment as I continued to watch. Now I understood why the Tylers were willing to settle now. Not only would Calvin get a throne with 25,000 peons, but he was going to use Linda to build up the new church in Savannah, Georgia.

Linda worshiped Bishop Tyler like a God and she loved Calvin Jr. more than life itself. But the Tylers motto was much more heartless. Even though they didn't say it out loud, their motto was simple "money over bitches."

I remembered looking at the ledger and seeing all the money that Bishop Tyler spent on women and wondered if he felt guilty. Now I knew the truth. The Tylers' main concern was making mo money, mo money, and mo money.

Bishop Tyler continued to moan and squeal, whipping the church into a wild frenzy. "Sometimes your crop size dictates the size of your farm. Can I get an amen! I said sometimes your crop size dictates your farm! We already have a large crop growing in the barn, but God wants to increase our crop even more. You can't have one barn if the new crop exceeds it, can you? You need another barn!"

The organist's fingers began to slide up and down the keys making a rhythmic noise that started out slow and then sped up. As the drummer and other instruments caught the beat, the crowd started to sway faster and faster. I saw several members jerking as the Holy Ghost moved them. And others like Linda staggered around the church speaking in tongues. Bishop Tyler continued to holler and scream as more people filled the floor and began to shout.

Bishop Tyler allowed everyone to move with the spirit until he was ready to speak. He raised his hand and the organ immediately lowered the sound. Some people still appeared to be in the spirit, but they were being herded back to their seats by the ushers. The lights began to dim and pictures of the new church flashed on the screen.

Bishop Tyler explained that the new eight-million-dollar sanctuary in Savannah would be able to accommodate twenty-one thousand members. The auditorium would have state-of-the-art lighting and a sound and video system. The atrium would house a one-hundred-fifty-foot musical fountain and be decorated like an Italian garden. Everyone was watching the pictures in amazement. Linda began to stagger around the stage speaking in tongues and bumping into chairs like she was drunk. Slowly she found her way to the microphone.

Bishop Tyler responded by handing her the microphone and stating, "God is trying to tell us something."

Slowly, Linda began to speak, "I have just had a vision from God. He wants me to take five thousand members to Savannah and help sow seeds of faith to the people."

The church grew silent as she glanced around the church looking for volunteers. When no one responded, I saw Calvin and his father step forward. They must have felt some of Linda's spirit, because all of sudden they were staggering around the stage in the spirit.

When they finally came to their senses, Bishop Tyler spoke. "God has just chosen who will go to Savannah with the prophetess."

He turned toward Calvin and he nodded in agreement.

Bishop Tyler turned toward the congregation and began to speak again. "When God chooses you, you don't have a choice."

I saw members in the audience quickly shake their heads in agreement. Bishop Tyler continued, "Each person chosen by God will be contacted by us personally to ensure that God's mission will be completed."

The whole scene was almost comical. I could almost imagine who would be going to Savannah. Those young church members who had absolutely nothing to lose. The well-established money members would probably stay at Solid Foundation with Calvin Jr. and his father.

I looked over at Sha'quonda and she stared back at me with a blank expression on her face.

I started laughing and Sha'quonda asked, "What so damn funny? I don't get it."

I placed my hands over my face and shook my head, and replied. "Sha'quonda! This is why they are ready to settle now. Can you imagine the backlash they would get, if the media found out about us? There's no way they can make a move this big with loose ends like us hanging around."

I looked at Sha'quonda and she still was not getting it. This changed everything for me. The pendulum was now swinging in my direction with full force. The Tylers had probably had instructed their lawyers to dispose of this situation as quickly and as quietly as possible. I stared at Sha'quonda as she cleaned her finger nails and looked at the television uninterested. Bishop Tyler was literally handing the world to Sha'quonda with this announcement, and this bitch was worried about scraping barbecue sauce off her nails.

I glanced down at her tummy and thought to myself, "If she only knew how much power she really had."

I turned away and shook my head in disbelief at her blasé attitude. I looked at the TV and saw the people pushing and shoving toward the stage with money in hand as Linda encouraged them to give until it hurt. I glared at Bishop Tyler, Calvin, and Linda with hatred and envy. I was angry because they were still getting over on people, but most of all I was jealous because they were doing it with such ease. Nobody was putting a gun to these people's heads. They were giving because they had so much love and admiration for them. I remember having that type of love and respect for them, but now my mind was only consumed with revenge. If Sha'quonda and the Tylers thought that tossing a couple of pennies my way would work, they were sadly mistaken. I was in it for the long dough or destruction there were no in betweens.

Chapter 16

The next day, I arrived at the law office energized by the new information that we had just received.

Sha'quonda looked around at the vaulted ceiling smacking her gum. After looking around for a while, she blurted out in her most annoying ghetto voice. "Dang! Da on one up in here."

I lowered my head in embarrassment as a perky girl with and outgoing smile approached us. She extended her hand and introduced herself as Amelia Stowe. We boarded a glass-walled elevator and quickly started to climb toward the thirty-second floor conference room. The view was absolutely breathtaking. I saw people walking get smaller as we soared toward the heavens.

I could hear Sha'quonda mumbling, "Oh my God! Girl, we gonna die! Dis too high."

I heard Amelia release a muffled laugh as we exited the elevator and came face-to-face with ten-foot French doors with frosted glass. I could hear muffled sounds coming from the conference room, but I could only see shadows. Amelia tapped on the door and waited until she was asked to enter. The room went from low muffled sounds to absolute silence.

I heard a deep baritone voice clear his throat and ask us to come in.

Amelia pushed a button on the wall and the doors quickly ejected backwards, allowing us to see in the room. As soon as we entered the room, I immediately sensed that Sha'quonda and I were over-matched.

I saw Calvin and his father strategically seated on the right side of the table with eight members of their legal team. Sha'quonda and I were asked to be seated on the left of the table facing Calvin and his father. Calvin Sr. had his hands crossed in front of him looking priestly as Calvin rocked back and forth with an evil "kill them all" glare on his face.

The conversation started out cordially with a heavy-set white man making introductions. My mind started to blank out as Calvin's legal team introduced themselves with titles included. The conversation quickly swung to us and I could feel Sha'quonda's leg nervously knocking against the bottom of the table.

I introduced myself and glanced over at Sha'quonda. I could tell that she would have preferred to be anywhere except in this conference room. Her voice quivered as she opened her mouth to introduce herself and I could see tears forming in her eyes. The thing about ghetto people is that they hate being out of their comfort zone. Sha'quonda would have been okay if we were having the meeting on her front porch, but we weren't. She was in a room full of college-educated people and her confidence was gone. It was almost like watching a two-hundred-fifty-pound bully shrink to a ninety-pound weakling.

The more questions the suits asked, the more intimidated she got. Calvin Jr. sensed the fear in Sha'quonda and started to exaggerate his power. Any time we spoke, he would lean over to his lawyer and whisper something, then he would turn to his father and smile. I could feel fear slowly crawling up my spine as the lawyers fired legal term after legal term in our direction. Some of the words I knew, but I was lost on the majority of them. Sha'quonda was nudging my leg on almost every word.

I could hear Sha'quonda's little feeble mind trying to kick start after automatic shutdown.

After about forty-five minutes of legal talk, a distinguished-looking man named Edward Schroder pushed the intercom button and spoke. "Amelia, can you please bring me those contracts."

Amelia appeared at the door five minutes later holding two dictionary-size folders full of paper. An ink pen and folder was placed in front Sha'quonda and me. Immediately, Sha'quonda grabbed her pen and opened her folder.

I glared at Sha'quonda as if to say, "What the fuck are you doing?"

She sheepishly smiled back and laid the pen back on the table.

Mr. Schroder sensed that the only way to get both contracts signed was to convince the strongest adversary, which was me, to sign first.

Mr. Schroder cracked a joke to lessen the tension. "Follow the pretty little post-its and sign your names."

All the suits glanced at each other and chuckled, but my frown brought the room to an abrupt silence.

I pushed my seat back and spoke, "Me and my friend need a little break to stretch our legs before we continue."

Mr. Schroder glanced at the wall clock and suggested that everyone take a ten-minute bathroom break and meet back at 11:30.

I looked at Sha'quonda who was shivering like a lost puppy and responded, "I was thinking more about taking lunch and meeting back at 1:00."

The eerie silence in the room was overshadowed by the gloom looks on the faces of Calvin and his father.

Mr. Schroder cleared his voice and suggested, "Why not work through lunch? I can order some food and we can get this wrapped up as soon as possible."

Bishop Tyler piggy-backed on Mr. Schroder's comment. "I can even pay for it. Lunch or dinner, you choose. I know the manager at the Sun Dial Restaurant. He is a very close friend of mine, and I would be happy to pick up the tab for both of you."

Sha'quonda smiled from ear to ear and nudged my arm and spoke. "Do you want to do that?"

I stared at Sha'quonda as if wanting to spit in her face. This bitch was about to give up her power over a twenty-dollar hamburger.

STEVEN DARRELL BATES

I kept my composure and responded to Bishop Tyler. "I think it would be best if we came back at 1:00. We both need to clear our heads before we make a bad decision."

Mr. Schroder quickly glanced at Calvin as if to say, "You better speak up and save this."

Calvin chimed in an attempt to sweet talk us. "Ladies, ladies, let's be reasonable. We all have more pressing things to do. I feel guilty because I have wasted so much of your time already. As soon as we get this paperwork out of the way, you can be on your way. I will have my driver escort both of you to the bank and you can cut a cashier's check today."

Calvin stared at me hoping I would break, but I remained silent.

Calvin glanced at his father and continued to talk. "Oh! I know what it is, Dad. We never told the young ladies how much they were receiving."

Calvin's father nodded his head in agreement and smiled. He took out his pen and wrote a number on a piece of paper. Bishop Tyler handed the paper to Mr. Schroder. Mr. Schroder's eyes beamed with pride as he showed the rest of the suits. After each of the men had nodded their heads in approval, the paper was slid to me.

I looked at the paper and immediately wanted to jump for joy. The three million dollar amount caught my attention and I heard Sha'quonda shriek in disbelieve. I could tell that Sha'quonda was ready to sign from all the kicks to my ankle. I asked for a ten-minute restroom break and everyone agreed.

Sha'quonda and I quickly hurried into the restroom and started dancing in a quiet celebratory manner because we had made it. I forgot all about holding out. I mean $1. 5 million apiece was nothing to sneeze at. We both agreed that the amount was reasonable, so we decided that we would go ahead and sign the contracts.

We had just finished powdering our noses when the bathroom door squeaked open and Amelia entered.

Our faces were still bubbling with joy when Amelia quietly started talking. "So what time are your attorneys arriving?"

Sha'quonda stared at Amelia in the mirror and then glanced at me.

I paused before answering and then I responded, "They should be here any minute."

Amelia responded, "That's good" and washed her hands in silence.

Sha'quonda glanced at me and started snickering as if she was at a comedy club. I, on the other hand, looked at Amelia and wondered if there was more to her comment.

What could she possible know that we didn't? Amelia turned the water off and found me staring at her in the mirror.

I looked Amelia squarely in the eye an asked, "Is there a reason that you asked about our lawyer?"

She smiled back at me and responded, "Nothing. Well I guess it's nothing. But you are aware that your friend's lawyer came to an appointment last week?"

Sha'quonda and I looked around at each other shocked and I asked, "What friend?"

Amelia looked at both Sha'quonda and I and said, "Are you kidding me?"

Amelia walked over to the bathroom door and turned the lock. She quickly shoved Sha'quonda and me toward the rear wall. She proceeded to lay out a trap that we never expected. "A gentleman by the name of Lazarus Goldstein came by with a signed document from a Patrick Jones."

Patrick Jones! Sha'quonda and I looked at each other confused. Why would the incarcerated father of our kids be involved with Calvin and his father?

Amelia continued to talk. "Patrick signed an affidavit stating that he was the father of both your unborn children. Calvin and his father had drawn the contracts up in a way that would void any future payments if it was discovered that the unborn children were not his."

Confused at what I was hearing, I glanced at Sha'quonda and she looked as puzzled as I was.

We turned our attention back to Amelia and she quickly clarified the confusion. "Look ladies, if you sign those contracts, you get nothing. Patrick is willing to lie under oath stating that he is the father of your children. The contracts are worded so that you both must have abortions within thirty days of the contract. Once the babies are aborted, there is no evidence that Calvin is the father. That's why you have so many people in that room rushing you to sign the contracts. Once the abortions are done, Patrick will be considered the father and no more payments will be given.

Sha'quonda quickly replied back to Amelia, "But we saw an amount for three million dollars."

Amelia responded quietly, "That's just a common practice. The money throws you off from looking at the entire contract. Once you sign the contract there is always some type of glitch that disqualifies you from ever getting all the money. They will give you a small portion of the money today and promise to give the rest later. But you rarely receive the full amount."

Amelia continued to tell us that Calvin's father had been doing the same trick on women for years.

I stared at Amelia not wanting to believe what I was hearing and asked, "How do you know about what they've been doing?"

Amelia winced with pain in her eyes as she responded. "My aunt was a victim of Bishop Tyler."

Amelia fought back tears as she revealed how Bishop Tyler destroyed her aunt. "My aunt fell in love with Calvin's father before he was a distinguished bishop. My aunt was a freshman in college when she met Bishop Tyler. Calvin Sr. would come to the local community college searching for young people to build his newly formed church. Bishop Tyler was new to the church game, but he was wise when it came to understanding hurt. My aunt was just coming out of a relationship that almost drove her insane and Calvin Sr. saw her pain. Calvin Sr. befriended my aunt and methodically changed into a person we no longer knew."

I looked at the pain on Amelia's face and understood completely. I remembered having the same feels when first Linda and then Calvin befriended me. I thought to myself, "How sick could a person really be to gain your trust through friendship and then turn around and use you?" Linda found me when I was alone and depressed. Calvin pushed closer to me after I was destroyed socially at the church. How ironic that all three knew exactly the right time to be your friend. As I continued to listen to Amelia, I wondered if this was a coincidence or whether it was something that was taught systemically by Bishop Tyler.

Amelia fought back tears as she continued her tragic story. "We all saw the change in my aunt, but we were completely blind. Most people in our family were happy that she was no longer depressed and that she was going to church. Bishop Tyler appeared to be a positive force in her life, but that was only a mirage for the family. The reality was that my aunt had become a robot for Calvin Sr. Calvin Sr. convinced my aunt to start attending his church. That church and Bishop Tyler became her God. Everything that she did was for the advancement of the church. Even after her grades dropped in college, she still promoted the church and Calvin Sr. He would call her and she would always be there for him. My family tried to make her understand that she was too caught up in the man, but she would not listen. It was only a matter of time before Calvin Sr. was "bonding" with her in a special way. Calvin Sr. would tell my aunt that "Christ is in him and he wanted Christ to be in her also."

My mind drifted off as Amelia finished her story. I bet the nigga was begging like, "Feel how the power of Christ thrust his unlimited power inside you. Behold, I stand at the door, and knock: if any woman hear my voice, and open the door, I will come in her, and will

266

sup with her, and she with me. Please baby, please let me come sup with you."

My mind zeroed back in as Amelia continued to speak"My aunt fell deeply in love with Bishop Tyler and soon he convinced her that the love between them was like a spiritual frontier. He convinced her that what they were doing was special and should only be between them. Not only was my aunt involved in a love affair with a married minister, but she was also reeling in new members. She was one of the founding members of Sold Out for Christ. She would go to different college campuses recruiting new members and Bishop Tyler would repay her by screwing her. It all came to an end after her pregnancy. Bishop Tyler denied being the father at first. Then gave her $12,000 through this same law office and convinced her to abort the child."

Sha'quonda and I glanced at each other because the story sounded all too real. It was like a generational blue print for the Tylers to stay out of trouble. Deny and then sweet talk them. If that didn't work, throw money at them. Bishop Tyler went on to become a mega bishop and Amelia's aunt committed suicide.

Now it was like she was our guardian angel trying to keep us from throwing our lives away. Sha'quonda tried to poke holes in Amelia's story, but everything just added up so perfectly. Amelia expressed her concern for us because she had never seen so many lawyers work so hard to destroy two girls.

Amelia's last words to us before she walked out of the bathroom made us really think. "I never said don't take the money. I said think first and get a lawyer."

She smiled at us and left us to our horrified thoughts. What if Amelia was right about all of this, were we actually signing away everything that we had worked for?

For the first time in her life, I think Sha'quonda finally had a logical idea come out of her mouth when she spoke. "Angela, I don't know about this. I mean we never really planned for the possibility that Calvin and his father just might be two steps ahead of us."

I stared at the vanity mirror and noticed a lighting bug scorched and stuck to one of the lights. I laughed to myself because I had a brief memory of when Steven and I were young and innocent chasing lightening bugs around the backyard in Baxley. Then it dawned on me—Steven!

Steven and I were not as close as we used to be, but I still could trust him. He found out by mistake what I was doing, and he eventually spilled the beans to my parents. Steven came over during a surprise visit and was shocked to find Sha'quonda and me sitting on the balcony talking like best friends. The cat was pretty much out the bag, so I only told him half the truth. I told him that Sha'quonda and I were discussing our options in regards to child support against Patrick. Steven being Steven did a little snooping and found out rather quickly that Sha'quonda and I might be pregnant.

Steven and my mother showed up banging on the door one Saturday morning spiting fire as they spoke to me. "I cannot believe you Angela! You barely come around and see RC and here you are pregnant with another baby."

I expected my father's reaction to be the worst of all, but I was surprised. My father quietly walked in as my mother and brother were admonishing me. He slumped down on the couch and stared at me as if I was a sick cancer patient.

My father asked my mother and brother to leave the room and then he spoke. "Baby girl, what's going on with your life? Do you even think about all the dreams that you had as a child. I know you've been through a lot, but there's got to be some type of logical explanation why you would allow your life to turn out like this? Always remember, no matter how far you run, God will always be their waiting."

I felt ashamed I never looked him in the eye. I just pulled at my fingernails with my teeth. I wanted to tell my father that I never really

268

got over all the hurtful things that Craig, Patrick, and Calvin had done to me. I wanted to tell my father that when I called for God, he destroyed me. Above all, I wanted to tell my father that never again would I be hurt by another man without destroying them first. I wanted to tell my father all these things, but I just sat in silence and stared at my jagged fingernails.

Steven and I still spoke on the phone sometimes, but I always felt like our relationship never was the same. I looked at Sha'quonda and then looked at the poor little lightning bug scorched on the light bulb and decided that we might be in a little over our heads. I quickly dialed Steven's number and the phone rang until his voicemail interrupted the slow steady ring. I left a message, hung my phone up, and slowly walked back toward the boardroom. I pushed through the door and saw that Calvin, his father, and the lawyers had already returned. The room became silent as Sha'quonda and I made our way back to our seats. Sha'quonda looked at me like she was a white girl trapped in a horror movie and I felt a lump slowly form in my throat.

Mr. Schroder sat quietly in the corner as a slender, dark-skinned gentlemen smiled and began to talk."Good afternoon, ladies. My name is Berry Mills and I'm in charge of financial litigation here at McCoy, Schroder and Mills. I will be representing your best interest as we move forward with this process. You may not understand some of the terminology because of the sheer volume of the paperwork but I'm hear to put your fears to rest. I refuse to allow my beautiful sisters to be railroaded by anyone."

I could see why Calvin and his father had hired this law firm. The number one thing about going into any situation is feeling comfortable, and Mr. Mills made you feel comfortable. He was not a stuffy, old, white man like Schroder. He was young, black, and handsome. He reminded me of Hill Harper with his engaging smile and movie star looks. Sha'quonda's nervous leg swinging had ceased. I felt comfortable asking him any question. The tension in the room started to melt as Mr. Mills offered to help invest the money in lucrative financial portfolios. Mr. Mills' engaging smile had Sha'quonda and me eating out of his hand. He drew the perfect picture and all we had to do was follow through with the abortions. The ink pens were almost in our hands when I saw Calvin lean toward Mr. Mills. He whispered something in his ear and Mr. Mills let out a haunted, bloodcurdling laugh. His eerie laugh reminded me of Vincent Price at the end of Michael Jackson's, Thriller song.

Sha'quonda quickly pulled the ink pen back from the paper almost as if she had seen a ghost and I followed suit.

Sha'quonda eyed Calvin and asked in a low, concerned voice, "I have one question. How will the payments be dispersed?"

I stared at Sha'quonda not knowing weather to smile with pride or laugh at her for all of sudden getting educated. Calvin and his father glanced back and forth at each other as if saying, "Did I hear that come out of this ghetto bitch's mouth?"

I had to admit, the question was the elephant in the room. Mr. Mills fell back into his "let me make it all better" persona and said, "It would be explained once the contracts were signed."

Both Sha'quonda and I twirled the ink pens in our hands not knowing whether to sign or walk out. Calvin and his father watched us with anticipation as the rest of the room fell silent. The silence was abruptly broken as the sound of T-pain and Kanye West bellowed out the words "Welcome to the Good Life," indicating that I had an incoming call. I glanced down at the phone and saw a picture of Steven staring back at me.

I excused myself from the conference table and walked into the hallway. I answered the phone and heard Steven's energetic voice. "What's up, baby sis? Whatcha into?"

Tears filled my eyes as thoughts of my brother filled my senses. No matter how upset Steven was with me, he would never let anyone hurt or take advantage of me. If only I had trusted Steven more, I probably would never have been in this predicament.

It must have been the distress in my voice message because Steven was all business as he spoke. "So what's going on, Angie? Are you okay?"

I wanted to scream, "No! I'm scared and afraid. I think I'm in some shit that I can't get out off."

Instead, I tried to make small talk. "Hey, Steven. I was just calling to see how you're doing."

Steven immediately cut me off and screamed, "Angela! Stop bullshiting me. You have to learn to stop trying to take on the world by yourself. I know you're hurting because I hear it in your voice. Now tell me what the fuck is going on."

Steven raising his voice at me forced more tears into my eyes, but he made his point. I guess my entire family was fed up with me. I was at a road block, and my brother was asking to help. It was time for me to open up and tell the truth. I took a deep breath and explained in graphic detail what Sha'quonda and I were up against. Some of the details made Steven cringe, especially the part about me faking a pregnancy.

I spoke to Steven in a low, desperate voice. "Steven, I don't know what to do. If I back out now, they'll probably sue me. If I keep going forward, I don't know what will happen. I'm scared, man! I think I really fucked up this time."

Instead of Steven cursing and judging me about poor decisions he screamed, "Definitely don't sign anything! And whatever you do, don't tell the truth. Baby girl, I hate to say this, but you have to ride it out. It's like peeling hot wax of hair. You have to rip it off fast and suffer through it."

I asked Steven what should I do, and without a pause, he told me to put him on speaker phone and go back in the room. I pulled the conference room door open like I was superman breaking out of a phone booth.

I looked at Sha'quonda and said, "Put the ink pen down. Our attorney is telling us not to sign anything."

The trivial chatter filtering throughout the room quickly came to a halt as all eyes were fixated on me.

Mr. Mills turned from the sweet southern confronter to Darth Vader as his voice boomed in my direction. "What the hell is going on? Five minutes ago we had an agreement. Now you come back after a phone call and the deal is off? What the hell is going on?"

I turned my phone's volume up to maximum and called for Steven.

Steven's normal, heavy southern accent was replaced by an articulate, baritone voice, custom made for the boardroom. "Sir, Ms. Anderson and Ms. Patterson will not be signing anything until we get more of a clarification about the document."

I heard a voice at the far end of the table finally come alive. A short, plump, elderly, white man leaned toward the cell phone and introduced himself. "Hello Sir. My name is Mitch McCoy, the owner of the firm. Who are you? And what are your credentials?"

Steven fired back in his most articulate voice, "Sir, that's really not relevant to this conversation. The most important thing to know is that no one will be signing anything today."

Angry that Steven was dismissing him as a nobody, Mr. McCoy quickly shouted back, "It is relevant!"

I laughed to myself because I had seen Steven play this game many times, and trust me, no one did it better.

Steven replied in a sarcastic voice. "Sir, if it was relevant, don't you think that those two young ladies would at least know the amount of money you are paying them?"

Mr. McCoy's voice came down a few octaves as he continued with a dry laugh and spoke back to Steven. "Sir, I don't know if you are fully aware of what's going on today. We are in the middle of negotiations to give these young ladies a substantial amount of money and you are interfering."

Steven paused for a few seconds and then replied, "What is the substantial amount?"

Mr. McCoy laughed again and replied, "Sir, we are not at liberty to disclose these proceedings."

I was quick to give an answer to the question. "They say they are going to give us $1. 5 million apiece."

Steven, quickly thinking two moves ahead like a chess match, responded with the same old dry laugh given to him by Mr. McCoy. "If they give you a casher's check for $1. 5 million today, I say sign the document and walk out happy."

I looked around the room locking eyes with each person, waiting to see if anyone would respond.

The room remained silent for what seemed like an eternity and then Bishop Tyler spoke. "Sir, we intend on paying these young ladies every cent that is due to them. But we need some assurance that these delicate issues won't come back to bite us. Our intentions are to give these young ladies $50,000 apiece today. We will release the full amount thirty days after the delicate matter is taken care of."

Calvin Jr. chimed in, "That's right! We need proof that the delicate matter is resolved."

You could tell that the discussion was annoying Mr. McCoy because he quickly jumped into the conversation. "But we are still in negotiations, so we can not deny or confirm the agreed upon payment."

Mr. McCoy was about to say something else when Steven interrupted, "Fax me over a copy of the contract and I will quickly view it."

There was a lot of mumbling coming from the Tylers and the suits.

Mr. McCoy responded, "Sir, I will not fax over a copy because it would be improper for my clients. Besides, I represent both parties in this legal matter. The young ladies were in the process of signing the paper work after they had obtained my colleague's services.

Mr. Mills flashed a large Bugs Bunny smile and leaned forward to talk.

273

Steven quickly interrupted before he could say anything. "Angela, you and Sha'quonda need your own attorneys. Call me back after you leave!"

Steven quickly hung up before any of the attorneys could rebut. Everyone in the room appeared to be confused. Bishop Tyler was frantically looking around the room hoping that someone would step in and save the day. The lawyers took turns at trying to convince us why it was important to deal with the issue now instead of bringing in strangers. Sha'quonda's nervous leg swinging had returned, and she looked as though she was about to throw up.

Every time I tried to say I think we need to get our own lawyer, Mr. McCoy would ignore me and offer more down payment money. "Our clients are willing to pay both of you $90,000 if we sign the contracts today. Did I say $90,000? Let's just do an even $100,000 and get this done today."

Everybody was running around trying to do their best to persuade Sha'quonda and me when I nearly missed another phone call. I looked at my phone not noticing the number but I felt like it was an important call. Again, I excused myself and answered the phone.

I was halfway out of the room when a heard the shrill of a familiar voice from long ago. "Skeee Wee Soror, this is number four asking if the tail might need a little assistance."

I felt the tears rush down my face as Kayla's voice continued to boom through the phone. "Hey girl, your brother called me and told me that you might need a little legal advice, so tell me was what's going   on."
I was so happy to hear Kayla's voice. I wanted to just talk about the good old days in college, but my mind was in fight or flight. I gave Kayla a general idea of what I and a friend were up against. I was too embarrassed to give names, so our conversation was a basic rundown on the current events.

Knowing how Kayla was, I knew she wanted more information. But she responded like a true friend, "I only want to know two things. What law firm are you at, and who's the father?"

I replied, "The first question is easy. I'm trapped on the thirty-second floor of McCoy, Schroder and Mills. These people will not let us leave unless I sign this document. They're throwing all types of numbers at me in order to get everything squared away today.

Kayla laughed and then spoke. "Don't worry about it! I'll handle it, girl."

I walked further away from the conference room door and began to speak again."Kayla, the second question is a little more complicated."

Kayla replied, "What's hard about the question? You do know who the baby's father is?"

I wanted to tell Kayla that I was lying about being pregnant. But that would have destroyed both me and Sha'quonda. Sha'quonda heard the lawyers' offers of ninety and $100,000. My telling the truth now would derail everything.

I thought for a brief minute and then whispered, "Calvin Tyler Jr. , the heir to the throne at Solid Foundation Cathedral."

I waited for Kayla to make a remark about my situation, but it never occurred. Instead of asking questions, Kayla instructed me to go back and wait for her signal. I walked back into the room and slumped down in the chair. I was hoping that Kayla would come through for me because the situation had gotten out of control. Sha'quonda was being wooed by Mr. Mills and it seemed to be working. The only person in the room with a long face was me. Everyone else was laughing at me and making comments about me being left out in the cold alone.

I was on the verge of snapping when I saw Amelia enter the conference room. Amelia walked over to Mr. McCoy and handed him a message. Mr. McCoy read the message to himself and then his pale, pink skin went completely flush. Mr. McCoy glanced at me and then back at the message.

Mr. McCoy cleared his voice and asked for quick five-minute break.

I don't know what the message said, but it was apparent that Bishop Tyler was involved. Mr. McCoy whispered in Bishop Tyler's ear and they both exited the room. Calvin stared at me as if he wanted to kill me. I stared back at him almost smiling because Kayla had made something big go down. Bishop Tyler stuck his head in the door and motioned for Calvin Jr. to come outside. The other five attorneys in the room made uneasy conversation amongst themselves while making quick glances towards the door.

I could hear voices getting louder in the hallway as if people were disagreeing. Sha'quonda glanced at me and gestured with her eyes as if to say, "Do you know what is going on?"

I smiled back at Sha'quonda and made a cut throat signal as if to say, "It's a wrap."

Calvin and his father reemerged from the hallway meeting looking as if the grim reaper had told them time's up.

Mr. McCoy started speaking in a low voice. "It has been brought to our attention that Ms. Anderson and Ms. Patterson have retained their own lawyers from the firm of Moore, Dukes and Price." The other attorneys in the room gasped for air as Mr. McCoy continued to talk. "The law Firm is prepared to file a cease and desist complaint against us if we continue this meeting. Ms. Anderson and Ms. Patterson, we would like to take this time to thank you for coming, and wish you good luck."

Sha'quonda and I walked out of the conference room to complete silence. As soon as the door closed, we heard an uproar of activity as the men started debating the best action to take.

We stepped on the elevator and Amelia quickly fell in behind us. "Damn! Girl, I didn't know you had it like that!

I looked at Amelia as if to say, "Can you please tell me what the hell is going on?"

Amelia looked at me first and then at Sha'quonda and spoke. "Do either one of you know what's going on." Sha'quonda and I stared back at Amelia with bewildered looks on our faces as she continued."You have the Law Firm of Moore, Dukes and Price in your corner and you don't know what's up?"

Again looking bewildered we shook our heads no.

Amelia blurted out, "Well let's just say you'll probably get a little bit more than $1 million. Moore, Dukes and Price only accept top money cases and high-profile clients. When you read headlines talking about baby mamas raping ballers' pockets, it's because of Moore, Dukes and Price."

I stared out the glass walled elevator trying to comprehend what was going on. I could hear the endless chatter between Sha'quonda and Amelia, but my mind was fixated on finding out what was going on.

The elevator slowly came to a stop on the lobby level, and the last thing I remember hearing was, "Congratulations! I'm glad you made the right decision."

Amelia smiled at us and we walked out the door. As soon as we were out the door, Sha'quonda was ready to celebrate. She was hugging me and screaming, "Paid in full, bitch!"

I was on the phone speed dialing Kayla with one hand and trying to calm Sha'quonda down with the other. I finally had Kayla on the other line so we quickly jumped into the car so we could hear.

Kayla started the conversation out sarcastically like always. "Well at least you are having a baby by a motherfucka with some money."

I managed a fake smile and asked her what was going on. Kayla proceeded to talk. "Solid Foundation is in a bit of a bind. My researchers tell me that Calvin and his father don't have much of a choice. The plans for Solid Foundation and the new church in

Savannah are tied together with your decision. If you had signed today, everything would have been hidden under the rug. They could have lied and said you were crazy because you would have had an abortion. Do you understand how many millions of dollars they can lose if they don't settle with you?"

Kayla calculated that Calvin and his father would be willing to pay as much as six or seven million dollars to keep this dirt on the down low. The thing about being a high-profile bishop is that you have to at least look squeaky clean to the public. Calvin had so much dirt on him that it was falling on his father. It would have been better for the church if Bishop Tyler would have simply thrown Calvin under the bus. But that greed and lust for more money could only be accomplished by protecting his son. Kayla told us that Calvin was still denying that he was the father.

Kayla started laughing and then spoke, "I wonder if he would be willing to roll the dice with a paternity suit."

I responded with a nervous laugh, but I was really horrified inside. Kayla told me that she would be in Atlanta in three weeks and we should do lunch. I acted excited but I was still thinking about the ramifications of a paternity test. I glanced over at Sha'quonda and she was swaying side to side as if listening to music. Her dreams were finally coming true. Three or four million dollars could go a very long way in her world. And I could see she was already spending it. It was time for me to start looking for an exit strategy. And meeting with Kayla would be my first step.

Chapter 17

It had been a while since I had had lunch on my old campus. I sipped on a small cup of water and watched as two girls flirted with a jock. I was daydreaming about all the fun times of campus life when I felt a sharp, stinging pinch on my arm. I turned around ready to scream bloody murder when I saw the face of my friend Kayla. We fell in each other's arms and hugged for what seemed like an eternity.

The thing about real friends is that no matter how far apart or how much time between contacts, that love will always be there. Kayla and I were no different. Kayla's hair was shorter than it was the last time I had seen her, but she still had the same big, brown eyes and engaging smile. We both sat down at the table smiling when a short, balding, white man surprised me by pulling his chair up to the table. I was even more surprised when he apologized to Kayla for running late and extended his hand to shake mine.

Kayla pointed toward the man and said, "This is Edward Potter. Ed, this is one of my best friends from college."

We both smiled at each other and shook hands as Kayla continued, "Ed is one of our private investigators who's been snooping around in Atlanta for me."

Kayla was never much for small talk, so she got right down to business.

Kayla whispered to Ed and motioned for him to get the briefcase near his leg. Ed opened the case and pulled out three brown folders. I felt like I was in a real spy movie as Ed spread the folders out on the table. Ed had gathered information on Calvin and his parents.

I glanced at the information that he had gathered on Calvin and I was surprised to see a photo of myself.

Ed began to talk. "Obviously, you two were a couple at one time. I spoke with people near your apartments and around the city, and they confirmed that you two dated at one time. I also found out through my contacts at the Tylers' law firm that there is possibly another woman pregnant by Calvin. I'm almost certain about this, but I need a little more time to get the woman's information."

I mumbled softly, "You are very thorough with your investigation."

I wanted to tell Kayla about Sha'quonda, but I knew how she felt about her. I mean really, how I could explain to her that Sha'quonda's ghetto ass and I had set Calvin up on purpose? I browsed through Bishop Tyler's information and was shocked when I saw his financial statement. The church ledgers that I had taken from Deacon Berry were only half of Papa Tyler's money. He had money coming in from books, jewelry, speaking engagements, and oversees ministry. When you look up the word "hustling" in a dictionary, there should be a picture of Bishop Tyler.

I chuckled to myself as I picked up the third folder, which read "Mrs. Leeann Tyler." I was shocked that Ed had information on Mrs. Tyler. Mrs. Tyler was so quiet and unassuming that you would think she was single. Mrs. Tyler would attend 11am service on Sundays, shake a couple of hands, and disappear for the week. I remember when I was trying to follow her. It was almost impossible to keep track of her. She rarely left the house and when she did it was to go to church or the airport.

My attention quickly returned to Kayla as she spoke about our plan of attack. "The church in Savannah is scheduled to open in four months, so that gives us approximately three months to get all our ducks in a row."

I looked at Kayla and asked, "Do you think this is going to get nasty?"

Kayla glanced at me from the top of her glasses looking like a hot ninth-grade school teacher and responded, "Angela, perception is everything. If I were representing the bishop and his son, I would turn over every rock until I found a fake rat."

I swallowed hard because after all, I was the fake rat. If Calvin's lawyer turned over enough rocks, they would definitely find me and my imaginary baby.

Kayla continued to talk. "But the good thing is that you have the upper hand. Calvin and his father were both banking on you signing off on the contracts as quickly as possible. He wanted you to sign off because there is a keep quiet clause in them. The last thing that Calvin needs is some hoochie mama coming forward talking about she's pregnant by him, no disrespect. And let's not even talk about his wife Linda Stanford. Prophetess Linda Stanford is being given an eight-million-dollar church based on her "I am a strong woman" pedestal. What would it look like if she stayed with Calvin? Hell, she'd probably look good to her audience, but the new church dreams would vanish like a pipe dream. Do you understand how much money they stand to lose if this comes out? We have to strike now so that we can get the best deal."

I was starting to see the big picture, but I wished I had followed Sha'quonda's lead and taken the money. This issue was starting to get bigger and bigger.

Kayla stared at me as if she were looking threw glass, "Angela, do you know who Calvin's other baby mama is?"

I froze not knowing weather to confirm or deny.

I finally came up with half an answer and spoke. "I got a pretty good idea."

Kayla glanced back at Ed and slammed her hand on the table. "Jackpot!"

Ed quickly chimed in. "Do you have a contact number? Do you know where she lives?"

Kayla cut Ed off and rephrased the question. "Better yet, do you think you can get her to Savannah in three months?"

Ed leaned into the table and nodded his head in agreement.

I glanced out the cafe window and spoke. "I'm certain I can get her to come to Savannah."

Kayla and Ed smiled at each other and then back at me. I could tell they were still curious about the mystery lady.

Kayla asked, "Hey Angela, how sure are you that this girl is pregnant by Calvin?"

I looked at Kayla and gave her the old AGA "Girl, you know it's true" look and responded, "I'm about 99.9% sure that he is the father."

Kayla leaned back in the chair and motioned to Ed. He tossed two first-class airplane tickets on the table towards me and smiled.

Kayla laughed and drummed on the table nervously as she spoke. "Alright, pretty girl, I'll see you in Savannah in three months."

I hugged Kayla as she dialed McCoy, Schroder and Mills to confirm a meeting that she had already planned. I smiled and exhaled a sigh of relief because I knew I had a bulldog that I trusted.

The smile on my face grew even wider as I heard Kayla scream into the phone. "Tell your clients if the money ain't right, get ready to do a lot more praying and crying."

And with that, she slammed the blackberry on the table. That girl Kayla's a beast.

I felt comfortable knowing that Kayla was in my corner, but I also had an uneasy feeling. I hated getting Kayla involved in my deception because I considered her a good friend. She would never forgive me if something went wrong. I would have destroyed the lives of friends and family all because of revenge. The Tylers could come back with a game plan to do nothing. They could just sit back and wait for us to show proof. That would be detrimental to us because trust would be out the door. I could easily be shown to be a fraud and Sha'quonda would be the only one with ammunition. There would be no reason for Sha'quonda to remain loyal once I was out of the way. In fact, there would be no reason for anyone to remain in my corner.

Through manipulation and sheer will power, I had everything I wanted and more within reach. All I had to do for the next few months was to keep Sha'quonda close and stay alert.

Chapter 18

After months of anticipation and waiting, the time finally arrived for Sha'quonda and me to put up or shut up. Kayla had stayed in touch with me weekly, giving me updates about our strategy. I was now comfortable wearing my prosthetic belly. My new belly was like my drivers license—I never left home without it. I felt good about faking my way through the negotiations because only I knew the truth. Kayla spared no expense to make us comfortable. She had followed through with everything she had promised. Now it was time for us to step up and present evidence. Kayla, finally finding out that Sha'quonda was the unknown mother of Calvin's baby, was already jeopardizing the plans.

The expression on Kayla's face told the whole story as she stared at Sha'quonda. Sha'quonda was not exactly the person she envisioned as being the mother of Calvin's baby. I could tell that Sha'quonda was annoying the hell out of Kayla. Every time Sha'quonda opened her mouth to eat or talk, Kayla rolled her eyes in disgust.

Kayla looked at me and motioned for me to meet her on the balcony. Kayla and I leaving the room didn't bother Sha'quonda. She was chopping on chicken wings and smacking with every annoying bite.

As soon as we closed the balcony door, Kayla held her hands up as if to say, "What the fuck is going on?"

The normally cool and collected Kayla seemed upset as she spoke. "How in God's name did that tramp become part of this?"

I flashed a nervous smile at Kayla and responded, "It just happened! We found out that Calvin was playing us both. I guess it was destiny."

Kayla twitched her mouth in disbelief as she responded. "Destiny, umm hum. I just bet it was destiny."

I turned away from her with a deceitful smile on my face. Kayla was reading me like an open book, but I could not tell her everything. She was upset because I was withholding details on important issues. Kayla was very meticulous when it came to her cases. She wanted all of her ducks in a row before the negotiations started. The only thing that kept her from panicking was the sex tapes.

We walked back into the room and I showed Kayla our most damaging evidence. My sex tape was not as graphic, but it clearly showed Calvin in a different light. The loving bishop's son was replaced by a cruel, sex-induced monster. The tape showed him cursing and swearing until he was sexually satisfied. The featured act showed Calvin looking pitiful with a mangled condom around his penis.

Kayla shook her head and spoke. "Girl, I know you had something to do with all of this."

Sha'quonda and I glanced at each other and started laughing

Kayla turned the TV off and started to speak. "Okay ladies, let's go over the game plan, because I don't want any slip ups tomorrow."

Kayla went over every possible scenario that she thought would be thrown at us. She grilled us on our backgrounds, which appeared to be our greatest weakness. If one of us cracked during the negotiation, it could cost us millions. Kayla's biggest concerns were both of us having a baby by Patrick and the dates of the conception with Calvin. It was already assumed that Patrick was on their team. He had already showed that he was willing to lie as long as the price was right. I couldn't blame him. He was only looking out for himself. Once he was released from prison he needed something to fall back on.

We had to prove to Calvin's lawyers that we weren't conspiring to trap Calvin. Calvin was swearing to anybody who listened that he wore a condom with Sha'quonda. And he was outright denying that he ever had sex with me during the listed conception period. Kayla figured that the videotaped sex act with Calvin was the key to the entire case. There was no way Calvin or his father was going to allow that sex tape to be plastered all over the place.

Kayla turned to me with a grim look on her face and quietly mentioned what I was thinking. "Your story might be harder to prove. The last time Calvin and you had sex was almost ten months ago. And here you are claiming to be six months pregnant."

The only thing I could do was sit there and look stupid. I blamed myself for writing how far along I was on that Father's Day card. There was no way this would add up.

Kayla didn't want the public to see the sex tape first because any monetary value attached to the tape would be small compared to a settlement. Kayla agreed that the best move would be for Sha'quonda and me to go into the negotiations separately. I already knew what Kayla was thinking. At least Sha'quonda would get her settlement before I walked in with an immaculate conception.

Kayla smiled at me, but I also saw concern in her eyes. She knew once I stepped in that room, all bets were off. When the dates stop adding up, I would have to take the best deal offered. They could easily say I was a scorned lover who used a syringe to extract sperm from a condom. Even worse, they could pull my shirt up and see a fake pregnancy belly. I guessed it was time to start looking for a lifeline. I fell asleep thinking of the worst-case scenario and decided I was not going down without a fight.

I woke up the next morning felling like Rocky Balboa. I jumped in the shower and prepared myself for the long day. While Sha'quonda was still sleeping like a baby, I was practicing worst-case scenarios. I met with Kayla for breakfast and we talked about the good old days in college.

We arrived at the scheduled negotiations late because Sha'quonda couldn't find her platinum hair weave. For whatever reason, Sha'quonda went in the meeting looking as ghetto as possible.

Maybe it was on purpose. She probably wanted to rub it in the face of Bishop Tyler. Your high-class son was all up in this ghetto pussy.

Kayla quickly disappeared into a conference room with the word "Reserved" across the door. Sha'quonda and I waited anxiously for the proceedings to start. Ten minutes later, Kayla walked out of the room looking pale and sick.

She cleared her voice and said, "Well guys, they're starting out hard and low. It seems like they may have some good shit on one of you."

I felt the prosthetic belly shift a little and wondered if they were going to pull my shirt up or punch me in my fake belly. I had already vowed that I would run out of the proceedings if a doctor was in there.

Kayla motioned in our direction to follow her. I turned to Sha'quonda and wished her good luck.

I was immediately interrupted by Kayla. "Sorry babes, that plan went out the window yesterday. We are going in together. We're going to swing first and hard. We're going to show the tapes and hope they back down. Whatever's going down is going down right now."

Sha'quonda leaped out of chair charged and ready to go like she was in Super Bowl 20. I was a little more subdued. The only thing on my mind was that a doctor was hiding behind the door. All I could visualize was a doctor snatching my fake belly out and him saying, "You are not the baby's father."

Sha'quonda waddled in first and I tried to waddle just like her. Ed quickly jumped up and pulled our chairs out and we sat down. The same people were present for this meeting as the last except for a few new faces. The old faces really didn't intimidate me like the new ones. I was studying each new face looking for the doctor when I came eye-to-eye with two familiar faces: Prophetess Linda Stanford Tyler and Mother Leeann Tyler. We were seated on opposite sides of a long conference table.

Linda stared at me as if she wanted my head on a silver platter. She would look in our direction and then whisper something to

Mother Tyler. I could feel Sha'quonda's leg trembling as Mr. McCoy greeted everyone. He pointed in the direction of a stenographer and the stenographer started softly speaking into a mask-like object. Mr. McCoy went for the juggler as soon as the stenographer gave the okay.

He turned in our direction and pointed his finger at Kayla. "We have reason to believe that your clients have falsely accused my client of indiscretions. Your clients have willfully engaged in actions to discredit my client's name. They have made threats and accusations that are simply untrue. My client and I believe your clients have exaggerated about evidence pertaining to a pregnancy. If you have any evidence to discredit my client please present it, or let's pack it up and go home early.

Kayla confidently peeled out of her seat like a model on a cat walk. She walked toward the TV and plugged a jump drive into it. Calvin and his team shifted uneasily in their chairs as Kayla reached for the remote. Before the picture even came into view, you could hear Calvin grunting and cursing at Sha'quonda. When the picture finally appeared on the screen, it was in HD.

Kayla had taken my low-grade-quality tape and converted into a high definition masterpiece. Gasping sounds filled the room as Calvin pumped back and forth for what seemed like forever. Kayla was like a mad scientist, rewinding and then playing it in slow motion. The look on Calvin's face was priceless. Kayla's version had a close-up view of Calvin just after he discovered that the rubber had broken. You could hear Sha'quonda's annoying voice mumbling about birth control in the video.

I glanced over at Linda and Leeann and they were studying the video like two pros. The date stamp was clearly visible, and Calvin's dumb ass had a shredded condom hanging from his penis. In the immortal words of Johnny Cochran, "If the rubber bust away, you must pay."

The silence in the room was eerie as Sha'quonda proudly stared at each member of Calvin's team. It was almost like she was taunting them by saying, "Yea, that's right. This is some good pussy. You wanna try it."

Calvin simply stared blankly at the table hoping that this nightmare would be over soon. Mr. McCoy wrote something on a piece of paper and handed it to Calvin and his father.

Then he turned his attention towards me and spoke. "Ms. Anderson, do you have any evidence that shows my client with you?"

The silence was broken when Kayla ejected one tape and immediately popped in another. As my brother Steven so eloquently put it, "All you saw was assholse and elbows"

Calvin was so deep off in my pudding that we looked like we were glued together. Thank God for Sha'quonda because she forgot to put the date stamp on the camcorder. Nobody in the room was paying attention to that. All the lawyers saw was Calvin grunting and growling to ejaculation. I glanced over at Calvin and he was still staring down at the table.

Mother Tyler was visibly upset about what she was seeing. She stood up and excused herself from the conference room. Linda also stood and slammed her chair against the table as she followed closely behind her.

Mr. McCoy whispered something to Bishop Tyler and he cleared his voice in an uneasy manner. I could see the little gears in Calvin's head working on overtime as he attempted to calculate when he last screwed me. With all the hoes he had hit, I was hoping that he wouldn't figure it out.

All of a sudden a look came across his face as if he smelled rotten cheese. He leaned over and whispered to his father and Mr. McCoy. They all looked in my direction and closely studied my face.

The first thing that popped up in my mind was, "Oh shit, time to run."

I was trying to remain calm and hold my poker face, but my nerves were going into overdrive. I felt my fake belly starting to shift as my heart rate increased.

Mr. McCoy opened his mouth to speak just as Mother Tyler reentered the room with Linda following like a lap puppy.

Mr. McCoy started speaking. "Ms. Anderson, are you sure that you conceived your baby during this encounter?"

I was about to open my mouth and say, "What had happened was." When Mother Tyler slammed her hand on the table and shouted, "Enough of this!"

I had never heard Leeann Tyler speak at church, but you could tell she was like EF Hutton. Everybody listened.

Bishop Tyler tried to quietly shush Leeann, but you could tell she was irritated. "Don't you shush me! If you two would keep it in your pants, we probably wouldn't be going through this every other month."

Kayla looked down and I could tell she was about to laugh as Leeann continued.

"Let's get straight down to business. Everybody in this room is in get money mode. The lawyers, the girls, and you two dummies. We are on the eve of opening one of the biggest churches in Georgia, and you two dummies choose now to start pinching pennies. We could give each of them ten million dollars and we would make it back in a year. We need to get on with this so that we can move forward. We cannot go into our new project with this hanging over our heads."

Linda quickly started shaking her head in agreement as Leeann stared at her, almost as if to say, "Bitch, remember what I told you." Both Calvin and his father wanted to say something, but it was like Leeann was on her soap box preaching.

I found myself silently agreeing with her and praying that everyone would listen. By the time Mama Tyler got finished, Calvin and his father were ready to concede defeat. The Tylers agreed to pay a lump sum of four million dollars to be split by both me and Sha'quonda. They also agreed to place two more million in separate escrow accounts for each child once they were born. Child support would be paid to us through the law firm. A silence clause was placed in the contract along with a special clause that only allowed the kids to know of their father's existence at age eighteen.

I was trying to remain calm, but I felt Sha'quonda nudging me over and over under the table. The nudges got harder and harder as the terms of the agreement were read. Kayla was asked to join a group of attorneys huddled near the stenographer. Contracts magically appeared as the attorneys continued to whisper.

Sha'quonda and I sat quietly at the table as Calvin, Linda, and Bishop Tyler stood to make their exit. None of them looked in our direction and quietly stormed out of the room, leaving Leeann standing near the table. Leeann smiled at us uncomfortably and walked around the table to get closer.

Kayla stopped Leeann's advancement by calling our names and motioning for us to come to her.

Kayla instructed us to sign some papers and then she spoke. "Look, Ed and I are going to stay here a few more hours to get everything squared away. If you too want to leave, that's fine."

Kayla waved at me and quickly returned to the pack of attorneys. Sha'quonda and I turned to leave and Leeann moved forward.

She shook hands with me and Sha'qounda and spoke. "I am so sorry that you girls had to go through this. No matter how carefully you raise your children, they sometimes stray. Had I known about this situation, it would have been handled months ago. You don't wait and tell at the last minute then try and play catch up. You girls were wronged by my son and now we have to move on."

As Leeann spoke to us, she reminded me of the actress Diane Carroll. She was tall and thin with mahogany skin. Her huge round eyes reminded me of Calvin. When she spoke, it was like listening to a world-class orator and Della Reece at the same time. She easily went from speaking perfect English to broken English without trying. She made you want to listen to her.

All three of us walked out of the conference room and just talked. Leeann made us feel extremely comfortable as she joked and laughed with us about her son. Leeann was about to leave when she pulled Sha'quonda and me in for a group hug.

It happened so fast that I forgot to hug her from the side. For a split second, I forgot about the fake belly. I could feel the fake stomach buckling from the weight of the hug. She slowly backed away from me and stared at my stomach, with a strange smile on her face. I tried to keep a fake grin on my face but I knew the gig was up.

Kayla and the pack of attorneys came through the door just as Sha'quonda and were leaving.

Leeann waved at us and spoke. "Sweetheart, let's do lunch, I'll call you."

This caught everybody by surprise because it was almost like the lion asking the lamb for lunch. I looked at Kayla with a stern look and whispered, "Do not give her my number."

Sha'quonda caught the first flight scheduled back to Atlanta. I could see that ghetto itch in her eyes that only Phillips Mall could satisfy. We hugged each other good bye and she caught the first cab to the airport. Kayla and I decided to have our own little slumber party in the hotel, which brought back memories of school. We talked, cried, and reminisced about everything from friend-of-me's to love lost. And for one magical night, it felt like we were transported back in time to the days when we had no worries.

The next morning, I was awakened by the low mummer of Kayla on her cell phone. It sounded serious as Kayla went through her logical progression of who, what, when, where, and why. The last thing I heard Kayla say was, "I'll catch the first flight out." Kayla bounced on the floor and started moving like a reverse hurricane packing her stuff and running her shower.

I rolled over still groggy from the night before and said, "Good morning. You got an emergency?"

Kayla looked at me sadly and responded, "Yeah girl, I have to get out of here. One of my rappers got arrested last night."

We both laughed as I sat up to hear more clearly. I was proud of Kayla as I watched her zoom around the room grabbing her stuff and getting prepared for another hectic day. Kayla looked around one final time and called for a bellhop. I felt the tears roll down my face as Kayla and I sat and talked quietly about the next time when we should get together.

There was a loud knock at the door which pushed us both over the emotional edge as we started bawling like little lost children. We hugged for what seemed like forever and I thanked Kayla for everything she he had done, and just like that, the door slammed shut.

I looked around at the shadows on the wall quietly thinking about Kayla when the sound of my phone chirped notifying me that I had a message. I automatically assumed that Kayla was shooting me a bye-bye email when I saw "bank alert" on the subject line. I opened the message expecting some type of overdraft when I saw "$4,000,000 deposit in account number 178392." I froze for a quick second and then I remembered that the money would be deposited at 8:00am.

The hotel alarm clock blinked at 5:56am, but my phone showed 8:02am. You can never describe the feeling when you go from broke to rich in a matter of seconds. Everything you ever wanted becomes incidental because now you can afford it. I lay back on the bed thinking about all the things I was going to buy when I was suddenly overcome with sleep. I drifted off to sleep thinking about all the bull that I had been through over the past few years. Tears of joy slowly trickled down my face as the low hum of the air conditioner softly rocked me back to sleep.

I felt the warm Savannah sun penetrate the curtains as my eyes focused on the 12:45pm scribbled across the clock. I pushed my prescription glasses towards my face as I read several text messages that were magically popping up out of nowhere. Out of the twenty-five messages sent to me, I only knew eight of the senders. The rest were from banks, investment firms, and other organizations aware of my newfound riches. I pulled myself slowly up from the bed and walked toward the bathroom. The first thing that I noticed lying on the floor was the fake pregnant belly. I must have taken it off while I was taking a nap. The thing had been attached to me for so long that I felt uncomfortable walking around without it.

I treated myself to a warm bubble bath, which quickly reinvigorated me. I couldn't wait to get back to Atlanta, but I also wanted to be cautious. I knew I couldn't just show up in Atlanta without a baby. People would start talking. I walked toward the computer and decided to purchase a seat on a private plane to Miami. I could do a little shopping and partying and sneak back to Atlanta in a few weeks, or even months.

I was about to purchase a ticket for a late evening flight when I heard a soft knock at the door. Instinctually, I responded, "Come back later," thinking it was housekeeping.

I settled in again to concentrate on my search when I heard the soft knock again. Annoyed by the interruption, I bounced from my seat cursing at the door. I knew housekeeping had heard me the first time.

I flung the door open and screamed, "Who the fuck is knocking?" Before I could finish my sentence, I almost fell over backwards in shock. My glasses were still on the dresser as I strained to focus. The image of Calvin's mother, Leeann Tyler was standing in front of me smiling. Leeann stood there smiling at me looking almost sinister.

She quickly glanced down at my belly and spoke. "I see you lost weight."

I quickly wrapped my arms around my stomach and moved backwards as she let herself in the room. I was afraid of what would happened next. Would she call her husband? Would she call the police? Or would she just call some old crony? Leeann quietly looked around the room as I uneasily watched every move she made. I had already decided that if she pulled her cell phone out, I would bash her head in with a vase, and take all the money out of the bank before anyone found out.

Leeann smiled at me again and asked if she could sit down. I quickly agreed. I sat down and positioned myself in front of her so that I could watch her every move. Leeann sighed loudly and I braced for whatever violent gesture she was about to make, but it never came.

Leeann leaned forward and smiled at me and spoke. "You know what? You remind me of me."

I didn't know weather to smile or just continue to stare at her like I was at a funeral.

She continued to talk. "You know, I remember when I was younger. I had game for days just like you. If I found a way to make money, I took advantage of it."

Leeann glanced at me and then glanced at the fake pregnant belly lying on the floor. I was still afraid to move, but Leeann waved her hand and continued to talk. "Ah girl, relax! I'm not here to hurt you. Shit, you did what you had to do and I applaud you for that. My cheating-ass husband taught my son to cheat, so it was just a matter of time before he got caught like his father. They're lucky they didn't run into a person like me. Shit, I would have taken all their money."

I still felt uncomfortable, but I managed a subdued smile.

Leeann started speaking again. "Obviously we not gonna be paying for a baby that don't exist. So when that two million dollars hits the escrow account in three months, don't expect it to stay there. I'll have someone contact you later today. You can forward me half of the money that hit your account this morning."

I glanced down at my hands as if somebody had just taken the cash out them. This bitch was leaving me with just two million dollars.

I started to say, "Damn bitch, you just as shiesty as your husband" when we came eye-to-eye.

I saw game written all over her face. I had seen that same expression so many times before from hustlers in the hood.

I don't know what it was, but I just decided to get bold with her when I spoke. "I'm sure we can work out a reasonable arrangement like a fifty-fifty split. You can take the two million dollars when it hits the escrow account and I'll give you a million today."

Leeann leaned back in the chair with a devilish grin and replied. "I'm sure we can work out an even better split and keep it at seventy-five-twenty-five. You played a good game right up to the last second and then missed your shot. You can either do it my way or get exposed the old-fashioned way."

We both stared at each other waiting for the other to blink. For all of my posturing, I knew I couldn't win. Leeann had me dead to center, and two million more dollars was all I was getting.

Still upset about what was occurring, I stood up and held my hand out. I had lost to a much better opponent.

Leeann firmly gripped my hand and said, "Nice doing business with you."

She turned to walk out the door and glanced at the fake belly on the floor.

She chuckled and spoke, "That was a good one. Will meet for drinks later to discuss the particulars."

I dreaded meeting Leeann for drinks for two reasons. One, I was embarrassed about being caught. And two, I didn't want to give away two million dollars.

When I arrived at the bar, Leeann was already seated and sipping wine. We exchanged pleasantries and she immediately went into business mode. I sat directly across from her and Leeann motioned to a young girl who appeared to be her assistant. The girl brought over a laptop computer and left. Leeann punched in some keys and swung the computer in my direction. I typed in my account number and pushed the computer back towards her. She typed in more numbers and showed me. I watched in agony as two million dollars disappeared from my account and reappeared in her private account in the Caymans.

I had to admit, Leeann was definitely not a dim-witted hussy. While Calvin Sr. was out plowing young hoes at the college campus, she was building herself a nice little nest egg. Everything for Leeann was paid for: vacation house, car, clothing, food, and jewelry. Everything was financed by little old ladies giving their last little pennies for tithes. Anything else that she received from her husband feeling guilty or marks like me was socked away. When I saw the twenty-five followed by six zeroes, I had to shake my head in disbelief. No wonder Leeann wanted to get rid of me and Sha'quonda. There was no way she was gone to allow two tricks to derail a multimillion-dollar train.

After Leeann finished tinkering with her computer, she closed it and spoke. "Angela, I have a proposition for you."

I responded to Leeann in a cautious manner. "Proposition. I don't know, Leeann. The last time we had deal, it cost me four million dollars."

Leeann laughed at my comment and responded, "That was just a teachable moment for you. You took something from me without my permission and I had to teach you a lesson. I'm not bitter about it because I would have done the same thing. I just didn't want you walking around thinking that you got over on me." A stern look came across Leeann's face as she leaned in and whispered. "No one gets over on me."

Leeann leaned back in the chair and her expression lightened as she continued to talk. "Now back to that proposition we were discussing."

I glanced around the bar and responded, "Yeah, I'm listening."

Leeann motioned in the direction of her assistant again and I looked at the wine menu.

I was about to order something to drink when I heard, "Good afternoon, Leeann."

My head quickly spun around to the familiar voice and face of Prophetess Linda Stanford-Tyler.

I turned toward Leeann and she had a weird smile plastered across her face. I stood as Linda sat beside Leeann.

Leeann pointed toward my chair and spoke. Everything's okay, Angela. Please have a seat. This is the proposition I was telling you about."

I glared at both Leeann and Linda as if warning them and responded, "What type of proposition are you talking about? I'm not on any of her bullshit."

Linda frowned back at me and responded, "Me on bullshit? You the one running around here setting people up, not me."

I held both arms out and responded, "Hey, I only give motherfuckers what's coming to them. And that motherfucker deserved everything he got."

Leeann cut me off in the middle of my sentence by saying, "Both of ya'll shut the fuck up. I'm up her trying to help both of you get rich, and you're bitching and moaning about my sorry-ass son. Now do ya'll want to make money, or talk about Calvin?"

Both Linda and I looked at each other and rolled our eyes.

Leeann continued to talk. "Here's the situation. We are scheduled to open a multimillion-dollar church in two days and we need to hit the ground running."

I looked at Linda and then back at Leeann confused.

Leeann continued to talk. "We have everything in place to attract members to the church except a marketing plan."

Leeann pointed at me and I knew what she was talking about. With Linda already following her around like a lap dog, it was just a matter of time before she had the opportunity to sock away more.

Linda was a powerful speaker who could control people's emotions. But what good is that if there's no one is at church to see her. That's where I came in. This went back to the Sold Out for Christ days. Not only was I good at strategy, but I was not shy about what I wanted. In short, Linda not only needed a hype man to proclaim her greatness, she needed a plan of attack.

Linda knew the Bible inside and out. But I knew the streets. Linda was the good shepherded who kept her flock happy. I was the evil rustler who brought her the flock. My tactics were like a Walmart superstore. I aimed to put everybody out of business. I was notorious for going into other churches and taking their members.

When I was with SOFC, I would go into small- and medium-sized churches and siphon off the members under thirty. I would testify, shout, and just generally get the young people excited about Christ. Once they arrived at Solid Foundation Cathedral, Linda, Calvin, and Bishop Tyler would quickly indoctrinate them. After three or four visits of being seated near celebrities, they were sold. It had been a while since I had did it, but it was like riding a bike. I could tell that Linda would have preferred someone else, but Leeann knew that no one could do it better.

Leeann leaned forward almost whispering, "I want you to lead our marketing team. I want to build this church up as soon as possible. My goal is to have ten thousand members by the end of the year and add ten thousand a year until we are overflowing. Calvin is donating five thousand members who I want you to train. I want them hungry like you were."

The plan sounded a little too good to be true and I responded, "I don't know about this, Leeann. It sounds good, but I'm not a hundred percent sure that Linda is on board. Plus, I'm not really interested in getting into another situation with your husband and son."

Leeann quickly shook her head and responded. "No, no, I understand. This is not that type of situation. This situation will only involve us three. Linda understands what type of man she has, now it's time for her to make the best decision for herself. I need you strictly for the marketing. If you choose not to come to service, that's fine."

Leeann pointed toward Linda without looking at her and continued to talk. "As for her, she will have no problem with our arrangement. She understands what her role is, and it will not have any effect on what you do. I don't care if you two are never friends.

This will be the perfect working relationship. I have no problem paying either of you six figures if you can keep it professional."

I shook my head still not believing it and promised to think about it. Leeann smiled as she pulled her designer shades over her eyes and stood to leave.

Linda quickly followed as Leeann began to speak. "No matter how upset you think I was about the situation, I can't knock your hustle. You deserve to be paid for using your mind, not your back."

She handed me her phone number and headed toward the door. Linda glared at me for a last time and followed Leeann without speaking.

I stayed at the bar and had a few more drinks. I may have gotten shaken down for some of my money, but I was still happy. The only thing weighing heavily on my mind was the offer from Leeann. Making six figures and starting over in Savannah was something positive. But I also had to think about the price. Was it really worth getting in bed with snakes like Linda and Leeann? I enjoyed watching Linda squirm. I especially loved the fact that she would always live with the vision of Calvin in freak mode. She probably would lie awake for the rest of their marriage asking the same question. "Why can't I bring the freak out of him like she did?"

The dilemma to accept the offer was still working its way through my head when I felt two hungry eyes peering at me from the corner. I really didn't care who it was because my mind was occupied by other thoughts.

I felt the eyes move closer and closer until I could smell the light, breezy aroma of his colognes. I tried to play coy with him and act like I didn't see him, but the stranger definitely had my attention.

I turned away from his presence in an attempt to ignore him and heard the voice of a someone from long ago. "Angela Anderson!

I turned toward the voice and went limp from shock as I saw Craig Harden's hand stretched toward me waiting for a response.

Chapter 19

Craig's gleaming, white smile and deep dimples were still an attractive feature on him. The thin body of long ago had been replaced with sexy muscles.

The initial shock wore off and I replied, "Well hello, stranger" not knowing if I was having another dream.

Three days ago, I was dreaming about him on an airplane. Now, like a mirage coming true, he was standing in front of me looking better then I had imagined.

I was still trying to get over the moment when Craig spoke. "Come on, Angela. You making me feel really bad. I know it hasn't been that long."

I continued to stare at Craig with a slight grin on my face and managed to respond by saying, "Wow! Craig Harden in the flesh."

Craig smiled back at me and spoke. "Angela, I'm sorry for approaching you so unexpectedly, but I was shocked when I saw you. Yesterday I saw you with an entourage of suits, and today I saw you in negotiations with Prophetess Linda Stanford."

Craig gently nudged me and continued to talk. "Look at you, all grown up. The last time I saw you, you had some thug chasing me out of the mall."

I almost spilled my drink as I leaned forward to laugh and responded, "Now, that was some funny shit. If you remember, you started it by walking up on me all crazy."

Craig leaned back and laughed as he responded. "You right, I thought I was God's gift to women back then. But seeing you in Atlanta made me understand that I still had some growing up to do."

We both laughed and I continued to sit there shocked as I stared at him from head to toe. I could tell that Craig had changed since we were younger. And changes appeared to be for the better. Craig was taller and his shoulders appeared to be a little broader. His attitude had also changed. The self-centered Craig had been replaced by a witty man who cared more about what I was going on in my life.

Craig moved closer and asked, "Is it okay if I sit down?"

I thought for a second and responded, "Sure!"

I stood up and brushed a few crumbs off my dress. As I turned to fix my chair, I heard Craig grumble, "Damn, Angela" as if he had seen something amazing.

I turned and questioned him. "What? What's wrong with you?"

Craig's eyes traced my body up and down and then he responded with a smile. "You filled out pretty good. I mean, you always had little bit back there, but it's real nice now. Real nice!"

I blushed at his comment and shook my head as I responded, "Boy, shut up!"

I have to admit that the attention that I was getting from Craig was refreshing. With all the stuff I had been through the past few days, I deserved a little attention from a man.

The conversation with Craig was easy because we were so much alike.

I was not even offended when the conversation switched to reminiscing about our intimate history. "You remember when I was trying to get a little? Boy, your legs slammed shut so fast."

I responded with a blushing smile, "Hold up Mr. Harden, if you going to tell a story, tell it right. My legs slammed shut because you called me another girl's name. What was her name? Christy, I believe. And speaking of Christy, where is your wife?"

Craig sadly looked at his hands and responded. Honestly, we never had a chance. I knew that I had made a mistake two years into the marriage. Christy wanted me to come home to her and the kids after a hard day at work. All I wanted to do was hang out with my friends. Can you imagine a nineteen-year-old kid having to worry about feeding a wife and two kids and your friends' only worries were how to sneak into the club? My friends would drop by the house and tell me about all the fun they were having, so I just started hanging out. The more I started hanging out, the more I realized I had made a mistake marrying so young. I started cheating and then she would cheat to get even. We hated each other so much, but the church was encouraging us to pray and hang in there. One day, I just felt like I couldn't breathe anymore, so I packed my shit up and moved to Miami with a friend. I just had to get the hell out of Baxley. People in the church, including my mother, felt like I should have stayed in the marriage for the kids. It really got bad when Christy started showing up at church asking for money. I really looked like a deadbeat even though I was paying court-ordered child support. I can't put all the blame on Christy because I didn't fight enough for my rights. The only time I could see the kids was when I went back to Baxley to visit my mother. After she passed, I had no contact at all with the kids."

I thought about all the times I tried to get him out of Baxley but his mother was in his ear.

I asked about his mother and he lowered his head almost in sorrow as he responded, "My mother died a year after I moved to Miami. We never had a chance to really hash out our differences. I was still angry about things that happened to me when I was younger. I felt she should have protected me more instead of being selfish."

Craig really didn't have to spell it out for me because I understood. I still remember how he changed after dealing with Elder Madison and the junior ministers.

I quickly changed the subject by saying, "Well sometimes things don't work out the way we want. We have to just keep moving on."

Craig glanced around the bar sadly and responded, "Yeah, I guess you're right."

Craig inquired about my life and I kind of hit and missed on certain things about my life. I just couldn't bring myself to tell Craig about all the pain and misery that blew through my life. And my ending up tricking on a bishop with a fake baby to get paid. I felt guilty listening to Craig talk about how he went from negative to positive while I was sitting on two million dollars worth of trick money.

My thoughts were interrupted by the sound of Craig's voice. "God has really blessed you. I guess that Bible verse is really true about the humble being exalted and the exalted being humbled."

The happiness of the moment was replaced with the grim facts of my reality.

I replied to Craig's comment in a low, melancholy voice. "Yeah, I guess I'm doing okay."

Craig noticed the glum look on my face and quickly changed the subject.

"You know, Angela we really had a lot of fun growing up in Baxley. You remember?"

I could see Craig's lips moving, but my mind was still stuck on his comment about my being exalted. The comment hurt more than anything because I felt like a fraud. I was looking like a million dollars, but I was broken inside. My thoughts were interrupted by Craig tapping me on my hand and getting my attention. Craig smiled at me and then lowered his head. An uneasy silence crept across the table as he nervously played with his napkin.

Craig broke the silence by asking, "Is everything okay?"

I responded by shaking my head yes, but my eyes were tearing up.

Craig responded by placing his hand on mine and speaking. "You know, Angela I've been where you're at. I know what it feels like to have nothing to live for. I know what it feels like to throw away your family because you're angry."

Those comments literally forced the tears down my face.

Craig moved his chair to my side of table and hugged me. His hug felt so genuine. He held me tight and just allowed me to cry. He didn't ask any questions or offer me something to clean my face. He just allowed me to release all the hurt and anger that was in me.

I could feel the same spirit that I had felt when I first received God as my personal savior. That was a time of innocence for me. I experienced new things and placed God first. I had often thought about searching for that feeling again, and ironically I was finding it in the least expected place. No matter how hard I tried to compose myself, I continued to cry.

Craig continued to hold me and whisper, "That's it, just let it go, just let it all go."

Finally I was able to calm down and say a few words while drying my face. "I'm sorry Craig, I didn't mean to mess up your shirt."

Craig pulled his chair to the opposite side of the table and spoke. "Don't worry about. It felt good letting you release."

I was preparing to answer some hard questions from Craig, but they never came. Craig just smiled at me and asked, "Do you want to go somewhere?"

I responded still trying to compose myself. "Craig, I'm really not in any condition to go anywhere. I just want to go to my room and relax."

Craig smiled at me and spoke. "Normally I wouldn't insist, but for this, I'm going to have to insist. I promise you it will make you feel like brand new."

I wanted to argue, but I was just mentally drained. All I could manage was a weak "yes" response.

I convinced him to at least let me go freshen up and reluctantly he agreed to escort me to my room.

Craig continued to talk about all the positive things going on in his life as we walked to the elevator. As I studied Craig's attire closer, I could tell that he was dressing a little snazzier than I last remembered. Craig explained that he was invited to Savannah to promote his new fashion brand. I looked at Craig in disbelief and responded, "Fashion? Boy, what do you know about fashion? The last I remember you were walking around with a raggedy John Deer cap on."

Craig laughed and explained how he had taken a small t-shirt idea and turned into a global icon for fashion.

Still confused, I stared at Craig and asked him the name. He responded, "My Life."

My head snapped back in shock as I remembered the eighty-dollar t-shirt that I fell in love with and bought.

I quickly opened my bag and pulled the "My Life" tee out. I looked at Craig in shock, asking, "Are you trying to tell me that you own this company?"

Craig looked bashfully at the floor and smiled as he responded, "Well yeah, I guess that's what I'm trying to say."

Craig continued to talk. I really wanted something that my kids could be proud of. It took me a while to get my life together, but with the help of God, I did it. I honestly can say that I have really been blessed. I was given a second chance with my kids and I have made the most of it."

Hearing how successful Craig was unleashed something in me that I thought was gone. I smiled as Craig continued to talk about his children attending private school and being on the dean's list. But deep inside, I felt jealously. People deal with their feelings in different ways. My way was always negative. The more positive he got, the more enraged I got.

Somewhere between the walk to the elevator and riding to the twelfth floor. I decided that my misery needed company. I interrupted Craig and asked, "So you're in the church real deep now?"

Craig smiled and responded, "I consider myself spiritual, not religious. I'm not into the church like I was when we grew up. I think people who place their faith in man will always be disappointed. I try to put God first in everything I do. I made a promise to God that he would remain first if he helped me. And I'm never going to break that promise."

Instead of me listening to Craig and supporting him, I began plotting. I wanted to test how spiritual he was. Mentally, that's what my life had been reduced to. I no longer cared about anything pure and positive because to me, it didn't exist. The only things that existed in my life for the past couple of years were desolation and revenge. Craig was at a happy place in his life and I hated it. I wanted him to wake up the next morning unhappy like me. The only way to impart my negativity to him was by seducing him. I wanted his God to watch in HD as I took his joy from him.

I walked closer to Craig and placed his hand inside mine. I could tell that Craig was uneasy because he immediately stopped talking. As the elevator came to a stop, I placed his hand on the small of my back. I smiled at Craig but he responded by nervously looking at the elevator numbers.

As the doors opened, I pulled his hand to follow me. By the time we got to my room, he was panicky. I opened my door and motioned for him to come in. The first thing that I saw was my fake pregnant belly folded neatly on my bed. I could only imagine the fun the housekeepers had with it. I quickly tossed a blanket over it and returned to Craig. Craig was still standing by the door looking terrified. I could tell that Craig wanted no part of me. I moved toward him and he quickly backed away. He moved so fast that his back slammed into the door, causing the room to shake. I used the door to my advantage and cornered him. I pushed him against the door and placed my hand on his penis.

Craig gently pushed me back and whispered, "I'm not ready for this right now."

Again, I advanced and shoved him into the door. This time, I clawed at his belt buckle and zipper until his pants loosened. I slid my hand down his underwear and slowly stroked his penis. Craig was still struggling to get away, but barley. I continued to stroke his penis until it was hard. Craig was breathing hard as to catch his breath as I slid down to my knees.

Craig quickly pulled away as I was guiding his penis toward my mouth.

He pulled his underwear and pants up and then spoke. "Angela, this is wrongI don't want to do you like this because I have too much respect for you."

Craig finished buckling his pants and urged me to get of my knees by pulling at my arm.

I yanked away from Craig angry because he had rejected me and said, "Damn, what's wrong with you? Are you gay or something?"

Those words had always guaranteed the reaction that I wanted. Those words were meant to hurt his manhood and force him to prove himself.

Instead of getting angry, Craig smiled at me and spoke. "No Angela, I'm not gay. I just think you deserve better than some random man throwing his dick down your throat. The Angela that I knew had way more respect for herself than that."

Craig opened the door to leave and gave me some parting words that tore through my soul. "No matter how bad you've been hurt, there's always something better. And no matter how much money you get, you'll never be satisfied because you're not happy. You have to see the worth in your life before you can make it better for someone else. Right now, you're lost. You probably think there's no way back, but there is. There is absolutely nothing that I can give you to make you happy. You have to find your way back."

Craig walked out the door and the door slowly closed. I was pissed and I wanted somebody to pay.

I quickly ran for the door and screamed toward Craig, "Whatever, little boy. You just can't handle a real woman!"

I waited for a response from Craig, but it never came. He simply continued to walk and disappeared onto the elevator. I backed into my room still angry but there was no one to vent too. I pushed the balcony door open and sat in a chair fuming.

The dusk across the Savannah sky slowly calmed me down. Craig's words began filtering back and forth in my head. It was like he knew what I was going through. Was he right? Had my life turned me into a spiteful person who only cared about revenge? I guess for the first time in a while, I felt embarrassed at the person I had become. Seeking revenge had driven me to places in my life that I had never imagined. I had lied to Kayla and family all because I wanted to get even. I had an eight-year-old son who considered his grandmother to be his mom. Had it really been worth it? People like the Tylers were desensitized to misery. For money, they were willing to destroy each other. They didn't care who they hurt in the process. It was just business to them. Had I really turned into that type of person? Was I willing to take away another person's joy and happiness to satisfy my own degradation?

That night was filled with a lot of soul searching as I looked for answers. I stayed awake all night thinking about who I had become. I was looking for answers, but I couldn't find any. I felt like a hamster trapped in a maze with no solution. I packed my clothes and tossed the bag in the corner, still hoping for answers. I wanted to make changes, but I didn't know how. When I was younger, I felt comfortable calling God. Now I was ashamed. What type of monster enjoys taking away another person's spirit then seeks comfort?

The rising of the sun did nothing to cure my gloom. I looked around my lonely room and started seeing my demon shadows from the past. Only this time, I was not afraid of them. I started feeling comfortable as they encouraged me to hurt others. My demons didn't care about my pride. They only wanted the end result. What type of spirit convinces its vessel to use her body to bequeath pain and misery to others?

I was at the point of accepting that very fate, when I heard a faint knock at my door. I could feel my demons begging me not to answer. But there still was a part of me pushing me to fight. There was something about the knock that seemed urgent. I staggered toward the door still deprived of sleep and opened it without looking. When I opened the door, I was surprised to see Craig standing there.

Craig held out his hand and said, "You need to come with me now."

The need to fight with Craig was gone. Craig's hand was like a lifeline giving me my life back. I took his hand and he quickly walked me toward the elevator. There was an uneasy silence as I looked around the elevator, still dazed.

I tried to break the eerie silence when I spoke. "Craig, I'm sorry for how I acted last night. I never meant to hurt your feelings. I don't know what I was thinking, but I never should have tried to take your spirit."

I continued to ramble on as tears started to fall from my eyes. Craig quickly escorted me out the door to a car waiting.

He helped me inside and responded, "Everything is okay, Angela. I'm taking you somewhere safe."

I leaned my face against the door and held his hand like a lost child. The tears flowed down my face as he walked back into the hotel.

The next few hours felt like I was in and out of a dream. I saw blurs and flashes of people I knew. I saw Craig, my brother Steven, my father, and most importantly, my mother. The contact with my mother seemed incredibly real as we hugged and kissed.

I was about to doze off again when I was startled by a small hand pushing my door open. The small hand was followed by two large brown eyes gazing at me with curiosity. My surroundings started to look more familiar as I smelled a familiar scent throughout the house. It felt like I was home. Not my empty apartment in Atlanta, but my home in Baxley.

A voice suddenly came from the crack in door. "Mama, are you up."

I quickly pulled myself up and responded, "Yes, I'm up. RC, is that you?"

The door pushed open and I saw the big bright smile of my son running toward me.

RC loudly proclaimed, "Grandma, Grandpa! Mama is up."

I heard what sounded like a stampede running up the steps as my mother, father, and Steven entered the room.

Steven was the first to speak. "Damn, girl! We thought you were going to sleep your life away."

My mother punched Steven and then shooed him out the room.

Steven waved at me as he was walking away and said, "We'll catch up. I'll talk to you later."

My father smiled at me and wiped away tears forming in my eyes and spoke. "We're glad you're home."

RC bounced around on the bed happy to see me. I could feel tears slowly falling down my face as everyone stood around gawking at me.

My mother finally had my father take RC out the room and then she spoke. "You had a long weekend, ah?"

I responded with a faint whisper, "How did I get here?"

My mother smiled and then spoke. "Craig. We got a call from Craig late Saturday concerned about you. Imagine our surprise when he said that he ran into you in Savannah. He called us because he was worried about you. You got here because he drove you here. No matter how much you hate Craig, we were glad he brought you home."

My mother held my hand tightly and continued talking. "I just didn't want you to go back to the condition that you were in before."

I gazed out the window as my mother walked toward the door.

She turned toward me and spoke. "If you get hungry, come on down. We got some food for you."

Easter weekend was always big growing up. But today was even more special because I was with my family.

My mother continued to talk. "Oh, Craig left a card beside the bed."

My mother left the room and I quickly opened the card.

The card read, "Angela, I hope you find what you're searching for. There is a positive spirit out there hoping that you will take the first step. I thought a good place to start was at home with people who love you."

311

Craig left his phone number and encouraged me to call when I finished my journey. Running into Craig turned out to be more exciting than I had anticipated. I slid out the bed just as RC bounced through the door again.

He ran toward me smiling and asked, "Ma, how long are you staying?"

I glanced at the card on my night stand and replied, "Until I finish my journey."

RC looked at me bewildered by my answer.

I smiled at him and pulled him close to me and spoke. "I will stay for as long as you want me to stay. Mama has a lot of time that she needs to make up with you. Do you think grandma and grandpa would mind if I moved back down here."

My father, mother, and Steven came into the room and surrounded me with a crushing hug.

Steven whispered in my ear, "It's never too late to start over."

I enjoyed the positive rays of energy coming from the hug of my family. The only thing I could do was look toward heaven and thank God for saving me from myself.

About the Author

Steven Darrell Bates Sr. is from Cincinnati, Ohio and attended the University of Cincinnati where he earned a degree in Criminal Justice. In 2004, he moved to Atlanta, Georgia to continue his career working with At-Risk Youth.

Being raised in the Pentecostal Holiness church and by a minister, he was on a strict regimen of religious beliefs. He was not allowed to watch TV, play cards, attend movie theaters, or listen to secular music. This lead Steve to gravitate towards reading and writing just as long as it was not church related. He always felt like he was held to a higher standard because his father was a minister and the beliefs placed on him by the church. While growing up, Steven was expected to become a minister but that was a frightening thought for him. As a young man, he had to stop living up to other people's expectations, and start living his own life.

Later in life, Steven Darrell Bates's artistic talents surfaced, inspiring him to become a writer. He writes to admit to himself that he can create a story where the church and the secular society come together. While in college, he developed a deep fascination for understanding the church, GOD, and the concept of spirituality.

While many of those thoughts still elude him, he was lucky enough to find his one true love, his wife, and he is living happily ever after with her and their two kids. He is currently working on his second book.

You can find Steven on social media at:
Website: http://www.stevendarrellbates.com
Twitter: http://www.twitter.com/stevendbatesatl
Facebook: http://www.facebook.com/stevendarrellbates